Rachel Lee was hooked ~~and practiced her craft as~~ all over the United States. ~~author now resides in Flo~~ full-time.

Lena Diaz was born in Kentucky and has also lived in California, Louisiana and Florida, where she now resides with her husband and two children. Before becoming a romantic suspense author, she was a computer programmer. A Romance Writers of America Golden Heart® Award finalist, she has also won the prestigious Daphne du Maurier Award for Excellence in Mystery/ Suspense. To get the latest news about Lena, please visit her website, lenadiaz.com

CONARD COUNTY: CHRISTMAS CRIME SPREE

RACHEL LEE

POLICE DOG PROCEDURAL

LENA DIAZ

MILLS & BOON

First Published in Great Britain 2022
by Mills & Boon, an imprint of HarperCollins*Publishers* Ltd
1 London Bridge Street, London, SE1 9GF

www.harpercollins.co.uk

HarperCollins*Publishers*
1st Floor, Watermarque Building,
Ringsend Road, Dublin 4, Ireland

Conard County: Christmas Crime Spree © 2022 Susan Civil-Brown
Police Dog Procedural © 2022 Harlequin Enterprises ULC.

Special thanks and acknowledgement are given to Lena Diaz for her contribution to the *K-9s on Patrol* series.

ISBN: 978-0-263-30361-2

1022

CONARD COUNTY: CHRISTMAS CRIME SPREE

RACHEL LEE

Chapter One

Reverend Molly Canton, pastor of Good Shepherd Church in Conard City, Wyoming, saw gently falling snow outside her study window. The snowflakes sparkled in the light gleaming from her window.

Enchanted, she rose, slipped into her red parka and stepped outside to enjoy a miracle of the Christmas season.

The cold nipped at her cheeks as she looked upward into the darkened night sky, but she hardly felt it. All that this perfection needed, she thought, was quiet Christmas carols in the background. With an inward giggle, she stuck out her tongue like a kid to catch a drifting flake.

To think, she would have missed this beauty if insomnia hadn't plagued her tonight. Snow floating down like this in the daytime carried little of the magic of lightly falling snow at night.

Turning, she looked up at the glowing steeple of the church, a soft light, meant to be a beacon to the faithful but faded a bit in the fog of the falling snow. Her heart soared with the rising steeple, lifting toward the heavens.

Cares and concerns vanished in the moment, making her feel as free as that shimmering snow. Almost as if she fell upward into it. Joy, never far from her at this time of year, flooded her now. Gratitude filled her.

She began to shiver and accepted the fact that she'd have to go back indoors, when she heard a sound.

It immediately caught her attention. Had it been a cry of some kind? Certainly not a baby; she'd recognize that sound. Did someone need help? Turning slowly, she strained her ears and held her breath as much as she could. The foggy clouds that had been issuing from her mouth and nose subsided to almost nothing.

Maybe she'd imagined it? Probably. Being alone in the near dark often stimulated the imagination. And she was certainly imaginative.

But just as she had decided she'd heard nothing at all, she heard the cry again. Someone *was* in trouble. A woman.

Her joy dropped away, replaced by a need for action. Adrenaline began to course through her, making her skin prickle. But where had the cry come from? Was it really distress? She pulled back her hood, hoping to hear better.

Near the church like this, sounds could echo off the high stone walls. At the same time, the increasing depth of the winter's snow muffled the world.

Unable to ignore the call, needing to place it, she stepped away from her parsonage and continued along the walkway to the church that a member of her congregation kept clear for her. Tonight it was lightly dusted with fresh snow between the banks of previous snows. Maybe standing somewhere else would localize the sound…if it came again.

That had sounded like a cry of distress, though. Not simply an exclamation. If someone was hurt, she had to find them. Quickly. The lack of sirens indicated no one had called 911. She must be alone—the woman who had cried out.

Urgency filled Molly. Her pace quickened, her snow

boots squeaking quietly on the wet pavement. The nights in this town were so quiet in the wee hours. There was no sound except trucks whizzing by on the state highway bypass.

She heard the cry again. From the far side of the church. She ran around the building, hoping she could find it. Then she saw a dim light in the upstairs bedroom of the house on the other side of the large churchyard.

Mabel Blix. A woman in her early thirties who lived alone, confined now to crutches and sometimes a wheelchair because of an auto accident.

Molly wasted no time running to Mabel's door. It was unlocked, so she raced inside, past family heirlooms, and charged up the stairs.

What she found made her pull out her cell phone and call the cops and the ambulance.

Mabel sprawled on the floor and she looked as if she had been beaten. Molly kneeled beside her, calling her name, letting her know she was not alone. That help was on the way.

DETECTIVE CALLUM McCLOUD arrived at the crime scene, dragged out of the most restful sleep he'd had in a while. Not that he hadn't once been used to these calls, but he'd hoped to find far fewer in this little out-of-the-way place. Now here he was in the thick of it again.

The crime-scene tape had already been strung around the house and environs. A small crowd had begun to collect despite the early hour, but no more than the county deputies and local police could hold easily at bay. From voices around him, he gathered that most of these people had known the victim. Small town, he reminded himself.

Crime-scene techs were already at work, bright lights flooded the yard and every light in the house had been turned on. As Callum reached the edge of the tape, one of the techs handed him a folded-up clean suit, gloves and booties to prevent contamination of the scene. He pulled them on, then yanked up the hood, tightening it with the drawstrings. Only then did he cross the barrier.

A path had been neatly delineated, with yellow tape laid on either side, indicating the areas the crime-scene team had already cleared. He stuck within those lines as he approached the front porch of the small two-story house. It was a routine entirely too familiar to him. Sickeningly familiar.

The pathway had been marked, up and into the house, where techs were busy at work. Floodlights glared over everything. Some of the team nodded briefly his way as he entered the home, and the lead technician approached.

"We cleared the stairs and the bedroom upstairs. You can go up if you want."

He definitely did. These hours after the home invasion could be the most important. "The victim?"

"Barely conscious. Blow to the head. She won't be able to tell you much right away."

Callum nodded, glancing around as flash cameras recorded every detail. Home invasion? Maybe. Objects had been smashed and thrown around. Items trampled.

But the biggest puzzle of all: a large-screen TV hanging from the wall. So what had the perp been seeking? Money in a rolled-up sock? Jewels that were probably mostly paste with the possible exception of an heirloom or two?

This didn't look right to his practiced eye.

He made his way into the bedroom and found more wanton destruction. Drawers pulled open or dumped, clothing thrown about. A jewelry box that appeared to have been shaken upside down. A few cheap pieces left behind. How did the perp know the difference, if there was one?

Blood on the pale blue rug, but not a dangerous amount.

Something nagged at him. He'd need to talk to the victim, study the crime-scene photos in detail. Well, that was standard procedure, but this time he felt there was something more he needed to figure out.

Returning outside, he asked the deputy who was standing just outside the door, Guy Redwing, "Who found the victim?"

"The pastor did."

Immediately, Callum scanned the crowd, searching among the men for a clerical collar. "The pastor?" he repeated.

Redwing pointed. "She's standing right there in the red parka."

She. Well, he hadn't expected that, not around here. Big cities were one thing, and they often still had trouble with female clerics. But a small area like this? It was also a sign of how little he'd come to know this community in the last few months.

There she stood, wrapped in her red parka, her hands stuffed in her pockets, her fur-lined hood pulled up but not tightened around her face. Jeans. Winter boots.

Bucking the image, he thought with dry amusement.

"Molly Canton," the deputy advised him. "Some call her 'Reverend,' most call her 'Pastor' and some call her names I won't repeat. Two years ain't long enough to change some attitudes around here."

Callum dragged up one corner of his mouth. "You got that right, Guy. Or anywhere."

He quickly stripped off his protective gear and tossed

it toward one of the crime scene crew, then headed to the pastor.

The crowd of lookie-loos had been growing steadily since he entered the house. Molly Canton wasn't being eased away from the tape, however. Her face reflected deep concern, and she didn't back away from him, but held out her gloved hand. He shook it.

"I'm Detective Callum McCloud, and you're Reverend Canton, right?"

"I am. I've seen you around a couple of times, Detective. I wish we'd met under better circumstances." At least she hadn't pressed him to join her flock.

"I'd like to have a few words with you, if you don't mind."

"I don't mind."

"Not out here, ma'am. Too many ears."

She nodded. "Come around to my cottage and I'll make coffee, or tea if you prefer."

He followed her along the shoveled walkway to the rear of the church. *Cottage* was a good name for it, he supposed. Maybe *cozy* in some people's parlance. Half the small stone house boasted a second floor that looked like a square tower, a single large room by itself. Unlike the rest of the cottage, it was covered in gray clapboard.

Inside the house was warm enough, but the rooms were small.

"I've often wondered how any of my predecessors could have raised a family in here," Molly remarked as she set about starting the coffee. "You a tea man?"

"Coffee for me."

"Easier." Then, as it began brewing, she doffed her parka and they sat down across from each other at a wooden table. "Any word on Mabel? The victim?"

"I'm told she's groggy. We won't be able to talk to her for at least a few hours."

"I'm so glad I found her alive." Molly's gentle face sagged.

Indeterminate age, Callum thought. Silver streaks in her dark hair. A bit plump around the middle, he'd noticed when she shed her jacket. She wore a pair of metal-rimmed glasses, "half-eyes" as they'd once been called. Middle-aged, maybe? Not to judge by her youthful face, a soft, pretty oval with a delicate nose. Curiosity pricked him.

"So you found Ms. Blix? How did that happen? Exactly."

"I was working in my study."

"At this hour?"

She gave him a crooked smile that wrinkled her nose just a tiny bit. "I'm sometimes an insomniac. This was one of those nights. Anyway, the light from my window caught a gentle snowfall, and it was just too beautiful to ignore. So I went outside to enjoy it. A little Christmas miracle."

He felt his face stiffen and hoped it didn't show. Miracles? He didn't believe in them, not the smallest of them.

Molly got up and poured their coffee, then leaned back against the counter to sip. "Regardless, I was enjoying the snow. This is my favorite time of year, and this was a touch of magic. For me, anyway. Then I thought I heard a cry. I wasn't sure, though. Then it came again and there was no mistaking it was a woman. She sounded in pain."

He nodded, pulled out his pocket notebook and scribbled some notes in it.

"Well, it's hard to tell where sounds come from, especially at night, when they can carry so far. I moved, hoping a different position would help. The stone walls of this church are famous for echoing."

He wrote some more.

"I came around the corner to the front of the church, and saw that Mabel's bedroom light was on which doesn't mean anything by itself. She was in a terrible car accident that left her needing crutches. The light usually stays on in case she needs to go to the bathroom. But I heard the cry again and knew it had to be her."

Molly paused to sip coffee and clearly collect herself. "I thought maybe she'd fallen and couldn't get up. I hurried over and the door was unlocked, so I charged in. I didn't much notice the mess downstairs I was in such a hurry. Then I found Mabel. It was obvious she'd been beaten. I gave what first aid I could until the ambulance arrived." Molly's face sagged.

"I noticed the mess when I was with Molly, then when I came downstairs." She looked directly at Callum. "It was a robbery, wasn't it? Although I can't think Mabel had a thing to steal."

"Jewelry?" Callum asked.

Molly shook her head. "She only had a couple of good pieces, heirlooms, and they weren't big enough to sell for much. Mostly sentimental value. Like a lot of people in this town, she was hanging by a financial thread, even talking about selling some of her antiques."

Callum nodded slowly and at last sipped some coffee. "Nobody who might have a problem with her?"

Molly shook her head. "Only the drunk who rammed into her car, and he's in jail right now. Although how he could blame *her*..." Molly frowned.

"You know her well?"

"She's a member of my congregation. I check in on her often, as do some of the other ladies. Being on crutches and in a wheelchair makes her life difficult. She hasn't had time to adjust to any of it yet. And I hope she never has to."

Callum nodded his agreement. But now, especially with a blow to the head, things might well grow more difficult for Mabel Blix.

He drained his coffee. "Thank you, Pastor. I may be in touch with more questions."

"No problem," she replied. "Often enough you'll have to drag me out of the middle of something, though."

"Busy?"

"The territory of this calling. Anyway, I'll be going to the hospital soon."

He hesitated as he reached for his jacket. "We don't want Ms. Blix's memory affected."

She screwed up her face. "Polluted, you mean. Well, I'm not going for any reason but to offer her comfort. And believe me, Detective McCloud, nobody will keep Mabel's pastor away."

WHAT A DOUR MAN, Molly thought as she changed into clerical garb. Black slacks in deference to the cold, black lace-up boots with respect to the snow and a long-sleeved black clerical shirt with plastic collar stuck in beneath the shirt tabs.

She hated that plastic collar—she preferred cotton—but the expense of keeping cotton pristine and starched had changed her thinking. She could keep plastic clean with an all-purpose cleaner. Didn't mean she had to like it.

Finally, she donned a dark gray wool coat and a scarf that could be pulled up over her head. Official-looking. The way people expected her to look, unlike the red parka she wore when the cold was brutal enough. Her own version of kicking over the traces.

But after nearly two years of working to win this county over to the idea of a female pastor, she wasn't about to blow it now. That task was far from completed. Her red parka might get a wink and a nudge, but it would have been foolish for her to go beyond that.

She thought of Detective Callum McCloud as she drove toward the hospital at the edge of town. His was not likely to be a face that Mabel would want to see on waking. Lord, how could a man look so unrelievedly grim? Tall, lanky but…grim. She'd seen him around a few times and was quite sure she'd never seen him smile.

But he was not her concern. Mabel was, and even if they weren't allowing friends to visit her yet, Molly could walk through those same doors as if they didn't exist.

She parked in a space reserved for clergy, although there weren't many of them around here, and entered the hospital. Here again, she knew most everyone by sight if not by name and they knew her. The advantage of being a pastor of the largest church in a small town. She would never be invisible.

But maybe that could be a disadvantage, too, she thought with a slight grimace. Not that she'd yet found a reason for it to be.

She was taken to Mabel's room without a problem, only to be told she'd have to wait. Mabel had gone to surgery for bleeding on the brain.

Molly didn't need a doctor to explain th danger to her. She'd seen it during her time in the National Guard. She folded her hands, closed her eyes and began a heartfelt prayer for Mabel Blix. The poor woman had suffered more than enough.

MIDMORNING, MABEL RETURNED to her room in a medically induced coma and the doctors had no idea when she might waken.

Molly left, truly distressed for Mabel, and headed back to the parsonage because she had other duties that required her attention. She claimed very little of her days solely for herself, which was fine by her. She'd always felt that busy was best.

There was a lunch that day at the bakery for the ladies who devoted so much time to keeping the church in excellent shape. They called themselves the Altar Society, and were a group of ten who managed busy lives in addition to helping out at the church with everything from cleaning to darning linens when they needed it.

The lunch was always an enjoyable experience, but so was the tea these same women presented monthly for other volunteers, such as ushers. A good group to share time with.

Today, however, the robbery of Mabel Blix was the subject of all conversation. They'd gathered in a small room reserved by Melinda, who owned the bakery, for group meetings. The pastries were hell on Molly's perennial diet.

"Surely you know something about last night, Pastor," Janice Remy remarked. She was an older woman with perfectly coiffed hair and a penchant for flowered dresses. She chaired the Altar Society and was often the most outspoken of the group. She was also the leading gossip in that she managed to ferret out the details of nearly everything that happened around here and wasn't shy about sharing them. It was a good thing she was not mean-spirited.

Nine other faces silently asked the same question. Molly debated how much she could share without crossing lines of confidentiality—lines she guarded stringently. She settled on the simplest answer.

"Just about Mabel. She needed some surgery and won't be awake for some time yet. No visitors. I'll check in this afternoon."

Claire AuCoin spoke. A gray-haired woman in her elder years, it hardly mattered that Janice was the titular head of the group. Claire had been serving so many years in the society that she was the de facto leader. It always amused Molly how any group, however small, had lines of authority.

Nor did Claire bow to formalities. For her, a patterned Western shirt and jeans were fine for anything except Sunday services.

"Tell Mabel we'll start a prayer circle for her," Claire said. "That woman has been through more than enough. I can't believe this has happened!"

The subtext being that crimes like this were rare in this city and county. Perhaps. But who knew what went on behind closed doors?

Janice took charge again. "The linens need dry cleaning again and, Georgia, I thought I saw some frayed edges that need mending."

Georgia, mender and darner par excellence, nodded her dark head. "I thought it was getting to be about time again." She was a woman with great skill, but was seriously overweight and always trying to hide the fact behind loose, flowy garments in dark colors. Molly thought of it as style.

The conversation moved on to lighter subjects, away from the church. Who was expecting a baby, how youngsters were getting along in school. The snowmen that were springing up in the city park. Whether the city's ice-skating rink, a depression filled with water every winter, was growing hard enough for the children to break out their skates, or the boys to bring out their hockey sticks and pucks. The general agreement was that the ice must be safe by now.

After the luncheon, Molly made two home visits, one to a dear woman in the last stages of breast cancer, Stacy Withers, who always said, "The mammogram didn't catch it."

Why this was so important to Stacy, Molly had no idea, and she didn't ask. She suspected that Stacy felt betrayed by medical science, but medical science had kept her going this long, and was now easing the pain of her last months. Molly's rule was never to pry unless a person said something that seemed to invite it.

This time, however, Stacy had something to add. "It happened too fast, Pastor. Too fast. Once a year for a mammogram wasn't often enough for me. Not nearly."

Molly took her hand. "Are you feeling you should have done more?" She hated to think that Stacy might in some way be feeling guilty about her illness. She already felt guilty about leaving her family behind.

"I guess I couldn't have," Stacy said after a few moments. "But I feel so betrayed. My family feels betrayed."

"Because you got sick?"

Stacy gave her a hollow-eyed look. "How can God do this to my children?"

A question with no decent answer, Molly thought sadly as she drove away. The usual bromides were useless. Certainly useless to Stacy.

Her next visit was to a man who worked hard at being a crusty curmudgeon from the confines of his recliner and wheelchair. He could have been amusing except that he took out most of his bad temper on his daughter, who looked ragged from caring for him.

"Get some help," Molly told her.

Marcia Lathrop just gave her an exhausted look. "My brother lives too far away."

"Not so far he can't get over here for a weekend. And I bet he could pay for some home care to give you a break once in a while."

Marcia simply shook her head.

"I can get some folks over here to give you a few hours from time to time."

Again, Marcia shook her head. "I can do this."

Molly decided to see how many volunteers she could rustle up to help Marcia, anyway. Enough of this, she thought with annoyance. She doubted anyone in her fold had the least idea that Marcia was handling this all alone. Marcia never, ever complained. Too bad if she didn't want to accept "charity" from the church. There was a point when independence reached self-immolation.

She swung by the hospital to check on Mabel Blix and ran in to Callum McCloud on his way out. She paused to greet him and he simply shook his head.

"She's still out, Pastor. The doc told me another day at least. I've called her family and they're flying in from Seattle. And before you think you should have done that, let me remind you that delivering the bad news when there's a crime is *my* job."

Molly studied the dour man and wondered how many times he'd had to face that hell, often in worse circumstances than this. "Thank you," she said finally.

For once, a corner of his mouth lifted. "Do I detect guilt? Don't bother. The family will need your services more when they arrive tomorrow."

Molly watched him walk away into snow that had begun to fall heavily, then she headed back to the church.

It was still the Christmas season, and one of her favorite things awaited her: after-school care.

Nearly thirty children, aged five to ten, crowded the church basement. Their high, piping voices shared the excitement they all felt as they worked on various projects. Some were stringing popcorn and others gluing together construction-paper rings, all to make garlands for their trees at home. A few concentrated with creased brows as they tried to make papier-mâché angels. Some painted small plaster images of bells, baubles and Santa Clauses. A few had brought in their school photos to make more personalized items.

Their excitement was infectious, and soon Molly shed the earlier part of the day to join them around their small tables and admire their artwork.

Laura Maskin, the retired teacher in charge, never stopped moving around the room, dispensing encouraging words. Her helper, Belinda Armistead, did the same.

It was beautiful, controlled chaos, and this excitement was part of what Molly loved so much about this season. These kids could barely contain themselves as Christmas drew nearer. Their cheer infused Molly.

She was sorry to see the children leave as their parents arrived to pick them up.

But after she helped clean up the church basement, the evening would be hers. This town, for whatever reason, didn't lend itself to evening prayers. She was often lucky to get a handful of people on weekday mornings. But Sundays made up for all that.

She decided to make one last swing through the church, then head back to her cottage for a bowl of hot soup and a good thriller. Her secret vice, those thrillers. Although she didn't know how secret it could be when they were stuffed on her bookshelf below all the religious texts. Anyone who came in would be bound to see them.

The hardest part of her current position was having to follow the straight and narrow so carefully. Moving here hadn't been easy, not when she found herself regarded with so much suspicion and sexism. Women shouldn't be pastors, evidently.

But that had been wearing off, and her biggest success to date had been suggesting they dress the figures in the crèche as the poor people they likely had been. Donations of tattered clothing had poured in, and the congregation had taken great pleasure in dressing the figures.

But it somehow seemed right in a county where so many people were living on a ragged economic edge. She guessed a lot of people must have felt the same. It also struck her that the Wise Men, who hadn't been present at the birth and hadn't shown up for two years, shouldn't be out there garbed in finery and bearing expensive gifts that had done the Holy Family little enough good.

Her personal rebellion.

With soup warm in her tummy, she grabbed a well-thumbed paperback and was about to dive in when she remembered that the Vestry was meeting in the morning.

That was *not* a joyous part of this season, or any season. They had hired her, but all she ever heard was a litany of how the church could be doing better, what oversights they deemed her guilty of and a bunch of other unpleasantries.

Oh, well. It came with the position.

But instead of reading, or thinking about the wardens, her thoughts turned to Detective Callum McCloud. Dour and grim, yes, but there was a story behind that disposition somewhere. A sad or ugly one. Someone with his experience and background didn't just choose an out-of-the-way place like this.

He was running from something, she decided. Hiding from it. Escaping it.

But he would have been one heck of a handsome man if he'd ever smiled. She'd caught just a glimpse of it that afternoon outside the hospital.

Well, maybe she could thaw him a bit with a touch of Christmas spirit. And tomorrow, she simply had to get that artificial tree out of the attic and set it up down here.

Bringing the season indoors was part of the joy. Twinkling lights, happy kids and mostly smiling parents.

Definitely the best time of year.

CALLUM MCCLOUD'S THOUGHTS drifted to Molly Canton as he sat in his rented house, with its ragged furniture, and sipped a bourbon. He'd sensed steel in her, a tensile strength that probably stood her in good stead even as she nurtured her flock.

That remark she made about how no one would keep the pastor away from Mabel Blix had included the subtext that not even he, a detective, could keep her away. The woman might bend some when she judged it necessary, but he doubted she ever broke.

He'd seen enough of her to know how pretty she was. That probably didn't help her cause any, although the streaks of early gray probably did.

In front of him, on a battered coffee table, he'd spread out the reports he had about the Blix attack. Neighbor interviews. Scene photos.

And nothing fit. During his long career, he'd seen enough home invasions to know when one was a burglary. This hadn't been. This kind of attack was something he'd only seen when the perp had a personal grudge.

But to hear the neighbors tell it, no one disliked her. She had a great many friends, and no current romantic relationship. She didn't even have an ex lingering in her background somewhere. No, she'd spent her entire young life here in this town and had lately worked as a recorder in the county's property office. Nothing in her job should have drawn this kind of ire.

Hell, he hated cases like this. Cases without an avenue to pursue. Cases that didn't yield immediate clues. Not one thing to hang his hat on.

He rose and went to refresh his bourbon, reminding himself it had to be his last. Drinking too much after his wife's death hadn't helped anything, but it had brought him close to some serious trouble. Angela would have hated that.

But he'd tried to leave Angela behind him, taking nothing with him when he left Boston except photo albums. No furniture, no mementos, no other reminders. And thus, he had brought himself to this one-horse town that shouldn't remind him of anything.

Until early this morning, anyway.

Cussing loudly because he didn't have to be quiet about it while he was alone like this, he went back to the coffee table and stood over it, wondering if a fan could blow all that paper and those photographs into something meaningful.

All too often, though, there *was* no meaning, as he knew from personal experience. Finding meaning in the violence of this world was like Diogenes searching for an honest man.

The only real meaning Callum had been able to find was that humans were brutes. Much of the time they kept it under control, but sometimes it burst out and it didn't need a meaning.

It might have a reason, but never a meaning. And most of the reasons were so half-baked they hardly bore repeating.

He passed a hand over his eyes, knowing full well that he wasn't going to find a clue or an answer tonight. No way.

Then his cell phone rang. It was the dispatcher at the sheriff's department, Velma, she of the indeterminate age and smoke-roughened voice.

"Hey, Detective," she said politely enough. "Pastor Canton wants you to call her. Need the number?"

He supposed the church number was written in capital letters on any web search, but he asked for it, anyway. People always liked to feel useful.

And what the hell did Molly Canton want from him, anyway? His heart quickened a bit. Had she found some kind of clue?

He tapped in her number immediately.

"Molly Canton," she answered cheerfully. Not even a title.

"This is Detective McCloud," he replied. "You wanted me to call?"

"Yes. I know I'm being forward and you have every right to tell me to get lost, but I realized I need a tall man for a bit of help. And you're tall."

He was hardly a ladder, he thought. "What is it?"

"I'm trying to get my Christmas tree out of the attic and I can't quite reach it."

Christmas tree? For several seconds he felt stunned.

"I understand it's an imposition and if you say no, I won't be offended. I promise."

He glanced at the clock—9:30 p.m. And she wanted a Christmas tree out of her attic. He shook his head and opened his mouth to say something sharp, then different words escaped him.

"I'll be right over, Pastor."

Damn it, he thought as he disconnected and reached for his cold-weather gear. What had come over him?

A freaking Christmas tree.

Chapter Two

Callum arrived at the parsonage five minutes later. To his surprise, Molly Canton was standing outside, parka unzipped, staring up into heavily falling snow.

When she heard him, she looked at him with a huge smile. "Best time of the year, don't you think?"

Not really. But he kept the thought to himself. "Where's this tree?"

"In the attic, like I said. One of the church handymen put it away for me last year and now I can't reach it. I can't thank you enough for coming over. I made some hot cocoa to warm you up, though. One benefit of doing a favor for a neighbor."

Hot cocoa? He hadn't had any of that in years. He wondered how it would mix with the bourbon in his stomach.

"But don't let me keep you longer than necessary," she said briskly, turning toward the door. "I'm really awful for having brought you out at this time of night. But as my congregants can tell you, once I get an idea, I don't let go easily."

He took a shot in the dark as he followed her into the warmly lit interior. "Like the crèche out front?"

She laughed as she shed her parka. "Like that."

"I kind of like it," he admitted reluctantly.

"A surprising number of people do, which is probably why I still have this job."

He dropped his jacket over the back of one of her kitchen chairs, then followed her up narrow stairs.

"A house of another era," she remarked. "No wasted space. I guess that's why the furniture is darn near as old as the house. Hard to remove."

"A little demolition and some build-it-yourself furniture might solve that problem."

"Agh. And here I had a lazy reason for leaving everything as it is."

Callum suspected this woman was in no way lazy. Not in this job. Not wanting her Christmas tree at an hour when most people were flopped in front of a TV or in bed. "Anything else up in that attic that you might need?"

She glanced at him with a smile. "One trip only?"

"I didn't say that." But he'd probably meant it. He didn't want to become anyone's errand boy.

"I don't plan to keep imposing," she replied as she pointed out the trapdoor overhead. "At least a former resident put in drop-down stairs. Can you imagine trying to reach in there from a wobbly ladder?"

"I'd probably become a statistic."

At least there was a pull-string light above the stairs. It wasn't bright, but bright enough. "That long box?" he asked when he was up to his waist in the small space.

"Please."

This was going to be fun. Neither the trapdoor nor the drop-down stairs would be wide enough to simply pull the box out and slide it down beside him. He'd have to back down while pulling the box.

"How many guys put this up here?" he asked.

"Two," she answered. "Is it too much for you to handle?"

Like he'd ever admit to that. "Just a little more complicated. Stand away from the bottom of the stairs."

Then he reached for the box and began his perilous journey, dragging it with him as he backed down. He was halfway down when he had enough of a grip to pull it out all the way and lower it. Molly reached for it.

"Thank you so much!"

He could hear the smile in her voice. Damn woman was too nice. "Anything else before I pull out of here?"

"Well, there are two other boxes. One with ornaments and one with garlands."

"You packed the garlands separately?"

"I didn't want them to get crushed. Besides, it meant smaller boxes."

Thank God for that. The first box barely fit through the opening and he barked his knuckles a little, but no big deal. The second box was easier. "Anything else?" he asked again.

"I hate to impose…"

As if she already hadn't. "What? Just tell me."

"There's another two boxes. Outdoor decorations. But it's not necessary…"

He gave up and climbed into the enclosed space. "Good thing I'm not claustrophobic." Crouched in the small space, he found the other two boxes. This time he dumped them slowly through the opening. Molly caught them.

"I can't thank you enough," she told him warmly.

His mother had raised him to be a gentleman, although sometimes he wondered why she had bothered. "No problem," he answered.

He climbed down, raised the stairs, then brushed himself off. "Someone needs to get up there to dust before it becomes a fire hazard. And no, I'm *not* volunteering."

"I'd think you were out of your mind if you did." But her mossy green eyes twinkled at him. "You're a kind man."

That was open to debate. "Where do you want these?"

"Oh, I can move them into the living room. You've already done enough."

He smothered a sigh, the gentleman in him rising to the fore again. "I'll do it."

The living room was small, just a few chairs and a fireplace that looked as if it hadn't been used in quite a while. It was too damn clean.

When he'd placed all the boxes out of the way as best he could, he brushed his hands together.

Molly spoke. "Now for that hot cocoa I promised you."

"That's not necessary."

"It's already almost done. Come to the kitchen, Detective."

"Just Callum," he told her.

"Then I'm just Molly."

When he was seated at the small table, she placed a large, steaming cup of cocoa in front of him. He couldn't remember the last time he'd had any. When he'd been a kid?

He eyed her as she sat across from him. "Aren't you having any?"

"Too many calories."

He paused with the mug halfway to his mouth. "What?"

She waved a hand, still smiling. "I need to take off fifteen pounds or so."

"According to who? Hollywood? TV commercials?"

"I don't like looking motherly. Although maybe that helps in my current position."

Callum shook his head. "You look just fine." Then he tasted the cocoa and was relieved it didn't go to war with the bourbon he'd swallowed earlier. In fact, it tasted wonderful.

"Great cocoa," he said.

"I'm glad you like it."

When he emptied his cup, she poured him another from the pan on the stove.

"It was awfully nice of you to come out this late at night," she said.

He eyed her over the rim of his mug and told the truth. "I wasn't relaxing."

"Looking over the case?"

"I don't let go easily."

She sighed and rested her chin in her hand. "I can't believe anyone would do that to Mabel. It would be hard to find a sweeter soul. And that car accident. Well, I'm not a vengeful person by nature, but I'm glad the drunk driver is in jail. Such lack of consideration for the lives of others in order to indulge an addiction. Or a quest for brief pleasure."

He didn't disagree and buried his own guilty conscience. At least he'd always summoned a cab.

"Now this," Molly continued. "I simply cannot fathom why anyone would want to hurt her. And they *wanted* to hurt her, didn't they?"

He couldn't answer that question even though he believed she was right. "I can't discuss the case."

"To think of Mabel being a case." Molly shook her head, then said, "I'm not trying to pry. Just ruminating. And I shouldn't be reminding you of work."

"It's not easy to put aside. Don't apologize." She had

a way about her, he thought. A nature that invited people to talk with her. He needed to be careful around her.

AFTER CALLUM LEFT, Molly stood in her living room surrounded by boxes she needed to unpack. Inviting Callum over to help get the items from the attic had been a brainstorm. She could have asked some of the men from church in the morning, but she'd thought of dour Callum, new in town, probably all alone.

It was the only way she could think of to get a chance to make him feel welcome.

But she'd been utterly surprised when he'd agreed. She hadn't expected that at all.

She flushed a bit when she thought of how difficult it had been for one man to handle those boxes. Hard enough for the guys last year to get them up there, but where else was she to put them?

Feeling not at all sleepy yet, and wondering if she faced another night of insomnia, she opened the box that contained the fiber-optic tree and placed the tree in the corner, in front of the bookcase and beside a small writing desk, the only place it would fit.

The tree had been left behind by her predecessor. It was an extravagance she never would have purchased herself, and the instant she plugged it in she felt the sparkle of magic once again. She went to her small CD player, popped in a disc of Christmas music and settled back into an overstuffed chair to let the beauty of the moments wash over her.

Decorating could wait for tomorrow. She'd probably need the enjoyment after meeting with the wardens.

At some point she drifted into sleep, "Silent Night" following her into her dreams.

For a little while, all was right with the world.

Chapter Three

All was right with the world until her meeting with the wardens. Sometimes she wanted to ask them outright why they'd hired her.

John Jason stepped onto his usual soapbox, bemoaning the fact that contributions had fallen off since Molly had taken over as pastor.

Daniel Alder wanted Molly to give a homily about the Christian duty to tithe to the church.

At that, Molly couldn't remain closemouthed. "Our primary duty is to help our fellow man," she said pleasantly. "There are a great many people in this county who need help. Regardless, my first responsibility is not to fill church coffers."

Silence greeted her. She was surprised only that no one erupted.

After a pregnant pause, John Jason spoke again. "This is the season of giving. Surely people can offer a little."

Callisto Manx, the only female member of the group, spoke. "Pastor Molly is supposed to be our spiritual guide, not our chief fundraiser."

John snorted. "Be that as it may, if the pastor wants to talk about helping our fellow man, at present there is no financial path to offering our annual Christmas baskets and the Christmas dinner."

Molly spoke again, disliking the way they were talking, as if she wasn't in the room. "I've spoken to the market. They're donating ten cooked turkeys for the dinner and a whole lot of canned ham for the baskets. Then, of course, we have the high school donating the use of their kitchen and cafeteria."

Silence fell again. John drummed his fingers on the long table. "Well, if you can do that, do more."

"I was thinking about asking our congregation to donate items for the baskets and for the dinner. A potluck sort of thing."

"That'll work," Callisto announced. "Some things are better than money, and folks feel better about giving them."

"The church has expenses," John reminded them with a glare in Molly's direction.

"And toys," Molly said, ignoring him. "A lot of children will need Christmas gifts. We need to put up the giving tree soon."

"And that still won't pay the light bill!"

"But candles will work." Molly smiled brightly. "Think how beautiful that would be."

When the meeting broke up in the early afternoon, Molly knew she was once again skating on thin ice. Nothing new about that, unfortunately.

She understood Good Shepherd's need for some cash flow, but the idea that people should be harangued about it from the pulpit truly bothered her. The pulpit was there to remind people of spirituality, not money.

How about starting a fundraiser toward a specific end? A time for people to enjoy each other's company and possibly make a donation? Something like Save Good Shepherd from the Cold and Dark.

Giving, she firmly believed, should be a choice and not forced under threat of hell.

After the meeting, she drove to the hospital to check in on Mabel Blix. The poor woman was still in her induced coma and that seriously worried Molly. She genuinely couldn't imagine the mind of anyone who would attack a woman in Mabel's condition. Or attack anyone at all, come to that.

Molly stayed for quite a while, sitting at Mabel's bedside, hoping for the slightest sign of consciousness before she decided she'd have to wait until tomorrow. She smiled and exchanged a few words with nurses and technicians as she left. The nicest thing about her job was that she had come to know quite a few people.

But as she was on her way back to the parsonage, her heart jammed into her throat.

Another house was surrounded by crime-scene tape. More lights swirled atop police cars. Tyra Lansing, one of Molly's closest friends, lived there.

And Callum's rangy figure, so unmistakable, was right in the middle of everything.

For several minutes, Molly sat with her hands gripping the steering wheel so tightly that they ached. Instead of murmuring the usual prayers, she had a stern one-sided conversation with God.

You may have set us loose with free will, but for Pete's sake, offer a hand from time to time. You protect the lilies of the field, but what about us two-legged organisms? Sure, we make our own misery, but You could still help out. That business about mankind being responsible for the world's suffering is beginning to wear thin with me.

She could have said a whole lot more, but even as she spouted her distress, she knew she was going over the top. God couldn't be blamed for violence generated by humans. Or by nature, for that matter.

Still, a visit from St. Michael with his flaming sword might do a bit of good.

She eased her car over until she was parked out of the way, then climbed out, into the waning winter afternoon, and walked to the tape, fearing what she'd hear.

Guy Redwing was standing there and greeted her with an angry face.

"Is it Tyra?" she asked, although in her heart of hearts she knew it was.

Guy nodded. "She's on her way to the hospital. I can't tell you more, Pastor."

"I know." Molly's heart squeezed until she felt as if it was being gripped by a giant fist. "What's going on?" A question without answer.

"If we knew that, we'd already have the perp. But that's obvious, isn't it." Guy's jaw tightened. "In all my years here, I've never seen the like of this. Now we have a vandal throwing rocks through store windows."

Molly gasped. "Really?"

"Drive down Main Street. Freitag's Mercantile lost three windows last night. Melinda's bakery window is cracked. Lucky, I guess, that she has a double-paned window."

What in the world was happening?

And it all seemed worse, somehow, given the time of year. Which was a ridiculous thought.

"Got any good ideas for Christmas?" Guy asked. "Right now I'm not feeling a whole lot of holiday spirit."

"Me, either." Thoughts of decorating her tree had fallen away.

Then she squared her shoulders. She had other people

to think about, people who might now grow scared. People who deserved to feel some of the joy of this season.

"Listen, Guy," she said after a moment, "I know Tyra wouldn't want anyone to lose their pleasure in the holiday. Especially the kids. They shouldn't have to deal with this."

Guy nodded slowly. "You're right, Pastor. Let's think of the kids."

It helped. Some. But Molly felt nearly crushed, anyway.

Tyra. Oh, God, Tyra, too? She still felt stunned and slammed the door after she reached the parsonage and stepped inside.

It was not a good time to be alone, but anger still trickled through her, and she had no desire to seek comfort in the church.

She looked upward again. "St. Michael. Just for a few minutes."

Then she eyed her tree and decided to get to it. This weekend, children would be coming by the church to enjoy hot drinks and to practice singing Christmas carols. Every year, the youngsters walked around town and sang on street corners. An old tradition that hadn't died here. A tradition she loved as much as she loved the others.

But some of those children would want to see her tree. She also needed to bake gingerbread men for them.

Mentally, she rolled up her sleeves, put on one of her CDs of carols and set to work.

Chapter Four

Night had deepened by the time Callum left the crime scene. One of the deputies had reported that Tyra Lansing was still unconscious. Head trauma. Broken ribs. A broken arm.

Whoever had done this was enjoying the pain he inflicted. Savoring it. Seeing it as the end in itself.

Because once again nothing of value had been taken as far as anyone could tell.

Neighbors had seen nothing. Well, why would they in the dark hours of winter? Every normal person was indoors, likely snuggled in bed. With windows closed, they wouldn't hear anything, either.

And all the police had were some heavy boot prints in the snow of the alley. All that told them was that the guy was big. Given how snow compressed, it was hard to guess how heavy he might be.

So okay, they likely had a male perp. Surprise, surprise.

Callum could have waited until morning, but he didn't want to. Simple as that.

He was chilled to the bone despite the high-quality winter gear he'd purchased for this climate. A sticky web of self-loathing tightened around him, even though he knew his guilt was unreasonable.

And he didn't want to spend another night with a glass of bourbon and a hideous spread of photos on his coffee table.

He had a reason for his visit, though. A number of neighbors had said that Tyra Lansing was good friends with Molly Canton. He definitely needed to talk to her and persuaded himself that she was probably a great deal less busy at this time of evening. Even though he had no idea how busy she was.

Half of him hoped she wouldn't answer her door when he knocked. That she was in the church building busy with something. Half of him knew damn well he shouldn't be here.

But the door opened and he faced a Molly Canton dusted with flour, a bit even smeared on her cheeks, and surrounded by a mouth-watering aroma.

She started to smile that warm smile but it died half-born, seemingly replaced by tension. "It's about Tyra. How bad?"

"I just have a few questions, that's all. No news about Ms. Lansing."

She nodded, relief flooding her face. "Well, come in out of the cold. I just pulled a batch of gingerbread men from the oven and I'm sure a few would taste good with coffee or tea."

Given the aroma, he figured they'd taste good with nothing at all. "Thanks," he said as he followed her into her tiny kitchen and unzipped his parka. "It sure does smell good in here."

"Well, hike up a chair and sit," she told him, her smile returning. She turned and used a spatula to move a few cookies from a cooling rack and onto a small floral plate. As she passed it to him, she asked, "Coffee or tea?"

"Don't go to any trouble for me."

She tsked. "Which is your poison? At this point I'd like either one myself. I have too many cookies left to bake, cool and put away to get sleepy now."

"Coffee, please. And why are you baking so many?"

She glanced over her shoulder as she started the coffee maker. "Children."

"Children?" Was she hiding them somewhere?

"On Saturday, the kids have a choir rehearsal to prepare for when they go caroling around town. Part of this is a tradition…well, I guess it's *my* tradition because I haven't been here that long and this is only my second Christmas. Anyway, after the rehearsal some of the kids come over to see my tree, and part of it is plucking gingerbread men off the tree to eat."

"Sounds like a good tradition."

"The rest of the cookies will go on the tree in the church hall in the basement. We'll see if I'm here long enough to make it traditional."

He had just been about to bite into one of the cookies but stopped. "Why wouldn't you be here long enough?"

"Let's just leave it that a woman pastor isn't exactly ideal for this county. In fairness, though, it's getting better." Smiling, she brought him coffee, then sat across from him.

Well, that stank, he thought. Must have been miserable to start here with a bunch of people resenting her.

"These are great," he told her sincerely after eating a cookie. Memories nearly swamped him. At this point he couldn't tell if they were uplifting or depressing, but Angela had always baked her way through the holidays. She'd absolutely loved to bake. God, he missed her.

"But about Tyra," Molly said, rising as a timer dinged. She bent to pull another sheet of cookies from the oven. "How is she? Really."

"Really? Really she's a mess and still unconscious, like Ms. Blix. This perp is loaded with anger, would be my guess, a cocked pistol. Or maybe he's just a serious sadist. Speculation on my part."

"You probably have the experience to speculate." Her expression grew so sad. "But you said you had some questions for me."

He nodded, reached for a paper napkin from a stack at the end of the table. "People are saying you're good friends with Ms. Lansing."

"I am. Drawn close, I think, because we're both outsiders." She slipped more cookies onto the cooling rack and another sheet into the oven. Tall stacks of cooled gingerbread men filled two large plates.

He arched an eyebrow. "Outsiders?"

"Well, you know about me," she answered, then her tone grew dry. "And, of course, Tyra is Black, which is not common in Conard County."

"Why should her race make a difference?" He knew it was a ridiculous question, but he wanted to hear her take.

Molly simply shook her head. "I'm sure it's different in Boston, but around here most people are Caucasian. We have a smattering of Indigenous people, of course, but Tyra is pretty much a singularity around here." Then she eyed him. "I doubt you're uneducated about race relations."

"I'm not. Plenty of tension that doesn't need to exist."

"We are in agreement about that."

"So how did Ms. Lansing get here and why doesn't she leave?"

"She came for a teaching job at the high school. She loves it. Anyway, there haven't been any problems and she's highly respected. Her students seem to love her as much as she loves her teaching. She's a great person."

He decided to reach for another cookie. "Any reason anyone would want to hurt her the way they hurt Ms. Blix? Enemies? Exes? Disputes?"

Molly's brow wrinkled. "Not that I'm aware of. Which doesn't mean anything, I guess. I'm sure I have enemies of my own but they haven't done anything to let me know."

Callum sat back, mug in hand, resisting the urge to eat that last cookie on the plate she'd given him. It must have been hard for her to be a pioneer, as the first woman pastor around here. Lonely. Frustrating. She had to be a stubborn and patient woman.

Molly spoke again. "So why did you come here from Boston?"

One corner of his mouth lifted reluctantly. "Less mayhem."

That drew a quiet laugh from her. "I guess I should wish you luck."

"So it seems."

The atmosphere was starting to get cozy, and Callum knew he should leave before the mood resurrected more memories. Like of the old house he and Angela had been slowly restoring to an earlier glory. Like the evenings in the kitchen, while Angela baked delights that she often gave away. He got the cleaning-up part. Other evenings in the living room with a glass of wine, music playing, easy, lazy conversation flowing.

Yeah, he'd better leave now. But just as he started to rise, Molly spoke.

"You know," she said slowly, "if Tyra had been the first victim instead of Mabel, I'd be harboring awful suspicions."

"Understandable." He relaxed into the chair again and

waited to see if there was more information. Focusing on his job got him through a lot of sad moments.

"Even so," she remarked briskly, "the suspicions are bad enough." Then she stood, clearly ending the evening.

He rose, too, and extended his hand for a shake. "Thanks for the cookies. And if you think of anything at all, let me know." He left his newly minted card on her table and headed for the front door.

As he stepped out and turned to close it behind himself, he saw Molly standing there.

She smiled. "I don't mean to be so abrupt, but in my position I have to be careful about perceptions."

"I should have thought of that before I came over." He should have, although coming from a very different world, it hadn't occurred to him.

"Not that I wouldn't stand up to them—" she shrugged "—but why look for a fight?"

She probably had enough of them already, he thought as he walked away into swirling snow. More than enough.

For nearly the first time since moving here, when Molly closed the door behind Callum she felt as if the house was big and empty. It was an odd sensation for such a small cottage.

Still, she felt it. The lights on the tree in the living room twinkled invitingly, and after she'd put the remaining dough in the refrigerator and covered the baked cookies with plastic wrap, she took full advantage of that tree.

Her predecessor had left it behind when he'd moved on to shepherd a large congregation in Omaha. With three kids, he probably needed the pay boost, she thought, grinning. Although he'd probably needed more living room, too. How he'd squeezed those three kids into this house she couldn't imagine. They'd had a dog as well.

Crowded. And probably a place they'd filled with love and laughter. Maybe. She'd heard that Reverend Stanton had belonged to the fire-breathing ranks. Maybe *that* was why the wardens had chosen a woman to fill the vacancy. A complete change of pace.

Some people, she'd discovered, vastly preferred a strict religion that promised endless punishment for failures. Others felt drawn to something much kinder and full of forgiveness. Both sides had their points, but catering to both schools could sometimes be a tightrope walk.

She sighed, wishing she could feel the least bit sleepy. Another insomnia night? Well, her homily would certainly get done well before time. Maybe she could even rustle up some fundraising ideas to settle the worried wardens.

Worried Wardens. She liked that and decided that was how she would think of them from now on. It took some of the sting out of the force they'd become in her life.

All of them meant well, she was sure, but more than one struck her as being on a bit of a power trip. Callisto Manx was the exception, but then Callisto was the exception to quite a lot. When Molly thought about it, she was still astonished that Callisto had even been elected a warden.

Maybe tides were changing even here. About time, when she considered that women were the heart and soul of every church she'd ever known.

ARTHUR KILLIAN HAD a pretty good thing going for a man who thirsted for vengeance and hadn't been able to think about much else for a long time now.

That bitch was gonna pay.

Especially since he couldn't locate the conniving, stupid, useless broad who'd been his wife. Man, he'd wasted a lot of time looking for her.

But finding Molly Canton, the only other possible object of his ire, had turned out to be comparatively easy. Oh, the National Guard hadn't been any help. Canton had been on duty when she tangled with him, but beyond the court papers, they were silent as clams.

The real eye-opener had been his web search. Only a handful of people in the entire country shared the name *Molly Canton*. Sifting through them had been easy enough—it had only taken a week to narrow his search down to those who fit the right age bracket with a military background. It cost him a few bucks to get that detailed information, but it had been worth it.

Sergeant Molly Canton, with a quick fist and well-aimed knee, had turned into a preacher. Soldier to saint. He invariably snickered when he thought about it. He bet she was soft now.

Anyway, he'd been able to settle into this small town without a problem. He'd rented a big box truck and parked it in the truck-stop lot, then had spent some time in the diner muttering about how he was stuck between the heavy snowfall and the delay in picking up his next load in Cheyenne. It easily explained his lingering, and he'd been able to find decent enough lodging at the La-Z-Rest motel. It had burned to the ground a few months ago and still stank of ash and fire, but a part of it had been rebuilt enough that he'd grabbed himself a discounted room.

Pretty well set, indeed, for the plans that he had to take care not to carry out too quickly.

But he'd taken out two women who were close to the bitch. At some point Molly Canton would realize he was after *her*. Or not. Once he got to her, it wouldn't matter.

But he thought breaking those windows had been a smart touch. Confusing the whole crime situation. Giving him plenty of ways to cover his tracks.

Chapter Five

The snowstorm overnight had delivered only six inches of snow. When Molly stepped out from the parsonage, she took a little time to admire the way the fresh white blanket gleamed and sparkled, acting like a prism so that many snowflakes reflected different colors.

Jimmy Dawson had apparently arrived bright and early, since the walkway from the parsonage to the rear entrance of the church was already cleared and sanded. A wonderful man, Jimmy.

Inside the relative warmth of the church, she found the church secretary already at her desk, busy with papers and the daily diary.

Henrietta Gilchrist was a woman in her late fifties with a head of short white hair and a face that seemed nearly ageless. She was decked out in an oversize dark green sweater and wool pants.

"Good morning, Pastor," she said brightly. Always formal was Henrietta.

"Good morning, Henrietta. How's the day look?"

The church office itself was spacious, full of dark antique furnishings except for the computer on Henrietta's desk. Molly much preferred her own little study at the parsonage.

"Not too full," the secretary answered. "Folks are busy

getting ready for Christmas. Tomorrow will be different, however. One wedding and two christenings."

Those were celebrations Molly would need to attend. "But I don't need to push anything aside? I'd like to go visit Mabel Blix and Tyra Lansing."

"Plenty of room today. I can clear more for tomorrow if you want. Some of these home visits can wait. But don't forget the choir rehearsal tonight."

"I can't miss that."

Henrietta shook her head. "Absolutely not. Oh, and the new market is offering precooked hams for the Christmas supper and quite a few boxes of stuffing and dried mashed potatoes. The volunteer list is on the rise."

That lifted Molly's heart. Being able to provide a special meal to those who couldn't provide their own was a good thing. The kind of thing they needed to do more often, but a regular soup kitchen was beyond them. It was hard enough to get dried goods to pass out the rest of the year.

"That's good news," she told Henrietta.

"I'll keep working on it. Some folks just need to be reminded. Now you take yourself over to the hospital. I'm so worried about those two women. I can't imagine why this happened."

Molly couldn't, either, but imagining why didn't change the facts one bit.

The hospital brought her more good news. Both women were awake. On pain meds, but still conscious. Molly headed for Mabel's room first, where she found Callum McCloud with his notebook out.

"I really don't know what happened," Mabel told him, her voice slightly slurred from the medication. "I'm not sure how much is that I can't remember. I just know I was sleeping. I always keep the lights on because it's safer for me to get around at night, so you would think I saw something, but all I remember was a blow to my head. I didn't see who did it. It came from behind while I was lying down. After that I don't recall a thing until I woke up."

Callum nodded and slipped his notebook into his jacket pocket. "If you remember anything more, will you be sure to have someone call me? We want to find this guy."

"Thank you," Mabel murmured, growing sleepier. "Pastor Molly..." Her voice trailed off completely.

"You can try coming back in an hour or so," the nurse told them. "She'll be in and out most of the day."

Outside the room, Molly looked at Callum. "Have you talked to Tyra?"

"I was just about to."

"Is it all right if I come?"

He offered her that half smile that didn't reach his eyes. "As if I could keep you out."

"Well, at least we have an understanding about that."

"They're part of your flock. You can do more for them than I can."

"At least for now."

Tyra was only three rooms down and was sitting up with a bed tray in front of her, her breakfast only half-touched. She smiled when she saw Molly. "Wondered when you'd get here, girl."

"I was here yesterday, but you ignored me."

Tyra gave a short, pained laugh. "I was ignoring everything." She looked at Callum.

"Detective Callum McCloud," he said, introducing himself.

"Oh, you're the new guy everyone wonders about.

You'd better tell them a little more about yourself or they'll be making up their own stories."

Molly sat in the chair beside the bed and took Tyra's hand gently. "How are you feeling?"

"Like a mule kicked me more than once. But I'll be fine. I just hate being away from the school right now. Those kids will be bouncing with excitement." She looked at Callum. "Even the older ones get wound up for Christmas. Some get irritated by it, but I just enjoy it. You'd be surprised how many of them don't get very happy the rest of the year."

"I wouldn't be surprised at all."

Tyra nodded, her long, intricate braids dancing on the pillow. "I bet you have questions for me."

"Anything at all that you can remember."

Tyra frowned and let her head fall back against the pillow. "Guy seemed to come out of nowhere."

"Guy?"

"Yeah. Kinda bulky, but who can be sure under those parkas. Just an impression. I couldn't sleep and was making a cup of tea. I saw something move in a reflection from the kitchen window, I turned around and then *boom!* Side of my head felt like it was imploding."

Callum spoke sympathetically. "It was a pretty bad blow."

"Tell me about it," Tyra said dryly.

"Was the man wearing anything that stood out to you?"

"No. All black with a balaclava under his parka hood."

"Eye color?"

Tyra closed her eyes. "Blueish, maybe. It was only a quick glimpse. They were certainly lighter than dark brown."

"Height?"

"A little taller than me. I'm five-nine."

"Can you think of anyone who might want to hurt you?"

Tyra gave it a minute's thought. "Not that I'm aware of, although I did get into quite an argument with a father who didn't think I should be passing out copies of *To Kill a Mockingbird* as an English assignment. I doubt anyone would want to do this to me over a book, though."

"His name?"

"Reedy. Gerry Reedy."

Callum put away his notebook, looking satisfied. "You've been a great help, Ms. Lansing. If you remember anything else, just call me." He placed a card on her table. "Or ask anyone at all to call me for you. I'll leave you with the pastor now."

Molly squeezed Tyra's hand as Callum walked out. "I wish I could give you a hug."

Tyra managed an impish smile. "Please don't. I'll take it as a given."

Molly felt the ache rising in her heart again, replacing the joy she'd first felt at learning both women were recovering. "I'm so sorry this happened to you."

"Me, too," Tyra answered frankly. "I just hope it doesn't happen to anyone else. How's Mabel doing?"

"Still in and out on the medications but improving."

"That's good news." Tyra sighed. "I'm getting sleepy again, but that's okay now. You get back to your duties and let me heal, girl. I'll be knocking on your door again before you know it."

"You better be."

"And Molly? Don't let this ruin your holiday for you. I know how much you love it. What you might do is drip some of that joy into that detective. Looks like he needs it."

That was Tyra, bless her. Always thinking of others.

Outside in the cold, she was surprised to see Callum, as if he was waiting for her.

"You need me?" she asked.

"Tyra's information was helpful," he remarked. "The eyes and height of the assailant. Interesting, though, that both women were attacked in the light. You'd expect someone like this to be working in the dark."

"That would make sense. Apparently none of this makes sense."

"No." He sighed. "Anyway, you know a whole lot of people. Do me a favor and pay attention to anything you hear or see. Someone might have some wisp of knowledge that could prove useful."

"I hope so."

The beautiful blue sky of the early morning had given way to pregnant clouds. A light snowfall swirled gently. Callum walked away, appearing lost in deep thought, and Molly headed back to the church. She was sure that Henrietta had been being kind when she said today's schedule was light. It wasn't often the case.

When she arrived back at Good Shepherd, she found Henrietta sitting with Callisto Manx in the church office. A couple of women occupied the pews, clearly deeply in prayer, so she left them alone while she closed the door and greeted Callisto.

Molly had always thought Callisto to be a striking woman—tall, strongly boned and wearing a black bob that appeared to be from another era. It suited the shape of Callisto's face perfectly.

"To what do I owe the honor?" Molly asked Callisto as she sat at her own desk.

"Friendship," Callisto said wryly. "I thought you should know that the ladies' Altar Society is in the middle of a tussle that's not getting any prettier. It's bound to spill on you, so take this as a heads-up so you can prepare yourself."

Molly nodded. The was not the first time she'd faced a set-to like this and it was bound not to be the last. "What's going on?"

"Janice Remy is titular head of the group, as you know. But Claire AuCoin is the de facto head. And by that, I mean everyone listens to Claire and follows her directions. I'm sure you've noticed. In any event, the problem blew up when Claire asked Georgia to darn the edges of the Christmas altar cloth and Janice announced that Claire had no right to do any such thing."

Molly nodded her head. "The group should be cooperative, shouldn't they?"

"You'd think. But it's the same trying to get the Senior Warden and Junior Warden to agree on anything except that you're wrong somehow. I personally believe that the church is no place for power struggles."

"But people will be people," Molly acknowledged.

"Sadly. I just wanted you to be ready for it when it really blows up. Then, I gave Daniel Alder a piece of my mind. For heaven's sake, as Junior Warden, finances are his headache. Why should he dump all that on you? So I told him to straighten up and do his job."

Molly drew a sharp breath, trying not to laugh. "You didn't."

"I did. And John Jason is next on my list. He's the Senior Warden but all he does is try to stir up trouble in one way or another."

Molly shook her head. "Be careful, Callisto. They could throw you off the Vestry."

"See if I care. They won't be able to shut my mouth

and I swear if they pull that I'll be talking outside vestry meetings."

With a *harrumph*, Callisto rose. Then she smiled at Molly. "You're doing a very good job, Pastor. Many of us have your back."

After the door closed, Henrietta made a sound of disapproval. Molly eyed her.

"What's wrong, Henrietta?"

"Bringing politics through this door is all."

"Politics are part of human nature."

"Be that as it may—" Henrietta frowned "—they don't belong in here."

"Seeing as how they are part of human nature, they *will* come in here, and my job is not to ignore it, but to try to keep this congregation together."

"Good luck dealing with this lot. The Vestry is bad enough but to have the Altar Society at each other's throats could spread all over the place."

Into factions. But Molly didn't say that. Like any other organization, there were groups of friends, tightly knit. If they started taking sides, life could get fractious indeed.

"No Christmas spirit," Henrietta muttered. "Ugly things have happened, and I know they burden your heart, but don't let them steal the joy from you. Don't let *anyone* do that."

"How's your Christmas spirit doing?" Molly asked.

Henrietta smiled brightly. "The family is coming! They weren't sure they could but I'll get to see my grandchildren."

"That's the best happiness of all."

CHOIR REHEARSAL THAT evening was beautiful. Good Shepherd had a wonderful choir, but the carols brought out something more in them. And at the candlelight service on Christmas Eve, with the entire congregation joining in, the experience would become indescribably moving.

She spoke to the choir afterward, telling them how beautiful they sounded and thanking them for the effort. She gave a short, impromptu homily about this time of love and peace, then shook hands at the door as everyone departed.

Only a few expressed concern about the victimization of two women, but she did her best to reassure them. As if anything short of arresting the creep could do that.

After a time spent in solitary prayer asking for blessings while kneeling before the altar, she headed back to the parsonage and stopped short when she saw Callum McCloud.

"Did something happen?" she asked immediately, her heart skipping a beat.

"Nothing worrisome." He tilted his head. "Like a kid, I came hoping for more cookies and coffee."

She laughed and opened the door to him. "I think that can be arranged."

But now she realized that Callum was truly a lonely man. A sad one.

She had to find a way to help him beyond cookies and coffee.

CALLUM FELT LIKE a bit of a fool, dropping in like this, but it was as if he'd been inexorably drawn. His bachelor pad had little to offer even when he didn't face bleak crimes, and something in him was reaching out. He didn't know if that was a good thing, but Molly's door seemed like a safe one to knock on.

This time she offered him coffee and cookies in her tiny living room, where they could see her Christmas tree. He settled on a recliner that had seen better days. It certainly needed at least one spring repaired. But nothing in this house appeared to be in much better condition.

When she had served and settled, she waxed about the choir rehearsal and how wonderful it had been. Then she made the inevitable invitation to the candlelight service.

He'd known he was going to be invited to her church sooner or later. The problem was that since his wife's death he had absolutely no desire to go into a church. Or anywhere near one.

When there was no hope in the world, faith seemed like a false promise. A delusion.

"I'll think about it," he answered her, offering no commitment but not refusing outright. There was no point in telling her what he really thought.

"Tomorrow's going to be busy," she remarked. "Two baptisms and a wedding. I'll have to be careful not to overindulge the bubbly at the celebrations afterward."

"One toast?" he asked.

"That's safe enough." Her smile was bright. "New beginnings. I love them!"

He nodded, wishing he could find the smile she deserved, but failing. He certainly didn't want to tell her this was the worst time of year for him. From everything he'd seen so far, he guessed this might be her favorite time.

"It's so beautiful," she continued, "the fresh snowfall last night. So clean and pristine, and I love the way the air smells. The way sounds are muffled. A hush seems to settle over the whole world."

"It does," he agreed. Then, before the gushing continued—mostly for his benefit, he thought—he said, "How's your congregation taking the two attacks?"

"We haven't had Sunday service yet, so I haven't seen most of them. But tonight after choir practice, only a few expressed fears. For most, that's human nature, thinking it can never happen to you."

"That may be true for women who don't live alone." He watched her face darken a bit. "I'm sorry, but you need to take extra care, Molly."

After a moment, she shook her head. "I'm not going to let this beast control me. As a pastor, I have important duties and my flock deserves a pastor who performs them, not one cowering in fear."

"I'm not suggesting cowering. I'm suggesting extra caution."

"Like what? Keeping my lights turned off?"

He stared at her. "I didn't say that."

"No, but you said earlier it was odd that both women had been attacked in lighted rooms. I'll grant that it's odd, but it doesn't seem like much protection to live in the dark. This guy could change his habit at any time."

He could hardly argue with that. Two similar crimes didn't even mean they'd been committed by the same perp. One could be a copycat. Or there could be one or more guys involved. Hell, even with a serial killer you couldn't even be sure you had one when there were only two crimes.

He ruminated quietly while sipping coffee and eating a second cookie. "Any link between these two victims?"

"They attend Good Shepherd. I don't even think they socialize except at church gatherings. Separate lives."

"And I bet Good Shepherd has hundreds of attendees, so that's meaningless."

Molly nodded. "All I can think of is that they're both women living alone."

"Easy targets in that sense." Time to shift gears, he decided. No reason to rain on her parade, such as it was. "Do you bake anything besides gingerbread cookies?"

"All I can say is that it's a good thing I have plenty of people to share my baking with. I may like making the stuff, but I can't eat much of it."

That weight thing again. He could have shaken his head.

"Anyway, I bake pies for the Christmas dinner, and I love to donate them wherever I can. There's a lot of satisfaction in that. It's nice to visit one of my flock with a pie. I'll bake you one soon."

"Don't go to any trouble."

"I just said I enjoy it," she replied a trifle tartly.

Again, that unusual urge to smile came over him, but he allowed only a small bit to show. "So tell me about Molly Canton. You must have done something before coming here."

"Well, I did, like most people." She rose, disappeared into her kitchen and returned with fresh coffee. "I grew up in an agnostic home," she said as she resumed her seat, a Boston rocker with a cushion. "Somehow, despite that, I found religion. Or it found me." She shrugged with a small smile.

"Then?"

"Off to college to major in social work. I joined the National Guard, too."

Callum arched an eyebrow. "Why?"

"Because I wanted to help during natural disasters."

He understood that. A lot of people felt the same—much good it did them during the war. "So how did you get here?"

"My religion became a calling. Seminary came next, followed by a church run by a pastor who *really* didn't like women of the cloth."

She flashed a grin. "Trial by fire. I survived him. Then a brief time at a smaller church with a more pleasant atmosphere. Then here. I'm still not sure why I was hired, but I'm never going to dive into that rat's nest. There are some things better left alone."

Callum nodded. "That can be very wise."

"But what about you?" she asked. "This is an odd place to come from Boston."

"Was I fired, you mean? No. I retired. Mostly I wanted to get away from those duties. Too much violence in a city." And one huge, bad memory, although his memory was already burdened with other violent crimes.

Molly sighed. "We aren't giving you a much better picture of us at the moment."

"Listen, I've been here barely three months and these are my first major crimes. No complaints."

Except he had many complaints, one of the foremost being that he didn't know the people and the area. He was working on it, but he still felt as if he had one hand tied behind his back. People knowledge had always been a great resource for him.

"It has to be hard for you to be an outsider, though," she remarked. "This area is tightly knit with relationships that go back for generations. Hard to break into, as I can attest. People are friendly enough, but I can't imagine how long you have to be here before you become a true part of the community."

"I think you're well on your way, Molly. Pastor, and all that. People must find you easier to talk with."

"I wish I could be sure." She shrugged one shoulder. "It doesn't matter. I like it here. Maybe I can finish out my career here."

Despite himself, a quiet chuckle escaped him. "Do you feel lucky?"

"Ha. We'll see. You can't please everyone."

He leaned back in the questionable chair and allowed

himself to enjoy the twinkling Christmas tree. He remembered store windows in Boston filled with snowy scenes and toys to entice kids. Once, he'd found strolling those streets to be special. Then he'd become blind to them.

He knew he needed to make some mental and emotional adjustments to the greatest loss of his life, to the fact that he was still living and breathing. It was difficult, and sometimes he just wanted to wallow.

"I've kept you long enough," he said suddenly, rising to carry his plate and cup to the kitchen. "Frankly, that chair needs some respringing."

She grinned. "Jimmy's going to get to it when he has time."

"Jimmy?"

"A wonderful jack-of-all-trades. He has a family and a full-time job to look after, though. The amazing thing is that he manages to keep my walkway shoveled, as well as the entrance to the church and the parking lot."

"Good man." But from his experience, not enough.

"I think so. There are a few in the world," she joked. "Anyway, if you don't want to come to the candlelight service, come for a choir practice. It's beautiful."

"I'll see." No promise.

As he headed back through the cold clear night, knowing what awaited him on his coffee table, he wondered why he didn't just carry the load of work back to the office.

A few deputies would be there. Unfortunately, from what he'd overheard, they were planning to decorate the office.

He'd probably get dragged in.

AFTER HE GATHERED UP all his materials, he drove to the station, anyway, and hauled everything inside. As he'd feared, the deputies who were night-staffing the squad room were cheerfully hanging up window stickers and spraying snowflake stencils to leave giant flakes behind. A stuffed Santa sat in one corner and a Christmas tree in another. He even saw pieces of a reindeer waiting to be assembled. No escaping it.

"Come on," Guy Redwing said to him. "Put that briefcase on your desk and come help. You can reach the higher spaces."

"I'm not a ladder," he said, not for the first time.

"Taller than any of us. We wouldn't need to break out the ladder. And there's some hot cider and cinnamon to share."

Two of the other deputies, Randy Webster and Stu Canaday, gave him looks suggesting he'd better join them.

Well, why not? he asked himself. It was one way to get to know more people around here. And it would keep him away from those horrific photos a while longer.

"Weird about those windows being broken," Stu remarked. "That hasn't happened before."

"I know," Randy said. "I grew up around here and I've never heard of it except graduation time, when some kids get too drunk for their own good."

"Too drunk for their age," Guy said. "How many bottles do we confiscate on average?"

"Does anyone count?"

Two laughs answered him.

Callum, instead of standing on a ladder, found himself on a window ledge pasting up stickers of Santa's sleigh and reindeer. "Hey," he said. "What about the bigger Santa and deer?"

"For the other window," Guy explained. "Every window is different."

Well, that made sense. The storefront-style office of the sheriff's department offered a panoramic view of the street in front through two windows on either side of the entry door, and another facing the Courthouse Square. Plenty of room for decoration.

The hot cider was pretty good, too, and finally even Callum, who tried to keep a distance from most people, fell into the camaraderie of the activity.

"Cleaning this up is going to be a mess," Randy remarked. "It always is. We can leave the cleanup to the day shift."

Guy snorted. "How can you be sure you won't be on the day shift by morning?"

"Can't," Randy remarked equably. "Just my hope."

After spreading puffy cotton snow around the feet of the big sleigh and reindeer, everyone stood back to look at their handiwork.

"Not bad," Stu pronounced. "Not perfect, but not bad."

"Perfection is overrated," Randy joked. "Come on, let's get more cider."

Yet another thermos was opened at the coffee table. Just then, a window shattered and a brick hit the floor hard.

"Well, hell," said one of the deputies as all four of the men took off after the miscreant.

In a hurry, they left their jackets behind as they raced up the street, peering into the dark spaces of doorways and an alley. No luck, and they finally grew too cold to stay outdoors.

Guy sent out a BOLO, not that it would do much good without a description.

Cold air sucked the heat right out of the office. Everyone pulled on jackets and then the hunt for plywood began. They found a piece and hammered it into place.

"Who the hell could be this crass?" Stu asked.

"Or this stupid," remarked Guy. "Hitting this office?"

Callum responded, "He got away, didn't he?"

Grim silence answered him.

After downing half a mug of cider, Randy said, "Well, that was the prettiest window. Of course."

Of course.

Chapter Six

In the morning, a larger-than-usual group of older women showed up for morning prayer. There were even some elderly men among them.

Wondering what was going on, Molly donned her surplice and stole, and led the prayers for the day.

But the attendees didn't leave directly afterward, and two of them came up to her. "Pastor, have you heard?"

Molly raised her eyebrows and her heart raced with dread—she hoped there hadn't been another vicious attack. "Heard what?"

"Someone threw a brick through the sheriff's office window," Belinda Armistead said.

"Right as they finished decorating," Claire AuCoin added. "What is this town coming to?"

A good question, Molly thought. She hadn't been here long, but it was long enough to realize this was becoming an unusual confluence of events.

"We must pray," she said, not for the first time, "for the safety of everyone in town."

"One of the deputies could have been hurt," Belinda said. "We all need safety, God willing."

Which led to nearly a dozen people kneeling before the altar while Molly led them in prayer. She hoped they felt better, but *she* didn't.

This most joyous time of the year was beginning to turn into a nightmare.

The afternoon wedding and christenings elevated her spirits considerably. A glass of champagne at each celebration afterward made her feel a little light-headed.

New beginnings. They were always welcome. And this was certainly the time of year for them.

TWO DAYS LATER, Tyra was released from the hospital. Molly wanted her to stay with her in her one tiny bedroom, but Tyra would have none of it.

"It's time to get back on my feet," she announced. "I refuse to get knocked down for long. I heard Mabel isn't doing as well."

Molly shook her head sadly. "She had to go to inpatient rehab. With all her earlier problems, I guess she's going to need more help."

"Now that really makes me mad," Tyra said. "*Very* mad. That poor woman has had more than her share of misery. We've got to catch this guy."

"Callum's on it."

Tyra waved a hand. "He doesn't know this area well enough. Folks have to help him."

"I'm sure he'll appreciate any hints we can give."

Tyra turned to look at her as Molly drove down the street. "This doesn't look like the way to my house."

"It's not. I figured you couldn't refuse an apple turnover fresh from the oven."

"Oh, girl, you *do* have my number!"

And Molly had every intention of making sure Tyra stayed with her for at least a few days. She couldn't imagine that her friend honestly wanted to be alone in her own house again. Not yet, anyway. Maybe not until they caught this beast.

Regardless, the turnovers were waiting, ready to be popped into the oven. Tyra winced as she sat at the table.

"Would you prefer to sit in the living room?"

Tyra shook her head. "On those torture devices you call chairs? I think not." Then she grinned. "Truth is, these cracked ribs hurt. You put me in one of those chairs and I'm not sure I'll be able to get up. No, this is more comfortable and it's less painful to breathe."

"Cool. And you want to go home? Are you actually going to try to sleep in bed? Or sleep sitting in any of those chairs you have?"

Tyra pursed her lips. "Do I sense pressure?"

"You might."

The turnovers were soon done, covered with a sprinkling of sugar. Molly put a hot one in front of Tyra. "Don't burn your mouth."

"As if."

Just then, someone knocked on the door. Molly promptly went to answer it and was surprised to see Callum.

"Come in and join us for turnovers," she invited. "I was about to make coffee, too."

"I'm a coffee fiend," Tyra said from the kitchen. "What brings you this way, Detective?"

He hung his jacket on a peg near the door, revealing a dark blue sweater and jeans, and entered the tiny kitchen. "I came to see how you're doing."

"And if I remember any more than I told you," Tyra retorted.

Callum tipped his head. "And that, too, although I was checking on Molly and didn't know you were here. I heard about Ms. Blix. Rehab?"

"Again." Molly frowned. "She's already been through it since her car accident. In fact, she was still getting in-home therapy. Now this. I'll be visiting her, for what little comfort I can offer at this point."

"She seems to have a big blank about the entire event."

Molly placed a turnover in front of him while the coffeepot gurgled behind her.

Tyra said, "Lucky her, actually. Who needs to remember any bit of it? Might be useful to you, Detective, but not to her."

"Callum, please. And you're right. But I have a job to do, and any scrap of information can help. Right now I don't have anything to work with except your description."

"Which could be anyone at all." Tyra sighed, but not deeply. "Well, there's one more little thing that probably won't help, either. The guy smelled like Bigfoot."

That brought a laugh from Molly and the faintest of smiles from Callum.

"You know Bigfoot?" he asked.

"Not personally, but I've heard about his smell. This guy smelled rank, like he hadn't showered in months. Of course, that could have been his clothes."

Callum nodded and pulled out his notebook from his shirt pocket, then made a note. "Smelling like that could make him very noticeable."

"Debatable around here," Tyra said dryly. "Some of these hired hands come to town and you wonder if they've ever heard of soap and water."

Conversation moved on to more pleasant matters, with Tyra complaining that she wasn't allowed to go back to work for a week. "I miss my kids, especially right now. You wouldn't believe a group of teens could get so excited about Christmas. I kind of expected them to be blasé about the entire subject. Nope."

"It shows up in church, too," Molly said. "We always

have so many volunteers for the youth choir. I wish they'd hang around for the rest of the year."

"These apple turnovers are the best," Callum remarked. "You trying to put Melinda's bakery out of business?"

"Not likely. These were specially made for Tyra." Then she had a thought. "Do you cook?"

"For myself, you mean? Not likely." He rose, thanking her for the coffee and turnover, then disappeared out the door like the shadow he seemed to try to remain.

"Something about that man," Tyra remarked.

"A heavy burden," Molly mused. "Very heavy."

ARTHUR KILLIAN FELT very proud of himself. That brick through the window of the sheriff's office had been brilliant. It had undoubtedly made a lot of deputies furious because it was a clear assault on their authority. More angry than the other broken windows. He was sure that more of them were busy hunting a vandal than the assailant of two women. Especially since he hadn't attacked anyone in a few days.

His hope was that they believed he had moved on. That angry or mischievous kids were responsible for the vandalism.

That suited his plan to perfection. *Distraction.* He'd wanted it all along to protect himself. To muddy the waters.

And this dang motel room wasn't that bad, despite the ashy smell. Hasty's diner across the road sure made some good meals.

If he didn't have another purpose, he could have stayed here until he was broke.

But some things were more important than his comfort. Far more important.

He popped open a carryout container and began to dive into a heap of fries and a couple of hamburgers. And tomorrow there'd be plenty of pancakes and syrup. A guy could definitely get used to this.

MOLLY WASN'T OVERWORKED. In one way, being at a smaller church had advantages. She had ample time to write her homilies, to spend with congregants who showed up wishing for some prayer or comfort. She also had time to visit those who were housebound.

Today was her day to go visit Stacy Withers, who was dying of cancer, and Marcia Lathrop, who needed some serious help dealing with her father, who was not only difficult, but also appeared to be sinking into some serious senility.

Finding people who were willing to make trips to these outlying ranches during the heavy winter season wasn't proving easy. Many murmured sympathy and concern, but none volunteered.

Too risky on these roads to undertake scheduled visits.

But today the roads were clear and Molly set out with some turnovers in tins beside her, some magazines and a couple of her thriller novels. Stacy seemed to like those.

In-town visits were so much easier, but these trips to outlying ranches were no less important. Maybe she even felt better about them because of the difficulties they presented.

Unfortunately, she now had time to think about Callum McCloud. He was, apart from his difficulty in smiling, an extremely attractive man. She tried not to notice such things. It wasn't as if a pastor couldn't fall in love, but being a woman made matters far more precarious for her.

She certainly couldn't have an affair. The thought

brought a furtive grin to her face. Such matters hadn't always been so difficult in her life. During her time in college and in the National Guard, she'd had several serious relationships. No concern about appearances back then.

But appearances ruled her life in many ways now. She sometimes had to remind herself that she'd chosen this life and its sacrifices.

And there were sacrifices. A penurious allowance, life in a cottage that needed some serious renovations and time that wasn't often her own.

She had to be available as much as possible. She had to remain in the church office in case someone needed to speak with her. Yes, she had some freedom, but for the sake of her flock, she kept that freedom on a short leash.

But Callum had caught her attention more than anyone else she remembered. And once again, she decided she needed to help him out somehow.

By the time she finished her visits and was on her way home, gentle snow had begun to fall once more. More snow than last year, she thought, but she didn't have much of a comparison.

It was with warmth that she saw Good Shepherd rise before her. She felt as if she was coming home.

CALLUM'S THOUGHTS WERE running along a different line. He kept getting the feeling that the window vandalism and the attacks on the two women were related somehow.

But such different crimes from the same perp? Even two?

How unlikely could that get?

Still, after all his years in policing, he was reluctant to ignore niggles of intuition. Something was going very wrong in Conard City from what he could determine, and his fellow officers were quick to share that feeling with him.

They were perplexed, as he was, but troubled because this seemed like a veritable crime wave in their small town. Maybe it was.

Even the sheriff, Gage Dalton, was growing cranky about it. "Get to it, people," he'd said only that morning. "This can't continue."

But even the brick that had come through the department's window offered no clues except that it must have come from the abandoned train depot on the edge of town. Dusting for fingerprints didn't help, of course. Gloves. In this weather, even foolish teens would be wearing gloves.

In the sheriff's private office, Gage regarded Callum across his desk. He spoke in a gravelly voice, no smile on his burn-scarred face. "It seems we've given you quite a conundrum for your first major case with us."

"So it seems," Callum answered. "Usually, though, someone screws up and leaves a useful clue behind."

"But how long do we have to wait for that?" Gage tapped his pencil on his desk, a habit Callum had already grown used to. "Lousy time of year to have our citizens getting upset and worried. The serious worry is going to start soon if we don't get a break. If there's another assault, fear will take over. Merry Christmas."

While Callum had plenty of reason not to care about Christmas, he knew others did and he didn't want it ruined for them. Not that he honestly felt any other time of year would be better.

"Poor Pastor Molly," Gage said, surprising him.

"Why 'poor pastor'?"

Gage managed a crooked smile. "She loves the Christmas season, and as we all saw last year, she does her best to make it magical for everyone else. This year is probably going to be harder for her."

Callum nodded, not knowing what else to say.

Gage sighed and leaned forward. "Connie's out front. You asked her to compile a list of women who live alone around here. I think she's completed it. One starting point, anyway. Maybe the only one."

CONNIE PARISH WAS USEFUL, not only in compiling the list, but she'd also offered to arrange drive-bys on a more regular basis by uniformed officers from both the city police and county sheriff's office.

Callum accepted the offer readily, but he doubted it would be helpful. This guy struck in the night, and apparently only in houses with lights on. The strangest modus operandi he'd ever seen or heard of.

"Connie, let's keep those patrols thickest at night around houses with lights on, okay?"

She nodded. "Makes sense. Will do."

"And I suggest these officers make a point of stopping at all the houses of the single women to encourage them to keep a better eye out. Or arrange pajama parties. Whatever."

When he stepped out of the office, into another quiet snowfall, he felt no more enlightened or useful than before.

Damn, there *had* to be a link between these two crimes. Some reason these two women had been chosen. Even serial killers had motives, however twisted they might be and there was no reason this type of perp should be any different.

When he reached the corner, before getting into his unmarked car, he stopped, barely aware of the snow falling around him. A bad, sad time of year, he thought. Full of promise for others, but not for him.

Angela. She was never far from his mind, a murder scene he'd stepped into before anyone could prevent him. A hideousness that haunted his days and nights. A horror that never quite slipped from his mind.

He knew he should be moving past it. With every breath he drew, with every step he took, he was choosing to live. But that life had to involve something more than work and memories, didn't it?

And maybe he had some kind of duty to find those things somehow. He thought of Molly baking gingerbread cookies to decorate her tree for children. Of sharing an apple turnover with him and Tyra.

Of the night he had simply gone there to ask for a cookie, like some kid. A night he had needed the comfort of another soul, and Molly had a cheerful, warm, welcoming heart.

It had been, he admitted, the first time he'd reached out to anyone for any kind of comfort since Angela. Not that people hadn't tried to offer it, but he hadn't been ready to accept any.

So he'd come here to be a stranger. Not to flee Angela—he'd never flee his memories of her. They meant too much. But to get away from the constant reminders, where every little thing held too many warm remembrances? Yes. To escape a job that had become overwhelming when it struck too close to home? Yes.

Now this. The case of these women was like walking back into his worst nightmare, and at the same time of year. It would have been easy to become a Scrooge, but Molly kept yanking him back from that even if she didn't know it.

Though she clearly identified him as a troubled man,

that didn't prevent her from smiling or talking about her delight in the season. He sure as hell didn't want to put a damper on that.

But his primary concern had to be the attacks on these two women. And the intuition that the broken windows were part of the larger whole.

But how and why? Nothing was adding up. Women in lighted rooms rather than dark ones. Why? Broken windows. Why?

Nothing fit, and that bothered him more than anything could.

A slightly taller man, Tyra had said. Coming from behind her while she stood at her kitchen sink. Stinking to high heaven.

Bigfoot. The name ought to stick, especially considering the size of the footprints they'd found at both scenes.

Bigfoot. And just about as elusive.

BACK IN THE church basement, Molly helped the children make angels out of paper doilies and pieces of ribbon. The figures lacked wings, but they were still identifiable by their shapes, and the kids had a great time. They all took some home with them for their own trees. Laura Maskin, the retired teacher, and her aide, Belinda Armistead, both looked happy as the kids departed and they began the inevitable cleanup. Somehow scissors and glue had gotten involved, although how Molly couldn't say, as she helped straighten everything up.

Then she went upstairs for evening prayer. Attendance was light, but there were some smiling faces who stayed after for a few minutes, and people invited her to various gatherings at their homes for a little good cheer.

It all sounded nice, but Molly couldn't think of a way to accept any of those invitations without eventually offending others that would follow if it became known she had accepted any. Instead, she suggested a gathering in the church hall in the next few days, one that wasn't scheduled, for anyone who cared to come.

"Don't forget the cider," she called after the departing families. "And let people know."

After a little straightening-up around the altar, Molly pulled on her jacket over her clerical garb and headed back to the parsonage. Time to do some more baking, especially if there was to be a gathering in a couple of days. Then there were the final touches around the church that she needed to think about.

No outdoor or indoor colored lights, of course, but more candlesticks to be wrapped with red and white bows. Maybe she could find those white wire angels that someone had donated last year. They carried big faux gold trumpets and added a nice touch outside the front doors.

Once indoors, warming up, she played "Hark! The Herald Angels Sing" because the song always cheered her up.

But why did she need cheering? Because of Mabel and Tyra, of course.

Tyra, who'd yielded to pleas to stay with Molly for a few days, stumbled out of the very tiny ground-floor bedroom, her robe wrapped tightly around her.

"What's got into you?" Tyra asked sleepily. "Trying to wake all the angels?"

Molly immediately felt guilty. "I'm sorry, I forgot you might be sleeping."

"You forgot I was here." Tyra yawned. "Which is good, I guess. Any possibility of tea?"

"Sure. Maybe you'll wake up enough to help me tie ribbons around the gingerbread men."

Tyra slid into a kitchen chair, yawning again. "As long as it's not around their necks. Not a pretty image."

"Under their arms," Molly assured her.

"But no frosting?"

"Heck no. Sticky fingers."

Tyra laughed carefully, sleepily. "Tea. Remember?"

Grateful for her electric kettle, Molly filled it with water and turned it on. "Green or black tea?"

"Green. Better for the heart, I hear."

Tyra slumped a little, resting her chin in her palm. "The good news is that I managed to get into bed without screaming from my ribs. The bad news is that I almost screamed when I got up."

Molly flushed. "I'm so sorry!"

"For what? For the fact that you're one of Santa's elves at this time of year? Be happy, enjoy it. Life provides little enough of those opportunities." She smiled drowsily. "It was nice to wake up to, all that musical joy. Have at it."

With the tea poured, Molly was about to sit with Tyra when someone knocked at her door. Glancing at the clock, she saw it was just before ten. "I hope it's not an emergency," she said as she hurried to answer it. Her heart always skipped a few beats when someone arrived so late. A death in the family? That was always her biggest worry.

Instead, she found Guy Redwing standing there, so buttoned up against the cold that he might have been a snowman himself.

"Sorry to bother you, Pastor, but Detective McCloud wants us to warn single women not to leave their lights on."

Molly nodded. "Sounds weird, but I understand why. Would you like to join Tyra and me for a few minutes to warm up?"

Guy flashed her a smile. "If I hold still too long I'll freeze in place. You might ask McCloud, though. I saw him just down the street. He's walking so you can bet he's colder than I am."

Molly laughed. "Well, tell him the welcome mat is out."

"Always is at your place." Guy gave her a mittened salute then turned and left.

"Poor guy," Tyra remarked. "I wouldn't want to be out there doing his job right now."

"Me, either, although I'd bet from what he said that *he's* got a car."

Tyra asked for more tea and if Molly had any turnovers left. Of course, she did, and it wasn't as if she was going to eat any herself.

"How many diets have you been on?" Tyra asked as she watched Molly serve only one plate.

"As many as have been invented. I think."

Tyra chuckled. "You are out of your mind."

"My stomach and the scale disagree. Frankly, I don't want to look matronly."

Tyra shook her head. "Probably helps in your job, though." Then she bit into a turnover. "You can make me a batch of these any time the urge overcomes you."

"Yeah, but you were blessed with being tall and lean."

"And you were blessed with being short and cute."

Another knock at the door interrupted them. This time it was Callum. "Guy said the welcome mat is out."

His cheeks were red from the cold and his hair was a bit tousled. Molly bet he hadn't even been wearing a hat.

Molly ushered him in with a smile. "Quickly. Don't let the heat out." Still in her clerical blouse and slacks, she felt just a bit self-conscious. She wondered if his aversion to the church extended to pastoral clothing.

He knocked snow off his boots before stepping inside, then saw Tyra as he was pulling off his jacket. "Hey, Tyra. How are you doing?"

"I've got some slightly used ribs I can sell cheap. Other than that, I'm doing much better. And these turnovers, unless I miss my bet, are still filling Molly's plastic container. We're drinking tea, though."

"I can make coffee," Molly said quickly. "It's not like it's a tough chore."

"Tea is fine," Callum assured her. "I was just here to check up on you two, but Guy caught up with me. I suppose I could have just left you in your peace."

"I'm glad you didn't," Molly said cheerfully. "The more the merrier. But what are you doing walking around out there so late?"

"Getting cold."

Molly laughed. Tyra could barely manage a snort.

"But seriously, what's going on?" Molly asked.

"Nothing at the moment, thankfully. No, just walking because it helps me think."

Tyra spoke. "No thinking in a frozen brain."

Molly placed tea and two turnovers in front of Callum. "Dig in. So no more attacks?"

"No. Maybe they're over. We did find a partial fingerprint at Mabel Blix's house, but just one. We've sent it in for analysis but that will take a while. And if the perp isn't on AFIS, the national database, no help at all. Regardless, we'd have to match the print to someone we think did the crime."

"Not as easy as on TV."

"Little is. So you're feeling better, Tyra?"

Tyra tossed her long black braids. "Better enough to get around. Although the bed is still an instrument of torture."

Callum winced. "I can imagine."

"It just takes time to mend," Tyra answered. "Although Molly woke me up with Christmas music. I swear there's no dampening of this woman's happiness at this time of year."

Callum looked at Molly, his face revealing nothing, as usual. "That's a good thing."

Molly bridled. "Is it? On the one hand I have a congregation that deserves to enjoy Christmas, and on the other I'm sickened by these attacks. Just sickened. I hope to heaven I never meet this guy because I might forget my Christian principles. Turning the other cheek is a great teaching but one of the hardest to follow, and I'm no different."

Tyra groaned softly as she reached over to cover Molly's hand with hers. "I'm sure you'd be forgiven."

"I wish I was as sure." She paused, her mind shooting into her past. "Life has taught me a lot of things, you know. Not every one of them is kind, trust me."

Silence answered her. Tyra glanced between Molly and Callum, then struggled to rise. "I'm awfully tired these days. I need to get back to bed."

"Can I help?" Molly asked.

"I need to do as much as I can for myself or I'll never get back on my feet. You're a sweetheart but quit trying to take care of the whole world."

Molly watched Tyra walk carefully down the short hallway, then looked at Callum.

That proved to be a mistake. At once she felt a zing of desire shoot through her, shortening her breath. No, she warned herself. No. This man wanted no one and nothing. More than once she'd wanted to help him somehow, but that was one of her problems. She couldn't help everyone, and certainly not unless they wanted it.

She looked down at the cooling tea in front of her, then dared another glance at Callum. To her surprise, he was looking straight at her, and deep in his brown eyes she thought she caught a reflection of what she felt.

You're a pastor, for heaven's sake. Cut it out. She could only imagine the repercussions if she had a relationship.

Callum rose, almost as if he sensed her reaction. "I'll say good night. Thanks for the turnovers and tea. You try to hang on to that happiness, like Tyra said. Little enough happiness comes to any of us."

Then he bundled himself up and disappeared out the door.

To walk the streets in lonely solitude again? Molly wondered. How sad. How very sad.

Tucked warmly away in his motel room that stank of fire, Arthur Killian was full of a great meal he'd brought from the diner across the highway, with a stack of snacks to keep him out of the cold overnight.

It was time to start hunting soon, he thought. It had been long enough that people had begun to calm down. Besides, he needed it.

Needed to punch and kick a woman around. Sort of like he'd taken care of that bitch who had been his wife. The need overcame him even now, as it had then. Only now he didn't need any excuse for his rage.

The rage existed all on its own, except for the bitch who'd ruined his marriage and helped put him in jail.

Moving on from his dinner to a packet of corn chips, he thought about it. He'd need to get his butt out in that cold soon. He'd need to look around.

And as much as he wanted to see those women while

he pummeled them, maybe it was time to do it in the dark. Break his routine. Confuse everything more.

Hell, he should have picked a better time of year. Except that damn pastor had beat him up during this very season. It was too much like the best payback to do it now.

Especially when, near as he could tell, she was having a great time with all the plans the church was making for Christmas. The announcement board out in front of the place announced everything from choir rehearsals to special dinners and Christmas basket giving. Who knew what was next?

But he'd certainly get some attention taking her out in the midst of all this. In the meantime, one more. Just one more to satisfy himself.

He didn't bother to think about what he'd do after he'd finished taking his vengeance. It didn't matter.

There'd be other women. They were easy enough to come by.

Chapter Seven

In the church office, Henrietta offered Molly a stack of papers to sign and a few checks. "Although why the Junior Warden isn't doing those checks I don't know." Henrietta sniffed.

"Most people do as little as they can get away with," Molly replied. "I'm happy to do the work. What's on for the day?"

"A visit from the Senior Warden, about funding, I make no doubt. Then there's the head of the new supermarket, the one that offered the hams. The letter for him is there, acknowledging the donation, but he hinted he might have more."

"That would be welcome. So many families are hard-pressed."

"Have been for a long time," Henrietta commented. "It just seems to be getting worse with each passing year."

"Sadly." And it was sad, the hardship that kept settling over this county. Molly wished there was a thing she could do about it.

The Senior Warden, John Jason, showed up promptly on time. "Pastor," he said, his voice a little short.

Molly indicated he should take a seat. "What can I do for you, John?"

"We need more volunteers to assemble the Christmas baskets. If you could appeal for some help?"

"I suppose I can do that."

"Then there's the Altar Society."

Molly sat up a bit straighter. "You have a complaint?"

"Only that the altar linens aren't in the best of shape for Christmas. *Someone* hasn't been taking care of the darning."

Meaning Georgia, Molly thought. "You may be aware that Georgia has been dealing with a family illness. Besides, I don't think Jesus will mind a bit of fraying. He didn't exactly wear wealthy clothing himself."

"That's not the point! This church has to present itself in the best light possible. We don't want to be looking ragged. That crèche out front is, well, hardly noteworthy. I said all along we needed something in better condition."

For the first time, Molly counted to ten. "If you recall, John, it was the people of this church who brought the clothing for it. Suitable for poor shepherds, I might remind you."

John's irritation grew. "You *can* be replaced."

"At any time," Molly observed. "I never did understand why you selected me in the first place."

Henrietta spoke dryly. "I think the warden has forgotten how few applicants we had for this position given our small population and the fact that we're out of the way. Not to mention a very poor stipend. No offense to you, Pastor Molly. I personally think you're the best thing that's happened to this church in a long time. A lot of other people agree with me."

John reddened and rose. "Then do the rest of your job, Pastor."

Henrietta didn't let that pass. "You should see the pastor's schedule. I'm sure it's busier than yours. And while we're at it, ask your wife if she can make some calls on the Lathrops and Stacy Withers. It seems wrong of her not to. Those folks need more help than Pastor Molly can provide."

Molly could almost see the steam coming out of John's ears as he stomped out of the office. She stared at her secretary. "Heavens, Henrietta!"

Henrietta looked self-satisfied. "You can't say those things yourself, Pastor. But *I* can. So I said them."

"There's too little I can say," Molly admitted.

"Certainly nothing like that. It's one thing to gently scold one of the flock, another to tell off the Senior Warden. How that man got elected I will never know. I wouldn't be surprised if some palms were greased."

"Henrietta!" Molly was appalled.

"You didn't hear me say that," Henrietta said, her anger subsiding. "But I still wonder. He's never been a pleasant man."

It was a point Molly couldn't argue.

But then, hard on his heels, the Junior Warden, Daniel Alder, arrived carrying the church's books. "I think you need to see this information, Pastor. To understand the financial problems we face. You may not be able to call for money from the pulpit, but if you have any fundraising ideas, I'd be happy to hear them. Right now we're close to running in the red."

More good news, Molly thought. But as life became more difficult around here, fewer people could afford to make offerings, let alone large ones.

"We could," said Daniel, "try to mortgage the church. The building must count something for equity."

Molly and Henrietta both gasped.

"Then come up with something better," Daniel said as he marched out.

"Good grief," Henrietta mumbled. "It never rains but it pours."

"It never snows but it's a blizzard," Molly said, causing Henrietta to laugh. "Let's put our heads together," she suggested. "Along with those supposedly troublesome ladies of the Altar Society."

"Particularly Claire," Henrietta added. "She's a smart one."

THAT EVENING, AFTER several counseling sessions in her office and a couple of in-town home visits, Molly felt worn out. Her shoulders weren't always big enough to bear the burdens of others, and sometimes she felt so helpless.

Seeking grace, she stood in front of the church, looking at the crèche and the facade of a building that had been built in the 1880s, during a brief gold rush up on Thunder Mountain. A truly magnificent construction of field stone, which, over the years, had been finished inside with smooth white walls and heavy beams. A stained-glass window had even been carted across mountains to stand behind the altar.

Amazing what faith could achieve. As a light snow started falling again, peace began to steal over her. A refreshing feeling of hope and even some renewed strength.

She had known this job wouldn't be easy, and that some days were going to be harder than others. She had prior experience, so there shouldn't have been a surprise on days like today, when grief and anger could be eased so little.

But sometimes she felt exhausted by the human misery she encountered, and sometimes she wondered if she was in the right job.

Just then, the scream of sirens from two blocks away startled her out of her self-preoccupation. Running at top speed, she raced around the church to her car parked near the parsonage. It didn't always start the first time in the cold, but this time it turned over immediately.

Moving as fast as she dared on these icy roads, she headed straight for the flashing lights.

Praying there hadn't been another attack.

CALLUM STOOD IN the circle of the police cordon, flood lamps lighting the area as bright as day. This time no lookie-loos showed up, possibly because fear had taken hold. He might be new to this area, but these people were in his care and it was killing him that he couldn't make them feel safe.

Another attack against a woman living alone. This one earlier in the night, but at a time that drove most people into their homes early because of the weather. A light snowfall again—acting like fog, it grayed out anything at a distance.

Police with flashlights circled the house for any kind of evidence. So far they hadn't even found signs of a break-in. There must have been an unlocked door.

As near as they could tell, the victim had been sitting in her living room in front of her TV when the attack occurred. Light again. Always in some light.

"Loretta Sanchez," said Guy Redwing, who approached him. "Older than the rest. Medics say it's not looking too good for her. Man must have got carried away."

Anger. This perp must be overflowing with anger. Nothing personal in these crimes as far as anyone could tell. Just fury.

"He wants to see what he's doing," Callum said. Randy Webster, another deputy, approached. A stubby man who didn't seem to be able to get rid of his beard shadow, he crunched his way across layers of snow.

"Detective? Medics think he broke her hands before the rest of it."

"God in heaven," Callum muttered. The cruelty, the pain. No justification. None. This had gone a step further than the others. "Listen, I don't care if the troops need magnifying glasses. Find me something besides smeared Bigfoot tracks in that snow."

Then, hearing tires crunch in the snow at the edge of the road, he turned to see Molly pulling up in her aging Taurus. Great. Now *she* would have nightmares tonight, too. Surely this news could have waited for morning.

Damn it all to hell. He tried so hard not to get emotionally involved in cases, but emotional distance was escaping him this time. Not good for his clarity of thought. Another reason he'd left Boston.

Molly emerged from her car to stand right behind the cordon. Reluctantly, he went to her.

"No point hanging out here," he told her flatly. "Ms. Sanchez is about to leave for the hospital and then we're getting down to the nitty-gritty inside. Nothing for you to do to help."

Molly bit her lower lip. "It's early. How was she found?"

"She managed to press the autodialer on her phone. Probably her last conscious act. Now get back to your church. Hold a vigil or something. This woman is going to need every prayer she can get."

Callum turned and went back to work, but he swore he could feel Molly's horrified gaze on his back. Nothing she could do about this, either. He pounded one gloved fist into the palm of the other, then forced himself to draw deep breaths.

A clear head. He *had* to keep a clear head.

BACK AT THE CHURCH, Molly found a few members of her congregation ahead of her. Henrietta had unlocked the doors and more than a dozen men and women sat in the pews, heads bowed, while John Jason read comforting passages from the Bible.

Molly walked slowly up the aisle, removing her jacket and gloves, revealing her clerical shirt and slacks. When she reached the front, she nodded to John then headed for the sacristy. Once there, she dumped her boots in favor of black flats. Then she donned a white ankle-length alb. Over it she wore her purple stole.

When she stepped out into the chancel, she discovered that the group in the pews had grown significantly. John had fallen silent, and the Bible was still open before him on the lectern. He saw her and nodded before stepping down to join the crowd.

Then she stood in the middle of the chancel, looking out at worried, hopeful faces. They must have heard about Loretta Sanchez and had come here for answers and comfort.

Neither of which Molly had to offer. She might be the pastor, but as so often happened, there were no easy answers that didn't sound trite. There was only one place to find a true answer, and all these people knew it.

Finally, she spoke. "We are here to pray for our sister Loretta Sanchez, to pray that she will recover swiftly from her injuries. We are here to pray for Mabel Blix, who is even now in rehabilitation. We are here to pray for Tyra Lansing, who, thanks be, is on the mend. We are here to pray for the police, that they will be swift in finding the criminal so that our women can feel safe in their homes again."

She paused and drew a breath. "We are called to remember that we do not walk alone, even in the darkest nights. At times like these, that can be hard to remember, but *we never walk alone.*"

With her hands folded, she looked out across the growing sea of faces and saw Callum McCloud standing at the very back of the narthex. Was he listening? Did he care?

Then she spread her arms wide, encompassing the group and inviting them to pray. A lovely thing happened then. A man stood and offered a memory of Loretta chasing his kids around the yard while they played Frisbee. Another woman recalled how Loretta had taught her how to make piecrust. Another spoke of Tyra and her free tutoring that had helped many children. One after another, many offered memories that were all good, that lightened the room.

Then, started by a single strong baritone, people began to sing "The First Noel," followed by "Away in a Manger."

Christmas tiptoed into the church.

CALLUM HAD FELT Christmas tiptoeing into that church, too, but he didn't need it. It wasn't useful, and that smarmy stuff might cloud his thinking. Although he had to admit that Molly had looked good standing up there, like an angel come to earth. She certainly appeared to belong there.

At that moment, he'd been more certain that Molly belonged in her chosen career than he belonged in his. The night's searches had turned up nothing. On the earlier cases, daytime hadn't proved any better. All they had were some messy bootprints and one lousy partial fingerprint that had come from a faucet, which could have come from anyone who had entered Mabel Blix's house. Certainly no word from AFIS.

And now the guy was changing it up, coming earlier

in the night, when his risks were higher. He was at least somewhat adaptable, which made the situation all that much worse from Callum's perspective.

Usually cases were surprisingly easy to solve. Mastermind criminals almost never existed and those who tried to get away with crimes always seemed to screw up somehow. Usually by talking too much to a friend, just a little bragging to the less than trustworthy. Other things gave them away, too. Things they never thought about until too late. Or maybe never got at all.

"No man is an island," to quote Donne, but especially not when it came to crime. There was always a trail somewhere, always a clue. It was Callum's job to find it.

A little more patience, he counseled himself. Just a little more. They hadn't finished doing up the forensics on the Sanchez scene, for one thing. And the cataloguing of Loretta Sanchez's wounds, to determine how she had been struck, was only about to begin. Looking for a weapon. Still hadn't found one.

Although Callum had the suspicion that there was no weapon. This creep was a hands-and-feet sort of guy. Nothing between him and the pain he inflicted.

Callum sometimes wondered if there were degrees of evil. He wondered if Molly could answer that one.

He checked in at the office only to find no calls had come over the tip line. Great. You'd think that by now people in this small town would be keeping eagle eyes out. Maybe even breaking out binoculars and old telescopes from the attic.

But then, who'd want to be leaving their curtains open between the cold and all that was going wrong around them?

Wandering around in the cold didn't seem to be helping his thought processes any, so he turned to walk back to his dismal rental. He promised himself that if he stayed here a year, he'd find better digs.

Truth was, he didn't care.

He was passing by the church once again when he caught a glimpse of light coming from the parsonage at the rear. Damn, Molly. She knew the warnings.

Annoyed, he stomped around to the back and banged on the door. She opened it, wrapped in a red bathrobe, looking startled. "Callum! Did something more happen?"

He couldn't keep the edge out of his voice. "No more than already has. What are you doing with your lights on?"

She was clearly taken aback. "I was just…"

"Is Tyra here with you? Tell me you're not alone."

"Tyra wanted to go home tonight."

"So she's gone?" He felt his frown deepen into a dark, unpleasant expression. "Turn those lights out, now. One mess tonight is enough! You think I want to be called here to find *you* a bloody mess? Or do you think your damn prayers are all the protection you need?"

She studied him, her face sad, her mossy green eyes soft. Then, quietly, she said, "Come in, Callum."

"And ding your reputation?" His laugh bordered on the bitter.

"Callum, please come in. It's cold out there."

Angrily, he stomped inside and nearly slammed the door behind him. "Do you ever take orders? Keeping yourself safe is important."

"So is taking care of my duties. It's Christmas. I have a lot I want to do to make this special for everyone. Except you, apparently. Take a seat in the kitchen. I just made coffee."

"At this time of night?"

"I'm plagued with insomnia sometimes. This is apparently one of those nights. I wouldn't mind some company."

He wasn't feeling like company as he tossed aside his jacket and gloves and pulled out a chair, sitting on it with a thud. Through his anger, a thought twisted its way to awareness. What the hell was he doing *here*?

Molly poured two cups of coffee. "Any word on Loretta's condition?"

"No. Except that she was beaten worse than the others. In short, she's in more danger. They're trying to stabilize her."

Molly sat, looking sad enough to cry. "My God," she whispered. "Oh, poor Loretta."

"Make sure it's not *poor Molly* next."

She shook her head, staring down into her cup, her silence possibly saying more than any words she could have spoken.

"I saw your little service at the church," he said finally. "I suppose you all think that will make anything better."

She looked up, her eyes snapping fire. "How could you possibly know that it doesn't?"

He couldn't, obviously. His anger was beginning to seep away and he didn't feel like getting into an argument with her about faith or the lack thereof.

But he still had something to say. "I hate Christmas. I hate it with a passion."

She moved sharply, tilting her head. "Why?"

"Because two weeks before Christmas I came home to find my wife dead. She'd been decorating the Christmas tree, as excited about it as any kid. I'll never forget that morning. She asked me to pick up some candy canes on the way home. Except I wish I'd never had to come home."

Molly reached across the table to touch one of his clenched fists. "I'm so sorry."

"Home invasion," he said shortly. "They caught the perps but it didn't matter. Angela was still dead. I hate Christmas, and this one, with all that's going on, is making me look into the maw of that horror again. Christmas? My worst nightmare."

Molly nodded gently, her hand tightening just a little on his. "I wish I could help."

"You're the pastor," he said, more bitterness creeping into his voice. "You ought to have the answer."

"I have as many questions as anyone, Callum. The only answer I have is faith."

He snorted. "Got any to share?"

Again she shook her head, just a little. "The thing people often misunderstand about faith is that it's not a choice. I believe, as do others, that it springs from a grace given by God. It's possible to ignore that grace, but it's not a choice to receive it."

He felt something internal shift a bit. "So what do you do about atheists?"

"Nothing. Welcome them as fellow travelers in a difficult world. They have as much right to their doubts and their questions as anyone else."

"You don't see them as sinners?"

"How could I?" She offered a small smile. "Faith springs from grace, remember? Besides, it's not my place to judge."

Callum sat back, sipping his coffee at last, his anger unwinding slowly. "You're unique."

"I hope not. In fact, I'm quite sure I'm not. These ideas are hardly original. They might be more accurately called interpretations, but they're interpretations I accept because they resound in me."

Well, he could understand that part. And here he was occupying her tiny kitchen at midnight, drinking her coffee, visiting her when she might get in trouble for it.

"I should go," he said. "It's late—I wouldn't want to cause you any gossip." Although he wondered how he possibly could after having seen her on the steps of the chancel tonight. The image of her with her arms outspread and her sleeves draping down from them almost like wings would stay with him forever. It must stay with everyone who saw it. An angel come to earth.

She didn't object, but as he turned one last time to look at her, he saw something he never would have imagined from all the strength she had shown tonight.

Overwhelming sorrow. A woman who looked as if she could bear no more. God!

Without thought, he swept her into his arms, into the tightest, most reassuring hug he could give her. This woman could be worn down, too. Could be overburdened.

"Molly," he said roughly. "We'll get to the bottom of this. But don't let it kill you. Don't wear yourself out."

She trembled slightly, in a way that whispered her need for strength to lean on. "I know," she said finally. "And I have to take care of my people as much as possible. This is *Advent*, for the love of God! A time of hope and joy and anticipation, and I'm not going to let this bum steal it from everyone!"

Her voice had grown stronger as she spoke against his chest, and she was no longer trembling like a leaf. He continued, however, to hold her close. "Much as I hate Christmas, I'll help in any way I can, Molly. Promise. Just let me know."

A sniffle issued from her, sounding precariously like a tear had escaped. "Come over tomorrow whenever you can and help me hang the last of those gingerbread men."

"And then?"

"Ask me then." She drew back and raised a hand to touch his cheek gently. "Thank you, Callum. From the bottom of my heart."

"Just turn off these damn lights. Work by a candle if you have to."

Then, grabbing his jacket, he disappeared again into the winter night.

WHAT AN INTERESTING MAN, she thought as the emptiness of the parsonage closed around her once again. She wished she could call Tyra to see how she was doing, but it was far too late and she didn't want to disturb her friend's sleep.

Her homily for Sunday waited on her small desk in her study, but she felt she was going to have to throw it out and start over after what had happened to Loretta Sanchez. Loretta was one of those quiet women, always with a ready smile, but generally so quiet she could pass unnoticed a lot of the time. Regardless, she was always there when any type of help was needed.

Somehow she had to address these tragedies without killing the holiday, especially for the children.

At last she dressed for the outdoors and stepped into air so cold that it threatened to take her breath away. Pulling up her fur-edged snorkel hood so there was only a small area open to the outside world, so that her breath would warm her face and keep it from freezing, she locked the door of the parsonage for the first time since she'd moved here, and walked around to the church's side door.

For a while, heedless of the chill that crept slowly through her outerwear, she stood looking up at the night sky, full of questions and hearing no answers, except possibly an internal quiet. Then she turned toward the church.

To conserve energy, the office wasn't a whole lot warmer than the outdoors, or so it felt. Disregarding the frigid temperature, Molly unzipped her jacket and stepped into the nave, pausing to light a candle before taking a seat in the front pew.

Tomorrow, she knew, was going to be a very busy day regardless of what might be on her calendar. Word would spread and her office would be full of people who needed only the comfort of being able to talk about what had happened.

And sometimes that was enough, just enough, to be able to talk freely without getting into an argument or dispute. Or find one's fears too closely echoed. People needed calming, not ramping up.

Although she was perilously close to ramping up herself. Rage, such as she had rarely felt, was eating at her. Memories of her National Guard days returned, bringing with them those times when violence had been willfully practiced.

A violence that now made her clench her fists. She had chosen this calling, but right now she wished she hadn't. She frankly wanted to smash someone or something.

IN THE PLEASANT warmth of one lousy motel room, Arthur Killian pigged out on French fries with a couple of sticky buns awaiting him on the small end table. That diner guy, Hasty, didn't mind filling a thermos with hot coffee, either. If he wanted to, he could run back and get a refill, no charge.

An odd way to run a business, Arthur thought.

But his thoughts didn't stay on his food or Hasty's coffee. No, they returned to the night's triumph. Man, had he enjoyed battering that woman. Part of him hoped she never woke up again.

But Arthur Killian didn't have any taste for murder. It was the easy way out for the victim, and Killian wasn't a guy who wanted to miss any sadistic pleasure he could find.

So he guessed he'd messed up tonight. But it had felt so good to kick and punch that mewling woman. Too good to stop until she fell silent. A beating he could really sink his teeth into.

In fact, he *had* bitten her, just to taste her fear, in a way he'd never done before. He liked it. Liked it enough that he was going to do it to that Molly Canton when he got around to her.

But that had to wait. He was pretty sure the cops were looking for him, so he should maybe wait until they thought the attacks had stopped. He sure was comfortable enough here. He could wait. Even if he wasn't good at it.

Tomorrow night, he decided, he'd break some windows. Keep the cops on two tracks, not just one. Divide and conquer, that was the thing. Maybe take some crap out of one of those stores. Like that jewelry store. He could take enough from there to make them think they had some robbers at work.

He liked that idea and gulped some more fries. Those sticky buns were smelling better by the moment. He didn't have to wait long for them.

Chapter Eight

Callum was walking the streets again, hating himself and feeling like a total failure. It was his job to find this bastard, his job to protect this whole damn town. And he was failing in a way he couldn't excuse in himself.

He avoided looking up at the cheerful holiday decorations that hung from nearly every lamppost. He avoided looking at the decorations that were filling yards and hanging from houses. All tinsel and glitter without meaning. All it did was burn energy unnecessarily.

And it sure didn't improve his mood any.

One new clue. He had one new clue, about as useless as the fingerprint. Boot marks stamped into the body of poor Loretta Sanchez. Partial prints of those soles, but at least another clue, better than the Bigfoot prints in the snow.

As for Ms. Sanchez, she'd had to be airlifted to a larger hospital in Cheyenne. Things were not looking good for her.

Failure. A woman sitting in front of her TV in the evening. She should have been as safe as a baby in its crib. She shouldn't have had a thing to fear in this entire world.

He ground his teeth, then caught himself. How many times had his dentist warned him he was grinding his way into dentures?

Not that he cared now if he became toothless in the next week. Whatever.

He'd been avoiding walking near the church for a couple of days, despite Molly's invitation to help hang gingerbread men on the tree. He wasn't the type for that kind of cutesiness.

But he was avoiding the church for another reason: Molly. He wanted to see her. Very much wanted to see her. No good. Not for her, especially, but bad in general. He was a husk of a man, and she'd find nothing worth risking her reputation for.

Before he realized what his feet were doing, he walked toward Good Shepherd. At first he didn't pay much attention, was mostly lost in thought and his steady strides, but then a bright field of red brought him to a dead stop.

By the side of the church was an old cemetery, and some of those teetering stones were likely as old as the church itself. But the stones didn't catch his attention.

No, at every single stone stood a bright red poinsettia. At first he could hardly believe his eyes, but then he felt his chest tighten, and he drew a deep breath, trying to ease the unwanted feeling.

Someone had done that. Someone had gone to all the trouble and expense to make those graves beautiful, to make sure they were remembered. Who did a thing like that?

Swallowing hard, a need he hadn't felt since the year after his wife died, he tried to move on, tried not to feel touched by this act. But he remained frozen, looking at that extensive field of red, trying to absorb everything it meant.

It tried to reach every part of him that had somehow been cut out.

Eventually, a movement in the corner of his eye caught his attention and he turned quickly, instinctively.

There was no mistaking that red parka amid a heap of snow. Molly. What the devil?

His legs unlocked and he walked her way, making sure to call her name so she wouldn't be startled.

She'd been bent over, but now she straightened and smiled. "Hi, Callum. You're out late."

"So are you. Insomnia?"

"It can be useful."

"What are you doing?"

"Trying to build a snowman for the kids. I'd like it to look like the kind that are always pictured in movies and cartoons, but I'm not sure I'm succeeding."

A snowman for the kids? For the second time in a half hour, surprise shook him. "Why are you building it? Don't they make their own?" He was quite sure he'd seen a couple of formless lumps in yards he'd passed.

"The snow is the problem." She bent and scooped up a couple of handfuls, then threw a snowball at him. He ducked, but before it could hit him, there was nothing left.

"See?" she said. "Too dry. It won't stick together."

He nodded. "So how are you getting around it?" Because her snowman looked as if it already had a head on it.

"Magic." Then she giggled. "Naw, not magic. The snow in the snowbanks is a lot firmer and stickier because of the pressure the plows put on it, so I'm using that."

"Great idea."

"So far it's working. But good mommas and daddies don't let their youngsters get into these banks so they don't have access to the packed stuff. Too many dangers. I, on the other hand, don't have to report to parents."

In spite of himself, he felt his face cracking into the weirdest expression he'd experienced in a very long time: a smile.

"Ah," Molly said. "So you *can* smile. I was beginning to wonder if you had nerve damage."

His smile grew and he scooped some snow from the nearest bank and patted it into a ball. "You ready, Pastor?"

"Nothing like a good snowball fight. Just look out for pebbles in that snow."

She had a good point, and, of course, that was one of the reasons parents didn't want kids playing with that snow. He lobbed his snowball to one side of her.

She tilted her head. "Chicken?" she asked.

"I'm not in the habit of bruising angels."

He had no idea where those words had come from but he didn't care. It had slipped out and he kind of liked the way her expression became embarrassed. He couldn't tell if she flushed because the cold had nipped her cheeks.

"I'm no angel," she said swiftly.

"Good, because perfection is boring."

That pulled a laugh from her—a rolling laugh that brought that stupid smile to his face again.

"Come on," she said. "I'm freezing. I want a hot drink, and then you can help me pick out a carrot, some buttons and a scarf for Snowy here."

"What, no hat?"

She replied dryly, "I don't think a balaclava would cut it."

THE INSIDE OF her kitchen was warm, possibly the warmest room in her small house. It was also redolent of vanilla and chocolate, and some other scents he couldn't identify. The counters and the table were full of cupcakes.

He looked around. "Have you been going crazy or something?"

She grinned. "Big events tomorrow. Kids will spend the morning finishing their decorations, then the children's choir will have a rehearsal followed by a practice by our Wassailers."

"Wassailers?" he asked.

"And old Norse term for a group of people who go around the neighborhoods singing Christmas carols. We have two groups but they practice together. And in the evening, the full choir will rehearse."

"That's a lot of singing," he remarked, not knowing what else to say.

"It's beautiful. Let me make a little room so we can have something hot to drink. I was beginning to feel frozen to the bone."

"Are you baking cupcakes for everyone?"

"Oh, no," she laughed. "Others are baking, too. These won't last long, not with so many people."

She made cocoa for him but tea for herself.

"Calories again?" he asked.

"A little caution. I can put on five pounds in a snap."

He just shook his head. "As hard as you work, I'm surprised you don't have to eat like an athlete."

"Metabolism. Say, why don't you join us tomorrow?"

He merely stared at her as he sipped the cocoa.

"Oh, come on," she persisted. "It's not only fun, but you can catch up on all the gossip."

The gossip part appealed to him. Maybe he'd overhear something useful. "Don't you folks disapprove of gossip?"

"Of course, we do, especially if it's malicious. It happens, anyway. What's more important is that you'll get to know more of the local people. It'd help your work, I'm sure, not to always be the stranger around here."

That was true. Very true. Once people got to know you, they started to trust you and might very well pass along information they wouldn't have otherwise. But all those Christmassy activities?

Oh, buck up, Callum, he told himself. Some things couldn't be avoided forever. Or hidden from.

"I know you have a problem with this season," Molly continued gently. "But Advent is a time of hope, of love, and the anticipation of a miracle."

He didn't believe in miracles, but for some reason her words didn't put him off. Whether he agreed with her or not, he liked her attitude.

"Maybe I will," he answered, making no promises.

"Good. The kids will start with the decorations about nine. Plenty of parents will be there."

He nodded. "Okay."

"Now," she said, "let's find that carrot and those buttons. I even think I have an old scarf I've used before." She cocked an amused eyebrow his way. "I'm not a very good knitter."

MOLLY WAS CONTENT with Callum's sort-of agreement to come to the festivities tomorrow. A minor victory, perhaps.

She had a stack of large, round black buttons she kept on hand for snowmen and who knew what else. They came in handy. The carrot was easy to find. The scarf was buried in a box of odds and ends from the knitting project she'd started so hopefully, only to discover she didn't have the hands for it.

A short while later the snowman was decorated and

she stood back to admire it. "The kids will love it in the morning."

"I'm sure they will."

Then Callum turned away. "See you, Molly."

Yeah, but when? Still content, Molly returned to the parsonage, remembering those two genuine smiles he'd let slip past his guard.

He was a remarkably attractive man. Gorgeous. He made her tingle. She yanked her thoughts away from *that* however. Not to be.

But those smiles were also a good sign. Maybe the man was softening up a bit.

Humming quietly, she went to her little office to work on her homily for Sunday. She might be cheating a bit, but she wasn't above cannibalizing her homilies from earlier years. There was only one way to say some things.

FOR HIS PART, Callum headed back to his own place trying not to think about Molly. That woman was getting under his skin and he wasn't sure he liked that. One thing he could say—her cheerful nature didn't seem to be forced. It was part of her.

At home, such as it was, weariness began to catch up with him. He was sure he'd only just closed his eyes when his cell phone rang.

The jewelry store had been burgled.

Chapter Nine

The predawn hours had grown cold enough and windy enough to cut through Callum's winter clothing. He wondered if he ought to ask someone around here for some advice about better gear.

But it was a mere passing thought. His eyes felt gritty, whether from lack of sleep or the cold he didn't know or care. Once again, standing in the middle of a police cordon with red, white and blue lights flashing off buildings and snow, he stared at the broken window and waited for the techs to gather evidence. Shortly they'd let him in to walk through a cleared area.

In the meantime, he began to wonder if he'd brought a crime wave to this town. From the talk at the office, they weren't used to having more than one major crime to deal with at a time. Now they had two, plus the vandalism.

Randy Webster approached him. "Ken Yost is on his way over."

"Yost?"

"The owner of the jewelry store."

"Good. That was my first question. You're right on top of it, Randy."

Randy shrugged. "No way else to know what was taken. From what I saw when we answered the alarm, a lot of display cases had been broken into."

Callum nodded, growing colder and more impatient by the minute. This was different than the earlier window breakings, which had seemed like mere vandalism—bad enough but not requiring the cavalry.

This was different. Breaking and entering. Probably grand theft. Either the original miscreants had upped their game or they had yet another perp running around.

God, he wouldn't have thought this place could have so much action all at once. Hell, he'd come here to escape this kind of constant activity, not to dive into it again.

But here he was, freezing his butt off, gloved hands shoved deep into jacket pockets and…well, Christmas slowly sucking him in, thanks to one enchanting lady at Good Shepherd Church. The whole nightmare he'd wanted to shake off.

"Randy?"

"Yo?"

"How does this town support a jewelry store?"

"Get used to Wyoming, Cal. People are spread out everywhere and there's only slightly more than six hundred thousand people in the state. This town is big compared to most. So a jewelry store can make it because folks come in from all over. Hell, that's how this whole town survives right now."

"*Survive* is evidently a good word for it."

Randy grimaced. "At least we are."

"That wasn't a criticism."

"Didn't think it was." Randy turned, looking toward the store. "A good target. Better than Freitag's, unless you want clothing and toys. The bakery, too. You wouldn't bother breaking in there unless you were damn hungry."

"And no money gone from the tills." Of course not. As far as they'd been able to discover, the windows had been broken but there'd been no entry. Strange, he thought, looking at the jewelry store. This one at least made some sense. The others seemed more like hijinks. The kind of thing bored kids might get up to.

He stifled a sigh, waiting for entry and for Mr. Yost to fill out the picture. And wishing for a thermos of Molly's excellent cocoa.

Lights came on in a storefront down the street. Maude's diner, which he'd learned was the local name for the café. Early to be starting work, he thought, but maybe not. He'd been here long enough to learn that Maude had a huge breakfast crowd. Mostly older people in the early hours, but older people tended to wake earlier.

Maybe he should spend more time in there. It was probably a hotbed of local gossip and knowledge.

He was still waiting for entry, wondering which part of him was going to get frostbite, when a heavyset woman, wrapped as if she was ready for a weekend at the north pole, came hurrying down the street. She stood at the edge of the cordon.

Then she called out. "Randy? Guy? If you can get away ten minutes, I got hot coffee for all of you. Can't carry it all myself."

Randy and Guy Redwing both looked at him and Callum nodded. Why not? They all needed some warmth and it didn't seem as if they were going to get inside very soon.

He walked over to Maude before she swept away with the two deputies in tow. "Maude?"

She turned to eye him. "McCloud, right?"

"Callum is fine. I was wondering if I could use your restaurant for a witness interview."

She barked out a laugh. "Wouldn't want Ken Yost freezing to death. His night is bad enough already. Come

along when you're ready. I'll keep Ken as calm as I can
until you get here."

"Thanks."

She looked him up and down. "Get you some better
clothes, Detective. Start with some long johns."

Evidently he *did* need advice.

The coffee showed up in short order—tall, insulated
cups of it—and was passed around to everyone who was
freezing on this damn street.

At last, one of the techies emerged through the door
and waved to him. Again a pathway had been laid out
inside—the safe places to go. Other techs kept at it. Callum doubted he'd ever have the patience they showed, or
their eye for minuscule details.

The rooms were all lit up, as bright as day, causing him
to blink a few times. Walking slowly along the marked
path, he unzipped his parka enough to pull out a pen and
his notebook. As if his fingers wanted to work.

A smash-and-grab if ever he'd seen one. Every case
had been shattered. The cash register had been yanked
open despite the lock.

The perp had wasted no time grabbing the easiest
pickings and getting out before the cops might come in
answer to a silent alarm. A hurried, poorly planned job.

He made unsteady notes as he moved through slowly,
his fingers almost refusing to grip the pen. Inexpert
smashing of the display cases, he thought. All broken
right in one spot, leaving lots of cracked glass that still
covered the contents. Leaving behind any jewelry that
would have been hard to reach. Not even taking time to
make more than one blow to the glass.

The cash register had probably been wrenched open
by the same tool that had smashed the cases. A crowbar?
Something heavy.

He spoke to one of the techs, who was kneeling by one case, dusting for fingerprints. "What type of glass?"

She looked up. "Glass. Just simple glass. Somebody needs to tell Ken Yost to go for some heavy-duty polycarbonate when he repairs all this."

Simple glass. Damn, he thought. Security consciousness in this store apparently hadn't gone beyond a silent alarm. Maybe the alarm had even seemed extreme in a place like this. Or maybe it had been required by insurance.

He finished his walk-through, looking forward to being able to walk around freely once the techs were done. Sometimes a practiced eye could see something in the bigger picture.

Randy called to tell him that Yost was in the diner. Yost wouldn't have much information to share until *he* could get in here, but he might have noticed something in the days before, if prompted to think about it.

When he entered the café, only one man was sitting there, looking as if he'd been dragged out of bed and hadn't even brushed his steel-colored hair. His narrow face was drawn, pale. He looked up immediately. "Detective?"

"Callum McCloud, and you're Mr. Yost?"

The man nodded. Callum pulled out a chair to face him and before he said another thing, Maude slapped another tall coffee in front of him. Thank God.

"How bad is it?" Yost asked.

"I can't say in detail until you look everything over, but it's bad. Every display case has been smashed, but each one still has some jewelry in it. Cash register has been emptied, too."

"I wish them luck with all those credit-card slips."

Yost shook his head, staring into space. Callum gave

him a few minutes. The man was experiencing some level of shock.

At last. Yost shook his head again, returning to the moment. "I'll be honest—I never expected anything like this. And most of the good stuff is in a vault in the back. Did they get into that, too?"

"I don't know yet."

Yost put his head in his hands.

Callum sipped hot coffee, waiting. Then he said, "I need to ask you a few questions."

Yost looked up immediately. "Sure."

"In the last few days have you noticed anything unusual?" Hope sprang eternal, Callum thought without amusement. At this point, though, anything might help.

"No, I don't think so."

"Someone hanging around. Outside, maybe? Or browsing too long in the store? Someone you don't know?"

Yost snorted. "I don't know everyone who comes in. Lots of my customers come from quite a distance and I only see them once or twice. People *do* just come to browse, maybe thinking of future purchases or deciding whether they can afford anything."

"Okay. But give it some thought, please? Maybe someone whose browsing was different from the usual. What about outside? Was someone propping up a lamppost for too long? Or too often?"

Yost's brow furrowed. "Maybe. Let me think."

So Callum let him think. He finished his coffee and another appeared on the table in front of him. He could get to like this café.

"Yeah," Yost said finally. "There was a guy. Can't tell you much because winter clothes hide a lot."

"Give me what you got." Callum pulled out his pocket notebook and pen.

"He was tall," Yost said finally. "Lots of folks are, but I noticed him. Just a bit mind you, because I wasn't paying much attention—but once or twice I thought he looked my way. *My way.*"

Callum nodded, scribbling. At least his fingers were working again. "Anything else?"

Yost closed his eyes, started shaking his head, then said suddenly, "He was big. Broad under them clothes. Wearing a balaclava, but lots of folks do. Nothing unusual about him, really."

Except that he was big, tall and wearing a balaclava. Callum's heart raced just a bit. Tyra's description of her assailant. Could it be? Could these crimes be linked?

But how and why?

And Yost was right. A lot of men around here probably fit that description.

But some instinct insisted that Callum had just gotten a description of the same man who had attacked Tyra, and by extension, Mabel Blix and Loretta Sanchez.

Still, how did that fit with the burglary of the jewelry store? Nothing had been taken during those attacks on the women.

But Callum couldn't let go of the possibility.

Maybe the guy was getting careless?

MOLLY HAD SNAGGED a few hours of sleep but then she heard the sirens.

A light sleeper, as well as an insomniac, she rose quickly. After jamming her feet into her snow boots and yanking on her jacket, she hurried out her door to look, fearing another woman had been attacked. Her heart was racing even as the cold night struck her across the face.

In just a minute, she located the center of the bright flashing lights and realized they were downtown. She steadied her breathing and turned to go back inside. Probably more broken windows, she thought. She thought of all the shopkeepers, most of whom she knew, facing a mess this early in the morning.

She stripped out of her jacket, kicked off her boots and wandered around her small house in her flannel pajamas, which were decorated with small rosebuds because she sometimes had a wild urge to feel feminine.

The thermostat had cooled the house for the night, though, so she pulled on her red terry robe and zipped it to her neck. That was better.

Screw it, she thought, and decided to make herself a cup of cocoa after all. Comfort and warmth, and just one cup might not appear on her hips, which to her way of thinking were a bit on the wide side.

Of course, maybe some of that feeling had come from her time in the National Guard. She'd always felt that she wasn't in quite good enough shape, although her shape hadn't kept her out, or kept her from performing as well as she needed to during highly physical activity. Still...

Sighing, she took the easy way out and made some instant cocoa. All well and good to make it from scratch when she had company, but for herself in the early hours? Nah.

It was going to be a long day, she thought as she leaned on her elbows over the steaming aromatic cup, surrounded by an array of cupcakes. She ought to put them in their carrying cases, but she could do that later and decided to let it go.

Just enjoy her cocoa. Just sit here and hope that the haze of sleep would begin to take over.

Instead of just relaxing, however, she thought about

Callum. He was probably out there in this cold, surrounded by the swirling lights. Probably standing there freezing and wondering why he'd ever left Boston. A bad winter storm was headed their way, too, on Monday, and if it arrived he was going to think a whole lot more kindly of Boston.

She sipped the cocoa as soon as it cooled enough and put her chin in her hand. Boston. She'd seen plenty of photos of it and had read about the Freedom Trail. The Old North Church. The Boston Common. So many interesting things to see. She'd always hoped to visit the city. Maybe someday. It sounded like a very different world than she was used to.

She hoped Tyra would feel well enough to attend some of the festivities here in Conard City. They'd talked earlier that morning and Tyra, while speaking bracingly about how well she was recovering, had nonetheless sounded weary. Healing took a toll.

But Tyra hadn't wanted her to come over to visit. "You have your hands already full with all the Advent activities. Plus, I'm not up to playing hostess yet, and I sure as hell don't want you over here waiting on me. We can talk well enough on the phone. Period. End of discussion. I *will*, however, try to make it to the children's choir rehearsal. I love those sweet young voices. Now get back to being everyone else's pastor."

That was Tyra, all right. Sweet as could be until she started handing out orders. Then she would brook no argument.

Smiling at the memory, Molly went to make another cup of cocoa. Maybe it would show up on her *other* hip and balance her out. Ha!

The four hours of sleep she'd managed to grab earlier in the night would at least help her get through the busy day ahead. Then, if she was lucky, she could leave the adult rehearsal and come home to collapse for about twelve hours. That sounded *so* good. And with her homily nearly completed, she wouldn't even feel bad about sleeping so much.

Her bouts of insomnia were often useful, but not this morning. This morning her mind just wanted to wander and drift. A mental break.

Then she thought of Callum again and wished she hadn't because thoughts of him were so stimulating. She'd even gotten to the point of noticing how he walked, an easy stride as if he was made for it.

She liked his rangy figure, too. Long and lean, a man who carried his strength out of sight. A man who liked to walk, evidently. She'd often seen him strolling around town since his arrival, but had only occasionally seen him in a patrol vehicle. But back then she hadn't been paying much attention.

Boy, had that changed. Now she was paying too much attention.

A sigh escaped her as she nodded to feelings and desires she hadn't allowed herself since choosing this calling. Sure, it would be okay for her to be married. But a courtship would probably start tongues wagging all the way to Cheyenne, and some people would start looking for moral slips. More reason to object to a female pastor.

The man had been in town for about three months and she'd never made one of her friendly self-introductions. Shame on her, but he certainly hadn't seemed like an approachable man.

In fact, it was almost as if he walked in a shield to hold everyone else at bay unless he had business with them.

That impression of him was gone now. She'd talked to him enough, she'd gotten a heartrending glimpse of his sorrow and now she'd seen him smile. Twice. The first time the expression had looked uncomfortable on his face, but the second time it had been easier for him.

A sad and lonely man.

At long last, she began to feel sleepy. She left the cup to deal with later and scuffed her way to bed. For once, sleep was kind.

CALLUM AND TWO uniforms had walked with Mr. Yost through his entire jewelry store while he catalogued the missing items. Callum kept track in his own pocket notebook, or PNB. The only time Yost's spirits seemed to lift a bit had been when he found his safe securely locked.

"The perp was in a hurry," Callum told him. "If he hadn't been, a lot more would be gone."

But damn, the guy looked sad. He must have put a whole lot of his life into this business. Callum could tell that his sorrow wasn't just a result of the monetary loss. The guy *must* have insurance, anyway, or he was stupid beyond belief. He'd recover financially.

But he might never recover from losing the sense of safety and trust that this break-in had thrust on him. Most people took a long time to get past it.

AT NINE, WITH the morning sunlight bright enough to hurt his eyes, Callum returned to the office. The place was full of deputies who looked absolutely exhausted.

And there, beside the coffee urns, the packets of sugar and no-cal sweeteners, stood a mound of cupcakes he recognized.

"Pastor Molly dropped them off," Guy Redwing said. "Nice lady, that one. We told her about the burglary. She was pretty upset."

"Yeah." He could imagine. Though not as upset as she'd been about the attacks on the women.

But as he looked at the clock one more time, he remembered. "I gotta run for a while. I promised to be at Good Shepherd for something or other. You guys start the paperwork, and I'll add anything I have when I get back. Okay?"

The *okay* wasn't necessary. It was their job, but he preferred not to toss around orders like some dictator.

Crap. He really did not feel like hanging out with some kids. Not right now. Not when he was so tired. But he'd half promised, and Molly had seemed so pleased that he was even considering it.

Well, he could handle it for a while. He actually liked youngsters and maybe he wouldn't fall asleep standing before the children's choir as they sang at least a song or two.

Besides, Molly was right. This was a good way to get to know people.

He rubbed the sleep from his eyes, downed three cups of the battery acid that passed for coffee in this office and snagged a cupcake. A very good cupcake, he thought, as he bit into it on the way to his police Blazer.

God, he must look like death warmed over. Didn't matter, he told himself. By now everyone would have heard about the Yost break-in and would rightly figure he'd been out there in the wee hours. If not, too bad.

It wasn't difficult to find his way to the church basement. The sound of excited piping voices guided him. When he reached the foot of the stairs, he entered a room swimming in red, green, white and silver. It was also swimming with kids who were running around or working hard at small tables, some of them with their tongues stuck out in concentration. They appeared, most of them, to be making cards out of colored paper. He saw a lot of strange-looking Santa Clauses.

Despite his fatigue and his desire to be anywhere else on the planet, he started to smile. The adults in the room began making their way to him, one at a time, as they could take their attention off kids with glue, scissors and markers for a minute or two. Molly's cupcakes held pride of place at the far end of the room, but there were also stacks of colorful Christmas cookies. Half-pint cartons of milk with straws stood on nearly every surface.

And soon, he was not only in the midst of kiddie mayhem, but also swamped by adult names he couldn't possibly remember under these circumstances. At least he always remembered faces.

Soon he was forgotten at one end of the basement, content to let the swirl continue while he watched.

At some point he noticed a little boy, maybe four, sitting alone at a small table. He had a card folded in front of him but was working on an angel, cut from a doily. He kept trying to cut more pieces from another doily, but something wasn't pleasing him. Finally he banged the scissors and said, "I can't do it!"

Nobody else seemed to notice, so Callum decided to step in. The kid looked so frustrated, and even close to tears. When he stood across the small table from the little boy, he pulled over one of those teensy chairs and sat facing the kid. His knees nearly reached his shoulders.

"Got a problem, kiddo?"

The little boy looked at him, his eyes widening. "You're the detective!"

"Sometimes, but not right now. What's your name?"

"Billy." Now the boy looked shy.

"You can call me Cal. So what's the problem?"

"I can't make the wings look right!"

Well, that did it, Callum thought, amused with himself. He'd just put himself into this up to his neck. "How do you want the wings to look?"

MOLLY CIRCULATED CONTINUOUSLY, talking with members of the congregation, talking to some she barely remembered seeing since the past Easter, and some she was sure had never entered the church. She thanked each and every parent for bringing their children to this event. That was the important thing.

She chatted about other matters as well, but she noticed uneasiness had seeped into the minds of some people. Hardly to be wondered at after the three attacks on women and all the vandalism. And now burglary. None of this was familiar to people who often didn't lock their doors. It hardly improved the enjoyment of Advent.

She talked to many of the children, too, some of them painfully shy. She didn't press them because she didn't want to make them uncomfortable.

Then she saw Callum sitting on a very small chair talking with Billy Carstairs. The two of them appeared intent on cutting a doily and comparing the pieces to an angel like the ones the children had recently made. A long night, probably because of the burglary, yet here he was where he'd almost refused to come. And he was engaged with a child.

That warmed her heart.

THE CHILDREN LEFT about an hour later, sticky from frosting, cookies and cupcakes. With the exception of a few of the youngest children who had become overtired or oversugared, the kids went out the door talking happily with their parents. Billy left with his dad, looking quite pleased with the angel he had glued to the front of the Christmas card he'd made.

Then the women of the Women's Club, a different group from the Altar Society, moved in to clean up. Women, of course. The mainstay of most churches. Molly made a point to thank them, but she couldn't help. The children's choir rehearsal was about to begin.

Upstairs in the choir loft, the singing had begun. The members stood straight and proud as they were led by Georgia, who was the organist. Georgia seemed to have built her life around the church and also seemed quite happy about that.

Standing between rows of pews, Molly looked up at the choir, all those shiny young faces, and felt peace flow through her.

CALLUM STOOD NEAR the altar of the church, eyes on Molly. She was wearing her clerical clothing, of course—this time not only the black shirt and white collar, but also a long loose skirt that reached her ankles. In fact, he thought, that woman gave new meaning to the term "clerical garb." Somehow stylish despite the limitations.

He decided not to disturb her and leave by the side door. God, he needed some sleep. But just as he'd turned to go, the choir began to sing "Silent Night." He froze, unable to move, as his throat tightened.

In those wonderful young voices, the song was extremely poignant, and he closed his eyes, lost in listening. For the first time in two years, he felt the touch of beauty. When the last of the song trailed away, his legs unlocked and he moved swiftly toward the door.

His eyes stung suspiciously, but damned if he was going to let tears fall. Those had been reserved for Angela and they always would be.

Chapter Ten

The Conard County Archives had begun to turn over information about any locals who might have been recently released from county, state or federal prisons. It had taken them a while to do the research, but now it sat on Callum's desk while he poured over a stack of photo images that had been made from microfiche or film. The number of them surprised him, given the nature of this town, but apparently some crimes were common enough to get a prison stint or time in the county jail.

Property crimes headed the list, probably because of the difficult economic times. The second thing on the list was spousal abuse. Quite a bit of it, actually. He'd ceased to be amazed by what went on behind closed doors.

He'd never caught that nap he'd hoped for, and his eyes were burning, as if someone had taken a match to them.

No more, he decided. He had to get some rest or he'd miss something important. Some little clue that was probably buried somewhere that only needed to be found by someone with the eyes to notice it. Right now he didn't have the eyes to see much.

The frigid air was bracing, and he figured it would be just his luck to have it wake him up. Long johns? He'd have to ask about them because he was getting cold entirely too quickly.

As he walked, he absently headed toward Good Shepherd. His mind was racing in a hamster wheel, refusing to stop, because if there was one thing Callum McCloud hated, it was an unsolved problem.

He saw Molly standing in front of the church, waving to a couple who were just leaving. He decided to turn around, but it was too late. Molly caught sight of him.

"Callum!"

Without being rude, he had to stay. "Hi, Molly," he said when she came closer.

"On one of your nightly rambles?" she asked.

"Heading home for some sleep." And now trying hard not to notice how tempting she looked, even all bundled up.

"You sure look like you need it." Her smile was gentle. "How about joining me for dinner?"

Shock opened his eyes wider and put him on alert. "What?" He started thinking how logistically impossible that would be, given her profession.

"I've got a nice frozen lasagna that I left on timed bake so it should just about be ready. Plenty for two, or even three."

That sounded a whole lot better than the peanut-butter sandwich he'd make for himself.

"Come on," she said. "It's just a frozen dinner. Maybe I'll even throw in some frozen garlic bread."

Now he was fully awake, trying to make up his mind, when she took his hand and tugged gently. "Come on," she said again. "You look like hell."

Startled, he asked, "Can you use that word?"

She laughed quietly. "Oh, I can. Judiciously."

He entered the parsonage with her, feeling almost guilty. Her reputation mattered, as she'd mentioned once when they'd first met. But she didn't seem concerned now.

Her house smelled good again, redolent of lasagna. Her cottage was always filled with enticing aromas.

"Grab a seat, Callum."

She pulled the lasagna out of the oven and put it on the counter while she took half a loaf of garlic bread and popped it in. Then she set the small table.

"You don't need to do all this, Molly."

She tilted her head. "I made the lasagna, anyway. The garlic bread's a snap. And I'd have to set the table regardless."

"Do you always eat frozen dinners?"

"I often don't have time to cook for myself. When I can, I do."

"But all your baking?" That must take a lot of hours, he thought.

"That's different. That's for the church."

He guessed he could see a difference there: one of generosity.

A few minutes later, Molly sat across from him. Lowering her head and folding her hands, she said Grace.

Boy, that took him back a long way. He murmured his "amen" at the appropriate time, then she started serving.

"The bread is for you," she told him.

"Oh, for Pete's sake, Molly, you look just fine. Far better than fine."

An instant silence filled the room. Molly didn't move a muscle. Callum felt awkward about letting that slip out and experienced a moment of gratitude that he hadn't said what he actually thought—that she was beautiful. Then he did the only thing he could think of. He put a slice of garlic bread on Molly's plate.

"Just continue to be thankful," he said, "and eat it. That's hardly going to add five pounds."

She blushed, which only made her prettier. His reactions had begun to disturb him. Since Angela's death, he'd been pretty much living in an emotional dead zone. Oh, grief and anger penetrated it, but not much else. Certainly not noticing how pretty a woman was.

"How's the case going?" Molly asked while they ate. "Or, I guess now, two cases."

The usual rule was to say something indefinite, something that revealed nothing. *We're working on it.*

But he didn't want to do that with Molly. This woman probably carried a whole ton of secrets about people and damn well knew how to keep them to herself.

"It's not going," he said bluntly. "If the evidence got any thinner on the ground you could see the grass under it."

"Wow," she breathed, forgetting her dinner. "That must be frustrating."

"It's more than frustrating. Women may still be in danger. That's the highest priority on my list. The jewelry store burglary is bad, but not on the same level. To me, anyway."

"I wouldn't think it was, either," she said, putting down her fork.

"This all stinks to high heaven and if anyone knows anything, they're not talking. What's worse, Mr. Yost gave me the description of a man he'd seen loitering outside his store on a couple of occasions. It's similar to Ms. Lansing's description of her attacker. That makes me nervous because if it's the same guy then the attacker is still in the area."

"Dear God," Molly murmured. "But such different crimes."

He reached for another piece of the garlic bread, eating it while the hamster wheel in his head revved up again.

"*Very* different crimes," he said when he'd finished the

bread. "Which makes it unlikely it's the same perp. So do we have two criminals running around at the same time? Or do we have a one-man crime wave? I don't know, but somehow I have the feeling it's one perp. Just one."

"But why?"

Callum shrugged. "There's no motive to the attacks that I can find. The jewelry store is obvious. But if it's one guy…"

He stopped. His plate was clean and he should just thank her and get the hell out. To save her. To save himself, perhaps, although he hadn't been much interested in saving himself for a long time.

"Callum? Can you put the two pieces together?"

"It's nonsense."

"I've heard nonsense before."

One corner of his mouth lifted. "I bet you have."

"So?"

"So maybe the jewelry store was a diversion. Or the other way around. To keep us looking for different perps. To make us stretch our resources. I don't know, obviously."

"It's an interesting idea."

"Maybe it's just forcing the puzzle pieces together. Anyway, thanks for the dinner. I guess I needed food, to judge by the disappearing garlic bread."

"I liked watching that," Molly answered, smiling. "But you still look beat."

He nodded, pushing away from the table. "I can wash up."

"You can just head home and find your bed. There's hardly a thing to do."

Their eyes locked, briefly, and Callum felt heat zing through him. For just a moment he thought he saw it reflected in her mossy green eyes.

Then she practically shooed him out the door, which amused him. First she'd taken him by the hand to get him here, and now she was sending him on his way. Good-naturedly, of course. That was Molly.

But she still sent him away when he very much wished he could stay.

MOLLY CLOSED THE door behind him, looking at the dinner remains with a smile. He'd polished off the food, which meant no leftovers and that he'd left with a decently full stomach.

It seemed like the least she could do, given the difficulty of his days right now.

Sending him on his way had been the right thing to do, but she wished she hadn't needed to. She'd have loved it if he could have stayed. If they had been able to get to know each other better. If they could have followed the usual course of a man and a woman who felt drawn together.

This was one of the times she intensely disliked the collar she wore. One of the very few times.

But like any normal woman, she hungered for a man's touch. For Callum's touch. Needs within her kept threatening to overwhelm her. That was not good.

Maybe she should just keep her distance. Her nature kept wanting to help the man with his grief, so she kept reaching out, and every time she reached out she knew she was making a mistake. Her position here was precarious enough.

She forced herself to think about something else. Like the fact that Jenny Clancy was coming over to clean the parsonage on Monday so she'd better have everything ready, including the clothes that needed to go to the dry cleaner. Jenny would also do her laundry, bless her.

She would conduct two Advent services in the morning, which meant she'd better find sleep soon. She needed to be rested and on the top of her form. Her day would be devoted to her congregants and the planning of the fundraiser she'd promised to produce so John Jason and Daniel Alder could stop worrying about cash flow.

They were justified in their concern and although Callista had scolded them, telling them that fundraising wasn't the pastor's job, Molly knew that in part, at least, it *was* her job.

After putting her clothing in the hamper and donning flannel pajamas, she crawled under the covers and rested her head on the pillow. She was tired—she *would* sleep.

Then the bed betrayed her. She kept imagining Callum beside her.

"Oh, man," she said aloud. "This *has* to stop."

Good luck, her body answered.

OUTSIDE IN THE miserable cold, Arthur Killian watched the detective leave Molly Canton's little house and felt a surge of anger.

The last thing he needed between him and his prize was a guard dog. As it was, Molly was never alone except when she was inside that cottage, and even then not all the time.

But during the night she was frequently alone. Unless that damn detective started staying overnight.

He was furious but unable to do anything about it because some guy with a snowblower started working on the walkway to the cottage.

Killian slipped away, telling himself his moment would come.

In the meantime, he decided that his move on the jewelry store had been brilliant. It sure had worked better than breaking windows. He'd enjoyed standing on that rooftop behind a chimney, watching the huge number of police officers that had turned out. As he'd hoped. Now they'd think they had someone to look for besides him.

Which went exactly according to his plan. *Divide and conquer.* He couldn't remember where he'd heard that, but he sure liked it. And he'd just accomplished it.

And the pieces of jewelry he'd taken could be fenced and he'd get some money out of it, too.

A double header. Oh, yeah.

Feeling better, he hiked his way to the truck-stop diner and ordered up a large meal while complaining that his pickup had been delayed again. "What's it with these companies?" he asked the waitress. "Like I don't have nothing better to do with my time and truck than wait around until they get their act together?"

The waitress made sounds of agreement as she served up his meal.

Yeah, he sure knew how to manage a situation.

Chapter Eleven

The morning had been exhilarating for Molly. The second Sunday in Advent and the church had been packed for both services. She hadn't expected so many until the Christmas services.

But standing in the doorway, speaking to members of her flock, she found among them a disturbing sense of worry. They had come in such large numbers at least in part because they sought some kind of reassurance in the face of the attacks and the burglary.

She hoped they'd found at least a small measure of comfort. She personally had very little to offer that would ease justifiable fears. The church offered them God, of course, but sometimes God could seem very far away and inscrutable.

She pondered that problem as she returned inside and headed for the church office, deciding that all she could do was remind them of the very real Presence in their lives, that they would never be abandoned. Even though they might think it sometimes.

Sighing, she entered the office to find Henrietta already there along with a couple who had promised to help with fundraising. Four more people were expected. Henrietta had made coffee and must have gone to the bakery for the donuts that filled a small tray.

Soon they were all gathered around the meeting table and tossing around ideas for the best way to raise funds.

"Thing is," Barney Rich said, "we did that fundraiser for the motel just recently. Add into that all the foods and gifts people want for Christmas and I think most folks are tapped out."

His wife, Marcy, agreed. "We need to set this up for late January, I think."

"Oh," said Henrietta in a foreboding voice, "won't the wardens love that."

Jesse Carlton snorted. "What do they want us to do? Pull teeth?"

That made Henrietta laugh. "Maybe we should offer that idea to them. Can't you just see their faces?"

Molly couldn't suppress a smile, though she refrained from criticizing the wardens in any way.

"Why aren't *they* here?" Barney asked. "Bunch of 'em want more money but they won't do a damn thing to help get it." He glanced at Molly. "Pardon me, Pastor."

She waved a hand. "As if I haven't heard cussing before, and I assure you, Barney, that was milder than some I've heard."

A laugh passed around the long conference table and brainstorming resumed. By the time they broke a couple of hours later, they had four ideas on the table. Several people had promised to look into the logistics.

They were off and running, as well as having something to report to the wardens.

Molly needed to attend to the stack of papers on her desk but told Henrietta to take the afternoon off. An hour later, she stepped into the church proper. Marvin was busy mopping floors and wiping the pews, and tomorrow the Altar Society, weather permitting, would come in to clean and polish the rest.

She stopped to speak to Marvin. "You aren't supposed to be here on Sunday." She smiled.

"We'll probably get that blizzard tomorrow. Wouldn't want the mess building up. With all the snow, slush has melted and gotten dirty from being walked on." He shook his head. "Won't do at all."

She returned to the parsonage, feeling her heart lightened. The rest of the day was her own unless something happened. Her afternoon of rest. Her afternoon of quiet contemplation, maybe even a good book. And a phone call with Tyra. It had been a while.

But Tyra wasn't at home. A good sign, Molly thought. She must be feeling well enough to get out for a little while. Still, she missed Tyra's voice and humor, which was always a lift.

She made a pot of tea for herself and decided to take it into the living room and settle in the Boston rocker with a good book. She'd finished her last one, even if it had taken weeks thanks to her duties, and was now ready for something fresh.

She thought of a walk to the library, which had afternoon hours on Sunday, then changed her mind. She wanted to be cozy and warm in her solitude, and the first signs of the approaching storm had begun to show. The wind had started to strengthen, sometimes gusting strongly enough to make the trees outside bend. Tomorrow promised to be a deadly day. She just hoped no one was careless of the cold.

There were plenty of books to choose from, a gift from prior pastors. She was searching the shelves for something that grabbed her attention when there was a knock at the door.

She went to open it and was surprised to see Gage Dalton standing there. "Sheriff! Is something wrong?" The frigid air began to reach her. "Come in out of the cold."

He gave his crooked smile, one that couldn't reach all the way because one side of his face was burn-scarred. Long ago he'd been an undercover DEA agent and had lost his entire family to a car bomb intended for him. He'd barely escaped himself.

"Nothing's wrong," he answered as he stepped inside and removed his cowboy hat, which was official headgear around here for the sheriff and his deputies.

"Can I offer you some tea or coffee? You must be cold, and that darn hat doesn't do a thing for your ears."

He chuckled. "It's getting time to switch to the watch cap. Or maybe past time."

He limped after her into the kitchen, accepting her offer of coffee, and claimed a chair at the table.

"So what's going on?" she asked after she started the coffee and sat with him. Her curiosity was killing her.

"Not as much as I'd like, but Callum is wearing himself out working on it. Last I saw he was neck-deep in reports about felons who've recently been released around here. It's a wonder his eyes don't fall out of his head. No, this visit is about you."

Her eyes widened and her heart skipped a beat. "About me?"

"Yup," he answered.

"Am I a suspect of some kind?"

"Not hardly."

She jumped up to get his coffee, then brought it over to him. "Then what? You're making me uneasy and you're taking your time about it."

He chuckled. "A chance to stay out of the cold. No, nothing you need to worry about. Not exactly."

"Oh, for heaven's sake, Sheriff!"

"You been here long enough to call me Gage. Anyhow, I was thinking about the security of women in this town. Then I got to thinking about you."

"Me?" This wasn't helping her at all. "You think I'm a target?"

"Not directly." He sipped his hot brew and sighed contentedly. "No, I'm thinking about it in a different way. You may think you're surrounded by good people here right next to the church, but I'm not so sure you're as safe as you think."

She didn't like the sound of that. "In what way?"

"Thanks to the parking lot and the graveyard, there are plenty of ways for someone to approach the parsonage without being seen."

"Oh." Her heart plummeted.

"I've seen enough of you, Pastor, to know that your picture is under the word *positive* in the dictionary. I want you to make sure you're protecting yourself as well as you can. You're more isolated than you think."

Isolation had never entered her head before. In her mind she was almost always surrounded by people, except for brief respites in the parsonage, and even then she knew all her neighbors. "Are you trying to frighten me?"

"Only enough to make sure you take precautions. Like turning off all your nights at night. Like locking up everything. In fact, Cal has ordered a new lock for your door. Something stronger."

"Callum has?" Molly was nearly stunned. "He didn't mention it."

"I think when he had dinner here last night he got concerned about that door of yours. I just saw it and he's right. That lock you have is little more than a latch from a century ago."

So how many people knew Callum had eaten a frozen dinner with her last night? Oh, man. All because of a generous impulse. *Mostly* generous, she added honestly. She needed to be more circumspect.

Gage continued his security dissection. "You need a stronger door, too, but I'll leave it up to the church to get you one. It's the least they can do."

Despite her surprise at all this, she could have laughed at the mental image she got of at least two wardens. Complaining about cash-flow problems, they'd never ante up to replace her door.

"I'll live with what I have," she said. "We have more important uses for money. This church isn't exactly swimming in it." Unable to resist, she added, "I hear about it all the time."

Gage chuckled and drained his coffee. "I bet you do. I know those wardens."

He shook his head at the offer of more coffee and eased himself up to his feet. "Just take all the care you can, okay?"

"I promise."

When Molly closed the door behind him, she paid close attention to the latch for the first time. He was right. Anyone could get through that. Worse, as a rule she didn't even try to lock it so her congregants could reach her.

Oh, heck. He'd left her with a sense of insecurity. She knew she could defend herself, but being caught in her sleep might well change the balance of power. Now what?

She tried to relax again with a book, but that didn't work very well. Her life seemed to have picked up some new complications.

Callum haunting her thoughts was the biggie, though.

CALLUM MANAGED A few hours of sleep, for which he was grateful. Very grateful.

Over a breakfast of oatmeal and a couple of eggs, he planned the day before him, as much as he could knowing so little. He needed some information from the crime lab about the Yost burglary. He needed some information from the medical doctors who were helping with photos and examinations of the patients, looking for something more useful than the partial boot prints they'd found on Loretta Sanchez. Scrapings from beneath her fingernails had been sent to the lab. Other small items and fibers had been as well.

There wasn't a big enough population around here to support extensive facilities, so much had been sent to the state's crime lab. Which meant inevitable delays.

The felons who'd been released recently weren't offering much, either. None of them, superficially at least, had a motive for going after those three women. The abusers, particularly, had no reason to go after anyone but their ex-spouses.

And the thieves among them didn't do smash-and-grabs. Although there was no reason to think they might not have changed their methods and approaches. Those were worth checking out.

Around ten, they held a meeting in the squad room—such as it was, being nearly the entire front of the office—and talked about their major crimes. They discussed the recently released felons, but nobody had any good ideas. Keep their ears out, listening for anything someone might say that could add to their pile of noninformation.

All the deputies present were as frustrated as Callum with the situation.

Guy Redwing expressed the general feeling. "How can anything happen in this town and no one knows about it? Even the least little things. What, are these guys ghosts?"

Callum kept silent about his own suspicion. He

couldn't begin to support it, and it might only muddy the waters.

The three attacked women apparently had no connections other than that they all attended Good Shepherd Church. Their circles of friends seemed to be different, although there might be some outliers the cops didn't know about yet.

Well, there had to be, Callum thought. People who were connected to all three ladies in some other way. So far they hadn't discovered any of those connections.

Except they all knew Molly through the church. The thought made his stomach churn.

But all those women attending the same church meant they had at least passing acquaintance with other members. Maybe he should get a church roster and have his men start questioning people about whether there'd been any conflicts at the church. So far they'd focused on stronger connections. Time to get to the passing ones.

When he suggested that, no one looked happy. Good Shepherd was a smaller community in this larger community of the town, but was still a community.

"We've got to examine *everything*, no matter how farfetched. These attacks were *personal* and they expressed rage. Time to look beyond the obvious."

As the men and women separated, Guy turned around. "Better stay inside today, Cal. Temp's going to drop to around thirty below, and it'll happen fast. The storm's already moving in. You'll feel it when you step outside."

Guy started to turn back, then said, "Oh, and don't stay here. It won't be a fun place to be stuck."

Callum looked around the room. No, it wouldn't.

"What about the patrols?" he asked.

"They're running same as usual. But they've got better gear than you have and they'll be in heated cars."

There it was again. *Learn to dress for the climate.* Damned embarrassing.

Guy spoke once more as he reached for the door. "And don't try to get gear at Freitag's right now. This storm is going to hit like an explosion. I've seen them drop the temp thirty degrees in twenty minutes. Not often, but it happens."

Thirty degrees in twenty minutes? Callum packed all the papers he could into his satchel then pulled on his outerwear.

He suspected he was about to get a lesson in the weather around here.

The instant he stepped out the door, he understood what Guy had meant. It was already colder than he'd felt here so far, and treetops had begun to sway hard. He decided he'd better take his official car. Walking was rapidly becoming dangerous.

He had just started the car and was letting the engine warm up a bit when his cell phone rang.

"Hi!" said Molly's cheerful voice.

"What's up?" he answered.

"It's going to get awfully cold today and probably through tomorrow. Anyway, wise people are staying inside. So I thought I'd invite you to the parsonage. Company is better when you're stuck inside and I *do* have a fire going on the hearth."

He should have refused. But instead, he accepted. Couldn't stop himself. He was losing the willpower battle with that woman.

"Just park as close as you can get," she warned him. "A few people have frozen to death in the coming temperatures because they weren't properly dressed. One woman froze going to her front door from the car. Just be careful."

Properly dressed. It was coming at him from all sides. He wouldn't have believed it was possible for people to tell that with a few glances. He must look like an idiot.

He parked behind the church in a parking lot that was empty of all, save Molly's sedan. Crap. How many people were watching him take this walk? When he looked up, however, all the curtains appeared to be drawn. In the middle of the day? Or maybe against the cold?

Molly opened the door quickly and let him in. She appeared to be wearing a blanket except she could stick her hands out of it. Like a poncho.

The first thing he said was "How can everyone see I'm underdressed for this?"

A smile tilted her mouth. "Your stuff just looks too *thin*, that's all."

He stood just inside the door, refusing to move any farther. "What about your reputation?" he asked, his voice hardening just a bit. "You don't want people talking because I spent all day here. And they will. You know they will."

"They will, if they look out their windows. Anyway, it doesn't matter. If you stayed all night, that would be a different thing altogether."

What was going on here? he wondered as he shed his jacket, gloves and scarf, and followed her into the kitchen. He pulled out a chair and sat reluctantly.

"Coffee or cocoa," she asked.

"Whichever is fine by me," he answered. Then he asked, "Why did you invite me over?"

She looked squarely at him. "Because I can't stop thinking about you."

Chapter Twelve

It seemed to Callum that all the air rushed from the room. He felt a slam of shock in his chest. "Molly—" he began hoarsely.

She cut him off, reaching for some mugs. "I figure a day together will be like an inoculation. Once we become more closely acquainted, the fascination will ease somewhat." She eyed him again. "That would be better, don't you think?"

Inoculation? It might become an addiction instead. A smart man would leave now, because Molly was the one who stood to get hurt by this impulse of hers.

He wasn't that smart.

"Do you want to go in and sit near the fire?" she asked. "I checked the weather. This storm is going to take us down to deadly temperatures. A nice warm fire is just the thing."

Then she winked. "I've even got a pillow to put on the seat of that darn recliner so you don't have to be poked by that spring."

Which was how he came to be sitting on the recliner in the living room of Pastor Molly Canton, enjoying the heat from a blazing fire. The warm mug of coffee in his hand felt good, too.

Molly sat in a Boston rocker, her face growing ruddy

in the glow from the fire. "I'm so blessed by my congregation," she said pleasantly. "My wood box is always full, I don't have to shovel my own walkway and the good ladies come over here to clean and do laundry for me. Most of my mortal needs are taken care of."

He nodded slowly. "What about the rest of your needs?"

He heard her draw a sharp breath. It was a couple of seconds before she answered. "I do my own grocery shopping."

Quick diversion, he thought, feeling amused.

"Anyway, I'm ready for this storm. A full refrigerator—"

"And freezer," he teased.

She laughed lightly. "Well, yes. But also a full pantry."

He finally dragged his gaze from the fire and dared to look at her. "Ready for the worst?"

"Ready not to have to go to the grocery in bad weather. Plus, finding a time to do it can be difficult."

"You must be awfully busy."

"Mostly," she answered, "but today's a wash. It'd be foolish to go out, so I canceled my home and hospital visits." She sighed. "I do so hate to do that. But me turning into a Popsicle wouldn't help anyone." She turned her head to look at him. "The full weight of the blizzard is going to be on us soon. The temperature is going to take a serious nosedive and from the speed this thing is moving, it's not going to be long before it's here."

"This must be a bad one to have folks heading for safety."

"It is. Blizzards happen, but the temperature doesn't usually sag this fast. Or this much all at once."

They sat in companionable silence as the fire crackled and danced. Mesmerizing shadows and orange light danced around the room.

After a bit, Callum asked, "What about Molly Canton. Who was she before this church?"

"Nothing exciting about my life story."

"I'd still like to know you better."

She glanced at him. "Happy childhood. I was lucky. Then, when I was in college, both my parents were killed by a drunk driver. He swerved off the road onto the sidewalk and hit four people. Sadly, my parents didn't survive."

"That's tragic. I'm sorry."

"I've grown used to it."

"Then?" he asked, prompting her.

"Well, the thing people seem to find most interesting about me is that I served in the National Guard. Did I mention it?"

"I think you may have."

When she said no more, he poked his nose further into her life. "It must have been an interesting journey from the National Guard to here."

She shrugged and smiled at him. "I think I told you, I joined the National Guard in part because I wanted to be able to help in disasters and because, much less altruistically, it helped pay for my education. The helping-in-disasters part, unfortunately, wasn't the only part."

Her face darkened, and he let her be. Unpleasant memories seemed to be plaguing her.

After a while, she shook herself. "After all that, I went to seminary, served in a few different churches as a deacon, and then I was offered this position." She turned her face his way and her voice grew dry. "I suppose I don't need to tell you how useless a woman in the clergy can be made to feel."

"I can guess." He admired Molly's determination to tough it out. She must be both stubborn and brave. But he felt sad, too, that following her dream must have cost her a lot. Yet here she was with her own church and her own flock.

"Want me to turn on the Christmas tree?" he asked when he decided he didn't want to pry any deeper.

Her head jerked a little in surprise. "I thought you hated stuff like that."

He looked at the tree and realized he didn't. Molly had managed to dig him out of his emotional grave, at least a little.

Rising, he went to turn on the tree. "It *does* look pretty," he remarked as fiber-optic lights danced with changing colors all over the tree. Then he turned and lifted his mug from the table. "I'm getting more coffee. Want some?"

She hadn't quite finished hers but nodded. "Sure. This is getting lukewarm. Thanks."

He could feel her gaze on him as he headed the short distance to the kitchen.

DURING THE FEW minutes that Callum was in the kitchen, Molly heard the wind pick up more. It was now whistling as it rounded the corners of the parsonage, reminding her that this was no ordinary blizzard. Her insulating curtains dampened the sound some, just the way they kept the heat inside. It was still afternoon, but the drapes kept the light out, too.

She thought about turning on a lamp, then decided against it. Between the fire and the Christmas tree, there was enough light to see by.

Callum returned with two steaming mugs and handed her one.

"Thanks," she said again, watching him settle into the recliner. He moved with such ease, a man comfortable in his body. She also liked that he was rangy rather than heavily muscled. And she sure liked the view when he bent over and the denim of his jeans stretched across his behind.

She could have laughed at herself. *Getting it bad, are you, girl?* as Tyra would have said. Well, yeah, but that didn't change anything.

He provided her with a good view of his behind as he bent to put another log on the fire.

"Mind if I look outside?" he asked. "It'll mean opening the door."

She laughed. "Just do it quick."

She heard the latch lift, but within thirty seconds she heard it close again. A draft of icy air twisted around her neck.

"Okay," he said. "The snow is blowing sideways. A great day to be indoors. Plus, it feels as if it's growing a lot colder."

"I'm not surprised. It's supposed to. Anyway, it's cozy in here."

"I can't disagree. You know, your life doesn't sound as boring as you might think. Guard training is no joke."

"I can't compare it to anything else. Now what about your life?"

He didn't answer for a while, as if there were things he didn't want to say, or if he was wondering where to start.

Presently he spoke. "I don't have any parents, either. Breast cancer took my mother at an early age. My dad made it long enough to retire."

"Retire from what?"

"He was a cop, too. I never thought about doing anything else."

"But why leave Boston to come here?"

"Because it got to be too much after my wife was killed. Oh, hell, maybe it was becoming too much even before that. I saw a lot of ugly things in my career. Too many, maybe. I kept at it after Angela died, but it really began to get to me. I thought coming to a small town might help. Less violence."

"And you walked right into this. You must be feeling you didn't get away from anything at all."

"At the moment, yeah. I've been assured that will change, once we get these cases solved."

Molly felt awful for him. His new life was turning into his old one. "I guess," she said slowly, "that neither of our lives is as boring as we said."

"Maybe not." He shook his head a little as if to shake something off.

"It *will* get better around here, I promise. We have our share of crime, but nothing like this. Of course, I haven't lived here that long."

"Doesn't matter. Like I said, the people at the office are saying the same thing, and most of them have been here almost their entire lives."

"They would know."

Silence fell again except for the whistling wind.

"The snowdrifts are going be deep," Molly said.

"How so?"

"Snow around here is usually dry. You saw that when I was building the snowman. The wind will push it around until anywhere there's a quiet place, it'll fall into a drift. Some folks are going to have to shovel just to get out their front doors."

"Fun."

He looked at her again and Molly felt an electrical crackle between them. She rose suddenly, driven by a need for self-protection. Not only would it not be good for her to have a brief sexual relationship—and given that he was still grieving, that's all that it could be—but she also didn't want that. She'd never want that.

"Have you eaten since breakfast, Callum?"

"No."

"Me, neither. I'll make us some lunch. Soup and sandwich? I warn you the soup is out of a can."

He half smiled. "Like I'm going to complain? I'm no chef. Soup and I are best friends."

She returned his smile. "I'll go see what I have in the cupboard."

She headed for her pantry and found some cans of New England clam chowder. Before pulling them off the shelf, she went to look around the door into the living room. "Can I insult you with canned clam chowder?"

"Why would that insult me?"

"You're from Boston," she pointed out. "You must have eaten better chowders. Crackers instead of sandwiches?"

"Sounds perfect."

Then she left him where he was, following his own paths of memory, she was sure.

As she stirred the soup on the stove, she thought about his wife, wondering what she'd been like. Her death had obviously gutted him in some essential way. He must have loved her very much.

And it had ruined the holiday season for him. Well, at least he'd been willing to help with the snowman. And hadn't he just turned on the tree? Then there was Billy, of course. Thinking about him taking the time to help that little boy with his Christmas card touched her. Everyone else in the room had been too preoccupied to notice that Billy was having a hard time, but Callum had noticed.

A good man, she thought. A very good man.

The soup was hot, so she asked him if he'd rather eat in the kitchen or off a TV tray in the living room.

He rose and stretched. "Kitchen would be easier."

"And colder," she warned him. "No insulating curtains in here."

"The soup will make up for it."

After filling two soup bowls, she found a smaller bowl and filled it with oyster crackers. "Help yourself."

He apparently liked them because he dumped a generous handful on his soup. "Smells like home," he remarked, then looked stricken. He started to put down his spoon.

"Callum?"

He glanced at her.

"This may not be home, but you're still allowed to eat some canned soup and crackers."

After a moment, he nodded and slipped his spoon into the bowl.

Molly spoke as she lifted a spoonful of soup. "I wish I knew the secret of eating soup without it dribbling on my chin."

He surprised her with a snort of laughter. "I sure don't. I won't tell if you don't."

"Deal," she told him.

Their lunch passed pleasantly enough while she shared some of her knowledge of the town and county.

"The county is huge," she said. "There are sheriff's substations scattered around. I don't think you'll see those deputies very often. Most of the communication with the office in town is by radio. Mostly there are tiny towns scattered around the ranch land. Some as small as two or three hundred people. And the ranches go on forever, it seems. I still get awed by it."

"I haven't had much of a chance to look out there."

"When the weather gets a lot better, take a few days to scout. You'll be amazed."

"And the town?"

"Five thousand people, give or take. That makes it a large town by Wyoming standards."

"And here, I thought this place was small," he said dryly.

"Not for this state. You'll get used to it. But, anyway, most everyone knows everyone. That's why getting hooked into the grapevine might be useful for you. Most of the gossip will probably bore you, but you never know when you might pick up a tidbit."

"So how do I get hooked in?"

She had to grin. "Hang around for a while. When people get used to you, they'll start sharing."

"Are you on the grapevine?"

"I think I've made it at least partway. But given I'm the pastor, I doubt I hear most of it."

He rose and carried their dishes to the sink. "Does your job make you feel lonely sometimes?"

She was about to say *no*, then realized that wasn't strictly true. "Sometimes," she admitted. "There's a distance at times. I don't know how exactly to describe it. And I don't know how much of that feeling comes from me being female."

"I'm sorry you face that kind of prejudice."

"Hey, I got through Guard training and I wasn't always welcomed by the men. A lot of them think it's tough-guy territory. That a woman can't measure up."

"But you did, obviously."

Her mouth twisted a bit. "Having to do twice as much as anyone else is annoying. Well, ask Tyra. She's faced a lot more of that than I have."

"That's sad, too. It's the same in the police force, you know. Female officers get too much crap and face a lot of doubt from some people. And as for Black officers... well, they must sometimes feel like they're living a nightmare. But they stick around and if you ask me, they're the toughest of the tough on the force to survive that bigotry and keep going."

"Being Black is an emotional battering. Tyra's amazing. She's had to be one of the best teachers in the high school and in the process she's gained a lot of respect. Maybe some of it grudging. The nice thing, she says, is that the kids love her."

"Hope for the world yet."

He filled the dishpan with hot soapy water, but Molly nudged him aside. "Let me," she said. "Just tell me about the cases. Any progress?"

He didn't answer immediately. Just as she was about to turn and find out if he was still there, she felt powerful arms slip around her from behind.

"Molly." His voice whispered in her ear.

She wanted to lean back into him, but warnings sounded in her head. "Callum..." Her voice sounded weak even to her.

"I understand," he murmured. "You told me. But damn it, woman, I can't stop wanting you."

She nearly melted but before she could turn into a puddle, his arms slipped away.

"You can trust me," he said in a firmer voice. "You and your reputation are safe with me. I think I should leave."

She swung around, forgetting the soapy water on her hands, and splattered it everywhere, even on Callum.

"Don't you dare leave! I don't want your corpse on my conscience!"

Again that half smile from him.

"Besides, I *do* trust you." Then she turned back to the dishpan, ignoring the way her hands trembled.

She wanted him, too, wanted to say "to hell with it all."

But she couldn't. She was too devoted to her calling.

A pastor couldn't have a fling, not if she wanted to keep her church and her flock.

ONCE AGAIN THEY sat in the living room with the twinkling tree and a hot fire.

The storm continued to blow with all the force it could muster. Molly wondered aloud if shingles would blow off her roof.

"They might," Callum answered. "Any idea how strong the wind gusts are?"

Molly hunted for the remote and turned on a flat-screen TV that she seldom used. It took her a minute to find the weather, then it popped up. It wasn't long before a crawler at the bottom of the screen began to report the unhappy news.

Temperatures in their part of Wyoming were dropping, down to about twenty-five below. The nighttime temperature was predicted to fall to minus thirty. Wind gusts were reaching sixty miles an hour.

Molly shook her head. "The cattle and sheep," she said. "This will devastate our ranchers. They can't possibly put most of their herds in shelter."

"I hadn't thought about that. It's one helluva storm. And yeah, you could lose some shingles."

She sighed. "So could a lot of other people. In fact, this storm is likely to hurt a lot of people. Want me to leave the TV on?"

"I really should go. I came in my official vehicle and it's been in the parking lot all this time."

She waved away his concern. "If anyone is nosy

enough to come out into this to count cars in the parking lot, he'd be a fool." She turned to look straight at him. "Unless you're desperate to get away, then stay put."

"It's not that far to my vehicle and you—"

"Oh, stop, Callum. If I was worried about that, I wouldn't have called you. And it may not be a great distance to your car, but this wind is enough to worry about even with a higher temperature."

"The car will protect me."

"From the wind, once you're in it, but I can guarantee your heater won't even start to work before you get home. Do you want me to remind you of that story about a woman who froze to death walking from her car to her front door? You might be better-dressed than she was, but look at those jeans. You can lose a lot of heat through your thigh muscles. Want to test how fast that can become deadly?"

He settled back on the recliner. "No, Pastor."

In spite of herself, she giggled. "You're a tough nut, Callum. Seriously, don't leave because of me. If you want to leave for other reasons, be my guest. I'm not trying to hog-tie you."

"You don't need to do that," he answered, his words freighted with meaning.

She felt her cheeks heat and didn't know how to respond. Almost desperately, she jumped to her feet. "Board game? Do you like *Scrabble*?"

"Sure. That'd be great."

She pulled out a card table and he opened it in the center of the tiny living room.

"I'll get the kitchen chairs," he said while she started to spread out the game.

"Thanks, Callum. I hope you're not too good at this because I frankly stink."

"Then we should be evenly matched. I have a talent for missing double word scores and I've never made a word out of seven tiles."

Molly laughed. "Sounds like me."

She made some popcorn, his buttered and hers not. That weight thing she had bothered him. Couldn't she see that she would provide a perfect armful? Couldn't she understand that a lot of men preferred to hold a soft woman rather than a bony one?

Apparently not, and there was nothing he could do about it.

But then, Molly, being a cleric, probably never thought in those terms. Or wouldn't allow herself to.

Silly words seemed to be the name of the game with Molly laughing a lot. Callum was amused enough that rare chuckles escaped him and he even made a few bad jokes.

Then, startling them both, someone banged on the front door.

Chapter Thirteen

Molly jumped up to answer the pounding. Callum stayed behind, clearly understanding the difficulty his presence could cause her.

Molly opened the door a careful crack. Fred Wilson, one of her congregation, stood there in a snowdrift more than two feet deep. Barely twenty-one, he still had the remains of a baby face.

"Fred!" she exclaimed. "What are you doing out in this weather?"

"Truck broke down."

"Well, come in!"

"Pastor, my wife and new baby are in the car in the back parking lot. They need to get in from the cold. The baby's gonna need nursing but I don't want Martha taking off her jacket. I thought you might know where we could stay."

"You can stay here, of course. We'll go get Martha and the baby. Get back to the car so your wife doesn't start worrying you froze to death."

Fred turned at once and headed back into the whiteout.

Molly closed the door and looked at Callum. He'd risen to his feet.

"I need to grab a few blankets," Molly said. "They're in my bedroom."

He followed her at once and together they pulled down quilts from the shelf in her closet. Then they dressed quickly for the outdoors.

"Let's not get lost out there," she remarked. "I hope Fred didn't."

Stepping out the door was like stepping into an icy whirlwind. Molly felt as if she'd be knocked off her feet at any moment. Leaning slightly backward, she forced herself to stay upright, no easy thing to do with the wind hammering her back. At least there was just enough visibility to see five feet or so, which should mean they wouldn't get lost out here.

Callum, leading the way, appeared to be having slightly less trouble.

God, her cheeks felt as if they were already freezing.

Then they came around behind the church and the building partially blocked the wind. The world became a little clearer and Molly had no difficulty seeing Fred's pickup truck. It was parked right beside her car. Callum's vehicle was invisible.

"There," she said loudly, her voice almost snatched away.

"I see it."

Fred and his family were safely tucked away in his cab, out of the wind.

Callum spoke loudly. "I'll help Mom and baby get out."

She watched briefly as he carried a couple of quilts toward the passenger side of the vehicle. She hurried to Fred to hand him another.

With both doors open, the wind ripped through the passenger cabin.

"Here," she said to Fred, passing him a blanket.

When their small band gathered in front of the truck,

Callum took charge. "Molly, you lead the way. Fred, you take care of your wife and baby. I'll follow behind in case anything happens."

And something *could* happen, Molly thought, with the wind blowing so hard and the snow getting so deep. She did her best to plow a trail along the path she and Callum had already followed, but their footprints were filling in fast. And looking into the wind was likely to turn her face into an ice cube. At least it was easier to walk by leaning forward.

She kept wanting to look behind to make certain everyone was there, but she was sure Callum would shout out if anything happened.

Then she reached the parsonage door and threw it open, not caring about the heat loss. They all stumbled into the warmth and Callum forced the door closed behind them. Blankets and quilts and outerwear fell all around them in a heap. Fred took his baby from Martha so she could doff her parka.

Martha was pretty, with dark hair but she looked far too young to be married with a child. Molly led her to the recliner, saw her settled and watched Fred pass the infant to her. By then she was as grateful as anyone could be for the blazing fire.

"Praise God," Martha said, visibly shivering. "It's so warm in here."

Molly spoke. "Fred, you take that rocking chair and let the fire warm you up. I'll make everyone something hot to drink. Cocoa?"

As she turned toward the kitchen, Molly remembered the table covered with the *Scrabble* game. Well, if that wasn't a dead giveaway that Callum had been here for a while. She might have groaned inwardly, but instead she smiled faintly. Maybe the time to kick over a trace or two had come. She sure as heck wasn't going to escape the speculation if Fred or Martha talked.

Shortly, Molly passed around cups of hot cocoa. "If you need to nurse," she told Martha, "just say the word and Callum and I will move to the kitchen. Okay?"

With her baby safely tucked in at her side, Martha nodded and began to sip her cocoa. "Oh, this is so good. I got so cold out there."

Molly and Callum sat in the two kitchen chairs they'd been using to play *Scrabble*.

"What happened?" Callum asked Fred.

"Dang engine overheated. You wouldn't think in this cold…" He shook his head. "I was stupid, anyway. They'd have kept Martha at the hospital, but I thought it was still clear enough to make it home. Then the engine." He spread his hands. "I'm a fool."

"I wanted to get home," Martha said. "Don't blame yourself, Fred. I kinda pushed you."

He grimaced then patted the large diaper bag Molly hadn't noticed in the heap of blankets. "At least I got the diapers."

Martha smiled at him with evident love. Then the baby started fussing and she said, "I think Andrea is hungry."

"She'll probably need a changing, too," Molly said. "Callum, let's get to the kitchen. When Andrea's done nursing I'll clear away the game to make a changing table."

"You're so kind," Martha said. "I can't thank you enough. We'll try not to put you out for too long."

"You're not putting me out at all."

CALLUM ENJOYED WATCHING Molly swing into action. Throughout her exchanges with the Wilsons, her voice had been so gentle, like a warm blanket that wrapped those around her. Callum was used to louder voices, sharp voices, angry voices. Even the voices of his best friends never sounded gentle like that.

He joined her in the kitchen on the two remaining chairs, which he'd carried back in.

She sat for a minute, drumming her fingers on the table. "I'll need to figure out what to make for dinner. This blizzard won't blow through before late tomorrow." Then she gave Callum a wry look. "No, not frozen dinners. But, man, I'm not used to cooking for so many. Well, I can figure it out."

She drummed her fingers a little longer. "They can have my bedroom. They'll need some privacy." Then she looked at him again. "Sorry, my planning must seem boring."

"Not at all," he answered truthfully. "But where will *you* sleep?"

"We'll make beds on the living-room floor. Can you handle it?"

Shock shook him. "You want me to stay the night? But—"

"Oh, forget about that. If there's going to be any talk, it started when I opened that front door. You saw what it's like out there, so you're staying here. Regardless, can you sleep on the floor?"

"Of course." Near to Molly, he probably could have slept on a bed of nails. He might have pointed out that he could probably get to his car and get home, even without the heater working, but he refrained. This situation was beginning to be fun. "Where else is there to sleep?"

"I'm beginning to wish I hadn't turned that second bedroom into an office. And the room in the addition upstairs gets way too cold in the winter, especially when there's a stiff wind."

"Maybe you should talk to the wardens about that, too."

Her face screwed up. "Yeah, right. Especially since we need some roof repairs to the church. And other things. Imagine me asking for more insulation and double-paned windows when I'm the only one living here."

He grinned at her response. "Hey, isn't this the season of giving?"

She shook her head. "Not for the parsonage, it isn't. I can just hear the scolding. Anyway, it usually doesn't matter at all. And I guess I'd better start thinking about dinner."

THEY SPENT A pleasant evening with the Wilsons in the living room by the fire. At least it remained pleasant until Fred asked about the attacks and the burglary at the jewelry store.

"How's that going?" he asked Callum. "Folks aren't really feeling safe right now."

"I'm not surprised," Callum answered. "We're working on it."

The typical police response. Information couldn't be shared with the public. Not that they had any useful information to share, Callum thought. "You hear anything that might be remotely useful? Any little thing no matter how small?"

Callum glanced at Molly. She was holding the infant to give Martha's arms a chance to rest, and her face had grown so soft. She could barely stop looking into the little sleeping face. There was a woman who wanted children, he thought. Shame she was denying herself that part of life, all to keep some misogynists from talking nasty.

He turned back to Fred, who was frowning thoughtfully.

"I don't know," the young man said.

Martha spoke. "But there's Sally at the truck-stop diner. She says there's this one trucker who's been hanging around for a while. Keeps complaining that his load isn't ready in Cheyenne. Says it's cheaper to stay here."

"That makes sense," Molly said as she handed little Andrea back to Martha, who was holding out her hands. "Madonna and Child," she remarked almost absently, then returned to her seat.

Callum put another log on the fire, keeping the room warm enough while the wind whistled outside. He made a mental note to check out that driver.

"The Christmas tree is so pretty," Martha said. "All we could afford was a teeny one with hardly any lights."

"We'll have a better one next year," Fred promised. "You'll see." He clearly meant it, too.

Callum liked the young couple. Too young, he thought, but life was probably different out here. "What do you do for a living, Fred?"

"Work road crews in the summer. And the rest of the year I'm a janitor at the elementary school." He smiled almost shyly. "I wanna be a cop."

Martha sighed. "I wish he'd get over that. Cops get killed."

"Not that many, and sure not around here."

She shook her head at her husband. "One is too many." Then she looked at Callum. "It happens, doesn't it?"

"It can," he said carefully. He didn't want to get into the middle of a marital disagreement, but he wouldn't lie.

"Have you ever been in a shootout?" Fred asked eagerly.

Oh, hell. Now he *did* want to lie, but he still couldn't. He wasn't a liar by nature. "Yes."

Martha looked at Fred. "See?"

Fred ignored her. "I bet none of the cops were killed, though."

Now how the hell did he answer that? He decided to skirt the issue. "None died."

Fred looked at Martha. "See?"

She shook her head and gave up, much to Callum's relief. None had died in those shootouts, but some had been wounded. Him among them. Just once. Once was enough and it could have been worse. Armor didn't protect every inch of the body, especially when cops were on the street. It could be different for a planned takedown, but when you got a call on duty, it wasn't the same. Chest protection wasn't always enough.

He felt Molly's gaze on him and looked at her. She didn't look any happier than Martha. Well, chalk that up as another reason not to get involved with her. Although he doubted there were many shootouts around here, if any.

But put a desperate armed man into a situation where he felt cornered and anything could happen.

It had taken a while for him to get past being wounded, and it had taken Angela a lot longer. Being a cop's wife was stressful. Callum sympathized with Martha.

But he could understand Fred, too. The job sounded exciting, but he could at least pour some cold water on that. "I hope you like paperwork, Fred. You'll spend a lot of time doing it."

"Really?"

"You ever see a cop in an empty parking lot behind a big store? He's sitting there taking care of paperwork so he doesn't have to do it when he finishes his shift. He's got his radio live, naturally, so he can answer any calls that come in, but he's busy filling out forms or tapping on a keyboard to save time."

"I didn't know that."

Callum produced a faint smile. "Now you do."

When he and Molly had gathered up blankets and

spare pillows from upstairs, the young family went to the bedroom down the hallway.

As he and Molly were spreading out the blankets, she said quietly, "You've been wounded, haven't you?"

He tensed, although he kept spreading a blanket. "What makes you think that?"

She sighed. "The way you looked when you were talking to Fred. Were you wounded?"

His jaw tightened. "Yes."

Then she totally astonished him. "Me, too."

He nearly gaped. "What?"

"There are some dangers to being in the National Guard, especially when we're at war and your unit gets called up."

He sat down on the floor, hard. "Tell me."

"Not much to tell about. I was in-country for all of six weeks. Short tour to say the least."

"Being wounded sent you home?"

She nodded. When her face raised to look at him, he saw the shimmer of tears. "You wouldn't believe the horrors I saw in just that little slice of time."

"I've probably seen some of it on the job."

"Maybe so." She plopped down her pillow and wiped her face with the sleeve of her sweater. "It's over. I rarely think about it anymore."

He doubted that was true, but he wasn't going to press her and drive her further into those memories.

She decided to leave the tree on, adding its light to the firelight.

"Why leave it on?" he asked.

"Because Advent only comes once a year. Because I only get a few weeks to enjoy the beauty."

Well, that was kind of sad, he thought.

Then, when they were stretched out on their blankets, he spoke. "There's something you have to do."

"What's that?"

"Tell the wardens you need a softer floor."

Her laughter made him feel a whole lot better about everything.

OUTSIDE, STANDING in the godawful blizzard and nearly freezing off his cojones, Arthur Killian watched the steadily growing group at the parsonage. That detective had been there all day, then those other people had come.

Hell. He'd thought the blizzard would give him cover to go after Molly. No way. Anyhow, all he could think about was getting back to that damn motel room.

He also realized he'd been stupid in coming out in this mess. Cover? It might kill *him* instead.

It wasn't long before he headed back to the car he'd "borrowed" from a distant corner of the truck-stop parking lot. Now his main need was to drive back and get to the motel alive.

Hell's bells.

Chapter Fourteen

Early in the morning, while the storm still raged outside, Molly and Martha made a breakfast of oatmeal and coffee for everyone. The baby slept blissfully in her car seat, rescued from the truck earlier by Callum.

Gathered around the small kitchen table, they conversed fitfully. While Molly usually found it easy to get to know new people, this morning she felt too groggy to manage.

Callum was right: she needed a softer floor.

With her elbows on the table, she held her mug of coffee in both hands and gazed at Callum over it. He seemed unaware, so she simply enjoyed the view.

"Can we get the weather report?" he asked.

"It's not looking good right now." As if to answer her, the wind started whistling again. "I'll turn on the TV in a few minutes."

Martha spoke. "I can't thank you enough for taking us in."

Molly smiled. "There's room at *this* inn."

That comment made both Fred and Martha smile. "I was hoping that Andrea would be born on Christmas," Martha said almost shyly. "She had her own thoughts about that."

"Evidently. I hear babies generally do. Which can sometimes drive a mother crazy when they're late."

"And worry them when they're early," Martha answered. "Andrea was early, but she's fine, thank God. And my labor was so fast. I was expecting it to take nearly a whole day, but it was only nine hours. My girlfriend said the next one would come faster so I'd better run to the hospital at the first twinge."

Molly chuckled. "I hadn't heard that."

A short while later, Fred said, "I don't even want to look out the window and see how bad it is out there."

"I'll go look," Callum said. "I'm curious."

He pulled the curtains back at two windows then returned to report, "It's still really bad. Horizontal snow. I can't imagine what's piled up in front of the door. It might be hard to get out of here."

"Jimmy will clear us out," Molly answered. "He clears the snow for the church. The whole front sidewalk, the steps, the path to my door, the parking lot. He'll get here as soon as he can. In the meantime, may I suggest we *don't* open the door? I honestly don't want to see the snow pour in if we do. Unless getting out is really urgent for some reason."

No one disagreed. Regardless of how much snow might have piled up, it was still too dangerous to go out.

But Molly couldn't help thinking of all the work she was missing. If this kept up for too long, she'd never catch up.

John Jason called. "How are you doing, Pastor? Got all the essentials? Not that I know how we could get anything to you right now, short of using an army tank."

She laughed. "All okay here, John. I always keep extra on hand for winter weather."

Boxes and cans and a freezer full of frozen meals. A

stove and heater that ran on natural gas. Even with three extra adults, they could make it two or three more days. By then, they'd be shoveled out.

"But you're okay?"

"Well," she said dryly, "I need a softer floor."

Callum suddenly grinned.

"What?" John exclaimed.

"Just joking. No, all's good here."

Right then, Andrea decided to wake up, fussing and crying. Even as Martha rose to take care of her, John's voice rose over the phone line.

"Do I hear a *baby*?"

"Yes, John, you do. The Wilsons and their newborn got caught out in the storm and they're staying with me. What did you think? That I have some dark secret?"

John practically spluttered at the other end of the phone. Callum grinned again.

"'Welcome the stranger,'" she said. For once she enjoyed stirring the man up. "I'll talk to you later. Thanks for checking on me."

Martha had disappeared to the bedroom with the baby. Fred spoke. "I'm sorry you're sleeping on the floor. We could sleep there and give you your bedroom back."

"Don't even think of it. It's good for the soul." *If not my hips and back.* But come to think of it, the mattress on that bed wasn't great, either.

With the bedding tucked away, they set up the folding table again and the four of them played a game of *Parcheesi*.

By late afternoon, the wind's howling had lessened. Callum went to the windows again and pulled back the curtains. "Winter wonderland," he announced. "But no more horizontal snow. Easing up, I think. What about that weather on the TV?"

Molly hunted up the remote. She so rarely watched television that she couldn't remember where she'd put it this time. She finally found it tucked between books on the shelf. At least it was easy enough to use. It was also easy to find the weather. Nearly every news channel was covering the storm, and the Wyoming stations were providing the forecast, as well as the dire stories emerging from the wintry blast.

"We're lucky," Fred said as they watched.

But the news was good in that the storm would finish blowing through around midnight.

"There," Molly said with satisfaction. "Life will start returning to normal tomorrow morning. Not much longer to be stuck. I bet you two want to get home with your baby."

Fred looked sheepish. "Well, yeah."

"Of course, you do. I don't think this is the way you visualized your first couple of days after you brought Martha and Andrea home."

After they had all curled up for the night, all Molly could think about was Callum's proximity. So near, yet so far. His male aromas reached her faintly, stirring desires she didn't want or need. Making her ache with hunger. To have a man's arms around her again would be heaven.

Well, she thought, forcing herself to remember her reasons for not getting involved, at least the presence of the Wilsons would prevent any gossip about what the preacher had been doing with a man in the parsonage.

Small blessings.

IN THE MORNING, the sun returned from its vacation, brightening the sky, making the snow blindingly bright. A gorgeous, cold day. The sound of snowplows and snowblowers reached inside the parsonage, reassuring in their promise that people could soon come out and drive again to the grocery.

By 10:00 a.m., a knock sounded at her door. Molly opened it to see Jimmy standing there with snow shovel in hand. She smiled at once.

"Your path is clear, Pastor. You can get to the side door of the church now. I'm getting the snowblower next and clearing the front, then the parking lot."

"I can't thank you enough, Jimmy."

He shrugged. "Least I can do to support Good Shepherd."

It was true, he didn't get paid for doing this. He'd added this of his own accord to doing minor repairs, a job that he did get paid for, and not nearly enough in Molly's opinion. But her control over such things was minimal, if not nonexistent.

The whole darn edifice depended on willing volunteers. Then she thought of something. "The Wilsons are staying with me. Their truck was overheating. Do you know who I might get over here to fix it?"

"I'll take a look at it," Jimmy said promptly. "If I can't fix it, I'll find someone to come over here."

There weren't enough thanks in the world for this man.

Then, all too soon, Callum said, "I can probably get to the office now. Thanks for your hospitality, Molly."

CALLUM, BY NATURE a bulldog with a bone when it came to crime, was for once reluctant to return to work. He plain didn't want to leave Molly.

But serious things had happened and they couldn't wait for his attention. He wasn't surprised that AFIS was taking so long with that one partial fingerprint. They were backlogged and, worse, they didn't have fingerprints on file for every felon because not all law-enforcement agencies forwarded them.

It wasn't like TV, where the cops had a fingerprint match within hours. Nor was DNA. Those matches never got done that fast. They took time to get results, and those labs were backed-up as well.

And with all of that, finding either one at a crime scene was useless unless they could be matched with someone.

He *did* make it to the office, though, along freshly plowed streets that were nevertheless coated with thin layers of snow. He imagined the sand trucks would follow.

In the meantime, he needed to figure out how to investigate the trucker that Sally, the waitress at the truck-stop diner, had mentioned to Fred. And he had to investigate somehow without raising the guy's suspicions. Last thing he wanted was a possible perp on the run.

Leaning back at his desk in the squad room, he folded his hands on his chest while he thought. Funny how hard it was to concentrate on the job when Molly kept popping into his thoughts.

Her good nature, her cheeriness, her warmth toward people, even her enjoyment of Christmas, were all enchanting him. Temptress.

He swallowed a smile, imagining how she might react to that word.

You think I'm Delilah or something?

Yup, that sounded like Molly.

Back to work, he told himself sternly. Women were depending on him. Now that trucker…

He leaned forward and reached for the landline, calling the truck-stop diner to ask when Sally would be on duty.

THAT TRUCKER WAS frustrated beyond words. He'd been kept from getting to Molly Canton during that blizzard, she still had those people staying with her and the likelihood he'd get a chance at her tonight was slim.

His fury was rising again, reaching a fever pitch. He *had* to get rid of it before it drove him into doing something really stupid. He wasn't good at impulse control, according to the prison psychologist, but he needed to practice it now. The patience he'd learned was strained to the max, getting ready to snap.

He had to take this anger out on something, a person or a place. Just about anything would do.

He started thinking about the possibilities open to him. Soon he thought he had one.

He rubbed his cold hands together.

That night, as always, he went to the diner for his dinner. While he was seated at the table eating, he froze in place.

The detective walked in and looked around. Killian could barely breathe. With difficulty, he stabbed his fork into a slab of meat. Then to his relief, the dick sat down and ordered coffee and a burger.

Okay. It was okay. But he couldn't completely relax.

FROM FIFTEEN FEET AWAY, Callum enjoyed his burger and coffee. But he hadn't missed the guy at the table near the back. Hadn't missed the way he'd frozen. The way he now seemed edgy, like he was ready to jump.

Maybe that was the trucker Sally had mentioned. If Callum's appearance had made the guy nervous, then he had something to hide. And Callum was pretty much sure he'd caused that attack of nerves. He'd watched enough people on the job to recognize the signs.

But what was the guy hiding? Had he stolen some

candy bars from the rack near the counter? Did he have weed in his pocket or maybe a load of it being transported in his truck? Was his truck improperly tagged? Nervousness didn't mean he'd attacked those women, and if he'd hit the jewelry store, he'd have long since left town.

But it could be a lot of things. Callum watched from the side of his eye, pretending to ignore everything except his food.

The guy ate in a hurry, dropped money on the table and disappeared out the door quickly.

Okay, then.

Callum rose and snagged a waitress. "You know who I am?"

She nodded, her eyes wide. She was a middle-aged woman who'd begun dying her hair that champagne color. He glanced at her nametag. "Sally."

"Yes."

"Was that man who just left the trucker you were talking about? If so, I need a favor from you. If you wouldn't mind."

She nodded, now looking excited.

"I want you to clear that man's table with a fresh pair of your rubber gloves. Carefully. Then carry it all to the back by itself, on a tray, or in a clean bus bin by itself. I'll meet you there."

"Wow," she whispered. "Okay, you got it. I knew there was something weird about that guy."

"Maybe so."

He spoke to the owner, Hasty by name, and had no trouble getting waved to the back. The advantage of a small town. He didn't have to flash his badge to get cooperation. It sure made something like this easier.

Sally brought the bus bin to the back and stood holding it while Callum pulled out several evidence bags and his own protective gloves. Then, taking everything by the safest spot, he lifted the coffee cup into a bag, then sealed it. After that came the fork in another bag.

He stood there marking them quickly then looked at Sally.

"Remember what we just did. Remember the items I took."

She looked at the two bags and nodded.

"If that guy did something that goes to trial, you may have to testify to the link between these items and that man."

Her eyes grew until they seemed to fill her entire face. "Wow. Really?"

"Really. And it would be a big help if you'd write down the date and time somewhere so you can't forget it. In fact, write everything down. Got it?"

She nodded and pulled out her order pad and pen. "Right now. I'll keep it safe."

"Got any idea what kind of truck that guy was driving?"

"A small truck, I think. At the back of the lot because the other trucks have been moving in and out. That one just stays there. White boxy thing, not like them big rigs out there."

He favored her with a smile. "Thank you."

"No need," she answered, her voice now growing firm. "If that guy did something bad, I want to help put him away."

ARTHUR KILLIAN DECIDED it was time to move out of the motel and start eating convenience-store sandwiches and chips. That detective had made him nervous, probably more nervous than he should be, but he wasn't going to take any chances. His goal was too close and he wasn't going to leave Molly Canton behind. Not now.

No, he needed to teach her a lesson, and the need was growing. It was hammering at him.

Well, he could move the truck out of town somewhere and sleep in it. Not too far from another car he could "borrow." He'd need a car.

Satisfied, he began to pack. Once that detective drove away, Killian would move. Fast.

BACK AT THE OFFICE, Callum asked one of the techs to try to lift prints from the cup and fork and match them to the partial they'd picked up at Mabel Blix's house.

Donna Henley shook her head a bit. "The comparison would be superficial, Callum, against a partial. We can look at it here, but we'd be better off asking the state lab to make the comparison."

"I'm not opposed to sending it on, but take a look with our software, anyway. Even a little bit might tell me if this guy could be our perp. He's hanging around. If he is, it means he isn't done."

"I'm on it," Donna answered, then headed toward the back and the limited forensic lab facilities.

And that was the downside of living in a small town, Callum thought. He simply didn't have the technical equipment he'd had in Boston.

He could have become frustrated by that but he'd chosen this path and he'd just have to deal.

And stop thinking about Molly Canton. About her easy joy in even little things, like holding that baby. Damned if she hadn't looked as if she wanted her own.

Chapter Fifteen

A few hours later, Donna returned with news.

"Well, Callum, you might be in luck."

He sat straight up. "How so?"

She laid two transparent sheets in front of him on his desk. "See that little scar on the thumb? Going sideways along the side?"

His heart quickened. "Yes."

She slid one sheet over the other. "Match."

"Fantastic. Now we just have to find out who he is." Which was the whole damn problem. Knowing the prints might match wasn't enough alone. There could be any reason the guy had been in the Blix house and a defense attorney could shred this evidence.

But he *could* bring the trucker in for questioning. Amazing how many people crumbled quickly. Or couldn't resist bragging. Regardless, it was time for a little third degree.

He called the motel and asked if they'd had a trucker staying with them for a week or more. He got the guy's name—Randy Cole.

Then he grabbed a uniform to go with him and headed out, feeling the first satisfaction he'd felt about these cases. Now he had something to work with.

Maybe.

No one answered the door when Callum knocked. "Hell," he muttered. Then he said to the uniform, Ben Staple, "I doubt he'll show up with a uniform present. Take a look around the truck-stop parking lot." He scribbled down the info he had, which wasn't much, and passed it to the deputy. "I'm gonna hang around a bit, over there." He pointed to the side of the motel entrance.

"You got it."

Staple walked across the highway and disappeared among the parked trucks, while Callum grew edgy. Had the guy flown the coop already?

Staple returned twenty minutes later. "The truck is gone, Detective. Fresh tire marks where the lot hasn't been plowed completely. They sure couldn't have plowed under it if it stayed parked. And all the other rigs are sitting there with their engines running and have been moving in and out today."

"Well, hell." What more could he say? "I don't think he's finished. We're going to need a stakeout, plain clothes. Let's go set it up." Because if the man was after another woman, then he'd come back.

Another woman. *Molly.* A mental map had grown in his head. Blix and Sanchez lived near the church. Tyra was her Molly's best friend. Little enough evidence of anything, possibly a coincidence, but his heart lurched, anyway. At night, Molly was usually all alone in the parsonage.

Then Donna came to him with the long-awaited results from AFIS. Now they knew who they were looking for.

THE WILSONS WERE STILL at Molly's because Jerry Jimmy had told them the radiator had cracked. "Old truck like that, things happen. Lew Franklin is getting one in as quick as he can. Maybe tomorrow."

Molly looked at Fred. "Where do you live? Maybe I can drive you home."

"About two miles west of town."

Molly frowned. "Any nearby neighbors?"

Fred shook his head. "We're on the edge of ranch country."

"Then you'll stay here. I can't leave you out there without any kind of transportation."

"But…"

"No *buts*," Molly said firmly. "What if your heater quits? Any kind of thing could turn into an emergency and there's no telling how long it would take for someone to get to you."

Fred stopped arguing. He eyed his wife and daughter, who were tucked up in the rocking chair. "You're right."

"I'm always right." Molly smiled. "I'm a pastor, remember?"

That made Fred laugh. Martha looked up from her absorption with her daughter. "Thank you," she said.

"It's no problem at all. I like having you here." Which was the truth. Somehow they made her cozy little house feel cozier.

But the path between the parsonage and the side door of the church had been cleared, so she supposed she ought to go over there and take care of some work.

Dang, it was cold outside, even bundled up as she was. She didn't expect Henrietta to be there, though. The woman had enough on her plate without risking her neck to drive here. With two young adopted boys and the school still closed, she couldn't leave them home, not while her husband was out of town.

The first thing she did when she settled at her desk was call Henrietta. She could hear excited boys' voices in the background.

"I hope school opens tomorrow," Henrietta said humorously. "These kids are running me ragged trying to keep them entertained."

"You have my sympathy," Molly answered, smiling into the phone. "I'm in the office. Is there anything I need to take care of today that isn't in the appointment book?" She knew that Henrietta, bless her heart, had the church calls forwarded to her home in the evening or on weekends.

"Not a thing, Pastor. I guess nobody wants to come out yet. Anyway, you'll find the appointments in the book aren't important and can be postponed."

Then Henrietta's voice grew concerned. "You shouldn't get on the roads, Pastor. Seriously. I'm hearing from my friends that the sand hasn't been spread everywhere yet, and that there's a black ice problem in places."

Well, that settled that, Molly thought. She spent some time making phone calls to the housebound, then the victims of the beatings. Loretta Sanchez was still in intensive care. Mabel Blix was at home but sounding tired. She had a friend staying with her and was fine, thank you for calling.

Then Tyra.

"Oh, hell, Molly," Tyra said. "Frankly I'm going out of my mind without school. I keep thinking of my students who live in miserable home situations, or whose families have trouble paying the bills and buying food. School is where they get fed. Where they get real care from people who actually give a damn. Where they can escape from it all for a few hours a day."

"You're breaking my heart, Tyra," Molly said honestly.

"Why? You folks at the church do a whole lot for these families." Then she gave a tired laugh. "SheeshMolly, you'd save the whole world if you could. And you weep that you can't. I know you."

Molly swiftly changed the subject to one that didn't embarrass her. "How are *you* doing otherwise, Tyra? That attack was nothing to sneeze at."

"Maybe not," Tyra answered forthrightly, "but you try growing up in a rough neighborhood. Been punched and kicked before."

What an awful commentary, Molly thought after she said goodbye. She stared blindly at nothing at all, until she shook herself out of her sudden mental funk. She'd be useless to everyone if she allowed herself to give way.

Then she rose and reached for the beauty and hope that made her life so blessed. Inside the church proper, she flicked switches and turned on the two Christmas trees and the strings of white lights strung from the choir loft. So beautiful.

A rack holding several rows of votive candles flickered with a few flames. She went over and lit one, then devoted herself to prayer for all the world's unfortunates.

She knew better than to blame God for the horrors. *These things result from the hard hearts of men.* People were capable of fixing all the problems of mankind.

They just refused to.

In the morning, the Wilsons went home. Molly missed them the minute they departed. Especially the baby. Those sounds and scents would be sorely missed.

Then off to the office again to catch up on work. At this time of year, there was plenty of it. Extra gatherings, extra practices, groups preparing the church with big red ribbons and enough pine boughs to scent the entire place, as well as making it pretty. A bake sale that smelled so delicious that as Molly wandered among the offerings, she figured she'd gained five pounds just from the aromas.

Then there were her usual calls to the housebound, and when she was in the office, a fair number of visitors who needed or wanted to talk with her.

It was a full life she enjoyed, for the most part. Today had been extra busy however, and she was glad to close the parsonage door behind her and slip into old jeans and a sweatshirt. And her silly, fuzzy pink slippers with eyes on them. After all this time, they still made her grin.

A frozen meal out of the fridge, one of those low-calorie ones. She hardly cared which. Only as she was warming the oven did she glance at it long enough to see it was supposedly pasta primavera. She didn't expect it to taste like the real thing, not with all those calories missing.

But what did it matter? Better than putting on weight.

She was just about to put the frozen tray in the oven when someone knocked on her door. Wondering who might need help at this hour, she went to answer.

There stood Callum, with a large brown bag in his hand. "Let me in," he said before she could say a word. "Or you're going to freeze in your own home and I'll be standing out here ready to be your next snowman."

A laugh bubbled up from her stomach and escaped her as she quickly stepped back to open the door more.

He headed straight for the kitchen without pulling off his jacket, gloves and watch cap. He placed the bag on the table and scanned her frozen meal.

He pointed to it. "Seriously?"

"I've got to mind my intake. I've told you."

"Not every single damn day," he said forcefully. "Besides, you need enough energy to stay warm."

She put her hands on her hips, feeling a flicker of resentiment. "You know, Callum, you could help me by not disparaging my diet. Respect my decisions."

He cocked an eye at her. "Okay, have your measly dinner and I'll shut up about it. But by the way?"

"Yes?"

"I *do* respect your decision. There's a big chef's salad in this bag."

She didn't even have to think about it. The frozen dinner went right back into the freezer.

Coffee and salad made a fairly good combination, Molly thought as she speared some lettuce with her fork. "Thanks so much, Callum."

"My pleasure. What, no dressing on that salad?"

She gave him a look that silenced him. But not for long.

"You know, Molly," he said, "you'd need a microscope to find many calories in those veggies. As for the ham and cheese in there, you'd need a magnifying glass."

It was true, the salad was lacking in the meats. She laughed. "Okay. But don't bug me."

He held up his hand, palm forward. "I won't." Then he pushed a thin slice of garlic bread toward her. "Croutons in their original shape, if you want them."

Oh, man, did she. Giving in, she took the slice and savored every mouthful. She could make up for her dietary sins tomorrow.

Callum, meanwhile, dug into his own dinner of a thick steak, mashed potatoes and a side of broccoli still green enough that it claimed it hadn't been overcooked.

"This salad is really good," Molly said. "A big thank-you."

He shrugged. "No biggie. Are you missing the Wilsons?"

"Actually, I am. Tiny as this cottage is, you'd think it

would have felt crowded, but it didn't. Maybe I'm getting an insight into my predecessor and his many children. I often wondered how they got by in this house."

"A lot of patience and love," Callum suggested.

Molly smiled at him. "I suspect you're right."

After they'd finished eating, the trash went into the wastebasket. No washing up.

They moved to the living room, where Callum built a fresh fire. Then he sat on the recliner while Molly claimed her favorite rocking chair.

"So," said Callum presently, "we think we know who our perp is, at least the one who beat those women."

"Thank goodness!" Molly felt a strong wave of relief, thinking that no other woman would face a horrific attack. "Have you caught him?"

"Not yet. He's not local and he might have skipped town."

"Oh." Her heart fell. "But you'll get him?"

"Soon, I hope. We've got a stakeout going on at that motel. Where Fred said the waitress said he was staying."

Molly's spirits lifted again. "But how did you find out who he is?"

"We had a partial print from Mabel Blix's house, which could have been anyone, but then Sally at the truck stop helped me get a full set of prints off that trucker's utensils. They match."

"Wonderful! But why would he suddenly run?"

Callum grimaced, his face etched by firelight. His strong chin, his straight nose, his...

Molly yanked herself back. Sheesh! Next she'd be climbing all over him.

Callum, apparently unaware of her gaze, shrugged. "Might have been my fault. I went to the diner specifically to get those prints and he got real nervous. Impossible to mistake."

"Especially for an experienced detective."

"Yeah, I think he recognized me. Anyhow, not being local, I can't understand why he'd come here to do this. It doesn't make sense. It would be hard to be any more out of the way than this town. And since he's not local, why in the world would he come here when he got out of prison so recently? That's how they matched his prints, by the way." He concealed his own ugly suspicion for which he had absolutely no evidence.

Molly nodded, rocking slowly as she thought about it. "Recently out of prison? You'd think he'd have bigger things on his mind."

"You'd think."

Molly, who'd been delighted to hear they'd identified the perpetrator, thought about the strange situation. Why, indeed, would some ex-con come to Conard City? Unless he knew someone here?

She bit her lower lip, wondering if she should question Callum any further. He wasn't supposed to talk in any detail about his cases, she was sure. But the question popped out, anyway.

"Do you think he might know someone here?"

Callum nodded slowly. "The question is crossing my mind."

"But *three* women?" It didn't make any sense to her.

"That's weird, all right. Especially since this guy was convicted of several charges of spousal abuse. Not the type to commit physical mayhem on random women."

Molly froze. "Spousal abuse?"

"Serious abuse."

"What's his name?" she asked, her voice barely above a whisper.

CALLUM SAW HER stiffen and her gaze grow distant as if she was remembering something. But she'd never been married as far as he knew. There was no way she could have been a victim of marital abuse.

"Molly," he said quietly.

Her eyes drifted toward him. "Callum, what was his name?"

He broke every rule in the book, hoping to make her feel better. Instead he made it worse, saying, "Arthur Jay Killian."

She drew a shaky breath and her face drained. "Oh, my God."

Callum leaned in her direction. "Molly? Do you know him?"

"I was instrumental in helping to put him in prison."

Chapter Sixteen

Callum remained silent. Well, that would explain the connection, he thought. She knew who the guy was, and he was here now. But that didn't explain the other women unless the guy was circling in on his prey, trying to unnerve her.

Nor was it necessary to know now. That could wait until they caught the beast. His concern for Molly grew by leaps and bounds.

"Molly," he said again.

Her eyes focused on him. She was no longer lost in memory.

"What happened? With this Killian guy."

She swallowed and tightened her lips, then spoke. "He was a vicious man. Unbelievably vicious. What he did to his wife? It was almost as bad as what he did to the women here. But he did it to her more than once."

She fell silent, once again traveling a path in her memory.

"Why isn't he after his wife?" Callum asked, wondering if she might have an answer. Abusers usually went after their wives, blaming them for everything.

"I guess she got as far away under a new name as I'd hoped."

"Which leaves you."

"That would be my guess. But why the other women? Why didn't he just come after *me*?"

"You'll have to ask *him* that when we cuff him. But what's the rest of the story?"

He was intensely curious now. Wanting to hear her part in this. How could she have made this man so furious with her that he'd attack other women? What caused the long-simmering boil?

She closed her eyes. "I was in the National Guard, serving during the week-long training. I heard something down an alley and I looked. I saw a man savagely beating a woman."

"You couldn't just walk away." He had no doubt of that. It wasn't a question.

Her eyes snapped open, suddenly looking like green fire. "Of course not! I tore down that alley and tried to pull him off her. He was strong with all that rage. When he wouldn't back off, but just kept hammering her and yelling horrible things at her, I managed to turn him around enough that he got a knee in his groin."

Callum managed to smother a grin. "Then?"

"I helped the woman away. I wasn't going to leave her with him. Dang, she was a bloody, bruised mess! But she was terrified, too. She freaked when I said I'd call the police. It took me some time to coax her into the coffee shop where I was meeting some of my buddies. I didn't even have to explain to them. They formed a phalanx around her, shielding her as much as they could from the other patrons. We got her settled under my jacket and with an icy drink to help the swelling in her mouth, and I swore I was taking her to a safe house."

Callum nodded, growing even more impressed with Molly. "But no police?"

She shook her head. "Of course, police. I wasn't going

to let that guy walk away. Eventually Carla—that was her name—grew less afraid. I think it helped that she was surrounded by seven men and women in uniform, all of them kind and understanding. She felt safe."

"I should think so." He began to understand more about Molly Canton. She simply couldn't walk away from someone in need even when she'd already rescued them.

"Anyway, the police took one look at her, got the information they needed and went after Killian. I gather he wasn't too hard to find. Idiot went home. The cops had given Carla the number of a women's shelter and I made her call it. I tell you, none of the people I was with were going to let her get out of it. You've never heard so much cajoling in your life."

"Good people." Very good people in a world where, as he knew all too well, people didn't want to get involved.

"We walked her down to the corner, where the car pulled up for her."

"How'd you know it was the right car?"

She smiled faintly. "They gave her a safe word."

Callum nodded. "Good thinking."

Molly sighed and looked miserable. "Well, the wheels of justice began grinding. A pile of hospital X-rays and all her excuses for them, recorded. I can't understand why no one at the hospital caught on and called the police themselves. But it was a wonder the woman was still alive."

"I can imagine. I've seen it."

"I guess you have." She shook herself. "And I had to be a witness, because I'd seen it with my own eyes. It would be my guess that's why he's here."

"Sounds like it might be. But Carla went through with the trial? That must have been hell for her."

"It's not easy to stand up against a man like that. Talk about courage! Anyway, I guess by then being in the shelter had helped strengthen her. She testified, all right. In excruciating detail. Horribly painful to listen to. But she also came to hear the verdict. Must have been a vindicating moment for her."

"Yeah." He could imagine the woman's relief—her relief at being believed. Her probable surprise that no one had believed her husband. The instant when she realized he would be gone for a long time.

"After that, people helped Carla get a new identity. She phoned to tell me that she was leaving and to thank me. And, no, I don't know how she got her new identity. I was just glad she did."

Callum had heard and seen so many stories like this it was almost blistering. And to find out that Molly had seen it happening like that? He wished he could erase her memory because she was clearly still troubled by it.

After Molly fell silent and turned to stare into the fire, Callum waited before speaking again.

"I'm sorry you had to see that, Molly."

"I've seen worse," she said tautly. "I've been to war however briefly, remember?"

When she turned her head toward him, he saw her tears glisten in the firelight.

"Why," she asked in a tremulous voice, "do people have to be so cruel? Why?"

"I wish I knew." But her tears touched him so deeply that he gave up trying to think about anything except Molly. Rising, he went to take her hands gently and tug her up from the rocker. Then he led her across the room, sat and pulled her into his lap.

"I guarantee I won't bite."

A small watery laugh escaped her, but then she turned her head into his shoulder and gave in to her tears. They dampened his shirt but he could only feel touched that she trusted him enough to let him see her like this.

Eventually, he began to rub her shoulder, trying to ease her grief, and realized that he could hold her like this for the rest of his life.

Oh, God, no. Her reputation. And his grief, which he hadn't quite absorbed yet. He couldn't do this to her.

As MOLLY QUIETED, her tears no longing running, she felt comforted. No one in a long time had offered her the comfort Callum gave her right then. Sitting on his lap, being held so gently, awakened a whole different kind of need than the desire she had felt before. She wanted to burrow into the warmth and strength he offered her.

She wanted it never to end. Dangerous. But she let herself enjoy it, anyway. It would end soon enough. Reality would return, as it always did.

Regardless, she'd realized in those minutes that although she was surrounded by people, by friends, she nearly always felt alone in some deep corner of her heart.

But at last, she had to move. Had to resume her life. Had to stand up and be the pastor again. As if to remind her, the phone rang.

Hardly able to smother a sigh, she eased off Callum's lap and then hurried to answer the phone in her kitchen. At the other end, she heard Tyra's voice.

"Molly, I don't know where that damn detective is, but I suspect you do. Tell him that Vera Holmes saw someone lurking in the back alley. She called me, heaven knows why. Am I a ninja?"

Her first concern was for her friend, then for Vera. "Tyra, are you okay?"

"I'm fine," Tyra said, sounding almost angry. "But I'm not sure you're safe! Now get to it, girl!"

Molly hung up and turned around to find Callum standing right behind her.

"What?" he demanded, as if he suspected the news.

"Vera Holmes. She lives on the other side of the alley behind the church parking lot. She saw a lurker and Tyra wanted me to tell you."

Right then, she didn't even think of what it meant that Tyra wanted her to tell Callum. She didn't care that apparently everyone knew right where he was. All she cared about was Vera Holmes.

THE EMOTIONS ROILING in Arthur Killian were like a pressure cooker ready to blow. They'd driven him out on this cold night to hunt at the parsonage only to see that that damn woman wasn't alone again. She used to be alone at night all the time since he'd arrived here to stalk her, but now she was never alone.

He shouldn't have wasted time working out his needs on those other women while circling in on Molly, hoping to frighten her. He shouldn't have tried to play the distraction game. He should have just gone for Molly Canton's throat.

Not so smart after all, he told himself. Man, he was almost stupid, playing his foolish little game while the rabbit kept avoiding the snare.

Standing in the alley, staring at the lights in her house, having seen that damn detective show up with a paper bag, he hated that woman more than ever.

But she wasn't alone. She *had* to be alone. He was smart enough to know he couldn't take down more people than that woman with anything but a gun. But a gun wouldn't satisfy him. Wouldn't satisfy his urges. He needed to beat her until her blood ran over the floor.

The other women hadn't been the same. They'd been

stopgaps, nothing more. Only Molly Canton could satisfy him.

He clenched his fists inside his gloves and resisted an urge to scream his fury.

Then he settled on the house right behind him. He knew a woman lived there alone. When he'd been picking out victims, he'd watched more than three. Alone. And this one had a light on, and he enjoyed seeing the blood spill. Until a dark shadow moved in the corner of his vision.

He melted away into trees and shrubs and took a roundabout route to his stolen car, knowing he was leaving prints in the snow, but he quickly reached a shoveled sidewalk. He crossed a street and melted into more shrubbery alongside the walk. Three minutes later he climbed into the car and drove away slowly.

Appearing to be just a local resident, not someone in a hurry. Another smart move. Maybe he wasn't a fool after all.

MOLLY WATCHED CALLUM swing into high gear, punching a button on his phone. Then he was speaking.

"Guy? You know Vera Holmes's house? Get some men in plainclothes over there as fast as you can. A man is standing in the alley between the church lot and her. Right."

Then he started to yank on his outwear as fast as he could. "Molly you stay here and lock the door. Prop a chair under the latch so it's not easy to get in. Then pick up the heaviest item you own and wait behind that door on the hinge side. Got it?"

Her fear, mostly for Vera, ramped up rapidly to nerve-stretching tension. "Got it."

Callum stopped just long enough to touch her arm. "Promise me."

"I promise. But get going."

She watched him slip out the door almost silently, then she did as he'd directed, all the while praying that Vera would be safe, that Callum wouldn't get hurt.

Then she picked up her fireplace poker. She doubted this creep had ever seen what military training taught a soldier to do with a rod. She sure as hell knew how to use it.

OUTSIDE, THE COLD air nearly snatched away Callum's breath. Moving as quietly as he could, keeping to the shadows, he slipped toward the alley, almost positive that this was their perp. He pushed down his throat-tightening fear for Molly to the furthest reaches of his mind. He needed every ounce of his focus on the minutes ahead.

He thought he saw a shadow move, blending into the night. Then hurrying feet came from his side.

He turned quickly, ready for anything, then recognized Guy Redwing, who spoke immediately, quietly. "I saw him slip into the shadows under the trees over there." He pointed.

"Ask Connie Parish to check on Vera Holmes. We can track this monster over the snow."

Guy tipped his head so that the radio microphone on his shoulder was close to his mouth, allowing him to speak quietly.

Then he turned to Callum. "Connie is going to Vera's."

Callum nodded, thinking that at this point Vera would respond better to a woman's voice outside her house. Then he and Guy moved toward the place where the man had disappeared. As he'd hoped, there were footprints clear in the snow.

Guy adjusted his flashlight to a pinpoint to lead the way. No moon tonight to guide them. No moon to illuminate that dark figure if he slipped deeper under the trees. Enough light, thanks to the snow, to give a pale, silvery sheen to the ground, but not enough to distinguish figures in the deep shadows.

Callum, his heart beating a steady but strong rhythm, walked beside Guy, taking care not to mess up the footprints.

They reached the street and everything changed. No prints in the frozen patina over the street.

"He had to go somewhere," Guy said.

"Yeah, but which way?" Callum turned on his own flashlight, widened the beam and began to sweep the street and sidewalks for a clue. Then he thought he found one at the edge of the far sidewalk, right up close to bushes and the shadowing trees. Then more. They followed them as rapidly as they could, as the prints disappeared then reappeared farther on down.

Callum jerked his head up as he heard a car start. On the night air, it probably sounded closer than it was, so he guessed it was at least a block away. But the engine didn't rev—instead, it sounded as if it was driving away slowly.

Nonetheless, he felt it in his gut. He turned to Guy Redwing. "That's him. He got away."

Guy answered with a reluctant nod, then a string of curses. "We don't know which way he went. We could get some cars over there…"

"Too late," Callum answered. "He could hide that car almost anywhere there are other cars because we don't know the make, color or model. He could hunker down so we couldn't tell he's inside unless we want to shine flashlights into every car in a five-mile radius."

"That'd be a whole lot of cars," Guy said grimly.

"Yeah." Callum shook his head, a relatively mild response to what he was feeling: overwhelming frustration. "We need to talk to Vera Holmes, find out how much she saw."

It was going to be a long night. Or morning. They'd have to question neighbors, too, all along the alley, in the hope that someone besides Vera had noticed something.

Guy spoke again as they walked back to the rear of the church. "You go check on the Pastor, Cal. Then we'll talk to Vera."

Shock jolted Callum. He'd believed he and Molly were being relatively circumspect, and damn, they were only friends, anyway.

But apparently the Conard County grapevine was busy, probably with a very different interpretation. One that Molly had wanted to avoid. One that might harm her position.

He gave himself a mental kick for being so careless after she'd warned him.

Then he headed for the parsonage door. Molly deserved to know that for right now she and Vera were safe.

MOLLY WAITED BESIDE the door, poker in hand, her heartbeat steady, her mood strangely calm. Adrenaline, she thought. Just adrenaline.

Her wait seemed to last an eternity before she heard a knock at the door, followed by Callum's voice. At once she pulled the bracing chair from beneath the latch and threw open the door.

Callum started to step in, then paused as he looked at her. "I figured some kind of candlestick or a cast-iron pan."

"What are you talking about?" Then she realized she was still holding the fireplace poker. "Oh."

"It's okay," he said, taking the poker from her and carrying it back to its stand. "He didn't have time to get to Vera, but she's probably pretty shaken. I need to go back to talk with her. But whoever was in that alley managed to escape, damn it."

Molly clapped her hand to her mouth, holding in her own instinctive string of curses. "Dang, Callum!"

"He caught sight of something. Maybe I didn't stick to the deep shadows well enough. Or maybe he glimpsed one of the deputies approaching. Whatever, he took off. We were able to track him at least part of the way but as near as I can tell, he took off in a car before we reached him."

"Oh, God. Oh, God."

Callum turned from the fireplace and wrapped her in his arms, holding her tightly against his still-cold jacket.

"I'm going to make you safe," he said tautly. "I promise."

"But what about other women?" she asked. "I can't stand that anyone else is suffering because of me. I can't stand it!"

He leaned back a bit and ran his gloved hand over her hair. "When we get him, everyone will be safe."

Then he let go of her. "I've got to go. This night isn't over." He paused. "I promised to make you safe, but I can't guarantee he won't find a way to swing around us and get back here. Keep that door locked and prop the chair against it. And stay close to that poker."

"And keep the lights off," she added shakily. "I will."

When Callum was gone, Molly stood alone in the cozy space that no longer felt cozy. Not in the least. She understood his promise, but she also understood that he couldn't guarantee anything.

Everything was too fluid. Knowing Killian's identity

wouldn't make him easier to find if he was in flight. And he could always come back later. A week. A month. Unless he was captured, she wouldn't be the only woman at risk from that monster.

The idea sickened her that she could be the cause of so much pain. *No good deed goes unpunished.* A depressing thought and so far from her usual nature that it disturbed her. She couldn't let Killian change her. That would be worse than being beaten. It would mean she'd lost.

By nature she was a fighter, not a quitter, and she wasn't going to let that man steal his way into her mind.

After locking up, as Callum wanted, she went to the kitchen and made herself some sugar-free cocoa. Which probably had as many calories one way or another as the real stuff, but it felt better to her diet-conscious self.

With the poker near at hand, she settled into her rocker in the dark to wait out the endless night hours. Any desire to sleep must have moved to the next state because her eyelids didn't feel even a bit heavy. Another time her insomnia was useful. The heat kicked on, sounding loud in the night's quiet. The Christmas tree shimmered in the corner, full of a promise that seemed to be escaping her.

Arthur Killian had not only beaten three women badly, but he was also stealing the sense of safety from every single woman in this town.

And he was stealing Christmas from all of them.

She half wished she'd get the chance to use the poker on him.

C ITY POLICE AND sheriff's deputies prowled the streets and alleys of Conard City even though they believed the search was useless. They *had* to try.

For a while, Callum sat with Connie Parish and Vera

Holmes. Vera had wrapped herself in a colorful afghan and held a mug full of hot tea in both her hands.

"Did you get the sense that anyone might be watching you or your house before tonight?" Callum asked.

Vera shook her head. "Not once. But that's not the kind of thing you think about around here, even with those attacks. Maybe we all wander around believing it won't happen to us."

"So just tonight?" Callum asked.

"Just seeing a man in the alley at that time of night, that was the only thing. He was pacing a little, but not much, as if he was waiting for something." Her eyes lifted from her mug. "I couldn't really see much more. He was like a black shadow. If he hadn't moved, I might never have noticed him at all."

"How did you see him?" Callum asked. "Wouldn't light inside make it hard to see out there?"

Vera sighed. "I was a fool, I guess. I turned off the light in the kitchen as I always do when I go to bed. Automatic. I woke up to go to the bathroom, then wanted a glass of water, and since I know my way around this house so well, I didn't even turn the kitchen light on again to get the water. That's when I saw him."

Little enough, Callum thought when he departed. Connie offered to stay the rest of the night with Vera, and the woman accepted gratefully.

Then he was back out in the cold and the only thing he felt good about was that they'd scared the creep. But the scare wouldn't keep him away for long, because he hadn't gotten his prize.

Callum picked up his vehicle from the church parking lot and headed toward the office. In the morning, the door knocking would start, over a wider area than the alley because the guy had gone somewhere and someone might have seen something just that little bit unusual.

This was going to take just about all the manpower they could spare. Back in the office, he listened to the crackling communications between officers, sparse at this time of night.

He had to get a picture of this Arthur Killian out to the public. Sticking it on a few windows wouldn't be enough.

He wondered if the Conard County weekly paper, full of ads and little news, could deliver the mug shot the way they delivered the paper: to nearly every driveway. Man, that would be a lot of copies but the paper, like many, was printed out of town. How many copiers would he be able to access around here? The schools, local businesses, the library. He was sure everyone would want to help. He needed to get that rolling first thing in the morning.

But maybe he could get some assistance from nearby television stations. All he had to do was call, explain and ask.

That was when he realized he was tired despite all the activity. He was running in circles trying to figure out how to get Killian's photo and description out there and trying to mentally count copy machines. Damn. Just call a few TV stations and tell 'em what was going on. Simple. Quick.

A hell of a lot faster than trying to string together every copy machine in town. What in the world had he been thinking?

He remembered the cot in the conference room. Usually folded against a wall, but occasionally used by a deputy who needed a nap after a long shift when he had to get back on the street soon. Sooner than he could reach his own bed. Not all of them lived in or near town.

Maybe he could catch some shut-eye back there. The

uniforms knew what they were doing. There was a dispatcher who'd wake him if he was needed.

But if he didn't catch some shut-eye he wouldn't be of any use at all.

MOLLY WAS STILL wide-awake when the first rosy light of dawn tried to peek around tiny cracks in her curtains. During the night she had grown chilled, so she headed for the kitchen to make some instant oatmeal.

The threat for this night was over. The daytime seemed to scare away that coward. Killian was certainly a coward, a man who beat up on people who were smaller than he was. Like his wife. And who knew how many others.

Like now, here in Conard City. Women, and women alone. Yeah, he was a coward, but feeling all tough inside his own mental delusion.

But what difference did that make? He was still hurting people. The kind of man he was or believed himself to be was irrelevant.

What she really needed was some plan to stop him.

Her cell phone rang just after she'd washed her oatmeal bowl and was drying her hands. Tyra. She answered quickly, glad to hear her friend's voice.

"I take it you're okay," Tyra said dryly. "The police presence back here has been astonishing. I never dreamed this small town had so many cops."

"You should take a head count."

Tyra laughed, a sound that was cut short. "Sorry, the damn ribs are still giving me a hard time. But not to worry. I'm healing. Just don't tell me any jokes."

"I doubt I could come up with a funny one right now. But at least Vera is all right."

"Yes, she is. Her guardian deputy, Connie Parish, I think, let me talk to her. What a change from when she first called me about the man in the alley. Right now she sounds ready to take him on. At least the bastard didn't try to get into her house. She wouldn't be feeling so feisty this morning."

No, he wanted to get into my house and couldn't because Callum was hanging around. Again, the thought sickened her, because what if Killian had decided to sate himself by going after Vera? What if he'd gotten inside?

"Molly? Where'd you go, girl?"

Molly realized she'd fallen silent. "Sorry. My insomnia again." She wasn't about to tell Tyra what she now knew about Killian. She didn't want Tyra worrying about her.

"I wish I could get back to school," Tyra said.

"Did the doctor tell you how long it would be?"

"I can't go back until I'm able to yell at the kids."

A surprised laugh escaped Molly. "You're kidding, right?"

"Of course, I'm kidding. Dang it, Molly, you *must* be sleepy. Anyway, Doc thinks another week. I won't be singing carols until then, I guess."

"I'm sorry."

"About what? That I won't be singing? The world will be grateful. Anyway, go find your pillow and catch some sleep, why don't you?"

"I've got a lot to do today."

"You always have a lot to do, and most of it can wait until you've had a few hours of sleep. I'm sure the inestimable Henrietta can hold the fort for a little while. Now scoot to bed or I'll come over there and sing at you."

Smiling, Molly said goodbye. Tyra was right. At last she was feeling sleepy. At last.

She wended her way to her bed, climbed into her pajamas and fell asleep almost as soon as her head touched the pillow.

ARTHUR KILLIAN WAS one furious man. Not only had he been thwarted last night and chased, but he also couldn't go back to that lousy motel room, where it was at least warm even if it did reek of ash. He'd spent most of the night curled up on the back seat under a blanket that stank of some kind of animal. Now he was freaking cold, sitting in a car he'd heisted, which would undoubtedly be reported, in a parking lot surrounded by other cars.

As daylight began to edge away the night with a ruddy glow, he decided that he needed to get farther away for just a little while. Let the heat die down.

He bit into another peanut-butter cracker and took a swig from a beer. Hell, he should have gotten coffee at that convenience store. At least it would be hot.

But as he thought about heading for a larger town, just to let the heat die down a bit, he knew he couldn't.

Something bigger than himself was driving him and he couldn't shake it, not for even a little while. He craved teaching that woman a lesson as much as he craved the air he breathed.

So he'd get another car, preferably one that could put out more heat that this little one. He'd need gas soon, anyway, if he was going to run the damn things nonstop.

But even buying gas was becoming more dangerous. He wondered if they'd somehow found out who he was. Nah. Then *maybe*. But how? He'd been so damn careful.

He tossed the cracker. It didn't taste good with the beer. He should have gotten some kind of chips or nuts. Next time.

As he sat there, shivering, he tried not to remember his brilliant plan to cause a distraction so nobody'd ever guess that Molly Canton was his intended target.

Because now it looked like major stupidity.

Hell. He dumped the beer into the snow and headed

back to the convenience store to get a couple of those giant mugs and fill them with coffee. He'd pick up a half dozen of those sweet rolls, too. At least they'd taste good with the coffee.

He didn't like the way the clerk looked at him, as if it was weird that he'd come back a second time.

Well, it was a free country, wasn't it?

Chapter Seventeen

Callum went to the parsonage that evening, unable to see any reason to avoid it. Near as he could tell, he and Molly had become an "item" in the minds of many people. If that caused her trouble, it was too late to fix it.

He was concerned about her reaction to recent events. He also wanted to be with her, but he told himself that was a minor thing compared to her state of mind, after how close that bastard had gotten to her.

Although he'd figured out she was a sturdy woman who could take a lot in her stride. So, okay, he mostly wanted to spend some time with her. Lying to himself rarely worked any better than people who tried to lie to him in an interrogation. But it was amazing how many stories people could invent. Stories that were as full of holes as Swiss cheese.

He stopped to eat beforehand so she wouldn't feel she needed to cook for him and could have one of her small frozen meals to appease her concern about weight.

He still didn't get it. She was a beautiful woman just as she was, and she'd still be beautiful if she gained more weight. But while he might not understand it, she'd sure made it clear that he should keep his opinion on that subject to himself, that it was her decision.

Fair enough.

She greeted him with that warm smile he was coming to love. The way it softened her face, made her look so gentle and kind and welcoming. How well it fit her nature.

"Want some dinner?" she asked him as he started pulling off his outerwear.

"I ate already, thanks, so just take care of yourself, please."

She laughed lightly. "I already ate, too. But I do have a pot of coffee. Odd that I have insomnia sometimes, but the amount of caffeine I drink in the evening seems to have no bearing on it."

"The coffee sounds great."

They moved into the living room, where the tree twinkled and the fire glowed with embers. Callum stirred them a bit with a poker, then took another log out of the large wood box that filled a back corner of the room. It wasn't long before fire lapped at the sides of the log.

"So tell me," he said, "do you go out and chop this wood yourself? It wouldn't surprise me."

She laughed quietly. "I thought I'd told you that Jimmy, Marvin, and a couple of other men keep that box well-stocked. People take care of me, Callum."

He returned to the recliner, adjusting the pillow before he sat. "Not well enough. They need to get you some new chairs, too."

"*You* talk to the wardens then. The church comes first."

"And you're part of that church. A very important part." He hesitated, then said, "You know people are talking. I shouldn't come here anymore."

"Oh, heck," she said irritably. "I'm not a cloistered nun. I'm entitled to a life and friends. If they can't take it, I'll move on."

"But you said…"

"I know what I said. Then I realized I've been tiptoeing too much because some people didn't like the idea of a woman pastor. Well, you know what? I finally got around to deciding that they *have* a woman pastor and they should be judging me on my performance in the job, not on my being female. It's independence day for me."

He had to laugh. "Good for you, Molly Canton."

"Well, it's true. It's not as if I'm getting drunk at the bar every night or swearing from the pulpit. Then they might have something to complain about."

He smiled at her because she always made him smile. He was coming out of his gloom at last. An odd feeling, one that brought a spark of guilt, but only a small one. He was getting past that, too.

And she was bringing him to this point. Her joy in life, her joy in the holiday season, had begun to thaw the ice that had encased him for so long.

And the desire he felt for her. A feeling he hadn't allowed himself since Angela. He felt it now and he didn't feel the least bit guilty about that, either.

He couldn't deny himself any longer. Rising, he held a hand out to her. She looked perplexed but took his hand and stood up. Then she looked into his eyes and he knew she could see the fire burning there. Fires he needed to quench. He wondered if she felt the same, but then she leaned into him, wrapping her arms around his waist.

"Oh, Callum," she breathed. "Please."

He needed no further invitation. Sweeping her along with him to the bedroom, where the chill was greater, but ignorable, he lifted her sweater over her head, exposing her plain cotton bra. Then with a flick, he unfastened it and let it fall to the floor.

Her breasts fell free, revealing a surprise to him. She

was not as small-breasted as she appeared when dressed. Another concession to her role?

She wasn't busty. No, her breasts were on the smaller side but perfect, tip-tilted with pink areolas and nipples. He circled her nipples with his thumbs, then kissed and sucked until she hardened. It didn't take long. She was coming along with him.

Her breaths quickened, quickening his body.

"Callum," she murmured. "Hurry up. It's chilly."

He almost laughed with pleasure, but he listened to her. Stripping her clothes away, he found more perfect delights. She was rounded, but it was womanly rounding, the kind that looked soft and had all the right curves.

"Get under the blanket," he said roughly. "Get warm while I get cold."

A happy but husky laugh escaped her as she slipped into the bed, devouring him with her eyes as he tossed his own clothing aside.

"You're gorgeous," she said quietly. "Gorgeous."

"Debatable." But he was glad she thought so. Then he slipped under the covers with her, drawing her heat toward him.

HE *WAS* GORGEOUS, she thought. Rangy and with lean muscles, as if he must run a lot, or walk a lot. A kind of muscling she liked.

But then, she was pressed against him while he stroked her and kissed her all over. She reciprocated as best she could, savoring the feel of his skin against her palms.

Perfect. Her insides throbbed so hard they almost hurt. He drove her wild, touching her most private places as if they had been made for him.

Then he slipped inside her, filling a space that had been empty for too long.

She felt as if she stopped breathing during those moments. Afterward she didn't remember breathing again until a cry of nearly painful pleasure escaped her.

He tumbled into completion with her.

TWO SWEATY BODIES wrapped in their own heat while winter lurked outside.

"Heaven," Molly murmured.

"Heaven can't hold a candle to this."

"Maybe not." She gave a soft laugh.

Then the parsonage phone rang in her little office across the hall.

"Ignore it," he suggested.

"I can't. People need help any hour of the day, even late at night. Or just someone to talk to."

She could feel his reluctance as he let her go. Unwrapping herself from him was painful, but the phone continued to ring.

Grabbing her bathrobe, ignoring her bare feet on the icy floor, she ran to grab the receiver.

"Hello, Pastor," said a man.

"Hello," she replied, trying to place that voice. It tickled the edge of her memory. "Can I help you?"

"Remember me? I'm coming for you," the voice said. "I'm coming for you and you won't live to regret it."

Then a slam and the line went dead.

She stood holding the receiver. Now she remembered the voice. The chill had begun to reach her heart.

"Molly?" Callum came into the office. "Molly? Do you need to go out?"

Slowly she hung up the phone. Her hand trembled and she felt ashamed of it.

"Molly?"

"That was Arthur Killian. He said he's coming for me."

Chapter Eighteen

It wasn't long before Molly showed her stubborn streak and became as immovable as the western mountains.

She refused to let Callum tell any of his colleagues.

"They'll just scare him away."

"That's good."

She shook her head. "Not if he goes after another woman. I cannot and will not be responsible for that. Do you hear me, Callum? I won't. I'd rather be beaten to a pulp."

He winced, his fists clenching and unclenching. "I can't allow that."

"You're going to have to. Because if you try to stop him to protect me, his future victims will be on your head. I know you wouldn't be able to bear that any more than I could."

He wished he could deny it, but she was right about that. Even if he protected Molly, he'd wind up hating himself if another woman was hurt.

He spread his hands, frustrated to the point of explosion. "So what are you going to do? Expose yourself to that bastard? Take that risk? How much do you think I'll be able to stand *that*?"

"It's *my* decision."

"You can't stop me from being a cop."

"Maybe not. But you've got other people to worry about, too. They count at least as much. He's not going to come for me when I'm not alone."

"How in the hell do you know that?"

"Because the man is a coward through and through. He might beat up on women who are alone, but he won't take the risk when she's not alone. Weaker, smaller, defenseless. That's what he wants. Well, he won't find me defenseless."

Callum stifled his anger, his fear for her. He had to handle this calmly. "Your National Guard training, right? That's what you're going to rely on?"

She nodded.

"Damn it, Molly that was years ago. You're rusty."

She tipped up one corner of her mouth. "Ever heard of muscle memory? It's like riding a bike."

"Riding a bike?" he repeated in disbelief.

"Yes," she said firmly. "Like riding a bike. When I picked up that poker I felt the muscle memory kick in. He's lucky he didn't come through that door, because my body knew exactly what to do with him, and that poker felt right in my hands. Now leave it, Callum."

"How am I supposed to leave it? I give a great big damn about you, Molly."

"Then go back to your office and do *your* thing. You can come to the curtain call."

The curtain call? She was serious. Deadly serious.

"I told you once not to interfere with my decisions, Callum. That includes right now."

Her damn independence. Problem was, if he honored it, this time she could get seriously hurt or dead. But if he didn't honor it, Molly might turn her back on him forever.

Damned if he did, damned if he didn't.

Her voice grew quieter even as it remained firm. "You

have to catch him before you can protect everyone. Trust me, I'll catch him for you."

He departed, as she'd demanded. But he was sure of one thing: Molly might appear to be alone, but he was going to make damn sure she wasn't. He'd wait outside in concealment every single night to make sure she wasn't.

Setting herself up as bait. For Pete's sake! All he could do was grind his teeth.

IT WAS THREE more days before Killian came for her. Three days in which she followed her normal routine. Choir rehearsals. Gathering more gifts for disadvantaged children and helping to wrap them. Keeping a friendly eye on the committee that was planning the Christmas dinner and getting volunteers from cooks to servers to cleanup. Asking local groceries for even more food, most of it willingly donated.

Visiting the homebound, like Stacy Withers, who was still feeling guilty about her terminal breast cancer and leaving her children behind. Like Marcia Lathrop, who was caring for the curmudgeonly father of hers who had the beginnings of Alzheimer's. So many people, so many problems, and she could do little except provide a kind ear, or try to rustle up a volunteer to help ease their burdens.

But every night she felt eyes on her as she walked alone to the pastorage. She might be imagining it but she feared she was not.

Once inside, she followed her usual routine, making a frozen dinner, going to her office to finish some routine paperwork, and work on next Sunday's sermon. The fourth Sunday in Advent. Christmas peeking right around the corner now.

Around ten, she turned the rocker to face the door and

put the poker beside it. Then she turned on all the downstairs lights and waited. She knew that Killian could see the light escaping even through the insulated curtains.

Her nerves stretched as the hours passed, but only a bit. She very much wanted to hit Killian a couple of times with that poker, maybe even get him in the family jewels again.

Not the kind of thoughts a pastor who taught forgiveness and turning the other cheek should have.

But she had them, anyway.

Not hers to judge? Killian deserved every bit of judgment this world could heap on him.

She was going to have to pray a whole lot for her own forgiveness, but she didn't care. Not right now. This man needed to be stopped.

It was on the third night two days after the third Sunday in Advent that her moment came.

CALLUM HAD MANAGED to secret himself in the shadow of one of the church's buttresses, facing Molly's cottage. He wore all black, his face as covered as the rest of him.

It was damn cold, but he didn't care if he turned into an icicle because he wasn't going to let Molly face this alone, whatever she wanted.

She'd get her licks in before he could reach her door. That ought to satisfy her. But then he'd be there to ensure she could take down Killian rather than lose the battle.

Too bad if she despised him for it, but nothing would make him allow her to face this threat alone. Nothing.

Each night, he'd watched her turn on lights and leave them on throughout the small house. She was waiting inside, waiting for a monster who wanted to hurt her savagely, even kill her. Waiting in the light for her hunter.

She probably wasn't sleeping at all, either. Nerves stretched as tightly as his.

He wished he could have persuaded her not to do this, but short of locking her in a holding cell, there was nothing. He admired her determination, understood her reasoning about more people getting hurt.

But he sure as hell didn't like it.

That pastor had a will of steel. He wondered if her congregation had any idea. Probably not. They'd probably never seen it and many most likely saw her in stereotypical terms. Her authority with them resided in her collar. It ought to reside in *her*.

And to think she'd been battling those attitudes since she arrived here. From what he could tell, she'd made significant headway, but he was willing to bet that none of those people had sensed her stubbornness and determination. Had realized that she hadn't left only because she didn't quit.

Now this. He wanted to get his hands around Arthur Killian's throat. He was used to this stuff, had learned to distance himself in order to keep his own mind clear and his life from going off the edge.

But with Molly, all that distance had vanished. She'd worked her way into his heart. What that meant he wasn't sure—he just knew there'd be a gaping hole inside him if anything happened to her.

God, for a hot cup of coffee. Something to warm him from the inside because the cold was sure stealing heat from his outside, even with the new thermal underwear he'd bought, even with felt-lined boots. He needed to move to stay warm, but he had to be very careful not to make noise, not to move enough that his shadow stood out among shadows.

Frostbite, here we come.

Then his eyes, well adapted to the dark by 2:00 a.m, caught sight of a movement just at the rear corner of the parsonage. Adrenaline slammed into him, pushing his heart to a fast beat. It flooded his limbs and made it extremely difficult to hold still.

No choice yet. No choice. As every muscle in his body coiled, he waited for the right moment. He had to get the guy *after* he broke in, when it could be proven that he was the perp by more than fingerprints alone. He'd had enough experience in court to know that just fingerprints couldn't bring about a conviction. One partial at one scene could have come from an ordinary visit. The prints he'd picked up at the diner were nearly useless because they didn't link Killian to any crime. They were good enough only to identify a possible perp. *Possible perp.* Enough for a defense lawyer to shred the case.

The dark figure moved again, slipping to Molly's door. Just another minute or two.

MOLLY HEARD THE fumbling at the latch. *Killian.* She picked up the poker and waited with it in her right hand hanging over the arm of the rocker. Out of sight. He wouldn't know.

Which was just what he wanted. Let him come in here and threaten her, take a swing at her. He'd live to regret it.

The door creaked open and she saw him as he hurried in and closed it behind him. All in black, head to foot.

"Well, well, Molly Canton," said a rough voice that could still cause anger to slither down her spine. "You're mine now."

"What the hell are you doing, Arthur? This could get you into trouble."

"You stole my wife from me. You hid her so well I can't find her to teach her a lesson." He pulled off his mask and scowled at her. "You sent me to prison. Now it's my turn to send you to hell."

He was still a tall fireplug of a man, too much beer showing on his belly. He had a shaved head that was an attempt to conceal his baldness and made up for that baldness with a scraggly beard. He reeked.

His fists were made for punching, though.

Molly tilted her head a bit, gauging the distance between them. "I think you've got that wrong, Arthur. If either of us goes to hell, it'll be you."

"I'm not talking about some fairy tale of an afterlife, Molly. I'm talking about the here and now. I'm going to rearrange your face. I'm going to kick you until you can't breathe. I've been debating whether to kill you, but I sure as hell want to see your blood all over the floor. I want to make sure you never forget what you did to me."

He was stepping closer, his hands clenching and unclenching. His bulky body leaning forward to give him the chance to swing a fist at her. Tough guy.

"What?" he asked. "Not going to try to defend yourself? Where's your fight?"

"You like women to fight back, do you?"

"A little feistiness makes it more fun, don't you think? At least you'll give yourself some stupid idea that you tried to save yourself. But there's no saving yourself now."

He raised his arm and she saw the punch coming toward the side of her head. She didn't even rise from the rocker as she swung the poker around and slammed his arm before his fist could reach her.

At once he cried out, punch forgotten.

Molly rose, still holding the poker. "How many more of your bones do you want me to break, Arthur? Maybe as many as you broke of your wife's bones? Maybe as many as you broke on the women around here? That could wind up being every single bone in your body."

She raised the poker again and watched Arthur cower backward with his good arm raised in front of his face. "I always knew you were a coward, Arthur. Now if you don't want me to swing again, get facedown on the floor."

Before he could comply, the door burst open and Callum barged in. In an instant he grabbed Killian's hands behind him and pulled out a zip cuff from his pocket. Killian yowled the whole time about his arm.

"You okay?" he asked Molly.

"It's him you should worry about. His arm is broken." Then quietly she added, "Callum, thank you."

He looked up from Arthur. "For what?"

"For waiting out there in spite of what I said. For saving me from beating him to death."

Then she turned her back on the scene, sickened by that man, and sickened by her own act of violence. Sickened by the seething urges she'd felt to keep on hurting Arthur Killian.

She had wanted to beat him to a pulp.

Chapter Nineteen

The Fourth Sunday in Advent. The lighting of the last purple candle in the Advent wreath. A full church, this time full of gratitude that women were finally safe from Killian.

The singing from the congregation sounded brighter, more voices joining in with the choir. "O Come, O Come, Emmanuel" felt as if it held extra significance this year.

Joy had returned to Molly. Her pleasure in the beauty and hope of the season filled her, restoring her. Christmas would not be stolen this year, not from anyone.

The church basement brimmed with wrapped presents for the less fortunate children. The Christmas meal planning was done, the volunteers in line. At her suggestion, families had begun to adopt "grandparents," the elderly who would be alone, and bring them into their homes for the holiday. Some of those "grandparents" would become long-term friends.

Molly couldn't have asked for more. The smiles she shared with people in the narthex as they left were broader than usual, warmer than ever. Her heart swelled.

As the crowd thinned, Callum came to stand beside her. She smiled at him then resumed talking to her congregants. When the last were gone, and as the Women's

Club along with the Altar Society began a quick cleaning, he spoke.

"It appears that the gossip hasn't damaged your reputation any."

"No, it doesn't seem to have."

"Good. When you're done here, can I meet you at the parsonage?"

"Of course." She was well past the point of worrying about it. She wanted to see Callum and that was the beginning and end of it.

As he walked away, she felt his absence like an empty hole inside her. How was she ever to stand this when he finally told her he was still grieving? That pain had left little room in his heart.

Yes, he wasn't as grim as he'd been when she first met him and her wish to share some of the joy of this time of year had worked, at least in part.

But he was still a man who had lost a woman he'd loved with his whole heart.

Sighing, she went to remove her robes, then headed to the parsonage in her black uniform of collar and slacks, with thermal underwear in deference to the winter. Her red parka hung open, hardly needed in the short distance.

Callum was inside waiting for her, smiling. He'd turned on the Christmas tree, much to her surprise, and had built a fire on the hearth. He'd even made a pot of coffee, the aroma reaching her, as did the scent of the fire. Cheerful, warm, cozy.

"Are you done for the day?" he asked.

"Pretty much. A few phone calls I should make later, but they're not urgent."

"Then maybe you should get comfortable. That collar must be annoying."

She shook her head. "I got used to it. Anyway, I'm proud of it."

"You should be. But go get comfortable, anyway. Something warm, of course."

She changed into her sweats and her silly fuzzy slippers, then met him in the kitchen for coffee. As they had so often, they faced each other across the table, which now felt like a gulf between them. For fear of what might show in her eyes, she kept her gaze down, even though she wanted to stare at him, at the face she'd become so fond of.

Callum cleared his throat. "I was wondering…"

"Yes?"

"Would you be willing to risk your reputation even more by dating me?"

Her heart slammed and at last she looked at him. "Of course."

A smile began to dawn on his face. "That's a good start. But there's more."

"More?" She couldn't imagine.

"Molly Canton, I have come to love you very much and I'd like to make an honest woman of you. You know, to keep your congregants happy and protect your reputation."

A laugh spilled out of her. "To keep *them* happy? What about *me*?"

His smile broadened, but he looked oddly nervous. "Well, that's what I was easing my way into."

Molly felt her jaw drop.

"Callum?" she whispered.

"I told you I love you. Heart and soul. But I want more than friendship and dating. I want you for the rest of my life. I want us to marry."

"Oh, Callum." But a dam inside her broke and her

heart filled with the love she felt for him. So fast, so sure, so true.

Unfortunately, he was beginning to look as if he believed she would refuse him.

But she couldn't, not for anything in this world. This was turning into her best Christmas ever.

"I love you," she said, her voice strengthening. "I love you and I definitely want to marry you."

A happy laugh escaped him. "Then what are we doing with this table between us?"

* * * * *

POLICE DOG PROCEDURAL

LENA DIAZ

This book is dedicated to my agent, Nalini Akolekar,
and my Mills & Boon editors, Allison Lyons and
Denise Zaza, for their patience and support when
I faced some tough family and health problems while
writing this book. Your kindness and understanding
mean everything to me. Thank you.

Chapter One

The painful echoes of the past whipped through Emma's mind, chilling her far more than the autumn winds funneling down from Idaho's Salmon River Mountains. She perched on the top step of her covered back deck, clutching a steaming coffee cup in her hands. The pre-dawn sky began to lighten to a soft gray, allowing a first glimpse of the rolling land around her. But it wasn't the K-9 training ring that she saw. Or the small horse paddock encircled by a white three-rail fence. Or even the golden larch trees just beginning to turn yellow amid the deep greens of the Douglas firs and western white pines. What she saw didn't exist, not anymore. And yet it was as brutally real this morning as it had been when she was a little girl.

Maybe it was the surprisingly crisp chill of this late-September morning that had triggered the memories she usually managed to keep locked away. It had been an unseasonably cool day much like this one when she'd last seen her biological parents. Her father had been using her as a punching bag—again—while her mother sat on the other side of the room in a drunken stupor, ignoring Emma's cries for help. She'd ignored Danny's and Katie's cries, too.

Emma had been the lucky one. She wasn't hurt so badly that she couldn't go to school. And her father hadn't been careful enough about where he'd hit her this time. When her second-grade teacher caught sight of suspicious-looking bruises peeking out from beneath Emma's long sleeves, she'd called the Jasper police. DCF, the Department of Child and Family Services, had taken Emma away. But they were too late to help her sister and brother.

Emma's hands tightened around her coffee mug as the dark memories swirled. After being released from the hospital, she'd been placed with foster parents, K-9 unit Officer Rick Daniels and his community-minded wife, Susan. If not for them, and the teacher who'd refused to ignore the signs that others had, Emma would have been sleeping with the angels by now. Just like Danny and Katie.

Swallowing past the tightness in her throat, she sent up a prayer of thanks that she, at least, was spared. And that her birth parents were both in prison where they could never hurt another child. Twenty-three years. Had it really been that long since that awful day when she'd lost her siblings?

Another chilly breeze had her taking a deep sip of the hot coffee. She reveled in the burn that warmed her insides—much as Rick and Susan's patient love and understanding had warmed her heart. Somehow, they'd eventually thawed out the ice around it that had enabled her to survive the eight long years of beatings, hunger and neglect. She thought about them, and missed them, every day. But it was the loss of her police officer father that hurt the most. Because he was the one who'd taught by example and helped her learn to trust again. He'd taught her that not all men were bad. He'd shown her that a real man, even if he was big and strong, used his strength to help others, not hurt them.

But even big, strong Rick Daniels wasn't impervious to a bullet.

When Officer Walters had broken the news that Rick and Duke, his K-9 partner, weren't ever coming home again, it had sent Emma into a dangerous tailspin. It had taken years for her to emerge from that dark place. And yet another police officer, like her dad, to help pull her out of it. Walters had done everything he could to turn her away from the destructive path she'd gone down. Thanks to him, and her dear mother, Susan, Emma had finally put her demons behind her.

Thank God the cancer had waited to take her mother until after Emma had straightened out. Susan had lived long enough to see Emma go to college. They'd made some wonderful memories that helped tide Emma over whenever grief reared its ugly head. Or when the other thoughts came, the ugly ones from her childhood.

She squeezed her eyes shut, wishing she could close her ears just as easily. The screams from her past were louder than ever, making her cringe against the sound of fear that had once been her constant companion.

Another scream tore through the air as the sun's first rays warmed her face. Her eyes flew open. Those weren't the sounds of her past. This was happening right now. Someone else was on the ranch, and they were crying, desperate for help.

She jumped to her feet, cursing when hot coffee sloshed onto her hand. She tossed the cup on the ground. The dogs were barking now, probably had been for a while. She'd been so caught up in her thoughts that she hadn't noticed. Something was wrong, horribly wrong.

And that mournful sound was coming from the *front* of the property.

She took off running, her boots digging into the grass and gravel as she whipped around the side of the house. Belatedly, she realized she should have gone inside and grabbed a gun first. No telling what she was about to find. But she couldn't ignore those anguished cries for even one more second. She rounded the corner and skidded to a halt in the gravel out front.

No one was there.

The cries had stopped.

The dogs were no longer barking.

She looked past the circular drive, past the wishing well in the middle, toward the arched entry to the ranch a good hundred yards west. Both her property manager and head trainer would be here soon. But their usual parking spaces to the left of the kennels just past the circular drive were empty except for Emma's rusty pickup truck. The only other vehicle was Shane's RV, backed into its usual spot between the kennels and the small barn that housed her two horses. All was silent. Everything looked as it should, and yet something seemed...off.

Was someone hiding just inside the clumps of evergreens on the far side of the clearing, watching her?

Or hunkered down behind the wishing well a few yards away?

Did they know about her past and make those awful cries, realizing she'd feel compelled to run out here to help?

She cautiously backed toward the porch steps behind her as she continued to scan the trees, hills and outbuildings. Unfortunately, trouble was no stranger here at the Daniels Canine Academy. Part of it had been Emma's fault, during her rebellious period after her father's death when she'd hooked up with a bad boy, Billy. But later, as an adult, she'd brought even more problems to the ranch when she'd fostered troubled youths. The Jasper police had already been familiar with DCA because Emma trained their K-9s. But they'd become even more familiar because of her calls for assistance on numerous occasions. But that was years ago. She hadn't fostered anyone for quite some time.

But she did have three at-risk high-school boys working part time here at DCA on weekends as part of their court-ordered community service.

William Shrader, Hugh Engel, and Kyle Norvell were a tight-knit group of friends. Emma had met with their families several times since the boys began working here to report on their progress. The parents all seemed nice enough and genuinely concerned about their sons. And the boys hadn't given her any trouble. But for only being in high school, they each had a shockingly long history of trouble with the law.

She slowed to a halt, hating where her mind was going. She didn't want to believe the worst. But experience told her she couldn't ignore the obvious—that the boys were forced by a judge to work here as part of an agreement to stay out of jail. They hadn't been working here for very long. Their resentment toward the judge could easily transfer to Emma. And she hadn't known them long enough to establish any real trust between them. She had no idea what they might be capable of.

If one of them was behind the screams, it could be a prank. It could also be something more sinister, dangerous. She *really* wished she'd gone inside for a gun.

She cautiously backed a few more steps toward the

covered porch that ran across the front of the little one-story house. A heart-wrenching cry sounded behind her. She whirled around. At the top of the steps, right outside the door, was a large wicker basket with a white blanket spilling out of it. Next to that was a pink vinyl bag.

Everything clicked together in her mind. The cries, the basket, that pink bag. No. *No, no, no.* Please. No one could be that cruel, that heartless, that...irresponsible, especially as cold as it was out here this morning. Could they? Well of course they could. She knew better than most that people could be cruel, heartless and downright *mean.*

She sprinted forward and fairly flew up the steps. Her pulse rushed in her ears as she dropped to her knees beside the basket and then flipped back the white blanket. The crying stopped. Tears spilled down Emma's cheeks as she yanked her cell phone out of her jacket pocket and dialed 911.

A chill wind ruffled her hair and made a piece of paper flutter where it had been taped to the top of the basket handle. It was a cryptic note.

Please take care of my Angel.

"Jasper police, what's your emergency?" a familiar-sounding young woman's voice asked through the phone.

"Jenny, it's Emma Daniels, at DCA. Someone trespassed on my property and—"

"Are you okay, Emma? Are they still at your ranch?"

"No, I mean, yes, I'm home. And yes, I'm fine. No one's here. At least, I don't think so, except—"

"I'm dispatching some deputies right now. I can send an ambulance, too, just to be sure you're okay. It's no trouble."

An ambulance? Did she need one? It was chilly, but

not freezing. And the temps would soar into the seventies as the sun rose higher. How long had the baby been left outside?

Dread had her heart lurching in her chest. She looked down again, then smiled through her tears as she lifted the precious bundle. "I don't think we need an ambulance. But, yes, please, send one. Just to be sure. I really think she's okay."

"Who's okay? Emma? Who's there with you?"

"Someone sneaked onto the ranch and left something by my front door—"

"What did they leave?"

She hugged the bundle closer and tugged her jacket around it, rocking back and forth as she looked into the baby's dark brown eyes. "An angel. They left me an angel."

Chapter Two

Lieutenant Macon Ridley slowed his Dodge Durango just enough to make the turn off South Elm onto 1 Daniels Way without fishtailing. As soon as he passed beneath the Daniels Canine Academy archway with its silhouette of a German shepherd, he gunned the engine. Dirt and gravel kicked up from his tires, spitting across the grass and pinging off nearby trees as he rushed up the long driveway. He didn't slow until he was a few car lengths from the modest, white-washed brick ranch house with its familiar green roof. He yanked the wheel, pulling the SUV to a rocking halt just short of the porch steps.

He was out in a flash, right hand resting on his holster as he scanned his surroundings. Off to the left, a concrete-and-wood building housed the dozen or so dog kennels as well as an office. There was an RV parked to the right of the kennels. That was new since he'd last been here. Next to the RV was a small white barn that he knew served as a home for Emma's two rescue horses. Past that, even though he couldn't see it, was a fenced-in area that he remembered doubled as an agility training arena for the K-9s and a paddock for the horses.

Everything seemed neat, orderly, pristine, which fit right in with his memories of Emma. But the place was quiet. Too quiet for a place where a 911 call had been placed just minutes earlier. Where was she? In the house? Alone? He didn't have much to go on from what dispatch had said. Just that some trespassers had allegedly left their surprise—a baby—on her porch and taken off. But they could have been hiding, waiting until Emma got off the phone. Jenny had tried to keep Emma on the line, per policy, but she'd insisted she was fine and needed to focus on caring for the infant. Macon had no way of knowing whether something else had happened after she hung up. She could be in trouble right now. And the decisions he made in the next few minutes were critical.

Please let her be okay.

A whimper sounded from the back seat. His black shepherd pressed his nose against the window, just as anxious as Macon to find out what was going on.

"Easy, Bogie." He yanked open the door and quickly attached the leash to the K-9's collar.

Bogie hopped out and Macon gave an instruction in German, adding the shepherd's more formal name at the end, Bogart. That had the dog's ears perking up. He was all business now, muscles taut as he strained on the leash, his gaze riveted on the house. Macon tightened his grip and together they bounded up the porch steps.

He drew his gun, holding it down by his right side while keeping a tight hold on Bogie's leash with his left hand.

"Police!" He shoved open the door without waiting for an answer and hurried inside.

He and Bogie were halfway across the main living area when a wide-eyed Emma rushed out of the kitchen opening at the back left corner of the house.

Cradling a baby against her chest.

If Jenny hadn't warned him, he'd have been surprised and confused to see Emma holding an infant. Judging by the shocked look on Emma's face, Jenny hadn't bothered to warn her about him. She definitely hadn't expected Macon to be the one who'd respond to her 911 call. Unfortunately, he didn't have time to explain.

He quickly scanned the room, making sure no one was hiding anywhere and paying special attention to his K-9 partner. Bogie was alert, but not giving an indication that he sensed anyone else aside from Emma…and the baby.

Macon strode forward and gently pushed Emma back so he and Bogie could make a quick sweep of the kitchen. After checking the walk-in pantry, he made sure the back door was locked, with the dead bolt engaged. Turning around, he moved past Emma again.

"Anyone else inside?" he called out as he and Bogie headed toward the hallway that opened off the back of the living room.

"No. No, it's just me. And Angel." Her voice wobbled, sounding strained, which wasn't characteristic of strong, confident Emma.

Keeping a watchful eye on the doors down the hallway, he gave Bogie another order in German. They quickly cleared the three small bedrooms, lone bathroom, and handful of closets before returning to the main room.

Emma was standing by the front door, which was now closed and dead-bolted.

He nodded his approval and holstered his gun. A quick command to Bogie had him sitting on the floor beside him. Gone was the tense, all-business K-9 ready to sacrifice himself to protect others. In his place was a hundred-pound teddy bear with his pink tongue lolling out, his adoring gaze fixed on Emma. Obviously Bogie hadn't forgotten her over the past two years any more than Macon had. And as she glanced from the dog to him, it was obvious that she hadn't forgotten them either.

Her brow knit with confusion as she clutched the bundle against her chest. "Macon? I don't understand. Did you come back here for more training and Jenny asked you to check on…" She seemed to suddenly take in his black uniform and the shield on his shoulder depicting the mountains and an eagle eyeing a salmon in the river. "That's a *Jasper PD* uniform. You're not with the canine task force in Boise anymore?"

Before he could answer, the dual sound of a siren out front and his radio squawking on his shoulder went off.

Emma turned toward the window. An ambulance was idling just past the archway at the end of the long drive. Lights flashed, but the siren was off now.

Macon reported in, letting Jenny know that the house was clear but to keep holding the ambulance at the entrance until he cleared the rest of the property.

"Emma, I need to check the outbuildings, make sure no one is hiding anywhere outside before the ambulance can come up here. Unless there's an urgency for medical attention for you, or the baby. If that's the case, I'll drive you both to the entrance—"

"No, no." She tightened her hold, shifting the bundle higher. "She seems fine. We'll wait. I didn't see anyone out there. I'm guessing they took off after they left Angel."

"The baby's name is Angel?"

She shrugged. "I'm not sure. But the note made it sound that way." She motioned toward a basket sitting off to the side with a piece of paper taped to the handle.

He wanted to read it, take the paper and the basket

into evidence. But he couldn't yet. First, he had to make sure Emma and the baby were safe. "That RV outside, is anyone—"

"No, no. It's empty. Shane keeps it here because there isn't any room to park it at his and Piper's place."

He nodded even though he had no clue who Shane was. Piper, he remembered, was a friend of Emma's who worked at DCA. "Flip the dead bolt behind me."

"Will do." She put her hand on his arm as he unlocked the door to leave. "Thanks, Macon. I don't know what's going on, why you're wearing a Jasper uniform, but it's good to see you. And with you and Bogie here, I know we're safe."

Her face pinkened with a light blush as if she regretted the uncharacteristic spilling of emotion.

He gave her a reassuring look, wishing he didn't have to leave her even for a few minutes. He'd never seen fear in her eyes until now. And it bothered him far more than he'd have expected.

"We'll be right back." After a quick command to *Bogart*, they were out the door, the shepherd once again on full alert.

It didn't take long to inspect the kennels and small barn and verify that the storage sheds on the property were locked tight. The RV was locked, too, and there were no signs that anyone had broken in. The lack of fresh footprints in the dirt beside the RV and Bogie's disinterest in it made him confident that no one was hiding inside.

The sound of a siren had him pausing by some bushes near the porch. Another Jasper PD SUV whipped past the idling ambulance and sped up the driveway. The backup that Jenny had promised had arrived. And as they neared, he realized it was Lieutenant Cal Hoover and rookie officer Jason Wright. Macon signaled, letting them know all was clear.

"Come on, boy." He tugged on Bogie's leash so they could greet the other officers. A whine had him turning to see why the dog wasn't following.

Bogie wasn't trained as a scent dog. He couldn't sniff out bombs or drugs, or track a lost child. He was trained for suspect apprehension and attack. But he had great instincts and had definitely smelled something he didn't like. He whined again, sniffing the air and pushing his body between Macon and the bushes.

Macon whipped his pistol out and trained it on the overgrown shrubs. Moments later, the two cops who'd just pulled up were shoulder to shoulder with him, their pistols also trained on the thick greenery where someone could easily hide. But it only took a few seconds for the three of them, along with the dog, to verify no one was there.

He exchanged a perplexed look with his brothers in blue and was just about to force Bogie away from the greenery when he realized what was bothering the shepherd. One of the lower branches on the bush closest to the edge of the porch was broken. And impaled on the sharp end was a small piece of white cloth that looked suspiciously similar to the blanket Emma had wrapped around the baby. Had the person who'd abandoned the baby hidden here and caught the blanket on the bush? If so, then the baby, and torn piece of blanket, weren't all they'd left.

They'd also left a smear of blood.

Chapter Three

Emma leaned to the side, trying to see past the two EMTs who were examining Angel on top of the kitchen table. "It can't be Angel's blood on those bushes. I checked her all over to make sure she was okay. There weren't any cuts."

The larger of the two men glanced up at her but didn't say anything as the other man pulled open the diaper.

Emma went rigid with fear as the reason for that part of the examination swept through her. "No," she whispered, pressing her hand to her mouth. "No. Please, God. Anything but that."

Suddenly Macon was beside her, his shoulder pressed to hers in a show of support. She clenched her hands together, waiting silently along with the two other officers—Cal Hoover and Jason Wright—who were squeezed into her tiny kitchen.

The first EMT re-taped the diaper into place and smiled at Emma. "A doctor will check her again, but I don't see any signs of trauma. I'm guessing she's a couple of months old, if that. Seems healthy."

Relief had her slumping against Macon. He stood strong and steady, giving her support in more ways than one. She smiled her thanks, then watched as Angel was bundled up again. The EMT who'd been examining the baby hurried out of the kitchen and strode toward the front door while the other one quickly repacked the box of supplies they'd brought inside.

"I want to ride along with her to the hospital," Emma said. "Just let me grab my purse."

"Not enough room," the EMT told her. "And the county insurance doesn't allow anyone else to ride back there."

"You won't even know I'm there," she insisted. "I'll stay out of your way. And I won't tell anyone."

He arched a brow and glanced at the three policemen in the room, then shook his head and snapped the box shut. "Sorry, but no."

"Get your purse, Emma." Macon's deep voice snapped her attention back to him instead of the second EMT who was now moving toward the front door.

She nodded, confident Macon would handle the situation, and hurried to her bedroom to grab her purse and phone. But when she got back to the living room, the house was empty. A quick glance out the front windows showed the ambulance speeding down the driveway away from the house.

She swore and rushed onto the porch just as Bogie hopped into the back of Macon's SUV. Macon shut the door and turned to face her as she hurried down the steps.

"Why did they leave without me?" she demanded. "I want to be there for Angel."

"And you will be. Just not in the ambulance. There really wasn't room back there and they wouldn't let you inside the emergency room with her anyway. Plus, you'll need a ride home from the hospital later. I figured I'd offer my services. We can sit in the waiting room together until the doctor finishes his exam. And I can take your official statement while we wait so you don't have to go to the station." He strode to the passenger side and opened the door, motioning behind her. "Cal and Jason will stay here to collect the blood evidence and search for other clues about who left the baby. They can lock up when they're done. I saw you had extra keys hanging by the front door. We'll talk about a safer place to keep them later. I assume one of them is a house key?"

She rolled her eyes and nodded, then turned to see Cal directing Jason, the rookie who was once a troubled teen she'd fostered here at DCA. She couldn't help smiling, remembering how good he'd been with the horses in particular. He'd absolutely adored her quarter horse, Presley. But what was even more rewarding was having watched him a few months earlier when he and a young woman she'd also fostered as a teen, Tashya, got married. But her smile faded in light of what Jason was doing right now, looking for evidence of whoever had trespassed on her property and abandoned a little baby.

They were examining the shrub that had gotten everyone so worried about Angel earlier. In a police force as small as the one in Jasper, with fewer than a dozen officers, they all wore many hats. And today, apparently it was Cal's and Jason's turns to be evidence technicians. Or, more likely, it was Jason's turn, but Cal came along because he was better than anyone else at training new hires. And he enjoyed it. He'd likely volunteered to come out to DCA when dispatch sent Jason as Macon's backup.

"Cal," she called out. "The house key is on one of the wall hooks just past the front door. I'm sure Jason remembers which one to use. But I doubt you'll need it. DCA's manager, Barbara Macy, should be here soon.

She'll take care of the place. Will you update her please, let her know why I'm not here?"

"No worries. Gotcha covered," he called back, not turning around. He was too intent on keeping an eye on Jason as the much younger officer used his gloved hand to carefully slide the piece of torn blanket into a paper evidence bag.

A shiver shot through her as she pictured someone hiding in those bushes, waiting. How long had they been there, watching her house?

"Emma?" Macon asked. "Are you okay?"

She forced the disconcerting image away and hurried to the passenger side of Macon's SUV, where he stood waiting with the door open. "I'm good." She motioned to Bogie in the back seat. "What about him? I don't think they'll want him inside the hospital."

"We'll drop him off at my place. It's on the way. Won't take but a minute."

"Your place?"

"A rental just outside of town, about a mile from the hospital."

"Then you really have left Boise? You're here to stay, not temporarily on loan to the department, like a task force?"

He studied her a moment. Something dark flickered in his light brown eyes, something she couldn't quite read. Was it sadness? Or something else?

"I'm not sure for how long," he said. "But yes, for now, I'm staying."

For now. She wondered why he'd come back if he didn't know his long-term plans. Did it have to do with that look she'd seen?

She climbed up into the passenger seat and he closed

her door. As he rounded the hood, he stopped to answer a question Cal asked him. She took advantage of the opportunity to admire his muscular build, those sexy biceps and long legs that she remembered so well. His six-foot-three height had even made her, at five foot seven, feel petite and extra feminine. His brown hair was the same as she remembered too, kept stylishly sideswept on the top with a fade on the side. But it was his gorgeous smile she'd always appreciated the most, framed by the light barely-there beard he sported.

That smile had been displayed quite a lot as they'd bantered back and forth for the weeks when he was here for training, both him and his K-9 partner, Bogie. She'd felt safe flirting with Macon, knowing that he'd return to Boise once the training was over and she wouldn't see him again. And now here he was, here for good. Or for however long he decided to stay. That could have been a problem if he'd walked in expecting to capitalize on all that flirting, to try to build a deeper relationship when she didn't know if she'd ever be ready for something like that, with anyone. But she didn't think she needed to worry. Nothing about him gave her the impression he even remembered that they'd ever flirted.

This Macon was different.

He seemed far more serious and quiet than he'd been over two years ago. Of course, a lot could take place in two years. Had something bad happened with his job? Was that what had put that indecipherable dark look in his gaze? Or was it his personal life that had changed him? Family troubles? Girlfriend troubles?

That last thought had her sobering. Did he have a girlfriend now? And why did that possibility bother her when she wasn't interested in that kind of relationship?

She wasn't good at relationships. Someone always got hurt, and that someone was usually her.

The driver's-side door opened and he hopped inside. "Seat belt," he reminded her, as he put his own on and then started the engine.

As soon as her belt was clicked into place, he sped down the driveway.

When he pulled off the road a few minutes later, he parked in front of a faded white cottage that looked even smaller than her ranch house. She'd probably passed it a hundred times and never even knew it was here, hidden around a slight curve in the road, with thick trees sheltering it from view.

She was relieved that he didn't ask her to come inside, even though she was curious to see it. But she was more anxious to get to the hospital. Even though Angel wasn't hers, or her responsibility at this point, she had to see for herself that the baby girl was okay. Maybe it was because of what she and her siblings had gone through when they were little. She couldn't stand the idea of not knowing for sure that Angel was going to be taken care of, that she wouldn't be dumped again on someone's porch without any concern for the weather or coyotes or other critters that could have hurt her when she was outside all alone.

True to his word, it only took Macon a few minutes to secure Bogie and get back in the SUV. He was on the phone when he got inside, barely glancing at her before pulling onto the road and speeding toward Memorial Hospital.

When they parked in a space near the emergency room, he ended the call and gave her his full attention. "That was DCF, the Department of Child and Family Services. They don't have any foster families available here in Jasper. And none of their caseworkers in Payette or Grangeville are available right now, so they're going to send one from the Boise office."

"Boise? That's three hours south of us."

"Might take even longer than that. They're scrambling to find a caseworker to come all the way to Jasper, not to mention line up a foster family who can fit one more child into an already full home. Seems like far more kids need help than there are homes and qualified people willing to take them in."

A twinge of guilt shot through her. But she ruthlessly shoved it away. She'd already done her fair share, fostered plenty of kids over the years. And while it had been incredibly rewarding, the emotional toll was overwhelming. Every time one of her foster kids was adopted or reunited with their birth family, a piece of her heart went with them. She didn't want to go through that again. That part of her life was over.

"Angel's a helpless little baby," she argued. "She can't be *fit in* with a family who already has all the kids they can handle. She needs someone who can devote time to her, give her the security and attention a baby needs."

He arched a brow. "Are you volunteering?"

She blinked. "What? No. No, no, no. I don't foster."

"But you have, in the past. Didn't you tell me you'd fostered nearly a dozen kids over the years? I know you fostered Jason Wright. Now he's a rookie police officer. You obviously did right by him. Are you still licensed with Family Services?"

She shook her head. "No. I mean, yes, I've kept my license current but I haven't fostered in years. The only reason my license is active is for emergency situations, if a child is in desperate need and there's no one to take them in—for a very limited time."

"This seems like an emergency to me."

"I meant emergencies for *older* kids, teens. I've never taken in a baby. I wouldn't. I couldn't. I'm not qualified."

"You seemed plenty qualified when you were taking care of Angel at your house."

"That's…that's different. It was…temporary. Like… taking care of a wounded animal. The basics. Food, warmth, reassurance. I wouldn't know what to do going forward. And why are we even discussing this? I don't have a crib or any of the baby things she'd need." She opened the passenger door. "Shouldn't we hurry? The doctor might be waiting to talk to us. And I don't want Angel left alone while waiting for Child Services to get here."

Cutting off any chance of him trying to convince her to foster Angel, she hopped out of the SUV and took off toward the emergency room.

Chapter Four

He'd spooked her. Macon stretched his legs out in front of
him and shifted in the too-narrow, barely padded wooden
chair as he studied Emma across from him in the ER
waiting room.

Other than giving him her official statement about
what had happened, she'd hardly looked at him since. It
had taken quite a bit of prodding for her to even admit
there were some people she didn't know well who'd
been working at DCA recently. William Shrader, Hugh
Engel, and Kyle Novell were exactly the kind of troubled
teens Macon wanted to check out in relation to Angel
being dumped on Emma's doorstep. But she hadn't been
pleased when he'd said he'd have to interview them to see
if they had alibis. That was nearly two hours ago. Now
he and Emma were stuck waiting for the young woman
at the information desk to let them know when the doctor finished examining the baby. Apparently, the ER was
short-staffed today. Macon didn't even know whether the
doctor had seen Angel yet.

He glanced at Emma. As anxious as he was for the
update about the baby, he was just as anxious to know
whether Emma was uncomfortable around him because

his showing up was so unexpected, or if she was worried he was going to try to talk her into fostering Angel again.

Uncomfortable was never something they'd been with each other in the past. The smiles, the laughter, had come easily between them. He hadn't missed the fact that she didn't laugh or smile as easily around anyone else. It had given him hope that maybe she'd been as attracted to him as he was to her. But then the training sessions were over. He and Bogie were both deemed ready to return to his K-9 task force in Boise.

Short of quitting his job, there really wasn't any reason to push for something more between them at that point, regardless of how much he'd wanted it. A long-distance relationship hadn't made sense considering there was a zero percent chance that she'd ever sell her ranch or he'd quit his job and move.

He sighed heavily and leaned back. So much for that zero percent chance. Here he was, living in Jasper. But after what had happened in Boise, he could no longer stay there. He'd had to leave, for his own sanity. And coming here had seemed the logical choice. He liked this sleepy little town. Jasper was close enough to the mountains for a spectacular view. Far enough away that he didn't have to deal with the dangerous turns and steep drop-offs that could be treacherous during the winter. He much preferred town life, or at least, being a few miles outside of town. It gave him access to everything he needed. But it also gave him the privacy he craved. It was a lot easier getting through the days, and long dark nights, when he didn't have to pretend everything was okay.

His stomach chose that moment to rumble. He checked the time on his phone. This was taking forever. He needed to check in with the chief and give him an update, and find out what was going on with DCF. Maybe he'd grab a snack while he was at it.

Emma glanced at him, her blue-eyed gaze locking onto his for a moment before flitting away. Dang, she was pretty, even prettier than he remembered. As usual, she'd pulled her shoulder-length light brown hair into a ponytail to keep it out of her way. But it only served to emphasize the delicate femininity of her golden-tanned face.

Her light jacket hung open in deference to the warm waiting room. And he knew, both in his older memories and the new ones formed hours ago, that her long legs still looked great in a pair of jeans. Her narrow waist only made her curves up top all the more appealing. But it was those eyes, more than anything, that had always been her best feature. Lashes that were dark and thick without the need for makeup framed slightly tilted ice-blue eyes that mirrored the intelligence behind them, and the empathy that was as much a part of her as breathing.

Perhaps his favorite thing about those incredible eyes was that they truly were a window to her soul. Every emotion she experienced flitted through them, like a movie playing out. Talking wasn't even necessary for him to see what she was thinking. As a cop, he was used to having people lie to him every day. It was beyond refreshing to know that he could always tell the truth about Emma just by looking in those expressive, gorgeous eyes.

She glanced at him again, then frowned. "Why are you smiling?"

"I'm not supposed to smile?"

"I didn't say that."

He chuckled and stood. "I'm going to grab us something from the cafeteria if it's open. Or a vending machine. Any requests? Preferences?"

She shook her head no.

"All right, be back soon."

When he returned, he divvied out the snacks and two bottles of water. She thanked him and nibbled on one of the sandwiches he'd gotten from a machine since the cafeteria had closed early, it being a Saturday. He didn't bother to tell her about the updates he'd received from his chief and Family Services. Basically, that initial inquiries had yielded no clues as to Angel's identity. And although a DCF caseworker was on his way here, no foster family had been found yet to take care of the baby.

Time seemed to drag while they waited. He checked with the volunteer at the information desk, twice, but she had no updates. The second time, when he took his seat again, he couldn't help noting how agitated Emma seemed. He leaned forward, resting his forearms on his knees. "She's going to be okay. Try not to worry."

"Who said I was worried?"

Your eyes said it. But instead of telling her that, he simply shrugged.

She didn't deny that she was concerned. Which was another thing he liked about her. Honesty. What she didn't want you to know, she wouldn't talk about. But she wouldn't lie about it. Some might call that lying by omission. He figured she was entitled to her privacy. It almost made him feel guilty that he could read her emotions so easily, even when she was trying to hide them.

"You're doing it again," she accused.

"What?"

"Smiling. Not that there's anything wrong with that. I just…"

"You just?"

"Well…you used to smile all the time. But you smiling

now, it's one of the few times since I've seen you again that I've noticed you smile. I guess I was just wondering why you stopped smiling so much."

Her words evoked the images he was trying so hard to keep locked away.

Her hand was suddenly on his as she leaned across the space between their chairs. "I'm sorry. Whatever it is, it's none of my business. I shouldn't have pried."

Unable to resist the impulse, he turned his hand beneath hers, lacing their fingers together. When she didn't pull away, something like relief swept through him. He'd missed her, their closeness, their easy friendship teetering on something deeper, richer. And, until now, he hadn't realized just how much he'd missed something as simple as holding someone's hand, of holding *Emma's* hand.

"It's okay," he told her. "It's not a secret, really. It was in the news all over Boise."

She blinked. "In the news?"

He nodded. "The K-9 task force Bogie and I were on, we ran into some trouble at the culmination of an investigation. We had over twenty officers and K-9s at a warehouse to swoop in and arrest the ring of criminals we were after. Everything was planned down to the minute. But…some things you can't plan for. Like a hidden room that our confidential informants didn't know about, that wasn't in the building's blueprints."

"Oh no."

"Oh no is right. Everyone had been arrested and was being taken outside when Bogie and Nemo, my human partner's dog, alerted to a sound behind us."

"Wait. Your human partner? Are you talking about Ken Bianca, the guy I met a few years ago when he came to DCA to check on your training?"

He nodded. "Nemo was Ken's K-9. They were both with me that day. Bullets were flying before we could even turn around. Three more thugs had been hiding in the room and thought the building had been emptied out. When they slid the door open and saw us, they panicked, started shooting. It was a disaster."

Her eyes widened and her gaze slid down his body as if searching for injuries. "Did you get hit?"

"Almost. If the bullet had gone to the left just a few more inches, it would have been me who died that day."

She blinked again. "Oh no. Ken?"

He nodded again, his throat tight.

She squeezed his hand tighter in hers. "Macon, I'm so sorry. Ken seemed like such a nice guy."

"He was."

"That's such an awful tragedy. I really am sorry. But I'm glad you're okay."

He gently tugged his hand free and sat back, feeling awkward being comforted when he felt guilty for even being alive. "Hard to believe it's already been six months."

"Was Ken married? Did he have kids?"

"Divorced. No kids. I guess in a way that's a blessing, that a wife and kids weren't left behind. But he had a huge family, five siblings, tons of aunts, uncles, cousins. His parents are still around, too. They were devastated, of course. They never expected to bury one of their children."

He forced a smile, pushing hard at the darkness that wanted to settle over him. "Boise's a big city, but I lived on the same street as Ken's parents and two of his sisters. We ran into each other all the time. They were gracious, always nice, never blamed me for what happened.

But I could see the truth in their eyes, that they wished it had been the other way around, that Ken had lived." He cleared his throat. "It was too hard, on all of us."

"That's why you left. Survivor's guilt."

"That's one way to put it, I guess. But there was another reason, too."

"Oh? What's that?"

You. That thought surprised him, but as soon as it occurred to him, he knew it was true. Part of the reason he'd returned to Jasper was the hope of seeing Emma again. Not to try to rekindle their fledgling relationship. He was too much of a wreck for that. But seeing a friendly face, someone who didn't look at him and wish he could trade places with their dead relative, was something he'd craved.

"Bogie," he finally answered. "I think he's got some PTSD or something, over the shooting. Sometimes he can be skittish. He's lost confidence, startles easily. Before all of this happened today, I was planning on dropping in sometime soon to let you know I was back in town. And I was going to ask if you'd be interested in working with Bogie again to help him out. Chief Walters already agreed, said the K-9 training fund at the station would pick up the tab for at least some training, when I have time to bring him by of course and in between callouts, or maybe training in the evenings if that's an option. Thankfully the chief didn't listen to Captain Arthur Rutledge, his second-in-command. As usual he was against everything to do with DCA and recommended against paying for any training."

She shook her head. "I've only met him a few times but I've heard how anti-K-9 program he is. I can't understand why he's so against it."

"Maybe he got bitten by a dog when he was a kid and can't get beyond it."

She laughed. "Maybe so."

"Anyway, I'm hoping we can work the training in as I get time. That is, if *you* have time."

"I'm pretty busy these days, with a full kennel right now."

Disappointment shot through him. "No problem. It's not an emergency or anything. The chief isn't relying on Bogie. He's letting him come up to speed gradually. I just thought—"

"You thought right. That I'd want to help him. And I do. Like I said, my schedule is really full. But I'll make adjustments, move things around. You said it's been six months since the shooting?"

He nodded.

"Then we need to get Bogie training again right away. That's a long time for him to be anxious and out of sorts. We need to rebuild his confidence as soon as possible." She cocked her head, studying him. "And yours."

"Um, mine?"

"Whether you want to admit it or not, you're probably suffering from some PTSD yourself or you wouldn't have left Boise and everything you'd worked for there. I remember that being your dream job. You need some retraining too, time to refocus and build your confidence along with your K-9 partner."

He crossed his arms. "I'm fine."

She gave him a doubtful look. "I'm not a head doctor. I won't press the issue. But I do hope that if you haven't seen anyone for what you went through, that you do soon. The problems you see manifesting in Bogie's behavior

can manifest in your own life as well, whether you realize it or not."

"Obviously Chief Walters doesn't agree with you. He
hired me without stipulations or reservations."

"As far as you know."

He stiffened.

"You said he's letting Bogie come up to speed slowly.
You sure you're not included in that assessment?"

Before he could respond, she held up her hands in a
placating gesture. "That was out of line. I'm sorry. Not
trying to start an argument. I just want to make sure you
and Bogie are both okay. Fair enough?"

He blew out a long breath and forced himself to relax.
"Fair enough."

"Good. Then I'll expect you and Bogie both to come
in for retraining, starting next week if that's okay with
the chief."

"Next week as in this Monday? Two days from now?"

She nodded. "That gives me the weekend to rearrange
my schedule, call in some favors from some other K-9
training facilities to help take on some of the load I have."

"I don't want to interfere with your previous obligations. Or cause you to lose income by switching things
around."

"I appreciate that, but you don't need to worry. Things
are good at DCA. And between the money my mom got
when dad was killed on duty, and the investments she
left me, I'm set. I'm not exactly buying Gucci purses or
a Maserati. But I have everything I need. Besides, if you
don't agree to show up sometime Monday for training,
you'll hurt my feelings. You wouldn't want to do that,
would you?"

He couldn't help but smile at her teasing. "No, I wouldn't want to hurt your feelings. That's for sure."

She slapped her hands on the tops of her thighs. "Good. It's settled. We'll—"

"Officer Ridley? Ms. Daniels?" The volunteer from the information desk in the waiting room approached them. "You're here for Baby Jane Doe, correct?"

"Angel," Emma corrected. "Yes, we're here for her. Is she okay?"

"I don't have any information on her status, just that the doctor is ready to speak to you." She motioned toward one of the doors on the far side of the room. "He'll meet you in there in just a few minutes."

The fear that flared in Emma's eyes had Macon standing and holding out his hand. "Come on. Whatever happens, we'll face it together."

Relief flooded her expression as she stood. "Together." She took his hand and they headed toward the door the volunteer had indicated.

Chapter Five

"I don't understand." Emma glanced from the doctor to the nurse he'd brought with him into the little privacy room off the main waiting area. "You said Angel appears to be a healthy two-month-old baby girl, that you didn't find anything concerning. But you're admitting her overnight?"

The doctor glanced at Macon before answering. "Unless the police can figure something out around the foster situation, we don't have a choice. There's nowhere to send Baby Doe—"

"Angel," Emma insisted.

"Right. Angel. Child Services isn't here yet. We can't keep the baby in the ER waiting for them when we need the beds for others with true emergencies."

The nurse beside him smiled at Emma. "She'll be well taken care of, Ms. Daniels. She'll be in the nursery on the maternity ward."

Emma fisted her hands in her lap. "Will someone hold her? Rock her? Reassure her? Or will they only give her attention when it's time for a feeding or diaper change? No offense. But everyone seems to be short-staffed and overworked these days. And it only makes sense that if other babies have medical needs, they'll receive the bulk of the attention. But that means that Angel, who has to be feeling out of sorts having already been abandoned once, may feel abandoned again. I don't want that to happen."

She turned to Macon. "Any updates on when Child Services will arrive? And whether they've found a family to take her in?"

His apologetic expression told her the answer before he even spoke.

"It's probably still going to be a little while before a caseworker gets here. And, no, the last text I got said they haven't lined up a foster family yet."

The doctor stood to leave. "I'm sorry, Ms. Daniels. But that's the best we can do. And I need to get back to the ER."

"I know. I understand. I really do. I appreciate everything you're both doing for her," Emma said. "Can I… can we see her?"

He motioned toward the nurse. "I'll leave that to Ms. Baker." He nodded at them and stepped out.

Ms. Baker, the nurse, held the door open. "They're getting a spot ready for her upstairs in the nursery. I can bring her in here for you to say goodbye."

"Thank you. I appreciate that."

When the door closed behind the nurse, Emma said, "Stop looking at me like that, Macon."

His brows arched. "Like what?"

"Like you still think I should volunteer to foster Angel."

"Well, you would be great at it. And if you foster her, you won't have to worry about her, because you'll know she's being taken care of."

"That's just it. If I took her home, I don't know that

she'll be taken care of." She clasped her hands around her waist and started pacing back and forth in the small room.

Macon sat in one of the two chairs, watching her. "Is it because of your busy schedule? You'd worry you wouldn't have enough time for her?"

She stopped in front of him, hands on her hips. "Of course I'd have time for her," she snapped. "As much as I love the dogs I'm training, people are more important. I'd make time for her."

"Then what's the issue, exactly?" He held up his hands to stop her angry retort. "I'm just playing devil's advocate, trying to understand your concerns. What has you so scared about taking care of Angel?"

She blinked, absorbing his words as she slowly sank into the other chair. "I *am* scared. You're right about that." She squeezed her eyes shut, breathing deep and even to try to calm her racing heart. The very idea of taking care of a baby, of being its foster parent, sent a cold chill through her. There were so many reasons that she'd never fostered any babies. And the very worst reason was something beyond her control—genetics.

A gentle hand lifted her chin until she was staring into Macon's light brown eyes. The kindness and empathy staring back at her almost made her lose her composure.

"Emma," he whispered, his deep voice soothing. "No pressure. Angel's going to be taken care of no matter what. But what, exactly, scares you about the thought of that person taking care of her being you?" He dropped his hand and waited, his gaze searching hers.

"Genetics," she finally blurted out. "And before you say that's crazy, I know how it sounds. But I can't help it. You know my biological parents were monsters. But the few stories I told you about them didn't begin to delve into the depth of their depravity. They were horrible, awful people. Still are, as far as I know, unless one of them has died in prison and no one told me." She shivered and rubbed her hands up and down her arms. "But the thing is, they didn't start out as monsters. I was the oldest, and I remember how it was, before my sister and brother were born. Back when my dad had a steady job, before Mom got hooked on drugs, they were nice, loving even. We had good times, good memories. But after the financial stress of two more kids, after Daddy got hurt and couldn't hold down a job anymore, and Mom turned to drugs and alcohol, they changed. Everything changed. Whatever love they'd once had died. They both became broken and took their disappointments in life out on the most innocent and vulnerable members of their family."

"Emma. You're nothing like your parents. I've seen the way you are with animals, with other people. You're empathetic and really care about them."

"My mom was loving once. How do I know I won't become like her? That the baby might cry and I get mad and—"

He took her hands in his. "Stop. It wouldn't happen. You'll never become what they became. I've seen you deal with animals who were belligerent, dangerous even. And you never raised your voice or your hand. Not once. Instead, you offered love and patience and security. And you won them over, calmed them, made them feel secure. I know you won't snap and become some awful person under extreme stress because I've *seen* you under extreme stress. You handled it far better than I ever could, than most people I know could. Genetics or not, you learned lessons from how your parents acted. You learned how it feels to be on the bad end of that, and made a point of never treating anyone, human or not, that way. You're a good person, Emma. Trust me on that."

She stared up at him, stunned at both what he'd said and the emotion behind his words. "You really believe that, don't you?"

Gently, ever so slowly, he cupped her face in his hands. "I really believe that." Then he shocked her by kissing her forehead before letting go and sitting back.

Who'd have thought a mere touch of someone's hand on her face, and a kiss on her forehead, could send a jolt of awareness straight through her body? Wow. But that was…chemistry. There'd always been an attraction between them. It didn't mean he was right about her, about whether heredity truly mattered or not.

She shook her head, rejecting his arguments. "I appreciate your confidence, your belief in me. But I can't do it. I can't risk it. The very idea of fostering Angel is ridiculous."

He looked like he was about to argue again, but a knock sounded on the door.

"Come in," Emma called out.

The nurse pushed open the door, cradling Angel in one hand and smiling. "Here you go. I'll give you some time to say goodbye."

Before Emma could even prepare herself, the baby was thrust in her arms and the nurse left.

She stared down at the precious bundle, the dark curly hair matting the top of her head, the pink bow lips seemingly smiling in her sleep. An adhesive bandage almost bigger than her hand was taped across the back where they'd probably drawn blood. Emma gently rubbed a finger across it, hoping the little baby hadn't felt the jab of the needle.

"Macon?"

"Hmm?" He leaned across her and gently tucked the blanket around one of the baby's feet that had been poking out.

"Has anyone made any progress in finding out who she is?"

"We've barely begun the investigation at this point. But we're keeping an open mind, in spite of that note that makes it appear that her mother is the one who left her. It's also possible there was a carjacking or something like that where someone ended up with a baby and didn't know what to do and left her on your doorstep. There aren't any missing persons reports or calls about a kidnapped baby as of yet. But, again, it's early. We're reaching out to neighboring counties, seeing if they've heard anything."

"How could a baby go unaccounted for and the parents, or grandparents, or even a concerned neighbor not immediately report it to the police? It's not like she's a teenager who could have stayed after school for some kind of extra-curricular activity. Babies are always with someone. A parent would have to know she was missing. It has to be a parent who abandoned her, don't you think? If not the mother, then the father?"

He shrugged. "Seems the most likely scenario. If that's the case, something made them desperate. Otherwise, I can't see them leaving her like that. Whoever was taking care of her was doing a good job."

She looked up at him. "She is well cared for, isn't she? I mean, no bruises. She's not too thin. The doctor said she was healthy."

He nodded. "I'm guessing if it wasn't the parents who left her, then someone stole her and the parents are too scared to go to the police—like if they're undocumented and are afraid they might be deported. Or…"

"Or?"

"Or, maybe they're down on their luck, unable to take care of Angel the way they want to and know you, or have heard about you. Maybe they left her on your porch hoping you'd take care of her, because they trust you."

She stared at him, shocked. "They trust me? So they left her there? Where a coyote could have come up on the porch and hurt her?"

"Maybe they were waiting for you to get her, and they were crouched in those bushes watching over her, ready to step in if a wild animal came along. The blood on the leaves tells us someone was there."

"I'm guessing it will take a while to trace the blood?"

"I wouldn't pin my hopes on anything useful any time soon. Getting a DNA profile can take weeks or longer, depending on the state lab's backlog."

"Weeks? Or longer?"

"Most likely, yes. And even with a profile, unless the contributor of that blood sample has committed a felony in the past and their DNA is in the databases, it won't do us any good. We're looking into those three teens you mentioned who work part-time at DCA so we can determine whether they're involved in some way. If any of them seem promising, I'll push the chief to try to get them to submit DNA samples to match against. It's expensive, though, and without probable cause we won't be able to force them to submit to the test. But we'll explore that angle and see where it leads."

She nodded. "They were the first ones I thought of when I found Angel. But it doesn't really make sense. They're so young. And I haven't heard about any of them even having a girlfriend. I sincerely doubt the baby is one of theirs."

"You know them well enough to know about potential girlfriends?"

"Well, no. Not really. I barely know them if I'm being completely honest here."

"How often do they come to DCA?"

"Two to three afternoons a week. They're all three seniors and only need a few classes to graduate high school. So they have early release. Kyle and Hugh usually show up in the early afternoon on Thursdays and Fridays. William is more sporadic because of extracurricular activities at school."

"I'll look into each of their backgrounds, see what I can find. In the meantime, someone needs to step up to take care of Angel."

She shook her head. "Even if you're right that someone trusts me and that's why they left her on my doorstep, it doesn't matter. What do I know about taking care of a baby? Nothing. I've never fostered anyone but teens. And it's not like I've got siblings and nieces and nephews to practice on. Rick and Susan showed me love, gave me role models for how to care for older kids, for other people. But babies?" She shook her head. "Never. Before this morning, I'd never even changed a diaper."

"I have."

She jerked her head up. "You've changed a diaper?"

He nodded. "I come from a large family, plenty of nieces and nephews. And I'm the oldest. I babysat my younger siblings hundreds of times. I could give you some pointers to try to avoid some messy leaks."

"No." She shook her head. "No, I told you. I'm not

qualified. There has to be someone else better at this, someone who can take care of her."

He placed a hand on her arm. "It's okay, Emma. You don't have to explain, or feel guilty about not taking her in. DCF will see that she's taken care of. She'll be okay."

A tear traced down her cheek. She wiped it away and stared down at the delicate face so content and happy-looking in sleep.

Another knock sounded on the door. The nurse must have come back to take Angel upstairs.

"Are you ready?" Macon asked, hand on the doorknob, prepared to open it.

She stiffened her back, gave him a crisp nod. "Ready."

He opened the door. But instead of the nurse, there was a man standing there. He was slightly balding and about a foot shorter than Macon, with a rumpled dress shirt tucked into a pair of faded jeans. The badge hanging on a lanyard around his neck probably showed his name, but it was too small for Emma to read. The three large letters stamped across the front, however, weren't. They read DCF.

She swallowed, automatically clutching Angel tighter as the man shook hands with Macon and they discussed the baby's situation.

A moment later, the nurse appeared behind them with another nurse who was wearing yellow scrubs with little ducks and bunnies all over them. And she was holding an infant carrier. They were here to take Angel upstairs to the maternity ward.

Where she'd be placed in a bassinet and left alone while the nurses tended to the other babies who needed medical attention.

The little room went silent. Emma realized they were all watching her.

"Ma'am," the nurse in yellow scrubs said. "I'm ready to take her." She held her hands out, smiling reassuringly.

Emma kissed Angel's cheek, then held her out toward the nurse, all the while trying to ignore the hot tears coursing down her face.

But just as the nurse started to take her, Emma snatched her back. "I've changed my mind. I'm keeping her." She grabbed her purse and took off down the hallway.

Chapter Six

"I'm keeping her?" Macon grinned at Emma in his SUV's rearview mirror as she rode beside the infant carrier holding Angel.

Her face turned a delightful shade of pink. "I just meant that I'd foster her, of course. Until they can find her rightful parents. Or another foster family to take her in."

"Lucky for you, Mr. Burns didn't call the police to swear out a complaint on behalf of DCF that you'd kidnapped her when you took off."

She rolled her eyes. "The police, *you*, were already there. And I didn't kidnap her. I just took her to the car to wait while you handled the paperwork."

He laughed but let it drop. It had taken considerably more than *paperwork* for him to calm everyone down when Emma ran off with Angel. The DCF caseworker had been livid and wanted her arrested, particularly since he'd driven four hours from his home to officially take custody of the baby and sign her in to the hospital until the desired foster family could be found. After Macon had told him Emma was a registered foster parent, and he'd explained Emma's background, just enough to gain some empathy from the caseworker, his anger had cooled. And then once Macon pointed out that DCF wouldn't have to pay for an overnight hospital stay, and that the caseworker no longer had to find an emergency foster placement, he'd ended up smiling and in a good mood. He'd signed on the dotted line so fast he'd almost forgotten to get Emma's signature. He'd transferred the infant car seat he'd brought to Macon's SUV, had Emma sign some forms, then took off, eager to head home.

"This is crazy," Emma said from the back seat. "I don't even have a crib. No diapers, no formula, well, except for what was left on my porch in that pink bag. What was I thinking?"

"You were thinking that you were the best option for little Angel right now. And I agree with you. As to the rest, that's being taken care of. There's a foster closet here in town."

"A foster what?"

"Closet. It's fairly new, no doubt created after you last fostered. It's a charity that works with DCF to help foster families get the supplies they need. The foster families exchange gently used clothing through the closet to other foster families. Donations of food and supplies, even furniture—like cribs and beds—are made by churches and others wanting to help. The caseworker, Mr. Burns, already put the call out. Someone from the foster closet is gathering up things for little Angel right now. They'll bring everything by later today."

"That's amazing. I always wondered how other foster parents were able to afford the clothes, games, food, everything you need when fostering. It's a struggle, even when you're doing okay financially like me. Goodness knows what DCF pays doesn't come close to covering expenses."

"Which makes it even more amazing that people like you agree to help."

"Stop. You're making me out to be a saint or something. Trust me. I'm far from it. If anything, I'm being selfish."

"Selfish? How?" He passed a slow-moving car and moved back into his lane.

"I'm in it for the rewards, like Angel's smiles when she looks up at me. I can't explain it. It just…it just feels so good to hold her, to see her happy."

"She's really too young to actually smile. It's probably gas."

She rolled her eyes again. "That's ridiculous. Of course she smiles. Besides, who made you the baby expert?"

"Younger siblings, and nieces and nephews, remember? If you ever need a break from watching her, I could help. As long as I'm not working a shift at the station, of course."

"Are you serious? You'd babysit her?"

"You don't have to act so surprised. I like kids, babies. Besides, you'll need me to show you how to change a diaper. I guess it's my turn to train you."

She laughed. "I guess it is. But Piper and Barb will help too. I texted them when you were talking to Mr. Burns. They both said they'd come over sometime this weekend to see her. Hey, wait, didn't we just pass your house?"

"I'm taking you straight to the ranch. No need to stop."

"What about Bogie? Won't he need to go out? We were at the hospital for several hours."

"There's a dog door. The back yard's fenced. He'll be okay, probably will sleep most of the time anyway."

A few minutes later, they turned into her long driveway. He glanced in the mirror at her and noticed her smiling at the metal cutout of a German shepherd on top of the arch over the entrance. He remembered her telling him once that it was supposed to be Duke, the K-9 cop partner of her father who'd been killed the same night as him. He'd expected that the daily reminder of her father would make her sad. But she'd explained to him it did just the opposite. It reminded her how blessed she'd been to be taken in by Rick and Susan Daniels.

A flash of orange off to his left disappeared so quickly into the trees that he half wondered whether he'd imagined it. But it was likely to be old Gus, the half-feral orange-and-white tabby who reigned supreme over the Daniels Canine Academy. Emma and a few others could occasionally pet him, but never pick him up. The closest Macon had ever gotten to Gus was a fly-by brush-up against his legs as the cat took off in search of his next meal. Not that he ever went hungry. Emma always made sure to keep fresh food and water in the outbuildings for him. But Gus reveled in the hunt. He preferred the kind of meals that squeaked and ran.

Now that he had time to really take things in, without being on the alert for a bad guy, Macon drank in the pristine, well-kept ranch as he drove up the long driveway. There were two familiar-looking cars parked to the left of the kennels by Emma's old pickup. Her friends had obviously made good already on their promise to come over this weekend and were likely waiting inside the house.

Piper Lambert's car was on the far left. Piper had been Emma's friend since college and had started helping her train dogs about four years ago. The other car belonged to Barbara Macy. Barb helped with paperwork, managing the business, and some light cleaning. He remembered she'd also been in charge of managing any volunteers who came out to DCA to socialize new pups or clean the kennels.

DCA was a fixture and well-liked by the little town of Jasper, Idaho. Especially since Emma ensured the small police force had the best-trained K-9s around—K-9s they couldn't even afford if it weren't for her generosity and her network of animal lovers around the state who donated to the cause.

Nothing much seemed to have changed, except himself. He definitely wasn't the man he used to be. When staying in Boise had become too painful, impossible to endure, he'd been desperate to escape. When he'd tried to figure out where to go, a place that was warm, welcoming, friendly but not intrusive, a name kept whispering through his mind—Jasper. And right on its heels was another name.

Emma.

He had no misconceptions that he was about to kindle anything romantic between them. He was too broken for that. But his battered soul craved a glimpse of her warm smile, and the easy friendship they'd once shared, if only for a little while. He'd been gifted with a few of those smiles at the hospital. But with a baby in the mix now, he imagined that would be it for a very long time. Emma was about to have her hands full. There'd be little time for a damaged cop who might or might not have the potential for something more in her life.

He pulled to a stop in the circular drive in front of her house, noting the absence of other police vehicles. Cal and Jason must have collected all the evidence they could find and left.

Emma was forced to wait for him to open the back door since it couldn't be opened from the inside. She smiled her thanks as he lifted out the infant in her carrier and brought everything up the stairs.

The door burst open and suddenly Emma and the baby were surrounded by Piper and Barb excitedly chattering and oohing and aahing over the baby.

Everyone was pretty much ignoring Macon, so he leaned against one of the posts that held up the roof over the porch and crossed his arms, waiting. As he watched Emma, he was sucker-punched all over again. *This* Emma, the one who was so happy and carefree, enamored with a newborn, had his heart thumping in his chest. Every cell in his body was tingling and buzzing, as if he was coming out of a deep freeze and sparking back to life.

At thirty-one, Emma could still pass for a college kid. If people in town didn't know her so well, they'd be asking to see her ID before selling her any alcohol. When his former partner from Boise had briefly met Emma when he'd traveled to DCA to check on Macon's training progress, he'd teased Macon that he'd finally found someone tall enough that she'd fit under his shoulder if they stood beside each other. Not that Emma was all that tall, but she was taller than average and Macon was a good six foot three. Ken had been right. She matched him perfectly, in a lot of ways.

Like him, she took care of herself, but not by working out in a gym. She had a lithe, toned body from her hard work on the ranch. And sun-kissed light brown hair that bounced behind her in a ponytail most days. Plus blue eyes that rivaled the blue of the skies over the Salmon River Mountains visible in the distance. But even more than her physical presence, it was her intelligence that drew him in. It was her quick wit, tenacity and soft heart that had him thinking about her long after he'd gone home to Boise, three hours south of Jasper.

He'd missed her even more than he'd realized.

Piper pulled the front door open for Barbara, who was now holding Angel. The three women rushed inside, their faces alight with excitement.

Macon grinned. Apparently Emma had forgotten he was here. The others were too smitten with the baby to notice or care. If that wasn't a signal for him to leave, he didn't know what was. He doubted Emma would need his help changing diapers after all, not with Piper and Barbara there to help. He'd check in with the foster closet again, make sure they were able to get everything together that Emma needed. If not, he'd head over to one of the box stores and get the rest himself after his shift was over.

He'd just started the engine when the front door burst open again. Emma came flying down the steps, her face red with embarrassment.

He rolled the window down as she reached the car.

"Macon, oh my gosh. I can't believe I was so rude and left you on the porch. I'm so sorry."

He chuckled. "Don't be. I'm glad you and your friends are enjoying Angel. You don't seem to need me right now and I have to head back anyway. I'm still on duty with a few hours left of my shift to work. I'll probably spend that writing up reports on everything that happened this morning."

She clutched the windowsill of his door, her eyes searching his. "You're wrong, you know. I do need you. I needed you so much today. And I appreciate everything you did. Maybe you can type up those reports some other time and come on inside? Piper and Barbara feel bad for ignoring you, too. Let us make it up to you. I'll cook dinner."

"That's a tempting offer. Rain check? Those reports really can't wait. The team will need the information for the investigation. And after that, I should head home. Bogie's going to eat my couch if I don't feed him soon."

She smiled. "Well, why didn't you say the life of your couch was at stake? Go. I wouldn't want to be responsible for its demise." She cocked her head in that way that was always so endearing. "You *are* coming back Monday, right? You and Bogie?"

"We'll be here, either before my shift or after, depending on the workload at the station. What time do you prefer?"

"The morning, if you can swing it. Ten o'clockish for our first lesson. Eight thirty if you want breakfast."

He grinned. "I'll move mountains to get here at eight thirty." He sobered. "Emma, I live just a few miles away. If you see or hear anything, anything at all that gives you cause for concern, don't hesitate to call me. Day or night. Doesn't matter what time. Okay?"

She nodded. "If it was just me, I wouldn't even think of bothering you like that. But with Angel as my responsibility, I wouldn't want to risk *not* calling if something happens."

"It's not a bother. Call me. I mean it. Day or night. Besides, I still need to give you my best diaper-changing tips at some point."

She laughed. "Okay. But it would help if I had your number."

"I guess it would." He pulled his phone out of his pocket. "I'll call your number since I got it from the report you gave me."

Her phone rang and she saved the incoming number. "Got it. Thanks. Oh, and Macon?"

"Yeah?"

"I really am sorry about your partner, Ken. But I'm glad you're here, that you came back to Jasper." With that, she turned and hurried up the steps and into the house, her sexy ponytail waving at him like a red flag at a bull.

Macon grinned, but then the bush where they'd found the blood sample caught his attention. It was too thick, too large and far too close to the foundation of the porch. Someone could be hiding there right now and he doubted that he'd see them. He'd have to talk to Emma about trimming back the bushes the next time he saw her.

He scanned the house, the outbuildings. But even though he didn't see any signs that someone was skulking around, he couldn't shake the feeling of unease as he drove down the driveway.

Chapter Seven

Macon pulled into the circular drive promptly at eight thirty on Monday morning. Emma was sitting in one of the rocking chairs on the front porch, smiling down at him. Angel wasn't with her. She was probably inside, being cuddled by Piper or Barbara since both of their cars were parked off to the left by the kennels.

Man, she sure looked good.

Clearing his tight throat, he stepped out of the car and glanced across the SUV's roof toward her as he opened the rear door.

Bogie leaped out, a blur of black fur and rabbit-worthy ears as the shepherd bounded around the vehicle toward the porch.

"Bogie, halt," he ordered, stopping the shepherd in his tracks near the bottom step. The dog stared adoringly up at Emma, but true to his training, other than his wagging tail, he didn't move.

Macon stopped beside him, resting a boot on the bottom step as he rubbed the top of Bogie's head. "Good morning, Emma."

She looked a bit overwhelmed, but also happy to see him. Or maybe it was his dog she was happy to see.

"Macon." Her smile widened. "And Bogart. One of my most favorite pupils ever."

"And here I thought I was your favorite," Macon teased. "How'd the weekend go? Are you worn out from midnight feedings yet?"

"Oh goodness, Angel isn't *that* little. The doctor estimated she was two months old, give or take. She sleeps through the night like the angel that she is. But I haven't been taking care of her all by myself. Piper and Barbara have been unbelievable, showing me the basics, how to change diapers without them leaking everywhere, giving me tons of useful tips. Barbara's daughter, Samantha, is grown and in college but she remembers plenty about taking care of babies. And even though Piper doesn't have any kids yet, she's babysat enough for friends and relatives that she seems like an expert to me. They were both here off and on this past weekend helping me. Barbara's inside with her right now. I'm building my confidence. Might even be able to go solo in a few days. Well, except for when I'm working. Barbara is going to use my guest room as her office for a while instead of using the office in the kennel building. That way she can alternate between management duties and watching over Angel when Piper and I are with the dogs. I think it's going to work out really well."

"Sounds like it. Were you able to lighten your training load like you hoped?"

"Barbara took care of that too already. Normally, she and Piper don't work here on weekends but she dove right in, contacting other K-9 training facilities. She off-loaded a third of our dogs to them and the clients were very understanding." She motioned toward his uniform. "I forgot to ask you how long you've been a Jasper policeman."

"I'm an old-timer. Been here a whole week."

She blinked. "A week. Wait, no way. Even transferring in from Boise, you'd still have to go through the academy here, wouldn't you? And you're a lieutenant, too, if I'm understanding the insignia on your uniform correctly. I would have thought you'd have to work your way up, prove you know the Jasper PD way of doing things before you made that rank."

He smiled. "Your foster dad taught you well about how police departments work."

She gave a little laugh. "He tried. But it was Chief Walters, *Officer* Walters back then, who taught me way more than I ever wanted to know about the police. Doing my community service at the police station kept me out of juvie, so I've got nothing to complain about."

He grinned. "I still can't imagine you as a juvenile delinquent."

"Yes, well. I didn't cope well after Dad's death and rebelled. I hung out with the local bad boy, Billy, and did some pretty awful things. I was as horrible as teenagers get. And so very lucky to have someone like the chief to straighten me out and remind me who I was, the adopted daughter of an amazing woman and her police officer husband who didn't deserve to have his memory tarnished with a daughter who was a budding criminal." She waved her hand again. "Sorry. Tripping down memory lane."

"I don't mind. And you're right about how police departments work. Normally someone transferring in would have to go through the usual training and start lower in the ranks than I did. But Chief Walters made an exception because of my previous experience working with Jasper officers as part of the task force. It also didn't hurt that

I had outstanding recommendations from my boss, and Walters had a soft spot for Bogie."

She laughed. "I can see Bogie tilting things in your favor, especially since the chief is such a huge supporter of having K-9s for every Jasper officer who wants one. I'm glad you didn't have to start from the bottom. And speaking of Bogie, poor little guy is dying to say hello. Release the hounds, Macon."

"You asked for it." He gave Bogie a command in German. The shepherd instantly bounded up the steps and skidded to a tail-wagging halt in front of Emma, excited to see her but too well-trained to jump on her like another dog might have done.

She knelt down and hugged him around the neck, ruffling his fur as he wiggled like a little puppy in her grasp.

"Have one of your own yet?" he asked as he climbed the steps and stopped a few feet away.

She gave Bogie one last pat and stood. "No reason to. My kennels are full of fur babies to love on. And as it is, I barely have enough time to give my horse rescues the attention they deserve. And Gus too, when he deems that I'm allowed to see him."

He chuckled. "I thought I saw a flash of that old orange cat heading into the trees when I was here Saturday. Wasn't sure if he was still around."

"Oh he's a fixture at DCA. And the way everyone caters to his every whim, trying to get him to let them pet him, he glories in the attention."

"You're still the only one who can get near him?"

"Pretty much." She cocked her head. "And you too, if I remember right."

"Yeah, well. He's rubbed against my legs before but that's as close as he'd let me get."

"Closer than most. Even Piper can't pet him and she's a wonder with all the other animals, feeding them, helping me with training. She and Barbara are my right and left hands around here." She crossed her arms, pulling her light jacket closed against the cool breeze that was much warmer than over the weekend. It would be in the midseventies by later in the afternoon. "Got any news about the investigation? I mean, if you had a chance to get an update on it before coming out here with Bogie."

"Since I'm the lead detective on this case, I definitely am in the loop on what everyone's doing."

"Lead detective? Really?"

He grinned. "It's not as impressive as it might sound. Jasper's so small we're basically *all* detectives, or evidence technicians as needed. Well, except the brand-new rookies like Jason. He's still in training. Otherwise, if we're the first to respond to a call from dispatch, it's our case. I've got some of the other officers digging into this one and keeping me posted. We've been meeting every morning to share status and brainstorm. I'll head over there to meet with them after we're done here." He leaned back against one of the thick wood posts on the porch. "As to what we've found out so far, not much. But not for lack of trying. The chief's all in on this one, approving shifts around the clock to figure out the baby's legal name, who her parents are. He's got a soft spot for kids. And you."

"The feeling's mutual. He's like a father to me." Her mouth turned down. "I don't count my bio dad anymore. Rick Daniels was my true father. Chief Walters is my bonus dad."

"Bonus dad. I like that. You could do much worse. He's a great guy. He did a lot of the searching himself into missing persons reports. Heck, even anti-DCA Captain Rutledge did some digging to help us out."

"I guess he's human after all, in spite of the rumors," she teased.

He smiled. "I combed through the database of the National Center for Missing and Exploited Children yesterday, trying to find a match. Nothing came close. Still no local missing persons reports. There's nothing logged in the entire state of Idaho for a baby girl her age with dark hair and dark eyes."

"Did you notice the birthmark on her upper right arm? It's an oval about the size of a quarter with ragged edges. That might help."

He nodded. "It was in the doctor's report from the ER. We included that in the flyers."

"Flyers?"

"Around town, and the neighboring counties. Next time you're in Jasper you'll see them. They're in store front windows, on lamp poles, restaurants. If she's from around here, someone's going to see her face and call it in. It's just a matter of time."

"I hope so."

"Your sad face doesn't match those words."

Her eyes widened. "Oh. Well, I mean I really do hope someone recognizes her because she needs to be with her family."

"I sense a but."

She idly patted Bogie's head; he was practically glued to her thighs, his muzzle tilted up to watch her. "Speaking from personal experience, just because someone's family, doesn't mean they're good people. If her family is who abandoned her, then I hope she doesn't go back to them."

She shook her head. "Here I am going on and on and

I promised you a hot breakfast. Meanwhile it's sitting on the table getting cold. Come on. Let's eat."

He reached the door before her and held it open. She smiled her thanks and headed inside. Bogie waited for Macon's permission. Normally Macon would ask someone if it was okay for the dog to come inside. But he knew Emma would be upset if he left Bogie on the porch.

"Come on, buddy. Let's go see what's cookin'." He stepped back and the shepherd eagerly trotted inside, heading straight toward the opening to the kitchen.

Macon detoured to the sink to wash his hands, then sat at the table that dominated the little room.

Emma grimaced when the back of his chair hit the wall. "Sorry. One of these days I'm going to add on to this place, or at least expand the kitchen. It's ridiculously small."

"It's cozy. And much bigger than my rental. Besides…" He motioned toward the food she'd set out in bowls in the middle. "You won't hear me complaining when you've cooked a feast like this. If you do this every morning, I'll always make sure to stop by on my way to the office."

She laughed. "Trust me. This is a rarity, or it *was*. Dinners are easier and more my style. But since Barbara agreed to watch Angel while I'm working and had to move all her papers and supplies up here to the house, I told her one of my ways of paying her back will be to provide a hot breakfast every morning she's here. And, before you ask, she made herself a plate as the food was coming off the stove. She's eating in my guest room slash office. Totally type A, wanting to get as much work done as she can before Angel wakes up from her morning nap." She motioned toward the bowls of food. "Now go on, get yourself a plate. You'll have to nuke it in the microwave to heat it up."

"Don't have to tell me twice." He quickly piled his plate high, then took both of their plates and reheated them.

True to her word, Emma had made a mouthwatering breakfast. Scrambled eggs with cheese, fried potatoes, biscuits, gravy, and some of the best salt-cured bacon he'd ever had. Bogie seemed to agree since he got several slices in the bowl of dog food that Emma had set out just for him. Even though Macon had already fed him before leaving the house, the bacon was too much for him to resist and he happily dove into his second breakfast.

Emma laughed and smiled down at Bogie. "With that kind of appetite, I'm surprised he's not fat and lazy by now."

"He's always been food-motivated, that's for sure. Luckily he gets plenty of exercise hanging with me at work."

"Well he'll get plenty today, for sure," she said. "We'll run him through the basics again, get him used to the routine of being here. It will help build his confidence, keeping it simple. In a couple of days, we can test him on some bad-guy takedowns, see how he does."

They were both quiet for a little while as they ate. But as Macon spooned a second helping of eggs onto his plate, Emma said, "You mentioned that Bogie hesitates. To help him get past that, I need to find out what it is that's specifically giving him anxiety. As much as we love our animals and think of them as if they were little humans, it's wrong to assume that we know why they react the way they do. We have to figure out what's making him anxious, and why, before we can work to correct it. Have you noticed he balks in specific kinds of circumstances?"

He took a quick sip of coffee before answering. "Sudden, loud noises, for sure. He'll cower against me, nearly knocking me over. I have to coax and reassure him to get him to move forward. Luckily, that hasn't happened during a call here so far. But I'm only starting my second week. Everything's been smooth, quiet for the most part."

"Interesting. Have you noticed any other issues, aside from how he reacts to loud noise?"

He shrugged. "I haven't really tried to narrow it down that way. I just know that back in Boise, at least, there were a ton of times in the months following the screwup at the warehouse where he'd back up against me and refuse to move. I knew his days working there were numbered at that point. I'm not even sure he'll be able to work successfully here, but when I called Chief Walters about it, he recommended I relocate and see if you could work a miracle. So I took a chunk of my 401K to buy Bogie from Boise PD, and here I am."

She blinked. "You bought him? Jasper PD didn't buy him for you to use here?"

"The chief offered, but that kind of budget wasn't available right away. It would have taken a while to pull the funds together. There was no guarantee what would happen to Bogie in the meantime. He wasn't fit to work in the kind of environment he'd been specifically trained for, and there really wasn't anywhere else for him there. They don't have the robust K-9 presence like we do in Jasper. They couldn't afford to let a work dog sit or gradually get back to one hundred percent. They would have sold him. I couldn't let that happen, couldn't risk him going somewhere else and me not being able to get him back."

"Police K-9s don't come cheap. That must have been a hefty hit to your investments."

He grimaced. "It hurt, no doubt about it. But Bogie was there for me more times than I can count. I wasn't going to abandon him just because it was the easier route to take."

Her eyes were suspiciously bright, as if she was holding back tears. "I sure wish there were more dog lovers like you. If there were, the pounds wouldn't be so full of neglected and abandoned animals." She rubbed the top of Bogie's head. "You're one lucky guy, sweet fella." She smiled at Macon. "As for me working a miracle with him, there aren't any miracles in what I do. Just hard work and years of experience. And if I've learned anything about K-9s, it's that you can't fix a problem if you don't know the cause. The easy explanation is that the gunshots scared him, so he's afraid of loud sounds. But working dogs like Bogie aren't easily intimidated. I'm betting there's more to it."

She motioned toward his plate. "Take your time and eat your fill. I'm going to check on the baby, and see whether Barbara needs anything before we head outside to reacclimate Bogie to the ranch. I don't want to do too much with him the first day back. He needs to feel comfortable before we start any real training."

Macon was about to answer when the radio on his shoulder squawked. It was Jenny, the dispatcher, requesting any available units to investigate a potential break-in. When he heard the address, he glanced up at Emma. "That's a couple of miles from here."

"Go on. It's okay. Come back anytime, or we can try again tomorrow."

He shoved back from the table as he let Jenny know

he'd take the call. "I'll stop by later today, for sure. Sorry about the mess. I would have helped clean up."

"I know you would." She made a shooing motion with her hands. "I understand a cop's obligations better than most. No apologies needed."

On an impulse, he leaned down and kissed her cheek. "Thanks, Emma."

For once, she was speechless, her eyes wide as she stared at him. And for once, he wasn't sure how to read her reaction. He guessed he'd figure it out later when he returned. Either she'd tell him to get lost or she'd overlook his impulsiveness. Or, if he was really lucky, she'd gladly welcome him back. He sincerely hoped it was the latter.

Chapter Eight

Emma couldn't resist one last stroke of the bloodhound's silky ears before closing the chain-link gate to his kennel. It had been a surprisingly typical Monday, long and hard getting the dogs back in the training routine after having the weekend off.

Beside her, Piper gave her a warning look. "Don't you dare try to get Red to like you more than me. I'm his favorite." She flipped her long red hair over her shoulder. "We gingers have to stick together."

Emma laughed. "No worries there. He was making puppy-dog eyes at you the whole time he drooled on me."

Piper grinned. "He's a beauty, isn't he? I think he's my favorite of the current batch of trainees. And judging by how quickly the two of you tracked and found me in the woods, I'd say he's ready to graduate."

"I was originally thinking he'd need another week. But his performance this afternoon tells me you're right. He's ready. He might be the best tracking dog we've ever worked with."

"No dog tracks better than Decoy."

Emma rolled her eyes. "You're biased since Decoy is Shane's search-and-rescue dog."

"Maybe. But I'll allow that Red has the potential to

be the second-best search-and-rescue hound in this area, maybe all of Idaho."

"Says the woman who did most of his training."

Piper held her hands out in an innocent gesture. "Ain't bragging if it's true."

Emma laughed and eyed the adorable hound as he slurped from his water bowl, long ears flopping and splashing the water onto the concrete floor. "I guess it's time to notify Shane that Red's ready to join his SAR team. We'll need Red's handler here for at least a couple of hours to put them both through their final paces before Red goes home. Can you tell Barbara before you leave, get her to set it up?"

Piper moved to the sink at the end of the run to wash her hands. "I can do that now. All the training we wanted to do today is done. I've finished cleaning the kennels and feeding everyone. Nothing left to do but go home, clean the stink off and veg on the couch."

"Ha," Emma said. "I'm sure you'll be doing more than just being a couch potato with that gorgeous Shane waiting for you."

Piper sighed and dried her hands on a towel, a lovesick look on her face. "He is gorgeous, isn't he?"

"If you like the tall, buff, dark-haired type, I suppose."

"Sort of like your Lieutenant Ridley? He's taller than Shane. And I swear his muscles have muscles. That man is *built*."

Emma arched a brow. "But he doesn't have dark hair."

They both laughed.

"See you tomorrow, boss." Piper waved and ducked out the doorway.

Emma spent a few more minutes in the kennel building, checking the gates on each dog enclosure, making sure they had clean bedding and water. But Piper was no slacker and she was doing an excellent job filling in on things Barbara normally did, in addition to Piper's regular training work. Everything was taken care of as she'd said. There was nothing else for Emma to do but check on the horses. Then she'd head inside, wash up and do what she'd been looking forward to all day—taking over babysitting duties from Barbara. She'd feed sweet little Angel her dinner and cuddle her until she fell asleep.

Gravel and dirt crunched beneath her feet as she crossed to the little barn that served as a stable and storage area. Her steps were sure and fast. She was anxious to get this last chore over with. And she couldn't lie to herself about why.

Angel.

It shocked Emma how much she enjoyed having the baby girl around, even though it had only been a few days. But she was determined not to become attached. If she did, then when they found Angel's parents, or a permanent home for her, it would break Emma's heart. She'd already suffered too many tragedies in her life to risk a broken heart. Losing someone else she cared about was more pain than she was willing to bear.

She slid open the heavy wooden barn door, then headed inside. The late-afternoon sunlight did little to illuminate the gloom of the interior, even with the ventilation windows open. But with a flip of a switch, the large overhead lights hanging down on poles chased away the shadows.

Like her K-9 building, the barn featured a center aisle. But where the other building had dog enclosures running down both sides, this barn was a combination of storage rooms on the right and only had two stalls on the left.

When Emma had used her inheritance to expand her family's property and build DCA, she'd planned on using the barn like her father had, to store the small tractor-mower and other equipment and tools. But when she'd found out that a neighbor was down on their luck and couldn't afford to feed their horses anymore, her plans had changed. She'd bought the horses for much more than they were worth, helping her neighbor and giving the horses a home. Thus, the barn became a stable.

Presley, an American quarter horse, extended his graceful neck over the top of the stall door. He snorted, his velvety muzzle snuffling against her shirt.

"Whoa there, boy. You know what I have for you, don't you?" She pulled two sugar cubes from her shirt pocket and placed them in the flat of her palm so he wouldn't accidentally take a couple of fingers along with the treats. "Don't tell Piper I gave you sugar. She wouldn't approve."

Presley chomped loudly and was soon pushing against her shirt pocket again.

She crooned and rubbed his forehead. But when he realized she wasn't feeding him anything else, he turned his attention to the pail of oats Piper had hung earlier.

"Guess I know what's more important to you. Food trumps Emma every time."

"Not in my book."

She turned around at the sound of the deep voice. Six foot three inches of tantalizing male stood in the open doorway, his skin turning a deep gold as the setting sun's ray slanted across him. Macon's smile flashed as he started toward her. His ever-present shadow, Bogie, trotted beside him.

"Hope you don't mind me dropping in on my way home without calling first."

She cleared her throat and moved to the next stall. "Of course not. You said you'd try to check on me after work. You're always welcome here." Her Appaloosa was already straining his neck toward her, anxious for the same treats he saw Presley get. "I was hoping you'd be able to come earlier in the day, though, so we could have worked with Bogie. I'm guessing it was a bad scene this morning? The break-in?"

He stopped just past the first stall and leaned against it while she fed Elton his two sugar cubes.

"False alarm. Literally. A rat chewed through a wire and set off the security alarm."

"How do you know it was a rat?"

"I found the crispy critter with his teeth still gripping the wire."

"Aw. Poor guy."

"Poor guy? Your barn cat eats rats all the time, I'll bet."

"True. But that's nature, the circle of life. A rat getting electrocuted isn't a natural death."

He idly patted Bogie's head. "You won't find me shedding any tears over a rodent. But I get it. Life is precious. Any time it's wasted or cut short isn't something to celebrate." He motioned toward the Appaloosa. "Elton, right? And the other one is Presley?"

"You remembered."

"Hard to forget. Elton John. Elvis Presley. Two great rockers in their time. But I don't get where the name Gus came from for your barn cat." He motioned toward the orange cat just as he darted under one of the stall doors.

"Gus is short for Angus," she said. "Angus Young, guitarist for AC/DC."

He grinned, his sexy smile lighting up the barn far

better than the overhead lights. "Gotta love consistency. I figure if I ever have another dog, I'll name it Bacall, to go along with Bogart."

"*Casablanca.* You could do worse."

"Actually it was Ingrid Bergman in *Casablanca.*"

She stopped petting Elton and stepped away from the stall. "That's right. I'm so used to hearing Bogie and Bacall, since they were in movies together and got married. What if your next dog is a boy? What would you name him?" She crouched down and gave Bogie a command to come. He eagerly sat in front of her, tail wagging, tongue lolling.

"Ernest, of course."

She blinked. "Ernest? Wait. Let me think." She tapped her hands on her jeans. "Oh, of course. Bogie and Bacall first met filming *To Have and Have Not*. It was based on the novel by Ernest Hemingway."

"Bingo."

She laughed. "Your mind works in odd ways, Macon."

"And yet your mind followed my line of reasoning. What does that say about you?" He winked and she laughed again.

Presley chose that moment to put his head over the half door and nudge against her pocket again. She pushed his head away, stepping back. "No more sugar cubes, boy. Not today."

He tossed his head and showed his displeasure by kicking the back wall in his stall.

Bogie jerked hard against Macon, forcing him to move away from the stall.

"Stop, Bogie. It's okay. There's nothing to be afraid of." He knelt down and started petting the shepherd, whispering soothing words. "This is what I was telling you about," he told Emma. "Loud, sudden noises scare him. He does this every time."

Emma crouched down in front of the shepherd. His eyes weren't wild. He wasn't shaking. But his fur was ruffled and he was staring at the stall door. She stood.

"Macon. He's not afraid. He's protecting you."

He gave her a doubtful look. "You think so? That's not how he's been trained to act when there's a threat. He's supposed to freeze in place, refuse to go forward. Or if there's an assailant, attack."

"Before the ambush, that's probably what he'd still do. But I've seen this kind of behavior before. He must be associating loud noises, like Presley kicking his stall, with the gunshot sounds when you and Ken were ambushed. So instead of going on the offensive, as he's supposed to do, he's being defensive. He's afraid, but not for himself. He's afraid for you."

He gently smoothed Bogie's fur. The shepherd had calmed now and sat down, panting happily as if nothing had happened.

"How do we fix him?" Macon asked.

She chuckled. "Fix him. Well, it's like we originally planned. He needs retraining. Not weeks or months like the last time. Well, maybe one week, or less if it goes well. Depends on how traumatized he is. I won't know until I work with him. Will you be able to bring him in tomorrow morning like we'd hoped to do today?"

"Possibly. Chief Walters has approved the training. But we're short on personnel right now with a couple of guys on vacation. So I still have to respond to calls when needed. Hard to predict. And I'm the lead investigating Angel, trying to find her family, and whether one of them or someone else left her at your doorstep. I'll bring him when I can but it might be spotty."

"I need to desensitize him. He needs to relearn that loud sounds aren't always bad and that you can handle yourself. One way to help him is to keep him on a regular routine. It will make him feel secure, that his environment is under control."

"If that's the case, then me not being able to commit to specific training times isn't doing him any favors."

"Exactly," she said. "How would you feel about dropping him off here in the mornings on your way to the police station? Then you can come train with him after your shifts are over and take him back home? It's imperative that he learn not to associate loud noises with you potentially dying, so he can stick to his training and go on the offensive and respond to your commands. To do that, I'll need you here during some of the training. But not the whole thing. We can compromise, have me work with him during the day and you come after work. I could throw in dinner afterward."

"Careful," he teased. "A home-cooked meal is a powerful bribe. And if it's even half as good as breakfast was this morning, you're in real trouble."

"I didn't say it would be home-cooked."

He smiled. "I should be able to come here most late afternoons or evenings. Dropping him off on my way into town before work sounds good too. That'll fit in better around the meetings I get pulled into and shift turnover every morning."

"Good." She led the way toward the barn door. "We can start our new routine right now, with dinner."

After securing the barn door behind them, they started toward the house, Bogie trotting happily at Macon's side.

"Unfortunately, in spite of what I just said, I can't to-night. I've got an appointment. But when I had to leave so quickly this morning, I'd promised to stop back by. So I'm keeping that promise. I wanted to let you know I can't train today, and of course to apologize for not re-turning earlier."

"Did you? Apologize?" She glanced up at him, laughed at his startled expression. "Kidding. No apology needed or expected."

He put his hand on her shoulder, stopping her in front of the porch. "I am, you know. Sorry. I should have called."

She put her hands on her hips. "Cop's daughter, re-member? Plus, my bonus dad is Chief Walters. I com-pletely understand that you aren't a nine-to-five desk guy. I know the job's constraints, that you can't control your hours even when you try. So, seriously, no apologies."

"Understanding the job doesn't mean apologies aren't necessary. So I'll continue to apologize when warranted."

She shook her head. "Fine. Whatever makes you feel better. What's this appointment you're off to? Or is it confidential?"

"Not at all. I've been trying to get interviews lined up with those teens who help DCA out as part of their court-ordered community service. Not having much luck so far. Even their parents aren't responding to police calls asking for interviews. So I'm going to surprise them, try to catch them at home, starting with the Norvells, Kyle's parents."

"Can't you just wait and talk to them when they're working here one afternoon?"

"You told me Kyle and Hugh work Thursdays and Fridays. And William's days are irregular, whenever he can get here. I can't wait all week to talk to them. I have an investigation to run."

"So, what, you're just going to show up at Kyle's house tonight, alone? Dressed like that?"

He frowned and glanced down. "Something wrong with my uniform?"

"And your car. They both scream police."

He arched a brow. "That's kind of the idea of the uniform and marked car."

She waved her hand impatiently. "What I'm saying is that if your goal is to get Kyle, or his parents, to give you any information, you need to be more low-key. In their neighborhood, the police are the enemy. Parking a police car in their driveway and showing up at their door in uniform is going to do one thing—ensure they don't talk to you. You don't survive living in that kind of environment looking like a snitch who talks to the cops. Even if his parents aren't involved in any criminal activities, a lot of their neighbors likely are. They can't risk being seen talking to you."

"I *have* to talk to them. We're hunting down every lead we can to find Angel's family. You're the one who told me about Kyle, Hugh and William. I'd be negligent if I *don't* talk to them as part of this investigation. I have to rule them out, or in, as being involved."

Bogie whined, drawing their attention. His huge shepherd ears were perked up and his head was tilted at an adorable angle as he looked up at them.

Macon sighed and knelt down, rubbing Bogie's neck. "Sorry, boy. It's okay. We're not really arguing."

"Sure we are."

He gave her an aggravated look. "No. We're not."

She laughed.

His frown deepened.

She held out her hands in a placating gesture. "Truce, Lieutenant Ridley. Look, I'm not trying to be difficult. I'm actually trying to be helpful. I don't want you to drive to Kyle's home only to be turned away."

He patted Bogie again then stood. "I'm sensing a suggestion coming on."

"Then you have excellent instincts. My recommendation is that you go home and change into civilian clothes before heading over there. And you don't show up in a police car. What kind of personal car do you drive?"

"A black Ford pickup."

"Oh, good. That will fit right in. What year?"

"This year. I bought it before leaving Boise."

"It's brand-new?"

"That's what this year means."

"Okay, now you're starting to annoy me. Cut the sarcasm."

He drew a deep breath, then let it out slowly. "Sorry."

"Apology accepted."

"I thought you never wanted me to apologize."

"For being a cop. Not for being a jerk."

His mouth twitched as if he wanted to smile but he didn't. "Point taken. Unfortunately, the only vehicles I have right now are the police SUV and my, apparently, *too-new* shiny pickup."

"You have a third choice." She motioned behind him toward the parking spots to the left of the kennel building.

A pained expression crossed his face. "Instead of driving my new truck, you want me to drive that olive-green rust bucket of bolts?"

"That rusted bucket of bolts is a 1952 Chevy half-ton pickup with the original 235 straight six engine and wood deck in the back. It's an antique. A collector's item, a classic. It's museum-worthy."

"It belongs in a junkyard."

"It belonged to my father, Rick Daniels. And green was his favorite color."

"It's beautiful. Perfect. I'd be honored to drive it."

"Smart man. But you're not driving it."

He turned around. "Then why offer it?"

"I'll drive. I'm going with you."

"No. Absolutely not. Besides, you need to stay home to take care of Angel."

"I'll ask Barbara if she can stay late to take care of Angel until I get back. Think about it, Macon. I admit I haven't known Kyle and the other two teens very long. I haven't really established a rapport with them quite yet. But they're starting to trust me. And if the neighbors see me there, the Norvells can honestly tell them I'm in charge of their son's community service to keep him out of jail. They can say I stopped by to discuss his work and no one will worry that they were snitching on someone for, well, anything."

"Makes sense. I get it," he said. "But what if Kyle is the one behind abducting Angel or maybe she's his daughter and he abandoned her. Either way, he'd be worried about being arrested for his part in whatever is going on with her. It could be dangerous. You shouldn't be there."

"If that's your argument then Kyle shouldn't even be allowed at DCA."

"Maybe he shouldn't. I could talk to the judge about that."

"Don't you dare. These kids need this job to stay out of jail and turn their lives around. If one of them is involved in what's going on with Angel, then they need our help more than ever. Besides, it's not like I'd be in that neighborhood, or in Kyle's home, by myself. You'd be with me. You'd protect me."

He shook his head. "No, Emma. You're not going with me. That's final."

Chapter Nine

Macon shook his head as Emma pulled her ancient pickup into the Norvells' driveway. "I can't believe I let you talk me into this."

"You're an intelligent man. You saw reason."

"I'm an idiot. I saw a beautiful woman and logic flew out the window."

She grinned. "Sweet of you to say that. Now let's go."

"Emma, I'm having second thoughts. I don't think this is a good—"

She jumped out of the truck and started toward the house.

Macon swore and hurried after her.

Once inside, Macon had to admit that Emma's strategy was correct. The Norvells admitted they wouldn't have opened the door except that Kyle recognized Emma. And while the parents weren't exactly warm and welcoming, they were civil and did seem to appreciate that Emma had agreed to let Kyle work at the Daniels Canine Academy as his required community service. Kyle, on the other hand, seemed indifferent and hadn't spoken more than to say hello since they'd come inside.

Since the teen seemed jumpy and anxious, and kept glancing at the front door as if he was going to make a run for it, Macon was glad he'd chosen a seat right beside the door. While Emma leaned forward in her chair making small talk with the parents on the couch, Macon kept his gaze trained on Kyle.

If Macon hadn't known the kid was seventeen, he'd have sworn he was in his early twenties. He was nearly as tall as Macon and had a world-weary look in his dark eyes whenever he actually made eye contact, which wasn't often. His hair looked as if it hadn't been washed in a few days and he kept shoving his too-long bangs back from his face.

The small home he and his family lived in spoke of a hard life without a lot of money. But it was neat and clean and showed pride in ownership. Everything seemed in good repair. Even the yard outside was well-maintained with some cheerful yellow flowers to the left and right of the front door.

While Kyle's parents' clothing looked worn and old, their son looked as if he'd just left a department store with brand-new sneakers, jeans and—surprisingly—a collared shirt. Macon had expected tattered jeans, holey shoes, and a T-shirt sporting some kind of profanity or reference to a heavy metal band. He'd based his expectations on the kid's rap sheet and mug shots. But maybe there was more to Kyle after all. Maybe he was struggling to make himself a life without the benefits of growing up in a family where money wasn't as hard to come by. And maybe he had nothing to do with Angel ending up on Emma's front porch. But if that was the case, why was he so nervous? And why did he look like he wanted to bolt?

"How do you like working at DCA, Kyle?" Macon asked.

Conversation on the other side of the room stopped and everyone looked at Macon. Except Kyle.

"Kyle," his father said, "answer the police officer."

Kyle frowned and crossed his arms, but he finally met Macon's gaze. "It's all right, I guess."

"Do you work with the dogs or the horses?"

"Not really. I mostly clean or make repairs." His gaze slid toward the door.

"Repairs," Macon said, trying to engage him in the conversation instead of hitting him up with hard questions he'd likely not answer. "I can see where there'd be a lot of things that need fixing on a spread of land like DCA. What kinds of things do you repair?"

He shrugged. "Fences. Doors. Siding. Junk like that."

"Siding. Like on the house?"

"The barn. It had some holes in it so Ms. Daniels asked me to replace some boards. No big deal. Dad, can I go now? You said I could hang out with my friends after dinner."

"That was before Officer Ridley showed up. Your friends can wait. Answer his questions."

Kyle sighed, his mouth tightening in a rebellious frown. "So ask me some questions, cop. Real questions. What do you want?"

"Kyle—"

"No, it's okay, Mr. Norvell," Macon told him. "Kyle has plans and I'm interfering. He's right. I should get to the point of my visit."

Instead of having built any trust or rapport in their short conversation, Macon could see Kyle tensing up in anticipation of whatever he was going to ask. Macon glanced at Emma, who was chewing her lip, but she only shrugged. She didn't have a long history with Kyle either, so they were both at a disadvantage.

"Do you have a girlfriend, Kyle?"

Kyle's eyes widened. Macon had definitely caught him off guard with that question.

"I, ah." The teen's gaze slid toward his parents before answering. "I got a few girls at school who like me. Nothing serious. What's that got to do with anything?"

"Did any of them have a baby about two months ago?"

Kyle's face reddened.

His father jumped to his feet. "What's going on here, Officer?"

Macon glanced at the father, but focused on Kyle as he answered. He didn't want to miss his reactions, verbal and nonverbal. "Last Saturday morning, someone left an approximately two-month-old baby girl on Ms. Daniels's front porch. We're trying to find out who the baby's parents are, and who left her at DCA."

"And you think that's me?" Kyle choked out, seemingly genuinely shocked.

Both of his parents were now standing and Emma was, too, speaking in low tones to Mrs. Norvell as if trying to soothe her anger. Before either of them could order him out of their house, Macon tried to lower the temperature in the room a few degrees.

"I have no idea who the baby's father is, or who left her there," Macon explained, keeping his voice calm. "But since you're at DCA several times a week, Ms. Daniels and I were hoping you could tell us if you've seen anyone suspicious lurking around. Or maybe while you've been out repairing fences, you've run across signs that someone's been watching the house. Footprints, broken branches in the shrubs near the house. That sort of thing. We're hoping you can help us. Even if you haven't seen signs of anyone else at the ranch, maybe you know about someone at school who had a baby recently and no one has seen the baby since."

Macon's little speech did what he'd hoped—it defused the situation. Mr. Norvell had stepped around the coffee table and was standing a few feet away now. But both he and Kyle seemed to have relaxed, if only a little. And it didn't seem as if the father was about to order Macon out of the house. Instead, he put his hand on his son's shoulder.

"Kyle, if you know anything, tell him. There's an innocent baby involved. He needs his family."

"She," Emma said, her voice quiet. She was holding Mrs. Norvell's hand as the two women watched them from across the room. "Her name is Angel. Or at least, that's what the note said that was left with her."

"She," Mr. Norvell corrected. "Kyle?"

Kyle held out his hands in a helpless gesture. "I don't know nothing. I swear. And I haven't seen anything to make me think someone was sneaking around DCA." He turned toward Emma. "I promise, Ms. Daniels. If I thought someone was trespassing, that you were in any danger, I'd tell you."

She smiled. "Thank you, Kyle. I appreciate that."

Something flickered in Kyle's expression. He was hiding something. The question was whether it had anything to do with Angel.

"What about your friends?" Macon asked. "William and Hugh. Do you think they could be involved?"

Kyle vigorously shook his head. "No way, man. You need to look at someone else."

"It's getting late, Officer Ridley." Mr. Norvell spoke in a hard tone, his meaning clear.

"Understood," Macon said. "I mean no offense to any

of you. I have to follow up on all possible leads to get Angel, the baby, to her mom and dad."

This time it was Mrs. Norvell who spoke up. "Of course you do." She nodded at Emma, then went to stand beside her husband and son. "And if any of us hear anything that might help, we'll definitely let you know."

"That's all I can ask." Macon shook their hands as Emma joined him by the door. "Thank you for your time." He handed a business card to the father. "If you think of anything that might help with the case, please call me."

When they were in Emma's truck again and back on the road, she shook her head. "That went about as bad as it could have gone."

"I think it went just fine."

She shot him a startled look. "Fine? We didn't get any information."

"Sure we did. I didn't expect anyone to tell us much during this initial interview, not given their history with the police. The family is bound to circle the wagons, try to protect their son. But even if they didn't say much, their body language was loud and clear. The parents were shocked to hear about Angel. Based on that, I'm inclined to believe the baby's not Kyle's. It would be hard to imagine him having a pregnant girlfriend who gave birth two months ago without the Norvells knowing about it. They seem like involved parents. And Kyle treats them with respect, more or less. They're aware of what's going on in his life. I think they'd know about a baby."

"I didn't think of it that way, but you're probably right. What about Kyle? What did you pick up from him?"

"Kyle's not as easy to read. He seemed shocked, too. But that might have been for his parents' benefit. I got the impression he was hiding something."

"Like what? You just said you don't think he's the father, that his parents would have known."

"It may not be related to the case. Maybe he's done something else that he didn't want the cops to know about. Or it could be something he's keeping from his parents, unrelated to this investigation. Still, I'm not convinced he doesn't know something about Angel and who's responsible for abandoning her."

"Or kidnapping her."

"I'm really not leaning in that direction right now. None of us working the case are. The parents would have filed a missing persons report even if they were leery of cops. I just can't see this as an abduction. I think whoever left Angel was the mother or father."

"That's a relief, actually. I'd rather believe that the person who trespassed on my property isn't some hardened criminal stealing someone's child."

"Don't get me wrong. We're looking at every possibility, keeping an open mind. I'm just saying that right now, it seems more likely that one of Angel's parents left her on your porch."

"I get it. And I appreciate that you're not jumping to conclusions. It's important to know exactly what's going on and why."

"Turn down that next road coming up."

She glanced toward where he was pointing. "That won't take us back to DCA."

"No. It won't." He glanced at the screen on his phone. "In spite of Mr. Norvell proclaiming that it was getting late, it's only going on eight o'clock. Hugh Engel's home isn't far from here, down that road. How do you feel about doing one more interview tonight?"

In answer, she slowed and made the requested turn. "If it helps with the investigation, I'm all for it. I've spoken to Hugh's parents before but it was at DCA. I've never been to his house. Give me the address and then you can call Barbara to make sure everything's okay with the baby."

"On it."

While Hugh wasn't home because he was out somewhere with his father, his mother was. And she didn't have the same reservations about talking to a police officer that the Norvells had. She readily answered every question that Macon asked. And she promised him that she'd check with other parents at the school to see if anyone had a baby in the past couple of months. She told Macon to expect a call tomorrow with the results of her inquiries. And she also said she'd have Hugh call him and arrange a meeting.

"That was refreshing," Emma said, when they were in her truck again, driving down the highway.

"Agreed. It's nice to question someone who doesn't seem to be hiding anything. Hopefully I'll get the same kind of cooperation from Hugh himself once I speak with him. Now for William Shrader." He checked the time on his phone again. "It really is getting late. I may have to try to interview him tomorrow. Let me look up his address and see how far away he lives."

"No need." Emma slowed and turned into a long driveway much like her own. "I've been here before. That SUV in front of the house belongs to William's dad. And that—" she pointed toward the right side of the long ranch home where a light shone in a window "—is William's room. He's home."

Chapter Ten

Emma shifted her weight in her kitchen chair, trying to ease the ache in her arms from holding the sleeping baby. She glanced at Macon, who was loading the dishwasher a few feet away, just as he'd done Tuesday and Wednesday after she'd fixed them dinner. The week was flying by.

She enjoyed seeing him each night, and during the day when he was able to fit in some training time with Bogie. But she was becoming increasingly frustrated that he was being so vague about the investigation, especially about what was going on with Kyle, William, and Hugh.

Back on Monday night, when she and Macon had stopped at William's home, it hadn't turned out as she'd expected. His parents claimed he wasn't there, in spite of the light in his window. And they hadn't even invited Macon and Emma inside.

Macon had reminded her that he couldn't force the parents to let him check William's bedroom without a warrant. Given Emma's own teenaged experiences on the wrong side of law enforcement, she'd known that. But she hadn't expected the family to refuse them entry. She'd thought her earlier meetings with them and reassurances that she wanted to help their son would have made a difference. Her being with Macon should have, in theory, eased their fears and made them want to co-operate. It hadn't.

When Macon finished putting the dirty dishes in the dishwasher and turned it on, she shifted in her chair again. Now, maybe she could finally get that update.

"Careful," she teased. "I could get used to having a man clean my kitchen every night."

He dried his hands on the dish towel hanging from her oven door and turned around, bracing his hands against the counter on either side of him as he stretched out his long legs. "It's the least I can do when you're the one providing the food." He nodded toward Bogie, who was resting by the back kitchen door. "To both of us. I may stop soon anyway if you continue to refuse to let me pay you."

"Sharing with Bogie isn't a burden. I buy dog food in bulk at Sampson's Feed and Grain just outside of town. Plus, Jasper PD is compensating me for training him. As for feeding you, I've never learned how to make dinner just for one. And I enjoy having you here."

Her face flushed warm at that admission, especially since his eyes widened slightly. He had to know she was wildly attracted to him, since she'd made no secret about that when they'd first met. And she was confident he felt the same way about her. They'd fallen back into their easy banter as if he hadn't been living in Boise for the past two years, as if he'd never left. But that didn't mean she wanted things to go further. She had to guard her heart against getting hurt.

It wasn't that he had a girlfriend. She'd nonchalantly worked that question into one of their conversations and knew he wasn't currently seeing anyone. The problem was her fear that she could fall for him and then he'd decide to move back to Boise.

His very large extended family was there. It made sense he'd probably want to return, once he healed more from the loss of his friend and survivor's guilt. She didn't want to be a fling in his memories or be left pining over him. No, it was better if she was careful. Encouraging a relationship beyond their easy friendship wasn't fair to either of them.

She cleared her throat. "Bogie is doing much better already. I don't think his trauma was nearly as bad as we both initially thought."

His warm brown eyes flickered toward the dog again, who was now lightly snoring. "I was thinking the same thing. This afternoon's session went really well. It's a relief to know he hasn't been scarred for life."

"Unlike you?" she asked softly.

He winced. "Maybe. But I can handle it. If losing one of my best friends *didn't* affect me, I'd be a cold loser."

"Well, you definitely aren't that."

Angel smacked her lips and burrowed her head deeper into the blanket covering her.

Macon sidled over and smiled down at the sleeping baby. "I swear she's grown already since I first saw her."

"You're probably right. I'm just relieved she's so healthy." She sighed wistfully. "It's hard to remember sometimes that she's not mine. She belongs to someone else. We need to find her family."

"Before you become too attached?"

"Something like that." She swallowed at the lump in her throat. "How are your inquiries going? Did you ever speak to William? Did Hugh's mom have him call you? I know you don't want to share every detail of an ongoing case. But this one directly impacts me. And I'm working with those kids. They were all here today.

It was kind of awkward not knowing what's going on where they're concerned."

He hesitated, as if trying to figure out how to phrase his answer. Then he shrugged. "I suppose that's fair. Hugh's mom finally called me back and provided an alibi for him for when Angel was left here. She provided pictures from a fishing trip he and his dad went on the weekend she was abandoned. They left Friday after school and didn't get back until Sunday night. We pulled cell phone records to verify it, and corroborated her claims with other witnesses. Hugh was definitely at a lake several hours away."

"That's good to know. And William? Did you speak to him yet?"

He nodded. "Several times, actually. Including earlier today. You were out in the field with Piper and the horses when I arrived. The boys were taking a break outside the kennel building. Honestly, I feel like none of them are very forthcoming. It could be their overall distrust of cops. But with Kyle, in particular, it seems as if he's hiding something. What I need to know is whether that has anything to do with Angel. All three of the boys claim they don't know anyone who's had a baby recently."

"Maybe they're telling the truth."

"Maybe. But I'm not letting them off the hook that easily. Kyle and the others seem really tight. I can't imagine that one of them is involved in this and the others don't know about it. The trick is in getting someone to crack."

She shifted her arm again. "I think you should leave them alone and explore other leads."

"It seems as if she gets heavier the longer you hold her, doesn't it? Let me take her and give you a break."

Before she could think of a reason to say no, he gently lifted Angel out of her arms and cuddled her against his chest. There was an ache in her own chest as she watched him smiling down at the baby. And she couldn't honestly say it was just because she selfishly wanted to hold Angel herself.

A full minute passed and the baby didn't so much as gurgle. Emma shook her head in wonder. "That wasn't fair. You distracted me to get me to stop asking questions."

He grinned, but didn't deny it.

She laughed and decided to let it drop. "She sure is comfortable with you. Piper can't even pick her up without Angel crying. Only Barbara and I can hold her and keep her happy, or so I thought."

"Maybe she still thinks you're holding her. She's asleep, after all."

"Trust me. It's something about you that makes her feel safe. I've tried transferring her to Piper while Angel was sleeping. And once to the veterinarian technician, Tashya, when she stopped by to vaccinate some of the dogs. As soon as she left my arms she jerked awake and started bawling. It didn't matter what Piper or Tashya said or tried. You really do have the magic touch. You'd be a good father."

His warm gaze flew to hers. "Thank you. You'd be a great mother, obviously."

She immediately shook her head. "No. No, I wouldn't. I'm not having children. Ever."

He frowned and looked like he wanted to argue with her, so she quickly slid her chair back. "I need to put her down for the night and shower and hit the hay soon myself. The dogs will be howling for breakfast if I oversleep."

"I thought Piper feeds them for you."

"Actually, Barbara used to do that and Piper mainly helped with the training. But with Angel being here, we've juggled the chores around. Piper and I clean, feed and train together while Barbara stays in the house with the baby and takes care of the administrative tasks for running this place. Regardless, the point is I help in the mornings, no matter who's feeding them. It's a big job."

She reached for the baby, and he seemed to reluctantly pass her back. After adjusting the blanket around the baby to make sure she was warm, Emma smiled up at Macon. "Thank you again, for everything. We're making great progress with Bogie. And hopefully the investigation will be resolved soon and we can all get back to our normal lives."

He stared at her a long moment, his gaze intense, questioning. "Is that what you want? For both of us to return to our normal lives, the way they were before Angel came along?"

Her chest tightened uncomfortably, well aware of what he really meant. He was asking about the possibility of them continuing their friendship and seeing where it might lead. But she wasn't ready for that, didn't think she'd ever be ready. And since she didn't even fully understand it herself, she didn't want to get into a discussion about it. So instead, she did what she'd always done when anyone got too close. She shut him down.

"Yes. I'm sure. I don't have time for a baby, not really. Or anything else right now. I'm too busy."

He stared at her until her face began to grow warm beneath the lie. Then he gave her a crisp nod. "Understood. Bogie, come on, boy."

The shepherd's ears perked up as he blinked his sleepy eyes.

Macon patted his thigh. "Come on. Home."

The word *home* had the shepherd eagerly rising to his feet, tail wagging, tongue lolling out. He trotted to Macon and looked up at him adoringly.

Emma followed the two of them to the front door.

Once on the porch, Macon paused as if to say something else, but seemed to think better of it. Instead, he jogged down the steps to his SUV.

Chapter Eleven

Emma jerked awake, bolting upright in her bed and covering her ears against the shrill, pulsating sound of her house's security alarm going off. The kennels erupted into frantic barking as the dogs reacted to the noise. Groggy and confused, she scanned her bedroom. It was pitch-dark, still nighttime. What was going on? Was the alarm malfunctioning? Or was someone trying to break in? Maybe they already had. A cold sweat broke out on her forehead in spite of the coolness of the house.

Desperate cries sounded from the guest room next door. *Angel!* Emma jumped out of bed and grabbed her Glock from the nightstand drawer. Her cell phone started ringing on top of the nightstand. She swiped it as she sprinted out of the bedroom and into Angel's room.

After slamming the door shut and locking it, she glanced at the screen, ready to send the call to voice mail so she could dial 911. But caller ID showed it was the alarm company. She put the phone on speaker mode and then pressed the screen to accept the call, before setting the phone on top of the chest of drawers so she could check on the baby.

"Ms. Daniels, this is—"

"The alarm company. I know. Please get the police out

here. I think someone is either trying to break into my house or is already inside. Tell the police that I'm locked in the baby's bedroom with her, front right corner of the house. And I've got a pistol. So they'd better announce themselves when they get here."

She leaned over the crib, her heart squeezing in her chest at the sight of Angel's red face and the tears tracking down her little cheeks. But she didn't dare pick her up yet. She trained her pistol on the bedroom door, ready to go down shooting if someone busted inside. She had to protect the baby.

"Ms. Daniels, I've notified Jasper PD. Please stay on the line while—"

"Sorry. Can't." She ended the call and pressed the favorites button on her phone. Then she hit the very first number.

The call picked up before the second ring. "Emma, what's wrong?"

Relief flooded through her. "Macon, the alarm—"

"Is going off. I hear it. I'll be there in two minutes." She could hear sounds, the rustling of fabric, keys jangling. "Where are you?"

"In the front bedroom, Angel's room. It's the last door down the hall on the right side."

"And the baby?"

"With me. The door's locked. I've got my pistol."

"Good." He sounded relieved. An engine roared to life. "Don't open that door to anyone but me."

"I'll need to let you in the front—"

"No. Stay in the bedroom until I get there."

She put the phone on speaker again and set it on top of the chest of drawers, keeping her pistol trained on the bedroom door the whole time. She couldn't hear Macon anymore if he was talking to her. But she had to focus, concentrate. The chaotic blaring of the alarm, the dogs barking and Angel screaming, along with the fear that someone was in the house, that they might try to break through the door at any second, had her shaking so hard she could barely hold the gun up.

"It's okay, baby girl," she called out toward the crib, her gaze glued on the door. "I'm so sorry I can't pick you up yet. This will all be over soon. Shh, shh, shh."

Bam! A door banged somewhere in the house.

She jumped at the new sound. Had Macon arrived? Had he busted down the front door to get to her? Or was someone else inside?

The pistol slipped. She grabbed it before it could fall and wrapped both hands around the grip, struggling to stop shaking. But even her teeth were chattering.

Another sound intruded between the ear-splitting pulses of the alarm. Footsteps. In the hallway.

Emma tensed, her finger tightening against the frame of the gun. She knew not to put it on the trigger until she was ready to fire. Her daddy had taught her that.

"Emma, it's Macon. I'm in the hallway. Are you okay?"

Relief nearly made her slump to the floor. "Yes. Yes, we're okay."

"The house is clear. Bogie's on guard in the main room. No one's getting past him. What's your alarm code?"

She told him, and moments later the sound blessedly stopped. The sudden quiet must have startled Angel, because she quit crying.

"You can open the door now," Macon called out.

Emma set the pistol down and ran to the door. Her

hands were still shaking so much it took two tries to unlock it. Then she flung it open and was immediately wrapped in Macon's arms. She didn't resist his tight hug. Instead, she reveled in it as he backed her into the room.

The sound of the door closing, then locking, had her stiffening against him.

"It's okay," he soothed. "I didn't see any intruders, but the back door had been jimmied open. That's how I got in. I'm guessing they didn't actually come inside because the alarm scared them away. But I'm not taking any chances that they're still on the property. We'll stay right here until more police arrive. I radioed them on my way here."

"Th-the…alarm…company called 911 t-too."

He gently pushed her back and held on to her shoulders. His brow furrowed with concern. "Are you sure you're okay?"

She laughed, or would have except her throat was so dry it came out as a raspy croak. She cleared her throat and tried again. "I'm fine. I really am. Thanks to you."

He gently squeezed her arms. "And the baby?"

She blinked. "Oh my gosh." About the time she spoke, Angel started screaming again. "Angel, poor baby. It's okay." She ran to the crib and scooped her up in her arms, rocking her against her chest. "It's okay, sweet girl. It's okay. Don't cry. Shh, shh, shh."

MACON NODDED AT what Chief Walters was telling him. But when Captain Rutledge interrupted to say something derogatory about DCA, Macon stepped away. Why Rutledge had even shown up was a mystery. He certainly wasn't contributing anything helpful to the situation. And he hadn't even bothered to ask whether Emma was okay, as pretty much every other officer on the scene had done.

Macon stopped near the end of the couch so he could see Emma through the kitchen opening. Still cradling Angel, she was sitting at the table listening to Piper and Barbara, who were sitting beside her. They'd both arrived shortly after dawn to begin their usual work routine and had been shocked to see all the police cars lining the driveway. Half of Jasper PD had shown up to make sure that Emma was safe. And Bogie wouldn't leave her side. He was curled up at her feet beneath the table.

"She's tougher than you think," Walters assured him, straightening the hat he always wore, even inside, thinking no one would realize he was going bald. "Emma will be fine."

"Tough or not, she's exhausted. We need to wrap this up."

Rutledge asked the chief a question, drawing his attention.

Cal Hoover stepped through the front door with his rookie-in-training, Jason, at his side. He glanced at the chief, but Walters pointed at Macon and went back to his conversation with Rutledge.

Hoover stopped in front of Macon and handed him a set of keys. "I've sent the team back to the station. We've collected all the evidence we could find. Nothing else we can do here. The inside of the RV doesn't look like it's been touched in weeks, maybe longer. There weren't any prints on the outside, either. This whole place is pristine. Even the kennels didn't yield many prints. We dusted the gates, doorways, the faucets on the sinks in both the kennels and the barn. Got a few prints, not many. But I'm betting those belong to the staff, not our perpetrator. Because whoever started to break in through the back door didn't leave any prints."

"He wore gloves."

"That's my guess. He did leave a few shoeprints, a trail, more or less. It starts by the front porch, which means he probably stuck to the gravel prior to that or I'd have found some more prints out front in the grass. Then he left a few shoeprints around the side of the house, and at the bottom of the deck. Well, assuming they don't turn out to belong to anyone who works here."

Macon stared at him. "By the front porch? Someone hid behind the shrubs? Again?"

"Yep."

"Those dang things need to be chopped down. They're like a welcome sign to a wanna-be intruder." Macon scratched the stubble along his jaw. "None of this makes sense. Someone goes to the trouble of wearing gloves but is careless enough to leave shoeprints. And he doesn't case the place before trying to break in or he'd have known there was a security alarm. What does that sound like to you?"

"A budding criminal who isn't very smart?"

"Or a budding criminal who isn't very experienced. Yet." Visions of the three teens—Kyle, William and Hugh—danced in Macon's head. Every time he told himself they weren't involved in what was going on at DCA, something else happened to keep them on his persons of interest list. "What I don't get is why. If it's to rob the place, why try breaking in when Emma's truck is here? Everyone in town knows about DCA, that Emma lives out here, alone. Why not wait until she goes into town on a weekend, when Piper and Barbara aren't around, and rob it then?" Macon's blood ran cold as the answer came to him. And from the worried expression on Cal's face, he'd come to the same conclusion.

"The bastard knew Emma was alone this time of night, or this time of morning, I guess." Macon fisted his hands beside him. "He wasn't here to rob. He was here for Emma. Or Angel."

Cal cursed beneath his breath and glanced toward the kitchen. He moved closer, keeping his voice low. "I'm right with you on that train of thought. It's too big a coincidence that someone trespasses and drops off a kid. Then someone else trespasses trying to break in a handful of days later."

"We may have two perpetrators," Macon said. "Someone wanting to get rid of a baby, and someone else wanting her back?"

"Could be," Cal agreed.

"The question is, are they both bad guys, or is one a good guy? If it was Angel's mother who left her here, maybe she was trying to protect her from someone else. And that someone else has figured out where she left the baby."

"Another twist on that," Cal took up the theory, "could be that the person who tried to break in tonight was either trying to *save* the baby—"

"Or *kill* her."

Cal grimaced. "This is bad. Really bad. And getting more complicated by the minute." He motioned to Jason behind him. "Recall the team. I want to go over this place again. Look for more evidence. There has to be something we've missed." He put his hand on Macon's shoulder as Jason hurried out the front door. "We'll figure it out. We'll get this guy." He shook his head. "Or both of them."

When Cal headed outside, Macon updated the chief and the captain. They discussed strategies and where the investigation was going. They left shortly after that to return to the station, while Macon stayed behind.

He glanced toward the kitchen again. Piper was holding Angel while Barbara stood at the stove, stirring something in a frying pan. It appeared that she was making Emma breakfast. She was in good hands for now. Which meant Macon could do what he'd been wanting to do ever since he got here.

Confront Kyle and his friends.

If they didn't have alibis for early this morning, he was going to personally drag them into the station to answer his questions. Either they were involved, or they weren't. But he dang well wanted to know which way to go with that so he could stop wasting time on them if they were innocent and had no helpful information.

A few hours later, Macon turned his truck up Emma's now-empty driveway, disappointed to see that everyone from Jasper PD was gone. Piper's and Barbara's vehicles were still parked beside Emma's truck, so at least she wasn't alone. But he didn't like not having an officer stationed at her home with what had happened in the early hours before sunrise. Thankfully Bogie was here since Macon had left him to guard her before leaving earlier. But still, one of his fellow officers should have stuck around, per his discussion with Chief Walters.

He jogged up the front steps, barely pausing long enough to rap on the door before opening it.

Emma stopped in the middle of the family room, a thick stack of papers clutched in one hand and a smile on her face. "Macon, hi. I didn't realize you were coming back. I figured you'd wrap up things this morning at the station and then go home to catch up on your sleep. That's what I'm going to do as soon as I finish reviewing some paperwork Barbara needs me to sign."

"I have a few things to take care of, too, before I can take a nap. Where's Bogie?"

"At the kennels, for training. Piper and I talked about how I've been working with him. She's taking over for the morning."

"And Barbara?" He glanced around. "Where is she?"

"Well, ah, she's in the office in the kennel building, with Angel. She knew I was tired and she didn't want Angel to cry and wake me up once I lie down. Otherwise she'd be in my office here." She frowned. "Is something wrong?"

"Other than the fact that someone tried to break into your home early this morning? And I can't find your community-service kids to check their alibis? And you're in this house, alone, without anyone to protect you?"

"Hold it. Stop. Back up. *Community-service kids?* You mean Kyle, William and Hugh? You think one of them is responsible for the break-in?"

"Maybe. Maybe not. But I sure would like to ask them about it. Funny thing is, no one seems to know where they are, even though it's a school day."

"O…kay. Well, Kyle and Hugh should be here this afternoon. You could try talking to them then."

"I plan on it. That doesn't resolve the problem of you being here alone."

"Oh, for Pete's sake. I'm not alone. Piper's here. Barbara's here. Kyle and Hugh, possibly William too, will be here later—"

"Which is exactly why you shouldn't be here without

protection. One or all of those kids could be involved in what's going on."

She tossed her stack of papers on one of the end tables and put her hands on her hips. "And what exactly *is* going on, Macon? Does anyone know? Because I sure don't. What's happening with the investigation about Angel? Do you have any leads aside from your police bias against troubled youths, jumping to conclusions and always assuming they're behind anything bad that happens? Even though you supposedly cleared Hugh earlier?"

He stiffened. "Police bias? You think that, what, I'm harassing Kyle and the others? For no reason?"

She crossed her arms. "Are you? I'm struggling to build trust with them, to help them turn their lives around. And they see me working every day with the police officer who keeps showing up at their houses and throwing accusations at them. Don't you have any adults to interview for this case? It can't be that hard to figure out who gave birth to a baby girl two months ago and suddenly doesn't have the child with them anymore. Who are Angel's parents? Are you *ever* going to find out? Are you even trying?"

The sound of someone clearing their throat had Macon slowly turning around. Cal stood in the doorway, his troubled gaze flickering back and forth between them.

"Hey," Cal said, his expression smoothing into a smile. "The door was open. Macon, what's with the saws, pruning shears and garbage bags in the back of your pickup? You here to attack the shrubs like you threatened earlier this morning?"

Macon cleared his throat, taking a moment before he trusted himself to speak. "If Emma approves it, yes."

Emma stepped forward as Cal joined Macon. Her face was a light red, which could mean she was either still angry or embarrassed. Macon didn't even try to figure out which one. He was too angry to care.

"Hi, Cal." She looked at Macon. "Attack my shrubs?"

He drew a calming breath. Then two, before speaking again. "The perpetrator this morning hid behind them in almost the same place as the person who hid there before abandoning Angel. I want to prune them low to the ground so no one can hide anymore. If you give me your permission. It won't hurt them. They'll grow back. But I obviously recommend you keep them trimmed low in the future."

"I, ah, okay."

Macon gave her a curt nod and faced Cal. "Are you here for the security detail?"

"Security detail?" Emma echoed. "What are you talking about? Macon? Cal?"

Cal glanced at Macon as if for permission. Macon was too disgusted and tired to do more than nod.

"Two 911 calls out here in less than a week is troubling," Cal told Emma. "Especially since someone actually tried to break into your home. Macon asked the chief to post someone here when he's not around. Having a police car out front is a good deterrent. And having an officer here just in case something else happens will make all of us feel better. Things got a little mixed up in the chaos earlier and we all bugged out at the same time. I'm back to watch out for you until Jason arrives. He volunteered to take first shift."

"Oh. Well, thank you. That does ease my mind. I appreciate it. And thank you, Macon, for setting it up."

"I have some bushes to trim." He strode out of the house.

EMMA STARED AT the now-empty doorway Macon had just gone through, her face turning hot as she faced Cal. She offered him a wobbly smile. "Sorry you walked in during my tirade. I'm way too tired to be thinking straight, obviously. I never intended to say any of that out loud. But I'm so frustrated that Macon's investigation seems to be focused entirely on the teens helping me out around here. I wish he'd focus on someone else."

Cal squeezed her shoulder, then dropped his hand. "You've known me for years, Emma. You know how we police work, from watching your dad, then Walters when he took you under his wing and helped you avoid juvie."

She didn't think her face could get any hotter. "I'd rather forget my rebellious criminal days."

"I'm sure you would. And I'm not trying to throw that in your face. I'm just pointing out that you have the background, on both sides of this. You know how investigations work, that most of what the police do is kept close to the vest. On the surface, it may seem like not much is being done. But under the water, we're paddling like crazy."

She nodded. "I shouldn't have gone off on him like that. I'm aggravated, and tired."

"We all are. Macon more than the rest of us. He's barely had any sleep since this whole thing started. He's convinced the chief to let everyone, and I mean everyone, work this thing as time permits, in between other cases going on. But, Emma, it's not just about those three kids you're so protective of. Macon's doing due diligence with them, looking into potential alibis. It would be negligent not to. They have criminal records. They're here a lot so they know the place, where to hide, when you're alone. They may resent you because they're forced to work here

She s... continued.

small fract...

all of us l... "We have a status meeting every ... hea... tion, so believe me, I know what all is being done. ... it's a lot. We've interviewed dozens of people so far and that number goes up every day. We're coordinating with other counties, the hospitals, to find Angel's mother. You can't just call up an administrator and say, hey, give me the names of all the women who had a baby there in the past few months. We have to work with judges to force them to do it. That's not easy when we don't have anything pointing to a specific person as a suspect. We're looking for similar crimes, anyone who's gotten out of jail recently who might be in the area causing trouble. We're investigating you too."

"Wait, me? What do you mean? Why?"

"Angel, her being left here. It could be random, but it could be personal, someone who knows you. We're looking at everyone who was fostered here, their families, their friends. That's not easy either. People scatter, get married, change names, move away. It's not like on TV where you press a magic button on a computer and someone's entire life history pops up on a screen. We have to dig, pound the pavement, go all over the county, neighboring counties, talking to anyone who will listen to us. Every time we do hit on potential suspects, and we have, it's a tedious, huge amount of work to rule them out, or keep looking at them. It all takes time. But trust me, Emma. We're putting in the hours, doing the work. We're following every bread crumb. Macon's not stopping until we resolve this thing. He's going to make sure you're safe

...ead, even when

and he's going to d...ng to happen overnight."

it means que...k onto the couch and wrapped her arms

this out. B...

Sh...r middle. "If you're trying to make me feel mis-

are...

erable. you've succeeded."

He sighed and sat beside her. "Emma, I'm not trying to make you feel bad. I just wanted you to know the truth. Macon's not the type to praise himself or expound on all the hard work he's doing, and that he's got us doing, on your behalf. He's working harder on this than anyone. And he doesn't deserve to be accused of basically being lazy and conducting a shoddy investigation."

She winced and drew a shaky breath. "I screwed up. I really screwed up."

He took her hand in his. "You reacted to a stressful situation with very little information to go on, with only a few hours of sleep. It's entirely understandable. But now you know the truth." He squeezed her hand and let it go. "I'm going outside to see what's taking Jason so long to get here. In the meantime, think about taking a nap. I can see how tired you are. You don't have to worry about being safe. We've got this."

"I know you do. I know Macon does." She cleared her throat. "Thanks, Cal."

He smiled, then headed outside.

A few moments later, Emma crossed to the front windows. Cal was standing by his police SUV in the circular driveway talking on his cell phone, presumably to Jason. Macon was tossing several full garbage bags into the back of his black pickup truck. It was a surprisingly large pile of bags for the short amount of time

Lena Diaz

Because of her.

"I really messed up," she whispered, hating herself in that moment. Here was a man who'd suffered a terrible loss, the death of his best friend. And he'd nearly been killed himself. Then he'd come here, looking to start a new, quieter life. But that didn't happen. Instead, he was doing everything he could to help her, to make her safe, to make her life better. And she'd paid him back by doubting him, questioning him, forgetting everything she knew about police work. He didn't deserve to be treated that way, especially by someone who knew him as well as she did. She knew the kind of person he was, knew he wasn't the type to look for the easy way out. He was exactly what Cal had portrayed, a driven detective who wouldn't stop until he solved this case and made sure Emma was okay.

She pressed a hand against the window as Macon bent to yank out some of the branches he'd just cut. She needed to apologize. But how? She'd been awful. She watched him for several minutes as he loaded more bags into the back of the truck. In spite of the mild temperatures outside, he was sweating, which was understandable given the hard work he was doing. He paused to wipe his forehead before turning back to the last shrub. A drink. He needed a cold drink. Not sure whether he preferred pop or iced tea, she took a gamble and decided he'd want tea. She'd have to make a fresh pitcher.

Chapter Twelve

"She really is a good baby." Emma raised the side rail on the crib. It had been a long day for all of them, especially Angel, having been jolted awake by the shrill blaring of the house alarm. But in spite of that, and so many people in and out of the house all day, she'd settled down for the night with almost no fuss.

"The best." Barbara leaned past Emma and adjusted the blanket. "I can't help thinking about her mom. That's who you think left her, right?"

"Seems to make the most sense. The police are keeping an open mind on that point, but they're leaning toward it being the mother. Macon said as much the last time we spoke about it." She fisted her hands, wondering when she'd speak to him again. After he'd chopped up her shrubs and left this morning, he hadn't even called to check on her. Before she'd been so horrible to him, he'd definitely have called.

Barbara nodded. "Even if she left her because she felt forced to, to protect her somehow, she still has to be missing her, wondering how she's doing."

Emma led the way out of the room, back into the family room before replying. "I've thought about this so many times, doubting that a mother would leave her child in that way. But door to door in her neighborhood ... the mother ... Polic..., she'd have been calling would be an... doesn't... word that her baby was missing. We'd have 911, ...ard something."

"Agreed. Angel must have been abandoned by her mother."

"Or the father." Officer Jason Wright, who'd been assigned guard duty this afternoon, stepped inside with Bogie at his heels. The shepherd instantly went to Emma, as was his habit now, and lay down on the floor beside her. "Just did my rounds. Nothing to report. Everything looks okay."

"Thanks, Jason." Emma bent down to pet Bogie before standing again. "And you're right. It could be the father, too. But I still think the mom has to know, or it would have been reported."

"What if there is no mother?" Jason asked. "Maybe something happened to her. A car accident or something like that. And the dad can't handle a baby on his own. Maybe he heard about DCA, knows you've fostered before, and thought she'd have better care if left with you than left at the door of a fire station or hospital. Macon's gone over those possibilities and more with us. It's all part of the different theories we're pursuing."

"I'm not surprised." Barbara grabbed her purse from the decorative table near the front door. "He seems to be on top of things from what I've seen. He'll get this figured out soon enough. You need anything, Emma, give me a call. I'm not far away."

"I think we'll be fine. But I really appreciate it, Barb. Thanks for everything."

The guilt that had been churning inside her ~~fingers and headed~~ ~~" Jason anno~~ over how she'd treated Macon took a back seat to the worry that now flared with Jason's announcement. She knew how much Piper adored Chipper. She'd been so excited to get him.

"Hopefully the little guy will be okay." She motioned toward the kitchen. "It's getting on to dinner time. I've gotten in the habit of cooking lately, but no one else is here to share it with. Can I tempt you with some spaghetti and garlic knots? I've got fresh tea and pop, too."

"Oh, man. That sounds great. But Tashya would kill me. I'm taking her to that fancy new seafood place off Salmon River Road tonight. Rain check maybe?"

"Of course. Wouldn't want your new bride to get mad at you already." She smiled to hide her disappointment. She really missed not having Macon here to share tonight's meal. "Guess I'll make myself a sandwich. No point in going to all that work for one person."

"Sorry, Emma."

"Hey, you're doing me a favor. Saving me a lot of trouble. Why don't you head on home to Tashya now? I'm sure whoever is assigned second shift will be here soon."

"No way. Macon would have my head if I left before he gets here."

"Macon's coming back? Tonight?"

"That's my understanding. Is that a problem? You sound worried."

"No, just surprised. I, ah, said a few things in anger

earlier without rea~~~ ~ncomfortable. "I
he'd want to se~~~ ~ut that. But I do know he was
He blink ne made up the schedule that he be the
haven't ~~~ere for the night shift. He said if someone tried
insi~ person to bust into your place again he wanted to be here to take
them down." He motioned over his shoulder. "Speaking
of Macon, I forgot to check the RV. I'll walk the grounds
one more time so I can be doubly sure there isn't any
sign of another trespasser. I want to be able to answer
any questions Macon has when he gets here. You have
my cell. Call if you need me. I won't be far."

"Thanks, Jason."

With the news that Macon was coming over, Emma
headed into the kitchen and started making the spaghetti
she'd originally offered Jason. If Macon had already eaten
before he got here, she could easily reheat the spaghetti
later. Piper and Barbara would enjoy it for lunch tomorrow. But she hoped he hadn't eaten, because he deserved
a hot, home-cooked meal. And an apology.

The sound of a car engine out front half an hour later
had both her and Bogie rushing to the front window. Jason's SUV was hurrying down the driveway. No doubt he
was eager to take his new love out on the town as promised. Another SUV was parked right out front. And moments later, a very tall, buff, gorgeous male stood in her
doorway, practically stealing her breath.

"Macon. Hi, it's good to see you."

He arched a brow in surprise. "I'm here for the next
shift. But if it makes you uncomfortable, I can get one
of the others to switch with me."

"Not at all. Come in." She opened the door for him,

which was sad given that he would normally knock and just come in without waiting. That was her fault, that their easy camaraderie had suffered. Hopefully she could fix it.

When he stepped inside, he locked the door behind him, then set a backpack on the floor at the end of the couch and knelt down to pat Bogie before taking a seat. He glanced up as Emma sat in the chair across from him, his expression stoic, unreadable. "I hope Bogie's still improving. I know I've been sporadic about training with him."

"He's doing great. Piper and I both worked with him today. And I can well understand your hours being unpredictable. I know you've been working really hard."

He frowned, as if confused, or maybe just surprised, by her declaration. But he nodded anyway and glanced around. "Is Angel sleeping?"

She smiled. "Just like the angel that she is. I fed her and put her down just a little while ago. Speaking of which, I just made some spaghetti. I can pop some garlic knots in the oven, too. It'll only take a few minutes. Want me to fix you a plate?" She stood to cross to the kitchen.

"No thanks," he said. "I appreciate it, really. It smells wonderful in here. But I had a quick bite with the chief downtown while we reviewed the case."

She slowly sat back down. "Okay. Well, if you get hungry later, I'll be sure to portion it out in different containers to make it easy to reheat."

"Thanks." He patted Bogie's head again. The shepherd had parked himself at Macon's feet and kept pressing his nose against his jeans.

Emma chuckled. "You'd think he never got any attention the way he acts. But I swear he gets more attention than any of the other animals around here. He's spoiled."

Macon ruffled his fur. "He deserves to be spoiled, don't ya, Bogie?"

Bogie's deep bark filled the room.

"Shh, not in the house." Macon scratched the top of the dog's head. "Not unless there's a bad guy outside."

Emma stood, hating the awkwardness between them. He'd barely looked at her since coming inside. Maybe she'd wait for a better time to apologize. "I'm going to put the spaghetti up. Want a beer? Or tea?"

"I'll get myself something later. Thanks." He grabbed his backpack and unzipped it. "If you don't mind, I'm going to sit here and look over some paperwork."

Just like strangers. All polite and distant.

"Of course. You can use my office if you want."

"No need." He pulled a thick folder out and set it on the couch beside him.

Emma slowly sat back down. "Is that the case file? On Angel?"

He glanced up at her. "One of them. Everything we've got fills a lot more than this folder. Mostly, this has the latest status updates, plus the reports on the break-in."

"I see. I, ah, spoke to Cal about the investigation. He mentioned you have a lot of people you're looking into, like ones associated with me, back when I was fostering pretty regularly. Mind telling me who you're looking at? Maybe I could help. I can tell you about each person, what I remember, anyway."

"I'd planned on talking to you once I narrowed the list down a little more. I suppose I can show you the list now. If someone strikes you as more likely than the others to be involved in something criminal, let me know."

He flipped through the thick folder and pulled out a piece of paper.

She took it, her eyes widening. "This is some list. I only fostered a dozen or so kids over the years. There must be—"

"Thirty-seven names. It's the people you fostered plus others we've linked them to with criminal records."

"And there are males and females. I guess this covers potential moms who left Angel, as well as guys who might have tried to break in?"

He nodded. "It could have been a woman who tried breaking in. But given the large shoeprints we saw, it's doubtful. Once the DNA comes back on the blood sample we collected, at least we'll know for sure whether a man or a woman left Angel here. But we still can't assume the two incidents were done by the same person. So we have to keep an open mind, look at every lead, every potential suspect, until we can clear them or move them higher up in priority so we can focus more on them."

"That's a ton of work. Let's see…" She scanned the list, smiling at some of the good memories many of the names evoked. "You can cross these first four off right now. I know all of them even though only that first one was one of my fosters. They're as honest as they come and would never be involved in anything criminal."

"I won't cross them off but I'll note them as a lower priority." He handed her his pen from the side table. "Put an *L* by those and any others you feel strongly about."

She was able to put an *L* by a good third of them, but a few of the names had her grimacing. "This one, Ricky Enos, he was my one for-sure failure. I never could gain his trust. I put up with his bad behavior for a while, but after he stole a few hundred dollars from Barbara's purse, it was out of my hands. He went to juvie. Never heard from him again after that."

"Put an *H* by him," Macon said. "But I remember the name. I'm pretty sure I already have a ton of information on him back at the station."

Her guilt from earlier was riding her hard as she reviewed other names and Macon commented on several of them. Just as Cal had said, Macon and his team had done a lot more investigating than she'd given them credit for. But it still bothered her that William, Hugh and Kyle were still mentioned with the others. They seemed more in need of support than suspicion.

"Here are a few more I'll note as high priority," she said as she marked the page. "I always tried to meet my fosters' friends so I could try to steer my kids away from bad influences." She read off the names she'd just marked. "Maria Loretto. David Timmons. Kelvin Armstrong. Josh Basham. He hung out a lot with Wanda Mickelson. The two of them were a terror, but Josh finally came around and broke up with her. Still, she was a bad influence and he struggled. I don't know what happened to him later. He's probably someone you should look at. Oh, look, Celia Banks is on here. I haven't thought about her in ages. She was so sweet. Like Josh, she had an onagain, off-again relationship with a bad influence. Sean something." She frowned. "Hopper. Yeah, I'll write his name here as someone to look at, high priority. Celia's an *L* for sure, though." She updated the sheet and handed the paper and pen to Macon.

"Thanks." He slid the paper into the folder and flipped back to the front. "I'll look over those later, after I review the status reports."

"I'm sorry."

He frowned. "That I have to review the reports?"

"No. I mean, yes, actually. I'm sorry that you're having to work so hard. You're clearly exhausted. Did you not take a nap today?"

He leaned back against the couch. "Haven't had time. I'll catch up on my sleep tonight."

"You're welcome to use the bed in the second guest room, the one that doubles as my office. It's on the left down the hall."

"I appreciate it. I probably will. Later." He started reading one of the papers in the folder.

"Macon?"

"Hmm?"

"Can you look at me please?"

He glanced at her in question.

"I am so, so sorry for how I acted earlier. For how I spoke to you. I know better, know how police work is, as I've said before. I never should have second-guessed how you're handling the investigation, or that you *are* handling it. That was wrong of me and, well, I'm really sorry."

He shook his head. "Don't apologize. We're both tired and maybe not as tactful as we'd otherwise be right now. But you said what you felt, can't fault you for that. Did it tick me off? Sure. But I'd rather have honesty than false emotions any day of the week. And I've always gotten honesty from you."

She blinked. "But I was terrible."

He shrugged. "You had valid concerns. Besides, didn't we agree never to apologize?"

"Not if I'm a jerk."

He grinned. "Apology accepted then."

She rolled her eyes, then laughed. "You made that way too easy. I thought you were furious with me."

"Fury is way too strong. I was angry, no doubt. But that was this morning. I'm past that now."

"But when you came in, you didn't even smile. Are you sure you aren't still mad?"

He blew out a deep breath. "I'm not mad. I'm tired. I got about two hours of sleep last night because I was up late, then got your call. It's not personal. Promise."

"Then we're good?"

He smiled, a real smile that lit up his eyes and had her heart swelling in her chest. "We're good."

She stood again, feeling so much better and relieved he'd forgiven her. "Well, okay. I'll go put up dinner now. And I'll bring you back an iced tea. Going through that thick folder is bound to work up your thirst."

Emma was so relieved to have cleared the air between them that she was grinning like a fool the entire time she worked on the kitchen. Bogie chomped on the food she gave him and curled up in the corner a few minutes later on the dog bed she'd brought in.

Once all the food was put up and the kitchen was spotless again, she made the promised iced tea and headed into the family room. And once again she was left holding the glass. Macon was sound asleep, still sitting upright on the couch.

The case folder was in serious danger of falling off his lap onto the floor. Emma managed to rescue it just before it fell, without spilling the tea, which she felt was quite a feat. After setting both the folder and the glass out of harm's way, she stood looking down at him.

The man was too handsome by far. She loved how he kept just enough stubble to form a light beard and mustache that were barely there. Her fingers itched to trace the angles of his face, feel the scratchiness of the stubble beneath them. If she had free rein, she'd smooth her hands up the sides of his head and bury them in the upswept hair on top. Of course, if she was really allowing herself to fantasize, she'd have to admit that she'd like to rip that shirt off over his head and feast her eyes on the muscles underneath. There was a tantalizing glimpse of a tattoo on his left biceps, barely visible beneath the edges of his collared shirt. She'd love to see the whole tattoo and find out whether he had any more.

She shivered and bit her lip. This was crazy. Macon was exhausted and sleeping and here she was ogling him like a Peeping Tom. He deserved his privacy. And she needed to get a grip on her infatuation with him. That's what it was, no denying it. She was completely infatuated with him. And she hadn't even realized how hung up on him she was until she'd spent the entire day feeling horrible for how she'd treated him. She'd felt guilty because she cared about his feelings, and she regretted hurting him. If she didn't care so much, she sure wouldn't have felt so bad all day.

Stop it, Emma. Just stop it.

She had to rein in her fascination with him before it was too late. She'd loved and lost too many people in her life already. And the last man she'd thought she'd loved had gotten her in trouble with the law and nearly destroyed her. He'd broken her trust, broken *her*. It had taken years to get over that. No, she'd do well to remember the lessons of the past. Don't risk your heart and you won't get hurt. Period. She had a life here, a good life, a satisfying life. And she didn't have to have a man in it to make her feel fulfilled. Macon was a friend, a very good friend. But that's all she could allow him to be.

Which meant, she needed to head back to her office. Or better yet go check on Angel instead of mooning after a man who would never be hers.

Still, he looked so uncomfortable slouched back like that with his head at an awkward angle. She grabbed a pillow from the other end of the couch and carefully tucked it up under his chin. Was it too cold in here? The cold snap earlier had given way to warmer temps again, so she had the air-conditioning on. She pulled the quilted throw from one of the other chairs and gently covered him.

In spite of her vow to keep everything in the friend-ship zone, she couldn't resist one last thing. She leaned down and ever so softly pressed a kiss against his cheek. A pleasant shiver ran down her spine. Just touching Macon's face was enough to make her dizzy with pleasure. This infatuation was bad, really bad. And she needed to do everything she could to fight it until he did what everyone else she'd ever loved did. Left her. But when Macon left, she promised herself it would be with her heart and her pride intact.

MACON SLOWLY OPENED his eyes, watching Emma leave the room and turn down the hallway. Being woken up with a kiss wasn't something he'd ever have expected, certainly not after the way things had been going today. Part of him wanted to jump up and follow her, kiss her the way he'd always wanted to. But that insanity was quickly squelched by the fact that he was so exhausted he wasn't even sure he could get up. His eyes closed and he drifted back to sleep.

Chapter Thirteen

No one was slowing down with Emma's case, least of
all Macon. It had been a long day of interviews and
dead ends. He was more than ready to return to Emma's, maybe do some training with Bogie to burn off
some of the tension inside him. He was on his way there
right now, having gone home only to shower and change
clothes.

Even though technically he was off the clock now,
he was driving his police-issued SUV in his continued
hope of using it as a warning sign to would-be intruders. Would Emma be glad to see him? Hard to say after
how they'd left things.

Yes, they'd supposedly made their peace with each
other last night. But this morning, their conversations had
been stilted and awkward. Emma must have spent most
of the night mulling over what had happened, because
she kept apologizing. That had him apologizing to her
for making her feel like she even needed to apologize.
What a mess. He'd tried to assure her that it was okay.
And it really was. He understood how she felt. Someone
going through the things she'd experienced had every
right to be upset. It was just unfortunate that he'd been
so tired he let himself get angry in response. Being tired

was never an excuse to act in a way that upset someone else. He should have been more understanding.

Hopefully they could move past this blip and go back to the easy friendship they shared. Although more and more, he was having trouble separating that friendship from the idea of something far more intimate and lasting. Especially since Emma had awakened him with that far too chaste kiss. He hadn't mentioned it, not wanting to embarrass her since she obviously hadn't intended for him to even know about it. But he couldn't quit thinking about it and wondering what it meant, and wishing for so much more. Which was really confusing since a few days ago she'd talked about them going back to the ways things used to be, meaning just friends, once the case was resolved. Was she fighting their attraction for a reason he didn't know about? Or did she truly not want to be more than friends?

He shook his head, not sure what to make of everything. It didn't seem possible that so little time had passed since they'd come back into each others' lives. And that so much had changed inside him as a result. Where before, he'd been hurting and wanted nothing more than to be by himself, now he couldn't imagine a day without Emma in it. But until he resolved the investigations around Angel and the attempted break-in, there wasn't any point in thinking about pursuing a relationship. Above everything else, he needed to focus on what was most important—keeping Emma safe and getting Angel back to her family.

He knew from experience that all it would take was one solid lead to break the investigation wide open. But the problem was they had so many tips, generated from the flyers around town and knock-and-talks he and his team had conducted throughout Jasper, that it was nearly impossible to weed out any real tips from the noise.

He turned onto Emma's driveway and hit the brakes. What was going on? Was the entire police force here? There were SUVs and police-issued sedans end to end in the circular drive in front of her house. And several more squeezed in between some trees by Piper's and Barbara's vehicles. If someone had hurt Emma and no one had called him, there'd be hell to pay.

He zipped up the driveway, coming to a rocking halt behind the last vehicle. He was almost to the front porch when the door opened and Barbara stepped out, cradling Angel in her arms. Weaving around her feet was a little corgi puppy.

"Hey, Macon. I saw your SUV through the window."

"Hi, Barbara. Who's that little guy trying to eat your shoes?"

"Eat my…oh good grief. Stop it, Chipper." She chuckled and pushed him back inside before pulling the door closed behind her. "That's Piper's new puppy. He swallowed something he shouldn't have and ended up at the vet's. He's doing okay but she wanted him close by so she can check on him when she takes breaks. Are you looking for Emma? If so, she's in the training ring out back."

He frowned. "The training ring? Then, nothing happened? Nothing's wrong?"

"What do you—oh, all the police cars." She grinned. "Amazing isn't it, how loved and accepted Emma is in the police community? Apparently after everyone recovered from yesterday's antics they wanted to come over and show their support for Emma and DCA. It's practically a county fair out there. Go on. Everything's fine.

If Angel and I need anything, which I'm sure we won't, we'll holler out the back door."

He hesitated, thinking about the various leads he and his fellow officers were wading through. With all the police cars out front, the likelihood of anyone trying to break into the house right now was about zero. But still. He didn't want Barbara left unprotected if someone was intent on coming after Angel.

"Where's Bogie? Is he out back, too?"

"No, he's inside with Jason. We're totally secure here. You're welcome to come in if you want."

Relief eased the tension in his shoulders. "No, that's good. Just wanted to make sure all was well. Thanks."

He strode around the left side of the house. County fair seemed an apt description as he stopped to take everything in. Emma was sitting on her Appaloosa in the middle of the ring. Piper was several yards away, walking down a row of happy-looking K-9s. Most of them were perfectly behaved, sitting and staying as instructed. Two, a pair of black Labs he remembered were being trained for a SAR team in Boise, were anything but obeying orders. Instead of sitting, they were doing their own version of search-and-rescue, pouncing on anything that moved in the dirt. Macon chuckled as they both went for a dragonfly and fell on top of each other.

Their audience, sitting on top of or lounging against the white three-rail fence, egged the Labs on, laughing and whistling.

Piper aimed an exasperated look at the worst offenders in her audience, who simply shrugged and laughed. She rolled her eyes and went after the two rebel K-9s, determined to get them to line up with the others.

Macon waited by the back deck, taking inventory of

everyone there, human and otherwise. He was surprised to see Chief Walters with his K-9, Buddy. The dog's face was so white and he was so slow getting up and down these days that he was basically already retired. He was also mostly deaf and none of the shenanigans were making a dent in his nap as he lay on the grass at the chief's feet.

Even more surprising than seeing the chief here was that the office manager, Theresa Norwood, was there. She rarely ever left the office. It was her own little fiefdom. But then again, she was the chief's shadow. If he was out having fun, she was usually with him. There was no secret that she was head over heels for him and he for her. But they'd never admit it and seemed to think no one else knew.

Cal Hoover was there with his German shepherd, Ruby, whom Emma had trained years ago. Brady Nichols had his yellow lab, Winnie, sitting at his feet. And while their best detective, Margaret Avery, didn't have a K-9, the rookie beside her, Ava Callan, did. Her dog was yet another German shepherd, Lacey.

A few of the officers and K-9s weren't there, like Jenny in dispatch. No doubt she was at the station, handling the phones until the night shift dispatcher arrived. Dillon Diaz wasn't there either, but he probably would have been if he could be. Like most at Jasper PD, he was a fan of the Daniels Canine Academy. Emma had not only trained most of the dogs for their police department, she'd worked with charities and did fundraisers to purchase and pay for the training. Since police-quality trained K-9s could run anywhere from a few thousand dollars to nearly twenty, depending on how specialized they were, that was no small savings. The little town of

Jasper had a higher K-9 to human officer ratio than any other department in Idaho because of Emma's firm belief in the benefits of having K-9s in law enforcement.

The one person not here who was definitely no surprise was Captain Rutledge. He alone was the voice *against* the K-9 program. He disliked dogs in general and felt they were a distraction from what he called "real" police work. His attitude was puzzling, given that the Jasper K-9s had saved so many lives over the years. And they were critical to the success of the drug enforcement efforts in the county. But Rutledge made no secret that he'd eliminate the program once he became chief.

If he became chief.

Rutledge seemed to think it was a foregone conclusion that once Walters retired, he would take his place. And it did seem as if the chief was leaning that way. Again, understandable since Rutledge was so smart and had an incredible knack for strategic planning. His photographic memory and ability to solve problems was a gift. And he knew it. But his condescending attitude and lack of interpersonal skills meant that most of the officers couldn't stand to be around him.

Macon had tried not to let the whispers and gripes around the station influence his own opinion of Rutledge. But the man seemed to go out of his way to try to annoy Macon. Maybe it was his way of razzing the new guy. But that high school bully attitude had no place in a professional environment where trusting your fellow officer could mean the difference between life and death. Macon, like many others, fervently hoped that the chief chose someone else to succeed him.

Macon headed toward the others. A cheer went up just as he leaned against the fence. At first he thought his fellow officers were teasing him for finally showing up. But they weren't cheering *him*. They were cheering Emma. She was taking her bows at the end of the K-9 line beside the two rebellious Labs. Both of them were now sitting upright like the other dogs, the picture of perfect obedience.

Piper was shaking her head, but grinning. She bowed in deference to Emma's training expertise, then mounted the Appaloosa.

Macon leaned against the fence beside Cal. "Why is the horse there?"

Cal nodded in greeting. "I'm not really sure. I thought Emma had taken the horse out for exercise. But then Piper brought out the dogs. It's impressive, isn't it? How the horse doesn't shy away from the dogs even when they bark? And the dogs don't mind the horse even when Emma had it trotting around the ring earlier."

"Desensitizing training."

Cal gave him a funny look. "What?"

"Special training Emma does to keep the animals comfortable in certain situations, like around sudden loud noises. Since she trains K-9s for a variety of police departments, they need to be conditioned to work around horses in case they ever work with equestrian units."

"Makes sense, I suppose."

"In addition to training all the dogs on the basics of police work and taking down bad guys, she specializes in scent training for some of the dogs, for drug detection and bomb-sniffing. It just depends on the needs of the department that owns each dog. That yellow Lab on the end is going to work with a bomb unit in McCall. She and Piper just finished certifying a bloodhound for search-and-rescue. They take turns hiding in the foothills past the kennels and teach dogs to find them and alert on their position." He was going to say more, but when he glanced at Cal again, he saw him grinning and shaking his head. "What's so amusing?"

Cal chuckled. "It's just that you've been with Jasper PD for all of a hot minute. I've been here for years. Emma trained my dog, all of our dogs except the chief's old guy, Buddy. And you're telling me what types of training she does. It's just…funny. It's also telling."

Macon turned to face him. "Telling?"

"You like her."

Macon snorted and turned back toward the fence. "All of Jasper PD likes her or they wouldn't be here showing their support."

"Um-hmm."

"Shut up, Cal."

Cal laughed and clasped him on the shoulder. "See you tomorrow, Macon. The wife and kids are waiting dinner on me. I'd say take good care of Emma when we all leave, but I know you will. Come on, Ruby. Heel." He was laughing as he headed toward his car with his K-9 trotting happily alongside him.

Macon greeted a few of the others but his attention was mainly centered on the incredibly gifted woman putting the dogs through their paces for her audience. He didn't know who had organized this impromptu session, but the happiness on Emma's face was the reward. He didn't realize how stressed the recent events had made her until he saw her like this, with her guard down, just enjoying life. Which had him itching to get back to his case files. He wanted this thing done, closed, so she could continue to laugh and smile the way she was right now.

Then she looked at him.

Her smile, if anything, became more bright. Her eyes danced with pleasure as she gave him a wave. Someone next to him shoved him good-naturedly and he returned Emma's wave. They could tease him all they wanted. All he cared about right now was seeing more of that smile of hers. And making her safe.

"Why didn't anyone tell me we were having a party?"

Macon stiffened at the unwelcome voice behind him. The ring went silent. The smiles on everyone's faces disappeared.

Captain Rutledge had shown up after all.

Chapter Fourteen

When Rutledge arrived at the training ring, Emma could have sworn the temperature outside dropped ten degrees. She hadn't spoken to him much over the years and he hadn't sought her out, no doubt because of his reputation of complaining that the K-9 program was too much overhead for a small police force like Jasper's. Never mind that the initial cost of obtaining each dog had been covered by Emma's fundraising efforts. Or that her continued fundraising provided reduced-cost veterinarian care to the K-9s. And that the officers themselves footed the bills for their food. None of that seemed to sway Rutledge's negative opinion. Still, even knowing his views, and having heard officers complain about him, it had been shocking to see the negative effect he had on their morale the moment he'd appeared.

Rutledge was speaking to Chief Walters and Cal Hoover about something. The other officers had edged away from the group. Emma glanced at Macon, curious about his reaction. His expression appeared to be carefully blank, but he, too, had moved away from the trio. Was it to give them privacy? Or because he didn't want to be near Rutledge, either? He pulled out his cell phone and looked at the screen before putting the phone to his ear. Maybe he'd stepped away to take a call.

Everyone's reactions to the captain had her wondering about the rumors that Walters was going to choose Rutledge as his successor. From what she'd seen, Hoover inspired much more respect from his fellow officers. And he got along with everyone. Of course, Emma was biased. Cal had been a friend of her father's. And he was a huge supporter of her K-9 program.

Whatever Rutledge had come here to discuss must have been important, because all three men—Rutledge, the chief and Cal—turned and headed toward their cars. The station manager, Theresa, nudged Buddy awake and snapped a leash onto his collar. She gently urged the aging dog along, then stopped to tell Macon something. He nodded and she headed to her car, too.

"Emma, are we going to do more training today?" Piper asked as she crossed the ring. She'd just finished putting Elton back in his stall.

Emma glanced at the remaining officers, gauging their interest. But Rutledge's appearance, and the chief and Cal leaving, had changed the atmosphere. It was getting late anyway. She'd thoroughly enjoyed the camaraderie and levity her unexpected visitors had created. It was a welcome respite from the stress she'd been under. But that was over now. However, it didn't have to be over forever. She had an idea of how she could recapture that closeness and fun again.

"We're done for today," she told Piper. "If you'll lead the dogs back inside, I'll be there in a few minutes to help feed them and settle them down for the night."

"Sounds good." Piper opened the gate at the far end of the ring that led directly into the kennel building. A quick command and the dogs came running. The ones more toward the end of their training at DCA were more sedate and calm about leaving the ring. The rest of them, particularly the two SAR Labs, lost all signs of decorum and were barking and spinning around like a circus act.

Piper resorted to bribing the last of the stragglers with treats to get them to leave the ring. A few smiles and scattered laughs followed her departure. But it was clear everyone was getting ready to leave.

Emma hurried to the fence to catch them before they took off. "Thank you all for coming. It was an unexpected pleasure. You're welcome to stop by any time. And if you ever want refresher training for you and your K-9 partners, please let me know and I'll get you on the schedule. I'd also like to make an announcement. Since the DCA ten-year anniversary celebration we had several months ago was so fun, I've decided to make it an annual affair. I hope you'll all come for the eleventh anniversary party next year."

A cheer went up and she laughed. "We'll make it even bigger and better than the last one. I'd like to plan a K-9 skill demonstration for you and your families, too. Is that something you'd like?"

Macon smiled and nodded as the others assured her they'd love it.

"Great. Since I've never put on an official demonstration before, I'll have to plan everything out and get some practice in ahead of time. Would anyone be interested in an anniversary-planning cookout in a month or two? I might even make some of my mom's famous huckleberry pie."

The enthusiastic response to her impromptu plan was so overwhelming that she was wiping away tears of gratitude in between the hugs and offers of help. She was still trying to hide her tears and wipe her eyes as the last of the officers drove away; everyone, that is, except Macon. He took one look at her tear-streaked face and immediately climbed over the three-rail fence and dropped down at her side. Before she could ask him what he was doing, he gently pulled her against his chest and wrapped his arms around her.

The hug was so unexpected, but so wonderful, that she immediately sank into the embrace and tightened her arms around his waist.

"It's okay, Emma," he whispered against the top of her head as he gently rubbed her back. "I know you're under tremendous stress right now. But I promise this is all going to end soon. I'm doing everything I can to find Angel's family and catch whoever tried to break into your home. And until I do, I'll make sure you're never alone. Okay?"

She blinked in surprise, still hugging him close. "Thank you, Macon."

"Any time."

Rather than correct his assumption that she'd cried because of stress or fear, she decided to let him think that was the cause. Mainly because she didn't want to end the hug to tell him.

The tears were because she was so overwhelmed by the acceptance and love she'd received today. She'd always felt close and friendly with the Jasper PD officers. But the way they'd circled the wagons to help her in her time of need was beyond anything she'd have ever expected. It had her missing Rick and Susan so much. But it also had her so very grateful for the people in her life, and newly aware that there were more people who cared about her than she'd ever realized.

And one of them, whether he admitted it openly or not, was Macon.

That shouldn't matter. In spite of all her admonitions to herself that she didn't want to risk her heart, or risk getting hurt, she didn't want this hug to end. But she'd held on to him so long it was going to get awkward if she didn't let go soon. And Piper would start wondering why she hadn't gone to the kennels yet to help her.

She loosened her arms and pulled back to thank him for caring, for wanting to make sure she was okay. But the second she looked up into those warm brown eyes staring down at her with raw male hunger, she was lost. She didn't know which of them reached for the other first, but suddenly they were in each other's arms and she was happily drowning in the hottest, most all-consuming kiss she'd ever experienced.

Holy fry sauce, did this man know how to stoke a fire.

He was so gentle, achingly sweet. And yet there was a raw hunger she sensed in him, just beneath the surface, as if he was struggling to hold himself back. This wasn't a man who wanted to overpower her with his strength and size. Instead, he was focused on giving her pleasure and allowing her to take it as far as she was willing to go. That combination, his focus on her needs, was heady, like a drug. And she wanted more, so much more.

She slid her greedy fingers across his face, reveling in the raspiness of the light stubble as her tongue dueled with his. He groaned low in his throat and tightened his hold, answering her hunger with more of his own. The beauty of it nearly made her weep. She could not get enough of this incredible man.

"Hey, Emma, are you—oh! Sorry! My bad."

Piper's voice was like a bucket of ice water across Emma's nerve endings. She jerked back from Macon and whirled around just in time to see Piper ducking into the kennel building. She groaned.

Macon laughed.

She turned back to face him and couldn't help laughing too. "That was…"

"Amazing?"

"Unexpected."

"I like amazing better," he said.

"How about hot?"

He grinned. "Definitely hot."

He was about to say something else when his phone buzzed in his pocket. His eyes widened in dismay. "Ah, shoot. I forgot." He yanked the phone out and checked the screen. "I'm so sorry, Emma. I need to take this. It's important." He stepped a few feet away. "Hello, yeah. No, I haven't left yet. Okay, yes."

Emma sighed and lifted a shaky hand to adjust her ponytail, which had come half-undone. Her heart was still racing and she drew slow, deep breaths trying to regain control. As Macon continued to talk to whoever was on the other end of the phone, she looked over her shoulder. No sign of Piper, but Emma knew what she was doing. Feeding and watering a dozen dogs, making sure their enclosures were clean and locking things up for the night. And she shouldn't have to do all of that alone. Guilt had her wanting to race to the building. But she couldn't run off without wrapping up whatever had just happened. And how exactly did one wrap up after that earth-tilting kiss? Should she just say, *hey, thanks, see ya later*?

She chuckled and he looked at her, a brow arched in

question. But since he was still talking on the phone, she simply stood and waited for him to finish.

Finally, he shoved the phone back in his pocket and crossed to her. "I really hate to—"

"Rock my world, then take off?"

He grinned with obvious male satisfaction. "Something like that." His smile faded. "A little earlier I got a lead in the investigation. I arranged for Jason to stay a little while longer and was supposed to meet my contact a few minutes ago. But I got distracted by all the activity in the ring. You put on an amazing show, by the way."

"Thanks. It was spur-of-the-moment but a ton of fun."

"It was. I really have to go, Emma. But I'll be back in a couple of hours. We should probably talk about what just happened. I know it was completely inappropriate since I'm supposed to be protecting you, not taking advantage of—"

"Don't," she told him. "Don't you dare say it was a mistake. Do what you need to do. But don't ruin a kiss like that with an apology."

"Emma—"

She waggled her fingers in the air in answer as she hurried toward the kennels.

Chapter Fifteen

Macon passed a slow-moving car, anxious to return to Emma's place. He'd been gone much longer than he'd meant to, but at least he knew Jason was there watching after her. Having Jason's police car parked in front of the house was a great deterrent, but Macon wouldn't feel completely secure about her safety unless he was there.

His hands tightened on the steering wheel. At least he'd made some progress tonight. He could finally cross Hugh and William off his list of people connected to Angel *and* the break-in attempt. His source's information had been spot-on about where the teens would be tonight. That had allowed Macon to surprise them and he'd finally gotten to confront them about inconsistencies in their stories. A few calls later and he'd corroborated their alibis. They were in the clear.

Kyle Norvell, on the other hand, definitely was *not* in the clear.

The kid was avoiding him at every turn. He hadn't shown up for his most recently scheduled work days at DCA. And his parents were covering for him, making excuses. If they'd just get Kyle to sit down with him and be honest about where he kept disappearing every night, per the tip that Macon had received from William, then Kyle could be cleared, too.

Or he could become the number one suspect.

He glanced at the clock on the SUV's dash and grimaced. He needed to reassure Jason that he'd be there soon. The kid was a newlywed and would be champing at the bit to get home. This wasn't the first time he'd been late because of Macon. He'd have to make it up to Jason by assigning someone else his shift tomorrow.

Pulling to the shoulder of the road to make the call, he got out his phone, then frowned. He'd turned it off earlier tonight, not wanting to risk any noise that might alert the teens as he sneaked up on their little campsite in the woods. He'd meant to turn it back on when he'd left and had forgot.

As soon as he powered it up, messages started filling his screen. He chuckled when he saw all of them were from Jason, and most of them were telling him that Tashya was going to put him in the doghouse if he didn't get home soon.

When Macon read Jason's last message, he swore. Tashya's parents were at her and Jason's house for a visit and she'd insisted he come home. The young rookie had made the assumption, based on Macon's original plan on when he'd return, that it would be okay to head home. He'd reasoned that Macon would arrive a few minutes after he left, so he hoped it would be all right.

Hell, no, it was *not* all right.

Jason had left two hours ago. Other than Bogie, there was no one else there protecting Emma.

He swore again and was just about to call Emma when she called him. Relief flooded through him as he answered and pulled back onto the road.

"Emma, hey. Sorry for the delay. I'm on my way and—"

"Macon. Someone's on the property. They must have broken into the kennel buildings. The dogs are loose and running all over the place. Should I call 911?"

A cold chill ran down Macon's spine. He slammed the accelerator, making the SUV jump forward. "Have you seen anyone? Have they tried to break inside?"

"No. All I've seen, and heard, are the dogs. I suppose Piper could have accidentally left the main gate open. But each of the kennels inside also has a gate. It's hard to imagine her being that careless."

"Agreed. Someone's definitely behind this. They're probably trying to draw you outside. Where are you?"

"The family room right now. I put Angel in her crib and grabbed my pistol. I turned out all the lights and have been peeking through the blinds. Jason already left. Bogie's inside, with me."

He was totally going to murder Jason Wright.

"Good. Stay inside. Call 911, but I'm not waiting around. I'm almost there. Might as well take advantage of this opportunity to try to sneak up and catch whoever is terrorizing you. Let Jenny know I'll park my SUV on Elm Street, just before the entrance to DCA. She'll need to alert the other officers to go in silent and be aware there's an armed officer already on the premises. I'd rather not get hit by friendly fire."

"Macon, maybe you should wait. I don't want you to get hurt."

The concern in her voice was almost his undoing. He wanted nothing more than to run inside the house and hold her close, to see for himself that she was safe. But being in fear every day was no way to live. He needed to end this. So instead, he tried to reassure her, even as he crept along the tree line on the left side of the property.

"That's my job, Emma. Don't worry about me. I'm going in on foot so I don't scare the intruder off. Stay inside, keep the doors locked. If anything, and I mean *anything* happens that makes you worry about your own safety, call me and barricade yourself with Angel in her room. I'll come running."

"Thanks, Macon. And please, please be careful."

"You too. Make that call. I'm at DCA now."

"Calling dispatch."

He left the phone and ringer on this time, just in case Emma needed to call him. It's not like it would add much to the noise outside if it did ring. The dogs were barking and he could see several of them off in the distance, milling around the outside of the kennel building and the barn. Hopefully they wouldn't come running toward him and give away his presence until he figured out where the intruder was—assuming they were still on the property. He was betting they were and that the stunt with the dogs was to trick Emma into going outside—especially since there wasn't a police car parked in front of her house anymore.

Jason would be lucky to have a job tomorrow once Macon was through with him.

Banking on the assumption that the dogs were hanging around the outbuildings because that's where the intruder was, he hurried toward that location, using the trees, bushes and darkness for cover.

His weapon was drawn and he had a small flashlight at the ready to flick on and illuminate a target.

A distant bark sounded from inside the house. Bogie. He was getting nervous. Either he'd sensed the intruder, or he'd sensed Macon. Or maybe backup was already here, following in Macon's footsteps. He needed to find the intruder, fast, before the dogs alerted on anyone else and revealed their positions.

Crouching down behind some trees about ten yards off to the side of the kennels, Macon scanned the outside of the building. There, on the far side nearest the barn, a shadow moved. Was it one of the dogs? No, a dog wouldn't crouch down like that and stay in one spot.

Macon eased around another tree. Closer. Closer. Ten yards away. Nine. Eight.

Suddenly two of the dogs came running toward him, howling like a couple of coyotes. It was the black Labs Piper had struggled to keep under control in the training ring. The shadow by the building jumped up and took off toward the barn.

Macon leaped over the two dogs and sprinted after him. "Police, stop!" He snapped the flashlight on as he rounded the barn.

The fleeing figure was dressed completely in black, with a hoodie covering his head. But he hadn't thought to wear black shoes. The flash of his white sneakers was like a beacon, shining in the beam of Macon's flashlight.

"Stop or I'll shoot," Macon yelled, putting on a burst of speed.

The man ignored him and ran past the barn. He tried to leap over the three-rail fence enclosing the training ring. Instead, he slammed against it and fell in the dirt. He swore and scrambled to his feet, then started climbing.

Macon shoved his pistol in his holster and vaulted over the fence, landing on top of the suspect on the other side. The other man cried out as they both crashed to the ground. The flashlight skittered across the dirt a few feet away.

"Freeze, you scumbag," Macon yelled as he wrestled with the flailing man.

They rolled several times until Macon slammed him onto his stomach. Macon straddled his back and shoved the suspect's right arm up between his shoulder blades.

The suspect cried out in pain. "Okay, okay, please, stop!"

Macon leaned across him and snagged his flashlight. After snatching off the man's hoodie, Macon grabbed his hair and yanked back his head, shining the light on his face.

"Don't shoot! Don't shoot! Please!" Tears streaked down his pale face as he begged for his life.

Macon swore in disgust.

It was Kyle Norvell.

Chapter Sixteen

Emma paced back and forth in her family room, watching the blue and red lights flashing against the closed blinds. Once again her driveway had several Jasper police vehicles. But other than Cal letting her know a few minutes ago that everything was secure and that they were rounding up the K-9s, no one was telling her anything. She was told to wait inside.

It was frustrating not knowing what was happening on her own property. Bogie was handling the situation far better than her. He'd parked himself near the front door, ears cocked forward like a neon sign on top of a taxi saying *on-duty*. No one was getting inside the house unless Bogie let them. Even Cal had been forced to wait to talk to her until she'd ordered Bogie to stand down.

She appreciated the K-9's protection and loyalty. But she didn't appreciate having to wait for more updates. Cal had said Macon caught the suspect and was okay. That was a relief, all the way around. But what did it really mean? He'd caught the suspect who'd let the dogs out? Or the suspect who was responsible for all the strange happenings lately? Most importantly, what did this mean for Angel? Emma had just gotten used to the idea that the person who left her must have been her mother. But would her mother do all these crazy things, like let the dogs out of their kennels?

If this latest occurrence was related to Angel, that could mean the police knew who she belonged to. That could also mean Angel wouldn't be here much longer with Emma taking care of her.

Just thinking about that possibility had her throat tightening and her heart squeezing in her chest. She'd been trying so hard not to become attached. But when you fed, bathed, clothed and cuddled a precious, sweet little baby how the heck were you not supposed to care about her and what might happen to her? She deserved to be loved and cherished, as all children did. Emma didn't know how she was going to survive giving her up. Especially if the parents turned out not to be the caring, loving people the baby deserved.

Calm down. You're making huge leaps in logic. Tonight's events may have nothing to do with Angel.

The motion-sensor floodlights flickered on outside. Voices sounded, along with the crunch of the gravel driveway beneath shoes. She rushed to the front windows. Bogie growled his displeasure as she peeked through the blinds.

"It's okay, boy," she reassured him. "I'm safe. Just trying to see what's happening."

As she watched, four Jasper police officers rounded the end of the house and headed toward one of the police cars. Relief swept through her as she recognized Macon with them. Even though Cal had said Macon was okay, she'd needed to see for herself. Cal was walking beside him. Brady and Dillon took up the rear. And in the middle, with his handcuffed arm being grasped by Macon, was Kyle Norvell.

Emma sucked in a sharp breath. No! Kyle couldn't be the one behind everything. He couldn't be. But as she watched, Macon opened the rear door of the closest police car and forced Kyle inside. Was Macon arresting him?

"Oh no, you don't." She threw open the front door, ignoring Bogie's barks, and jogged down the front steps. "Macon, stop. Let him go."

Macon shut the car door and turned around, frowning down at her. "Emma, you shouldn't be out here. What if Kyle's working with a partner? You could still be in danger." He motioned to Brady. "Get her inside."

Brady hurried to Emma.

A low-throated growl had him stopping as he reached for her. Bogie's teeth were bared as he stood in front of Emma, his hackles raised.

Macon issued a command in German along with "Bogart" and Bogie immediately stopped growling. But he didn't move away from Emma.

Macon exchanged a surprised look with her.

She crossed her arms and arched a brow. "Bogie knows I don't want to go back inside the house and no one is going to force me. Now what's going on? Why is Kyle in handcuffs?"

Macon's eyes narrowed. "Your resident juvenile delinquent is the one who trespassed on your property and let all the dogs out. Tomorrow, after the sun comes up, we'll search for more evidence. I won't be surprised if we find proof that he's the one who tried to break into your house."

A pounding noise sounded behind him.

Kyle was banging on the police car's window, his terrified gaze pleading with Emma.

Macon motioned to Dillon. "Take him to the station. I'll meet you there."

Dillon carefully avoided Bogie and got into the driver's seat.

Emma spoke a low command to Bogie. He ran and vaulted onto the hood of the car, barking and growling as if he was going to dive through the windshield to get Dillon.

"What the—" Macon whirled around toward Emma. "You've broken my dog."

She crossed her arms. "He's not broken. He's loyal to me *and* to you. But if either of us seems to be in danger, he's going to go with his instincts and protect us."

He shook his head in disgust and strode to the car. He gave Bogie a command in German and the dog immediately stopped growling and hopped off the car. Dillon started the engine, but hesitated, watching as Emma started forward.

Macon moved to block her path.

"Don't," she snapped.

"Don't what?"

"Don't let Dillon take Kyle to the station. Let me talk to him." She motioned toward the back window where Kyle was yelling and pleading for help. "He wants to tell us something."

"He wants to save his sorry butt by telling more lies."

"Where's your compassion for a young, scared kid?"

"Compassion? Look at how he's dressed, Emma. All in black so no one would see him in the dark. He had a hoodie pulled over his face to hide his identity. Today's been warm for this time of year so it sure as certain wasn't because he was cold. I found him skulking around the kennel building, hiding in the shadows. When

I identified myself as a police officer, he took off running, away from me. What do you think all that means? That he's innocent and just happened to be on a stroll on your property miles from his house at the same time that someone released all your very expensive K-9s?"

Emma's face flushed hot at the lecture. She glanced at Cal and Brady, who'd taken several steps back as if to distance themselves from the discussion.

She cleared her throat. "What if I refuse to press charges?"

Macon's jaw tightened. He motioned to Dillon to cut the engine.

"And why would you do that, Emma?" His voice was hard, cold.

She drew a deep, bracing breath and prayed that she could make him understand. "When I look at Kyle, I see myself. When my foster father was killed in the line of duty, I couldn't cope. I rebelled and fell in with the wrong crowd. I did some stupid, awful things. I deserved to go to jail, maybe even prison. But Chief Walters had compassion for me. He understood what I was going through and gave me a second chance. It's because of that compassion that I turned my life around. Kyle's been through some rocky times, too, and he deserves a second chance. If you arrest him now, the judge could revoke the conditions of his release for his last offense. He could go to prison."

Empathy had flickered in his gaze as she spoke. But when she finished, she could tell by his hard, unyielding look that the empathy wasn't for Kyle. It was for her.

"Kyle isn't you, Emma. And he already had a second chance, working community service at DCA. He threw that away when he trespassed on your property, jeopardizing thousands of dollars' worth of animals. And if he's behind everything else, he's done a heck of a lot more than that. If he ends up in prison, it's because he earned it."

Ignoring their audience, Emma stepped close and feathered her hand against his cheek. "Like you said, Kyle and I are different. Some people need more than a second chance to turn the corner, to make better choices. Please. Do this for me. Give Kyle an opportunity to explain what he was doing on my property tonight. That's all I'm asking. Just listen to him, *really* listen."

He stared down at her a long moment, his expression unreadable. Then he swore and, with a surprisingly gentle motion, pulled her hand down from his face. "If I do this, and he can't come up with anything plausible to explain his actions, will you agree to press charges?"

She glanced at Kyle's tear-streaked face, remembering another night much like this one when she'd been the one in the back of the police car.

"Emma?"

"I don't know, okay? I just need to hear his side before you lock him away. Please."

Obviously not happy with her reply, he glanced past her at Cal, as if silently asking the more senior officer's opinion. Emma turned to look at Cal, too, but Macon was already heading to the driver's door of the police car. He tapped on the window.

Dillon rolled it down, looking at him in question.

"Change of plans," Macon said. "We're going to interview Kyle here first. *Then* we'll take him to the station."

Macon issued a command to Bogie. Then he stalked to Emma and gestured toward the house. "I'm not convinced that Kyle doesn't have a partner in crime lurking in the trees out here watching what's going on. Let's take this inside where you'll be safe."

She glanced past the reach of the floodlights to the darkened silhouettes of trees at the edge of her property and suddenly felt very exposed and vulnerable.

Macon grabbed her hand and pulled her toward the steps while Bogie trotted after them.

A few minutes later everyone was seated in the family room and the interrogation had begun. In spite of Emma's protests, Kyle was still in handcuffs. But at least he was on the couch now instead of locked in the back of a patrol car.

Macon held up his hand, stopping Kyle mid-sentence. "That's a load of crap you're selling. You expect me to believe you took your mom's car, left it parked down the street so no one would see it, dressed like a burglar and sneaked onto this property...*to visit the dogs*?"

"It's the truth! I swear!" Kyle looked at Emma sitting by the fireplace on the other side of the room, his eyes silently pleading for help. Macon had insisted that she stay far away from Kyle, with Bogie once again on guard in front of her in full protection mode. But she wasn't going to ignore what was happening and remain silent.

She smiled reassuringly. "Go on, Kyle, tell Macon everything. He's a reasonable man, but you have to be honest."

Macon gave her an aggravated look, then turned back toward Kyle.

Kyle licked his lips. He nodded at Emma, then straightened instead of cowering against the back of the couch. His cheeks flushed a bright red as he spoke.

"I like the dogs, okay? The horses, too, but I really like the dogs. They don't yell at me or judge me. They're always in a good mood and happy to see me. They make me feel good, you know?" A single tear slid down his cheek and he brushed his face against his shoulder to wipe it away, his face flushing even redder.

"What's that got to do with you sneaking onto the property at night?" Macon demanded. But his voice had lost some of its edge.

"It's stupid, okay? I know it's stupid. But, well, you've been accusing me of things and keep wanting to question me so I've been avoiding you."

"No kidding."

"I've been avoiding you," Kyle continued. "And since you've been here every day, I haven't been able to see the dogs. So I…" He swallowed, looking miserable. "I've been sneaking out here at night to pet them and check on them."

"I don't believe you."

"It's true! I've been visiting them for weeks." His eyes widened at his admission and he aimed an apologetic look at Emma. "I'm sorry, Ms. Daniels. But it's true. I've been sneaking onto your property ever since I started working here. I'm the tough guy, you know? With Hugh and William. I can't act all soft and stuff in front of them. I've never had a dog of my own and they're really cool. I really do love those dogs."

Emma's throat was tight. The pain and embarrassment in his voice had her wanting to cross the room to wrap him in a tight hug. But she didn't dare try, positive that Macon or the others would stop her.

"I know you do, Kyle," she assured him. "You're saying you wanted to see the dogs but didn't want anyone else to know you liked them? Because you thought it would make you seem too soft, too vulnerable, if your friends knew?"

He nodded, looking miserable.

"If that's true, then why let the dogs out of the kennels?" Macon asked. "You endangered them. They could have run off, gone out to the road, maybe been hit by a car."

Kyle's eyes widened. "I didn't let them out. They were already out when I got here. I was going to try to round them up, get them back in their kennels. Then you came running at me so I took off."

"I announced that I was a police officer. Why didn't you stop?"

Kyle rolled his eyes. "You're kidding, right? I knew what would happen if you caught me. You'd assume I'd done something wrong and would throw me in the back of a police car." Kyle aimed a mutinous expression at Macon.

Dillon coughed as if to cover a laugh.

Before Macon could ask another question, Kyle volunteered, "Besides, I couldn't be sure you were a real cop in the dark. It could have been the other guy, trying to trick me."

The room went silent and every eye was suddenly watching Kyle intently.

"What other guy?" Macon asked.

Kyle rolled his eyes again. "Are you even *trying* to listen to me? I told you the dogs were out when I got here. There was another guy skulking around. He ran into the same trees where you came running out. I wasn't sure what to think and took off. But I swear I didn't let any of the dogs out. I was there to check on them. That's it."

Cal stepped forward. "You saw someone else out there tonight, aside from Lieutenant Ridley?"

"Yes, sir. He was wearing dark clothes. Like me. And like I said, he ran into the trees, just past the kennels."

"Kyle," Macon said, recapturing his attention. "Where was this other man when you first saw him?"

"Outside, out back. Running."

"Out back, meaning behind this house?"

"Yeah. He was running across the yard, sprinting past the paddock, the training ring. I ducked behind the kennels and he ran right past me."

"Did you get a good look at him? Did you recognize him?"

He shrugged. "It was pretty dark. I was just trying not to let anyone see me. And I wanted to get the dogs back in their kennels after he was gone, so I was waiting to make sure he'd left."

Cal drew his weapon and tapped Dillon on the shoulder. "Let's check it out." They headed outside.

Macon and Brady exchanged an uneasy glance before Macon continued the questioning. "Kyle, those two officers who just left are going to look for signs of this guy you supposedly saw. Are you wasting their time?"

He vigorously shook his head. "No, I swear. Like I said, I didn't do anything. Except…" His face reddened again and he glanced at Emma before looking down at the floor.

"Except what?" Macon asked.

"It's okay," Emma called out. "Whatever it is, it's okay. Just tell the truth, Kyle."

He let out a shaky breath. "I'm really sorry, Ms. Daniels. I know it was wrong. But I didn't think it would cause any real harm." Another tear slid down his cheek.

"Kyle—" Macon warned.

"I fed the dogs," Kyle blurted out, as if he was admitting to an egregious sin. "I know it's wrong because they belong to other people and all. And some of them are on specific diets. But they're so fun when you give them treats. They jump all over you and lick you and they really enjoy them. I feed them treats every time I sneak onto the property."

"Oh for Pete's sake," Macon said. "This is ridiculous. You do *not* sneak onto DCA property to feed the dogs."

"I do too! I'm telling the truth. And I can prove it! I keep the treats hidden in an old barrel behind the kennel, where Ms. Daniels grows flowers."

"In a barrel." Sarcasm and disbelief practically dripped from Macon's words.

"Yes, sir. Right outside the back door of the kennel building."

Macon muttered beneath his breath. "Brady, I hate to ask—"

"I'm on it. I'll radio Cal and Dillon to let them know I'm heading out to the kennel building."

Brady hurried outside, his boots echoing on the stairs.

"Kyle, if you really saw someone else—"

"I did. Cross my heart, hope to die."

"If you saw someone, do you think you could work with a sketch artist to come up with a picture of him?"

He shrugged. "I dunno. Maybe. It was dark. But there are lights out by the kennels, and the training ring. I caught a glimpse of his face here and there. He was tall. That I remember."

"As tall as me?"

He chuckled. "Dude. You're like the tallest cop in the

police department. Nah, shorter than you. But not by a whole lot. Maybe three or four inches."

"So, about six feet tall?"

"Or a little under. Yeah, seems about right. Skinny, too. White guy. That I'm sure of. He was real pale under the lights."

Macon's cell phone buzzed. "You're on speaker. Go ahead, Cal."

"We found a trail. It leads from the back deck of Emma's house, past the outbuildings, and into the trees. Comparing those shoe prints to the ones out where you tackled Kyle, I'd say they're different. The kid was right. Someone else was out here tonight, but they appear to be long gone."

Macon sighed and scrubbed the stubble on his chin. "Thanks, Cal." He ended the call.

The phone immediately buzzed again. "You're on speaker, Brady. Let us have it."

"I dug around in the barrel. There's a whole bunch of purple and white flowers. And one enormous bag of dog jerky, Meaty Bones and rawhide chews."

Macon shook his head in defeat. "Understood. Thanks, Brady."

"Should I bring the dog treats back to the house?"

"I don't give a flying—"

"Yes, please," Emma interrupted, trying not to laugh. "Some of the dogs really are on special diets. I give them treats, but I have to dole out specific ones to each dog."

"Will do."

Macon pitched his phone onto the side table and stood. "On your feet, Kyle."

Kyle's eyes widened. "You're still arresting me? For feeding the dogs?"

"No, Kyle. I'm not arresting you for feeding the dogs."
Emma hurried to the couch just as Macon jerked Kyle
up and turned him around. Her words of protest died unsaid as Macon unlocked Kyle's handcuffs.

Chapter Seventeen

Emma sipped her coffee, marveling at how beautiful the mountains looked through the kitchen back door. Living in Idaho was a nature lover's dream, with beauty around every corner. She loved everything about it. From the local festivals where everyone gorged on potatoes cooked a dozen different ways, drenched in fry sauce of course, to white water rafting down any of a dozen waterways just outside of Jasper.

Normally, on a gorgeous weekend like this one, she'd feed and water the animals since Piper and Barbara weren't here on weekends. After that, if the weather was this sunny, she'd be grabbing her backpack and hiking into the foothills. Or maybe she'd rent a canoe and enjoy a ride down the Salmon River. But those carefree days were over, at least for now. She had no intention of taking Angel on a raft or hiking in the mountains.

Of course, both Barbara and Piper had offered to help her on weekends because of Angel. But Emma had bought a baby monitor and assured them she would only go outside to do chores when Angel was sleeping. And she'd lock the house up tight. She also wouldn't be gone for more than a few minutes at a time, just to make certain the baby was safe. It would make her chores take a lot longer that way, but it was worth it to make sure that Angel was okay. Of course, she really didn't have to worry today since Macon had spent the night. She and the baby were both safe with him watching over them. All she really needed to worry about was keeping warm. Today had dawned chilly, almost cold, much like the morning Angel had been left on her doorstep.

Taking one last sip from her nearly empty coffee cup, she rinsed it and set it in the sink. Time to get Angel up and change and feed her. Once she was down for a nap, Emma would put the baby monitor receiver in her pocket and go feed the animals. If she didn't do that soon, the dogs would start barking and Presley would be kicking his stall down to get into the pasture.

It was surprising that Angel had slept this late. Normally she'd wake Emma at dawn, crying because of a wet diaper, or hungry for her bottle. It was a blessing that she hadn't this morning, because Emma had been exhausted after everything that had happened last night.

She'd taken advantage of Angel's late morning by taking a quick shower and enjoying a cup of coffee. But now she was starting to get worried. Angel had never slept this late before.

She headed down the hallway, passing Macon's closed door. He was sleeping late, too, for which she was also grateful. He'd still been awake when she'd gone to bed at midnight. The sleep would do him good.

When she opened the door to Angel's room, she stopped in surprise. Macon wasn't in the guest room. He was right here, in the rocking chair, cradling the baby against his chest as both of them slept.

The sight of big, powerful Macon so sweetly holding delicate little Angel had her heart going all gooey and warm. As she watched, the baby stirred, making happy gurgling sounds. Macon instinctively cuddled her closer, gently patting her back. Angel settled down, smacking her little mouth contentedly, and Macon's breaths resumed their deep, even sounds. He hadn't even woken up, and yet he'd automatically soothed the baby and held her protectively. Even Bogie, curled up on the floor, merely blinked his eyes at the interruption, then settled back down to sleep.

Emma pressed her hand to her chest as she watched them. It was such a beautiful sight, the quintessential perfect little family. A strong, handsome father who only used that strength to help others. The beautiful daughter whose innocence and happiness were jealously guarded and cherished. The family dog, curled up and protective of both of them. And the mother, watching it all, her heart near to bursting with joy at the wondrousness of it.

Of course, the Norman Rockwell fantasy wasn't reality. Emma wasn't a mother. Macon wasn't her husband or a father. And Angel was only here until her true parents could be found. Emma would do well to remember that. But the fantasy, as brief as it was, had touched her deeply and had her wondering whether she was wrong to resist her fierce attraction to Macon. And whether maybe the possibility of love, and a real family, was worth the risk of being hurt.

Was it? Worth the risk? Was this what she wanted out of life? Someone like Macon to hold her, to love her every day? A child they'd made together? There was no sense in denying that the idea felt wonderful. But was she really willing to risk allowing herself to love again, especially a policeman, knowing that knock could come on the door one night as it had for her mother, telling her that her husband was dead? She didn't know if she could even survive that kind of loss again, though the idea of a future with Macon had every nerve in her body singing and crying out, *go for it!*

The ringing of the doorbell shook her out of her thoughts. Macon's eyes flew open and his gaze locked onto her. His mouth curved in a smile that had her heart fluttering again.

"Morning," he said.

"Morning." Her voice came out a dry rasp. She cleared her throat. "Someone's at the door. I'll go see who it is."

He was shaking his head before she even finished talking. "I'll get the door. You stay here until I know it's safe." He stood and passed the baby to her, then hurried down the hall.

Emma changed Angel's diaper, then dressed her in a onesie with feet in it to keep her warm.

Footsteps sounded down the hall. Emma turned with the baby in her arms as Macon entered the room. She was just about to ask him who was at the door when he stepped back to let someone else in.

The smile Emma had for Macon faded as she recognized their early-morning surprise visitor. It was Mr. Burns, the caseworker from the Department of Child and Family Services.

MACON HAD HELPED Emma feed the animals or they wouldn't have made it to the police station this quickly, especially since she'd also had to pack a diaper bag for Angel and make up some bottles of formula. Emma was still fighting to hold back tears when he pulled the SUV into a parking spot.

She unclipped her seat belt. "I still can't believe DCF is allowed to show up like that and just steal her."

"He didn't steal her. He took her to a doctor for a routine checkup. You should know more than most that popping in unexpectedly like that is something DCF does on purpose, to catch the fosters off guard. They want to make sure the baby was being well cared for by surprising you. He certainly didn't have any complaints. And it worked out great anyway since our guys need to search your property for evidence from last night's happenings at your place. You won't have to be there while they're running around and you can attend this morning's status meeting. It's a win-win.

"Chief Walters has been asking me to bring you to one of our meetings so you could review some of the background information we've gathered. I just haven't had time to arrange it. Everything worked out for the best with Mr. Burns stopping by unexpectedly. You don't need to worry about Angel. Burns will call me when he's done and we'll pick her up, or have her brought here."

"It still seems fishy to me. What doctor works on Sundays?"

"The kind that works in a hospital. Mr. Burns said the doctor has a contract with DCF, so that's where he took her."

"I don't like it. Angel doesn't know him. She could be scared right now, wondering what's going on."

Macon gave her a droll look. "She was giggling when he strapped her into the car seat."

"She's too young to giggle. It was gas."

He laughed. "Probably so. I appreciate that you're okay not being at your place while our team looks for evidence.

A lot of people wouldn't consent to let us comb over everything when they weren't home."

"Jasper PD is like family to me. I'm not worried about them being out there unsupervised. And Jason's familiar with how I run things and where everything is. He can also help with the animals if something comes up."

"Jason." He practically spat the name. "I still need to talk to him about his failure to keep you safe. He shouldn't have left before I got there."

She put her hand on his. "No, you don't need to talk to him. Trust me, he feels awful and it won't happen again. He was eager to gain your trust again this morning by watching over things."

"He told you that?"

"I inferred it."

He laughed. "I'm still going to talk to him. Eventually. When I'm less angry." He checked the time on his phone. "Kyle and his parents should be here by now. I'll take you to the break room to wait while I speak to them. Then we'll head into the chief's meeting."

They both got out and headed toward the front doors.

"Why are you meeting with Kyle's parents?"

"I need them to sign a consent form so Kyle can work with the sketch artist this morning." He held one of the double doors open for her.

"Mind if I join you? I might be able to help smooth things over. You aren't exactly their favorite person right now."

"Tell me about it. When I drove Kyle home last night, his mother was so mad she wouldn't even talk to me. His father wasn't home, so I didn't get a chance to explain things to him. No telling what version of the story Kyle gave them after I left."

"They're good people. I think they mean well."

"They acted willing to cooperate when you and I went there, but since then, they've done the complete opposite. They lied for him, covered for him every time I tried to find him to ask him more questions."

"They love him and they were protecting him. Let's just get this over with."

Twenty minutes later, Kyle was working with a sketch artist and his parents had apologized repeatedly to Macon over their earlier behavior. It wasn't because of Emma's skills in getting them to calm down, either. It was because Macon had gotten impatient and told them that if they'd made Kyle talk to him instead of covering for him and allowing him to hide out, Macon may not have jumped to the wrong conclusions last night and nearly put Kyle in jail. That realization had them both sputtering. They couldn't sign the consent papers fast enough.

Macon led Emma into the main conference room where the chief, Rutledge, Cal and a few others were discussing all the happenings at DCA. Pens, bright yellow legal pads and folders were scattered around the table. A whiteboard hanging on the far wall displayed a smattering of pictures, including one of Angel and what appeared to be a satellite image of Emma's property showing the various buildings. She was a little disappointed there weren't red strings attaching everything in a spiderweb pattern like she'd seen on TV crime dramas. But she'd learned long ago from her father that real police work wasn't nearly as flashy as those television shows would have you believe.

Emma hadn't been sitting for more than a minute before Rutledge stood, giving her an annoyed look.

"I've seen what I needed to see for now. I'm not going

to waste any more time discussing a K-9 training facility. Cal, if something useful to the investigation comes up, let me know."

Macon squeezed Emma's hand reassuringly beneath the table as Rutledge left the room.

She put on a brave face and smiled as if it hadn't bothered her. But she couldn't help being annoyed by his attitude. She also couldn't help wondering if there may be something more behind his dislike of all things DCA related. For a man who professed that he despised her program, he'd seemingly gone out of his way to show up at her property recently. Was he keeping tabs on her for some reason? Could he be the one behind everything going on? While she couldn't see him as someone who'd kidnap or abandon a baby on her doorstep, she couldn't as easily dismiss the idea of him causing problems at her ranch. Maybe he was trying to harass her, scare her, to get her to close it down?

Macon spread out a group of folders in the middle of the table as he answered a question from the chief.

Emma glanced at the stack and immediately recognized the name on one of the tabs, Maria Loretto. She'd been on the list of foster kids he'd shown her yesterday. Did the entire folder contain information about her?

She leaned slightly forward to read some of the other folder tabs. She barely refrained from rolling her eyes when she saw folders for William, Hugh and Kyle. But there were many others she and Macon had discussed last night, including David Timmons, Kelvin Armstrong, Josh Basham and Wanda Mickelson. There was even one on Celia Banks, which seemed like a complete waste of time. Emma had marked her name with an *L* the other day for low priority. But that was the folder Macon reached for now.

As he browsed through it, the chief aimed a fatherly smile at Emma. "Thanks for coming to the meeting. Macon told me you gave him some insight about some of the people he's been investigating. When he and I spoke this morning, he relayed what you'd said about high and low priority potential suspects. So I had Cal here organize the folders along those lines and update them with recent interview sheets or pictures we've been collecting. As a result, he discovered something I felt that both you and Macon needed to see right away." He waved toward Macon. "From the look on Macon's face, I'm guessing he's seen what Cal pointed out to me. Go ahead. Show her."

Macon pulled two pictures from the folder and set one on the table in front of Emma. "That's what Celia Banks looks like today."

Emma nodded, smiling at the pretty dark-haired, dark-eyed girl she remembered so fondly. She hadn't changed much in the handful of years since Emma had last seen her.

"And this," Macon said, as he placed another picture on top of the first, "is what she looked like when she was a baby."

Emma froze, stunned as she stared at the photograph. If Macon hadn't told her it was Celia, she'd have sworn her last nickel that it was a picture of Angel.

Chapter Eighteen

"What happens now?" Emma was unable to keep her voice from shaking. "Obviously Angel is Celia's baby. Is DCF going to take her away?" Her face grew warm at the looks of sympathy aimed her way. There was no point in pretending she wasn't devastated over the prospect of giving up the baby. As hard as she'd tried not to, she'd grown to love her. And she was silently cursing herself for letting her heart get involved.

Which was another reason she needed to put the brakes on her Rockwell fantasy of Macon and her potentially becoming a family. She couldn't survive having him, then losing him. Her heart was already halfway his and she needed to protect herself from becoming even more entangled.

Macon reached for her hand again beneath the table and squeezed it as if to reassure her. She tugged her hand loose, her heart breaking just a little more at the surprised look on his face.

He crossed his forearms on top of the table. "That's not how it works. No one's taking Angel just yet. We'll interview Celia, find out what's going on and whether she says Angel is hers or denies it. Either way, a blood sample will be drawn so a lab can test it and prove whether she's Angel's mother."

"She is," Emma insisted. "Everyone in this room knows it. That picture is proof."

"A judge won't see it that way," Macon continued. "He'll want the blood test. But DCF is the legal guardian right now. They won't wait for the blood test results. They'll start investigating Celia right now, with the assumption that she's the mother to save time. Their goal will be to find out whether she's a fit parent. The answer to that seems like an obvious no. A fit parent would have reported their child missing, or wouldn't have abandoned her if Celia is the one who did that. If she hopes to regain custody, she'll likely have to jump through a ton of hoops to convince DCF and a judge that she'll make better decisions for her daughter here on out."

Emma glanced at him, hope flaring inside her. But as soon as it did, guilt slammed down hard. She shouldn't be rooting for a woman to fail DCF's tests so that Emma could keep her daughter a little longer. That was awful, especially given that Emma knew Celia, or had at one time. Something terrible must have happened to make her give up Angel. Or maybe someone had stolen her and Celia, for some unknown reason, was too afraid to report it. Either way, Celia would need Emma's support going forward. Not her jealousy and resentment.

She drew a bracing breath and forced a smile. "Celia is a good person. I'm sure there's a reasonable explanation, at least in her mind, as to why Angel ended up at my door. And I can't imagine, given the chance, that Celia wouldn't do everything she can to get her daughter back. We need to help her."

"First things first." Macon pulled a business card

out of his wallet and slid it across the table toward Dillon. "That's the DCF caseworker's card. Mr. Burns has Angel at the hospital seeing a pediatrician right now for a checkup. Would you mind telling him our suspicions? He can start an investigation on his end and order the blood test to prove whether or not Angel is Celia's baby while the baby is already at the hospital."

"No problem." Dillon took the card and left the room.

Macon grabbed a pen and legal pad from the middle of the table. "Emma, if you want to help Celia, then start by telling us everything you remember about her, not just the quick summary you gave me last night."

"I didn't actually foster her very long. She was seventeen when she came to live with me." Emma proceeded to tell them about the shy, sweet teenager who'd been left an orphan after her parents died in a car accident. Her only relatives were some aging grandparents with health issues. They were unwilling and unable to raise their granddaughter. And since they lived on the other side of the country, Celia had rarely seen them and barely even knew them. Foster care had been her only option until she turned eighteen and could live on her own.

"I helped her with her studies, showed her the ropes at DCA. But she was far more interested in boys than studying or helping with the animals. She got in trouble for skipping school quite a few times, always to hang out with some guy. But she always felt guilty later and made up for it. She got good grades, aced most of her tests. Still, with so many unexcused absences she was in danger of failing. I tried everything I could to help her graduate. But when her latest boyfriend came along, it was basically over. She failed twelfth grade and, as far as I know, never did go back and finish. A month later, she turned eighteen and aged out of foster care." She held her hands up in a helpless gesture. "I offered for her to stay with me but all she wanted was to go off with Sean. I haven't seen or heard about her since."

The chief leaned forward in his chair at the head of the rectangular table. "Wasn't there a Sean on that high priority list you discussed with Macon?"

"Sean Hopper, yes. That's the boy she fell the hardest for. He was several years older than her, working odd jobs to get by. He was cute and seemed cool to a girl like Celia. She didn't look much deeper than that. He was the resident bad boy, but not just by reputation. He really was bad. He'd been in trouble with the law for petty crimes for years. I imagine by now he's done some time in jail, maybe even prison. That's really all I can tell you. That folder has a lot of pieces of paper in it. You probably know a lot more than I've ever known about Celia and her old boyfriends."

Macon leaned forward. "A few things, nothing substantial. Until I saw that baby picture of Celia, I wasn't seriously considering her as the possible mother to Angel. But now we'll dig, hard, into both her background and, as you said, any guys she hangs with or once hung with. I do have a local address, so that will make it easier."

"When are you going to talk to her?" she asked.

He pushed his chair back. "I'm going to head over there right now. Given the circumstances, I'd rather surprise her and not give her a chance to make up a false story or go into hiding. I'll drop you off at your place on the way."

"No need." She pushed her own chair back and smiled her thanks at the others around the table. "I've been meaning to visit Jenny for a while. Seems like I haven't talked to her in ages. I can get someone else to take me home later."

Macon frowned. "Jenny Dix? The dispatcher?"

"One and the same. I know she gets a lot of downtime between calls. Or at least, she did before the latest spate of crimes at my place." She laughed nervously, avoiding Macon's questioning gaze as she escaped from the conference room.

Yes, she was a coward, avoiding him this way. But just thinking about losing Angel was splintering her into little pieces. If she allowed herself to spend more time alone with Macon, and fall for him even harder, then when he inevitably left her at some point—whether by choice or chance—it would obliterate what was left of her heart. She had to stop this…thing, this attraction between them, before it was too late.

If it wasn't already.

She'd only made it around the corner from the conference room when a hand grasped her elbow and gently turned her around.

Macon.

"What's wrong, Emma? What did I do to make you upset with me?"

Her heart cracked a little more. It was the hardest thing she'd ever done to stand there and force a confused look on her face.

And lie.

"I don't know what you mean, Macon. Everything's good. Looks like you may have solved the most important issue—finding Angel's mom. I agree with your theory that Angel is connected to the other events on my property. So you should be able to figure out who's behind it all in a matter of days, maybe even today. It's a relief. You won't have to come guard me anymore. Bogie is doing great and doesn't need additional training. It's been great seeing you again after all this time, but now we can each go back to our normal lives. Neither of us will have to see each other every day. We're free."

She forced herself to smile up at him in spite of the hurt and confusion in his gaze.

"Free? We can both go back to our separate lives, the way they were before all this? That's what you want?"

She frowned. "Well, of course. Don't you?"

He stood there for a long moment. Then his expression smoothed out, becoming unreadable. He gave her a curt nod. "I'll call you later with an update on the case. Jason's watching your place right now. I'll get someone else to cover the night shift instead of me since that appears to be your preference. If you wanted to be free of me, Emma, all you had to do was tell me. I'm not the kind of man who would ever force his presence on someone who doesn't want him." He turned around and strode back to the conference room.

As soon as the door closed behind him, the first sob hit. She covered her mouth and sprinted for the bathroom so she could fall apart in private.

Chapter Nineteen

Barbara leaned across the kitchen table and put her hand on top of Emma's. "Quit thanking me for coming over. That's what friends are for. My weekends aren't sacred. Goodness, I'm alone most of the time anyway. Samantha's away at college right now. And Bob would much rather go off with his buddies fishing than watch me work in my garden." She patted Emma's hand and sat back. "What you need to do is quit crying about Angel. She's not going anywhere, not right now anyway. That's what Macon said, right? These things take time."

Emma went along with Barbara's assumption that it was just Angel who had her upset. Macon was as much on her mind, and her heart, as the baby and accounted for at least half her tears. Emma felt awful for how she'd had to leave things with him. It was tearing her apart, even though she knew it was for the best. She just wished it didn't hurt so much.

"I know, I know," Emma said. "But even with her off with that Mr. Burns the house feels way too empty."

Jason leaned over from where he was sitting on the couch, watching TV. "I don't count? Is that it?" He grinned.

Barbara gave him an admonishing look. "Shouldn't

you be making rounds or something? Making sure no one's sneaking around the place?"

He chuckled and stood. "I can take a hint. I need to stretch my legs anyway."

"Sorry, Jason," Emma called out.

"No worries. Be back soon."

"Not too soon I hope," Barbara called after him as he shut the front door.

"You're so bad." Emma smiled.

"Nah, I've known Jason almost as long as you have. He gets me. And it was worth picking on him to see you smile again. What time are you expecting that family services guy to bring Angel back?"

"That's just it. I have no idea. This morning I thought it would be for a couple of hours. But it's late afternoon now and I haven't heard from Mr. Burns or anyone else. I don't know what's going on. I'm guessing the discovery that Celia is likely the mother changed everything."

"Macon hasn't called with any updates?"

She briefly closed her eyes. "Things were, ah, difficult at the station between us. He's probably giving me my space, hoping I snap out of it and go back to normal."

"You really care about him, don't you?"

Emma stared at her in surprise. "It's that obvious?"

Barbara laughed. "Are you kidding? Honey, it was obvious a couple of years ago when you were training him and that dog of his. I'm just surprised it took you this long to realize it."

She dropped her head in her hands. "What am I going to do? This is a disaster."

"Why? It's obvious he cares about you, too."

"You don't understand."

"Which is why I'm asking."

Emma sighed and sat back.

Barbara dunked a fry into the homemade fry sauce that Emma had made to thank her for coming over. After chasing it down with a sip of iced tea, she said, "Enlighten me. Because we both know you didn't ask me over here just because of what's going on with Angel. You're hurting, bad. And Macon is at the center of it."

"You're wrong. I hadn't planned on talking about him at all. I really did call you because I wanted to commiserate about the baby."

"Well, I'm not leaving until you spill the beans on why it's such a bad thing that you and Macon are obviously wild about each other. To my knowledge, other than that Billy guy who nearly destroyed your life during your rebellious phase—"

"Ugh. Please don't mention Billy."

"Just sayin', other than him, you've never let any other guys into your life that I know of. You deserve some fun, Emma. And if I read things right, Macon's a dang good one, a keeper. Talk to me. Bob won't be back from his fishing trip until tomorrow afternoon. I've got all night." She popped another drenched fry into her mouth.

Emma let out a shaky breath. "That's just it. Other than…the bad phase in my life, there's been no one. By choice. I've lost so many people I've loved and been hurt by the very people who were supposed to love me the most. The one time I took a chance was he who shall not be named again, and that nearly led to me going to prison. It took years for me to build a life, to create the Daniels Canine Academy, to learn to be happy again. I know Macon is a good man, the best. He'd never hurt me on purpose. But if I give him what's left of my heart, and he either moves back to Boise or something happened to him, I don't think I could survive."

"Oh, sweetie. Don't you see? You've already given him your heart. And you can't live your life trying to avoid pain. It's just not possible. And really, is that even a life, one without love? You remember how much you loved your siblings, and then your parents—Rick and Susan Daniels. And you're scared because you don't want to hurt the way you did when you lost them. But would you have rather never known your siblings? Never been taken in by Rick and Susan? Would your life really have been better if you'd never loved at all? The whole point of life is to share it with people you care about. And, heck, no way would Macon move off and leave you, not if you give him a chance to break past that wall of yours."

She squeezed Emma's hand again. "Love is a rare and precious gift. Not everyone gets a chance at it. You've got that chance right in front of you. What you have to ask yourself is whether you'd rather spend the rest of your life knowing you threw that chance away. I can tell you right now, if Bob died tomorrow it would be the hardest thing I've ever faced. But I wouldn't undo all our years together to avoid that pain. I cherish every moment we've had together. What's that cliché? Better to have loved and lost than to never have loved? It's true, Emma. It's so true."

Emma stared at her in dismay as her words sank in. "Even if you're right, it doesn't matter. I hurt him. And there's no way he'll ever be able to forgive what I did." She burst into tears.

Chapter Twenty

Riding her horses had always been Emma's favorite escape when she was stressed out, even more so than working with her beloved K-9s. And with the mess that her life had become, the only exercise Presley and Elton had gotten lately was when she let them out in the pasture on their own. So after convincing Barbara that she'd be all right and it was okay to leave, Emma had headed out to the barn.

Jason wasn't too happy about her decision since he felt compelled to sit with Bogie against the fence that circled the pasture to keep an eye on her. He was an excellent horseman, having helped her with Presley and Elton when he'd been a foster here. But he wanted to be able to scan their surroundings while she was outside to make sure no one sneaked up on them. Doing that on top of a trotting horse was a recipe for disaster. Plus, Bogie could be a problem if they were both on horses. He might get underfoot. So Jason was relegated to looking around and whiling away his time with the shepherd while also keeping an eye on her.

But Emma didn't mind being alone, or relatively alone. She was sick to death of being babysat and had told him he could wait for her up at the house rather than out here.

His insistence on watching her while she trotted Presley around the pasture was his decision. And she desperately needed this mindless exercise to try to come to terms with everything that was going on and pull herself together.

The names of everyone she'd loved and lost beat a mournful drum in her mind in rhythm with Presley's hooves.

Danny.

Little Katie.

Her biological mom and dad—before drugs and alcohol had turned them into monsters.

Rick Daniels.

Susan Daniels.

Countless fosters who'd broken her heart each and every time one of them left. At least with them, it wasn't the grief of complete loss like it had been for her loved ones who'd passed away. But it was still difficult, and there was only so much sorrow one person could bear. She'd vowed never to risk her heart like that again. She didn't really count bad boy Billy. That wasn't love. It was rebellion. There'd been no one else in her heart for so long.

Then Macon had shown up.

He was so handsome, charming. So fun to laugh with while she'd trained him and Bogie several years ago. She'd loosened up, enjoyed him, allowed herself to have fun knowing she'd never see him again. She'd reasoned that he was a "safe" man to flirt with because he'd return to Boise and that was that. But then he'd come back to Jasper, and the feelings she'd thought she'd buried so long ago had exploded to the surface.

Macon and Angel. She loved both of them. There was

no point in denying it now. And she was losing both of them. Just as she'd feared, it was tearing her apart. She knew Barbara was right, that love was really what made life worth living. Because her world had been gray, safe, before Macon and Angel had reawakened her to the wonderful colors all around her. How was she supposed to go back to life the way it had been now that she knew what she was missing?

Presley stumbled on the turn at the far end of the pasture. She eased up on the reins and patted his neck. She hadn't been paying attention and had been holding the reins too tightly, interfering with his gait and his ability to stretch out for the turn. Stupid, stupid. She could have caused him to break a leg and he'd have had to be put down. There was nothing more dangerous while riding a horse than to not be paying attention.

"I'm sorry, boy." She patted his neck again. "Goodness, you're all lathered up. Too much exercise after being cooped up so much, isn't that right? Come on. I'll give you extra oats for supper to make it up to you."

He whinnied as if he understood as she turned him toward the barn.

Jason caught her attention at the fence, motioning to her. Bogie was standing at attention as well. She looked past them and saw why. Two cars were coming up the driveway. One was a Jasper PD SUV. The other was a car she remembered from when she'd transferred the car seat from it to Macon's vehicle at the hospital. It belonged to Mr. Burns, the Child and Family Services caseworker.

She dismounted as Jason and Bogie joined her outside the barn.

"Who is it?" she asked, both dreading and hoping that Macon was in the SUV.

"I don't know. No one called to say they were coming." He sounded irritated about that fact.

Together they watched as Mr. Burns's car turned up the circular drive, disappearing when the house blocked their view. The SUV continued toward them, parking several yards away, probably so they wouldn't spook the horse or risk hitting Bogie. This close, even with the windows being darkly tinted, she could see who was driving. And the way Bogie was standing at attention, he knew, too.

Macon.

Seeing him again, so soon after their disastrous morning, and her falling apart in her kitchen after realizing she was in love with him, had her pulse rushing in her ears. But when both passenger doors opened and the chief and office manager, Theresa, stepped out, her trepidation turned to alarm.

"What's happened?" she demanded as they all moved toward her and Jason. "Is Angel okay? I saw Mr. Burns drive up to the house—"

"She's fine," Macon assured her, his voice gentle and soothing even though she didn't deserve for him to treat her so kindly. "Angel did great at her checkup, got a clean bill of health. And she had the blood test too. The doctor said she's thriving under your care. Mr. Burns brought her back. She's up at the house with him." He patted Bogie, who'd ducked under the fence rail to sit in the gravel beside him.

Relief had Emma pressing a shaky hand to her chest. "Thank goodness she's okay. Thank you, Macon."

He nodded, his smile fading as he gestured to the chief. "I asked Chief Walters to come with me to update you on the latest happenings."

The rest of his words went unsaid, but she understood his meaning. It was his case. He wanted to update her and answer her questions. But he'd brought the chief along to keep things on a more formal, less personal basis.

She really hated herself right now.

"And Theresa? You're always welcome here, but I'm wondering why you came. You rarely make the trip out this way."

Theresa smiled. "Macon will explain."

Jason took Presley's reins. "Ms. Daniels, how about I rub Presley down and get both of the horses settled for the night while y'all talk this out."

She smiled her gratitude and stepped through the gate to join the others.

"We found Celia Banks fairly easily," Macon told her. "The chief went with me since she's met him before. We thought it might put her more at ease. It didn't. She was really nervous, burst into tears the second we drove up. She didn't even try to deny the truth. She's the one who left Angel on your porch. And Angel is her child, only her real name is Anna."

Emma's stomach dropped as if she was on a roller coaster. "I guess the DNA test isn't necessary after all."

"Oh, it's necessary. It's required, actually. The chief secured a court order even before we got to Celia's place to compel her to provide a DNA sample. It's being driven to the state lab as we speak, along with a sample taken from the baby when she was at the hospital. The chief pulled some strings to put a rush on it. But it will still take longer than we'd like. We still don't have the DNA results back from the other sample we sent, from those shrubs by your porch. As to Angel, I mean Anna, Celia had pictures of her, as you'd expect. And DCF used the footprints on her birth certificate as a preliminary way to verify her identity. The prints match."

"No surprise there, but now I'm confused. Is... Anna...staying with me now or going back to Celia?"

The chief patted her shoulder as if she were his daughter. "For now, you're still watching little Anna. DCF trusts you to keep her safe until Celia can prove to the court that she's a fit mother. Right now, she's not, obviously, after having left her baby on someone's porch. But there *are* extenuating circumstances that are being taken into account. She'll have to take some parenting courses, maintain employment and do a host of other things in order to get Anna back. It could be months or longer before DCF recommends a hearing to transfer custody to her."

Emma struggled to take it all in, make sense of what they were saying. Everything was happening so quickly.

"Emma," Macon asked, "are you okay watching over the baby for that long? Especially knowing that you'll have to give her up if Celia is granted custody again?"

"Oh, yes," she said, without hesitation. And she realized it was true. She smiled. "I love Angel. I mean Anna. Wow, that's going to be hard to get used to, a new name. I love her and enjoy taking care of her. But what's most important is that we do what's best for her. I'll enjoy keeping her until her mom can take over."

Macon smiled. "If you weren't okay with that, Theresa had volunteered to take Anna until Mr. Burns could find another foster situation. They're still short on families in the area willing and able to take in babies."

Emma hugged Theresa. "That's so sweet of you. I really appreciate it. And now I know who to ask to babysit if I ever need a night off," she teased.

Theresa hugged her fiercely and stepped back, her eyes suspiciously misty. "My Henry and I, God rest his soul, were never blessed with children. I'd love to watch Anna for you any time."

The chief smiled, too, and patted Theresa's back. Then, as if suddenly realizing what he was doing, he dropped his hand and awkwardly cleared his throat.

Emma thought it was sweet that, once again, the chief and Theresa were trying to keep their relationship a secret. She glanced at Macon, who was watching her intently, as if trying to figure her out.

She nervously smoothed her hands down her jeans. "Did Celia tell you the name of Anna's father? I'd think he'd be given custody instead of leaving her with me, unless he has to go through everything Celia will to be deemed a fit parent too?"

Macon leaned against the wooden fence. "The father is her boyfriend, Sean Hopper, the same guy you remembered being a bad influence on her years ago."

Emma nodded, not really surprised, but sad too. She'd hoped for so much better for sweet Celia.

"They'll do a paternity test to confirm that Sean is the father, but there's no reason to doubt it. And, if everything Celia told us about Sean is true," Macon continued, "Sean is the reason she left Anna here. She was afraid of him, afraid he'd hurt her. Celia's life post–foster care has been rough. Sean is a small-time criminal and has been abusing Celia. She thought, mistakenly, that having a baby would calm him down, make him want to be better. Instead, the violence escalated after Anna was born and their financial struggles got worse. But until recently, he'd never hit Anna."

Emma pressed a hand to her mouth, afraid of what else he was going to say.

"He never hit the baby," he reassured her, his voice gentle again. "But he tried. When he went to punch her, Celia threw herself between them and took the beating instead. After that, she knew she had to leave. She couldn't risk Anna being hurt. But she didn't have money or a job. She was desperate. And she didn't trust the cops or anyone else, except you. She told me you're the only person after her parents' deaths who ever genuinely cared about her. Leaving Anna here, to her, wasn't abandonment. It was a second chance."

"Poor Celia," Emma whispered. "What happened to her after that? You said she didn't have a job or money."

"We found her in a women's shelter one county over. But since I found her so easily, I figure her boyfriend can also find her, if he's looking. So I took her with me when I left. She's at the station right now." He motioned to Theresa. "Theresa's going to pick her up after we leave and take Celia to her place."

"And I'll help her get back on her feet," Theresa added. "She certainly won't go hungry. And we'll try to find her a job. Of course, she'll have to delay starting one until Sean is found."

Emma shook her head. "She was such a good kid. I hate that she's mixed up with him. But she'll be okay. Theresa will make sure of it." She smiled her thanks again.

The chief nodded, as if in agreement that Theresa would take care of Celia. "I'll stop by and check on her after work every day." He cleared his throat. "To check on Celia. Just in case Sean is trying to find her. She's tried to leave him before and he always hunted her down and forced her to come back. Worried he'd do that again, she's been moving from shelter to shelter to keep a step ahead of him."

"And left Anna with me so she wouldn't be in danger." She glanced back and forth between the chief and Macon. "But it sounds like he must have figured out that Anna was here and has been sneaking around, trying to break in, cause me problems. Is that the going theory?"

Macon shifted against the fence. "It makes the most sense, when taking everything else into account. None of our other potential suspects have panned out. And the trouble here at DCA didn't start until Celia left Anna with you. When we asked her if she thought Sean would harass you if he thought you had Anna, she said that's exactly the kind of thing he'd do. He might not want Anna, but he wouldn't want someone else to have her, either. That's the kind of abusive, controlling person he is. If your alarm hadn't gone off that night when he broke in and scared him away, there's no telling what he might have done."

She shivered and wrapped her arms around her waist.

He moved closer, as if wanting to put his arm around her, but stopped, his expression hardening.

Grief and guilt—for what she'd done, for how she'd treated him—had her fighting back tears. How could she ever make this right? She swiped at her eyes. This wasn't the time to think about that. She needed to get to Anna, make sure she was okay. Feed her, give her a bath. There was so much to do when taking care of a little baby. And she looked forward to every minute she had left with her.

The chief motioned to Macon. "Show her the pictures."

"Oh, forgot about that."

"Pictures?" Emma asked.

Macon tapped his phone screen, then turned it around, revealing a typical police mugshot. "Recognize him?"

She frowned and moved closer. "No…wait. The eyes are the same, but it's been a few years. Is that Sean?"

He nodded and flipped to another photo before holding up his phone again. "Recognize this guy?"

"Well, of course. That's Sean, too. Why?"

He put his phone away. "That's the rendering the artist drew based on Kyle's eyewitness statements about the man he saw the night the dogs were let out. I sent a photo lineup to Kyle. He picked Sean out right away."

"That's great. I guess we can take Captain Rutledge off the suspect list now, huh?"

Macon's eyes widened.

"Rutledge?" The chief looked confused. "Arthur was on your suspect list?"

"No," Macon said.

"Yes," Emma said.

Macon rolled his eyes.

Emma relaxed, relief easing the tension in her shoulders. "Then it's over, really over, right, Macon? Celia is Anna's mom. And Sean is the one who's been trying to scare me, or worse."

"We know who, and have a guess as to why. But it's not over until Sean's locked up. We sent a team to arrest him but he wasn't home. His neighbors told us he's usually home this time of day, boozing it up with whatever money he made working. He might have seen the cop cars and got spooked. We've got a BOLO out on him and in the neighboring counties so law enforcement will be on the lookout both for him and his car. But until he's behind bars you're still in danger."

She muttered beneath her breath and leaned against the fence. "I'm still going to have a babysitter."

His mouth twitched as if he wanted to smile, but he held it back. "An officer needs to be here at DCA until Sean is put away, yes."

Jason stepped out of the barn as Macon was talking and joined them on the other side of the fence. "What did I miss?"

"Too much to repeat right now," Macon told him.

The sound of a car engine had all of them looking toward the driveway. Yet another police SUV rounded the circular drive and disappeared from sight when the house blocked the view.

"What's going on now?" Emma asked, exasperated at the thought of yet another emergency to deal with.

"I can answer that one." Jason waved his hand, smiling. "It's Dillon. He's taking night-shift duties today. He'll have Bentley with him, his Australian shepherd mix, so Bogie can head home with Macon. And, for once, I get to go home on time to my new bride." His grin widened.

Macon narrowed his eyes, making Jason sober. "Remind me to talk to you tomorrow about your duties and how your shift doesn't end until your replacement arrives, no matter how late they might be or who's waiting at home."

Jason swallowed. "Yes, sir. The horses are all set for the night, Ms. Daniels. Need me to do anything else?"

She shook her head. "You've been wonderful, Jason. Thanks so much for taking care of that. Thanks for everything."

"Of course. If you're done here, I'll walk you to the house."

She hesitated and looked at Macon.

"Good idea," Macon told him, even though he was looking at Emma as he spoke. "I'll drive the chief and Theresa to the station. Come, Bogie." He opened the passenger door and Bogie hopped inside. Then he assisted Theresa up into the SUV.

Emma's throat tightened. The chief gave her a sympathetic glance and hugged her.

"It will all work out," he whispered by her ear. "Have faith."

She nodded her thanks, not sure whether the chief was talking about the situation with Sean Hopper, or whether he'd figured out that she was upset about Macon.

"My bride's waiting," Jason teased.

She gave him a wobbly smile and started across the lawn toward the house, while Macon and the others drove away.

Chapter Twenty-One

Emma turned her pickup out of her driveway onto Elm Street. "Thanks for going with me to the feed store, Jason. With all the excitement lately, Barbara and I both forgot to put in our usual order for delivery and are about to run out of dog food."

He gave her a droll look. "Like I'd let you go anywhere without me by your side when it's my turn to guard you. Macon would kill me." He grimaced. "He may kill me anyway. I'm not looking forward to that talk he promised today."

She laughed and turned down another road, heading away from the more populated areas of Jasper. "Barbara was excited to get to stay at DCA with Anna instead of coming along. She really missed the baby. It's good to have her back."

"Tashya and I are thinking about having kids."

"What? Already?"

"Well, not right away. But we're talking about it. She's always wanted a big family. I guess I could handle a few if they're like Angel. I mean Anna. She's pretty cool."

"Yes. She is. I hope you and Tashya have a bunch of rug rats and a dozen grandkids."

"Whoa, whoa. You're already making me a grandpa? I only just got married."

She laughed and turned down the long road the feed store was on. This one wasn't paved and was full of potholes. Her truck squeaked and rattled like it was about to fall apart. But she knew better. It had been around for decades and would probably still be around for decades to come.

"Where is this place?" Jason asked, looking out the window. "It's like we're in Timbuktu or something."

"It's in a perfect location for its purposes. You can't see the houses because of all the trees along the road but there's prime pastureland out this way for families with horses and other livestock." She pointed off to the right. "There, Sampson's Feed and Grain. And it's not in Timbuktu."

"Nearly. Well, at least the parking lot is empty. Easier to keep an eye out for that Sean fellow that way. Still, I'm texting Macon the address just so he knows we're not at DCA. I'm not taking any chances with him. I need this job."

Her stomach tightened as she pulled into a parking space an aisle back from the building so no one could park behind them. They'd need the room to load the bags of feed into the bed of the pickup. "You don't really expect Sean to come all the way out here, do you?"

"Naw. Everyone's looking for him. A woman-beating scumbag like him is a coward. He'll lie low somewhere, waiting for the heat to die down."

"I hope they find him soon. I'm tired of looking over my shoulder."

"Don't worry, Ms. Daniels. I'll keep you safe."

"Are you ever going to call me Emma?"

He looked horrified. "You were like a mom to me when I was at DCA. I'd never call you by your first name. And we're too close in age in the grand scheme of things for me to call you mom."

She laughed. "Ms. Daniels it is. Let's get this over with and head back home. I don't want Barbara to usurp me in Anna's affections."

He chuckled and they headed inside.

Even though the store was obviously empty except for the man at the register, Jason made her wait while he checked both of the bathrooms. As he headed up the aisle toward her, she stared at him.

"Did you really just go into the women's bathroom?"

"Of course. That's a perfect place for a wanted man to hide, thinking no one would check."

"Wanted man?" the cashier asked. "Should I be worried?"

Jason shook his head. "If he shows up, I'll take care of him."

Emma smiled at his confidence, but she prayed he'd never be put to the test. She knew how dangerous being a cop could be, even in a relatively peaceful town like Jasper. After all, her father had been gunned down in the line of duty.

She arranged a delivery date for the supplies that she needed that wouldn't fit in the truck. Jason loaded the fifty-pound bags of dog food onto a rolling cart and followed her out of the store.

As he loaded them into the back of the truck, she headed around to the driver's side, then froze in shock. While they'd been in the store, someone had spray-painted filthy words across the door in big orange letters. She whirled around, but the parking lot was empty.

Their truck was the only vehicle parked out front. Was there an employee lot in the back? It hadn't occurred to her until now. The cashier must have a vehicle somewhere. Had Sean, or someone else, parked there too and vandalized her truck?

"Last one." The truck springs creaked as Jason hoisted the bag into the back, then slammed the tailgate. He headed around to her side, pushing the cart. "Something wrong? What are you looking—" He swore and shoved the cart out of the way. "Get in, get in." He drew his gun and scanned the parking lot and building, as he reached for the police-radio transmitter on his shoulder with his other hand.

"Get in the truck. Now."

His panicked order finally broke through her shock. She hurried to unlock the door, then yanked it open.

A man jumped up from where he'd been lying across the bench seat and aimed a gun at her face. Sean Hopper. She screamed and slammed the door, knocking his gun arm up.

"Jason, gun!"

He whirled around as she dived to the ground, her purse skittering underneath the truck. Two gunshots rang out, deafeningly loud over the top of her head. A look of shock crossed Jason's face. Then he crumpled to the ground, his pistol skittering across the pavement.

Emma sobbed his name even as she ran forward to grab the gun.

Another shot rang out. The bullet whistled past her so close she could feel its heat. She ducked down and ran to the other side of the truck, crouching behind the engine block. She needed to call 911, but her phone was in her purse, which was under the truck somewhere. She leaned down, trying to see where it was.

"You're just making it worse for yourself, you interfering witch," Sean yelled. "Where are you hiding Celia?"

Her purse was too far under the truck to reach, and she was nothing but a target out here. She needed to get away, hide. The store was surrounded by trees, but they weren't close to the building. She'd have to run a good twenty yards to reach them.

Her heart squeezed in her chest as she thought about poor Jason. Where had he been shot? She pictured him lying there, bleeding out. Had he radioed dispatch before Sean surprised them? She didn't think so. Somehow she had to get him help.

The truck bounced on its springs. The door flew open, its rusty hinges squeaking in protest. "I'm comin' for you. Give up now and I'll kill you fast. Make me work for it and I'll teach you a lesson before I kill you."

She had no choice. She couldn't wait here and let Sean kill her. The only way to help Jason was to survive and call the police. She took off, running in a zigzag pattern toward the store.

Bullets whined past her, burying themselves in the weathered siding of the building. She put on another burst of speed and shoved the glass door, slamming it back against the wall. She ran to the first aisle past the door and crouched down behind the metal shelves.

The cashier was nowhere to be seen. He'd probably heard the gunshots and was hiding. She prayed he'd had the sense to call 911. Where was he hiding? Was there a place she could hide, too? The shelves wouldn't offer her any real protection and they certainly wouldn't conceal her location.

No. She couldn't just hide and wait while Jason died out there. She had to call 911 just in case the cashier hadn't. And she needed to let them know to send an ambulance for Jason.

The glass in the front door shattered as another bullet crashed through it.

Emma let out a squeak of surprise, then took off running again for the back door beneath a neon red sign marked Exit.

The sound of Sean chuckling as he stalked across the wooden walkway out front had her sprinting forward and bursting through the exit door.

"Those bags of feed won't stop a bullet, Ms. Busybody," he called out from inside the store.

The sound of his laughter sent a frisson of fear up Emma's spine. But she wasn't looking for a place to hide now. She couldn't outrun a bullet. She had to fight fire with fire. She needed to go for Jason's gun and either try to operate the police radio on his uniform or find his phone.

Keeping to the side of the building, she moved as quickly and quietly as she could down the wooden walkway that circled the building like a wraparound porch. She didn't want to go too fast or Sean would hear her and know she'd doubled back, rather than run behind the stacks of feed behind the store. She made it down the side of the building, then stopped at the corner. She glanced behind her to make sure he wasn't there, then hurried to the front.

She raced down the steps toward the truck, hurrying to the driver's side. She skidded to a halt on the gravel, again in shock. Jason wasn't there. Neither was his gun. What did that mean? Had Sean thrown his body somewhere?

Cold fear clutched her chest. She was about to run to

the back of the truck to look, when the sound of boots running across the wooden walkway had her jumping into the pickup and slamming the door shut. She was reaching for the keys when Sean rounded the outside of the building and stopped by the ruined front doors. He grinned and held up something shiny and shook it, metal flashing in the sunlight, making a jingling sound.

Keys.

Emma grabbed for the steering column where the truck keys should have been. Sure enough, they were gone. A keening moan wheezed out of her clenched teeth. She was trapped.

Sean slowly raised his gun, grinning the whole time.

The ruined front door of the feed store jerked back, shards of glass flying and tinkling across the walkway. Jason stood half-crouched in the opening, as if in pain, clutching his pistol in front of him. "Freeze, scumbag. Police."

Sean swore, then raised his gun hand in the air, pointing his pistol at the sky. "You got me, copper."

"Throw the gun down away from you," Jason ordered.

"Whatever you say." Sean looked at Emma, his feral smile never wavering.

She tensed, keeping as still as possible so she didn't distract Jason.

Sean tossed the gun onto the gravel.

"On your knees," Jason ordered. "Hands out to your sides."

"Don't shoot, Officer." Sean chuckled, then lowered himself down onto one knee. He watched Emma the whole time, still smiling. Then he winked.

She sucked in a sharp breath.

Sean whirled around, another pistol seemingly magically appearing in his other hand. He squeezed off two shots before Jason could even squeeze off one. Jason collapsed forward onto the wooden deck.

"No, please, no." The words came out a raspy whisper as Emma stared in horror at Jason's crumpled body.

Sean laughed and kicked his gun away. "Why bring one gun to a gunfight when you can bring two, I always say. Now, let's make sure you don't get up this time, shall we?" He raised his gun, ready to deliver a kill shot, if Jason wasn't dead already.

Emma slammed her hand down on the horn.

Sean whirled around, swinging his pistol toward her.

She dived toward the floorboard. But instead of hearing more gunshots, she heard something else.

A siren.

Had the cashier called 911 after all?

The sound of a vehicle's tires crunching on gravel had Sean swearing.

Emma lay there frozen, afraid to move in case he was waiting to shoot at her.

The next sounds she heard were boots running across the wooden planks and a vehicle sliding across the gravel into the parking lot, siren blaring.

She edged up out of the floorboard, ready to duck down again if she saw Sean.

The truck door flew open and the bore of a pistol was suddenly pointing at her.

She bit her lip so hard, the metallic taste of blood filled her mouth.

The pistol jerked up and away. "Emma, what the hell?"

She blinked. "Macon? Thank God, Macon." She scrambled out of the floorboard and plopped onto the bench seat. "Careful, he's in the store. Or maybe hid-

ing around the left side of the building. He's got a gun."
She whipped back toward the windshield. "Jason." She
pointed, her throat so tight she could barely force the
words out. "He shot Jason, two different times. By the
truck, and in front of the store."

His jaw tightened as he looked toward the store. "Sean
Hopper?"

"Yes. He must have followed us here. But I never saw
a vehicle. I think he may have parked behind the building, maybe in an employee parking lot." She glanced past
him. "Are you alone? No backup?"

He stood with his pistol pointed at the store as he
scanned the building and nearby trees. "Backup's on the
way. Jason had texted me this address earlier and I was
already headed here to check on you when the call came
in. I was worried it would be a good place for an ambush."

"I'm so sorry," Emma whispered. "I should have
thought of that."

"No, Jason should have thought of that. And he should
have told you to let me pick up your supplies instead
of letting you come out here. Is anyone else inside the
store?"

"It's not Jason's fault, I—"

"Is anyone else in the store?"

"Sorry. The cashier, I assume. He disappeared when
the shots started. He must be hiding. I don't think Sean
did anything to him but I'm not sure."

"Get back down in the floorboard. The engine block
should stop any bullets if he shoots this way."

He radioed dispatch through his police transmitter, giving a quick update and telling them *officer down*. "Emma,
backup will be here soon. They're just a few minutes out.
I hate to leave you, but I have to check on Jason."

"Go. Help him."

"Wait here. Do not get out of the truck." He motioned behind him. "Bogart. Up."

Bogie hopped into the truck, forcing Emma to scrunch down into the floorboard again.

Macon issued a command in German. Bogie's demeanor changed instantly. Ears pricked forward, hackles raised. He stared through the windshield, alert for any sign of danger.

Macon shut the door.

"Wait," Emma called out. "You need Bogie more than me. Take him with you."

Her only answer was the sound of crunching gravel as he took off running.

Chapter Twenty-Two

Macon trained his gun toward the store as he crouched beside Jason. He risked a quick glance down, but didn't see any blood. A quick pat against Jason's chest sent a wave of relief through Macon. Jason was wearing his Kevlar vest. But that didn't mean a bullet hadn't entered through an armhole and hit something vital. It was rare, but it happened.

Continuing to scan the side of the building and store beyond, alert for any signs of movement, he ran his hand up Jason's vest to his neck where he pressed against the carotid artery, feeling for a pulse.

"Aren't you supposed to buy me dinner before getting this fresh?" Jason's voice wheezed out of him.

Macon couldn't help laughing. "Son of a… I thought you were dead."

"I *feel* dead." He coughed. "Hard…to breathe. Jerk hit me at least…" He gasped, obviously struggling. "Four… times."

"Probably broke a rib, punctured a lung. Help is on the way. Stop blabbing and save your air."

"Stop…being…so bossy."

Macon risked another quick glance down. "Cal's

going to be ticked if he has to train another recruit to replace you."

"Gee, excuse me…f…for incon…veniencing him."

"Danged straight. Better not die so you can pull your fair share around the station." He smiled to make sure Jason knew he was teasing.

Jason tried to smile back, but winced in pain. "I'll… think about it. Phone broken. Tried radio. Broken…too."

"Cal and the others will be here any minute. An ambulance is right behind them. Your initial radio call went through. Dispatch heard you, heard the gunshots."

"Did something…right…then. Didn't…leave… Ms. Daniels."

Macon squeezed Jason's hand. "You did fine before, too. I was too hard on you."

"Don't…p…patron…"

"Don't patronize you?"

Jason nodded.

"I'm not. You've done a fine job, Jason. Just hold on a few more minutes. That's what I need you to do now."

Macon hesitated. They were both sitting ducks if Sean came back. He looked toward the truck, saw Bogie still on alert. No one was anywhere near the truck. He scanned the trees again, then shoved his pistol into his holster. "This is gonna hurt like hell."

"What?" Jason cried out as Macon grabbed his vest and pulled him into the store.

He yanked him behind shelves that would hide them from view from the back door, then checked his pulse again. Thready, but even. He'd passed out from the pain but was still breathing. Barely. Keeping an eye out for Sean, he punched the police radio button on his shoulder.

"Officer down. Repeat, officer down. Possible collapsed lung, broken ribs and who knows what else. Where's that bus I called for?"

"The ambulance should be there any minute," Jenny assured him.

Macon gave her more details as he watched the truck outside, ready to take off running toward Emma if Sean came anywhere near it. As soon as he clicked off the radio, the welcome sound of sirens came from down the road out front.

A gunshot sounded outside. The bullet pinged off the metal shelving a few feet away. Macon swore and took a quick look past the end of the aisle. Sean was standing by a stack of feed visible through the now-propped-open back door, pointing his gun toward Macon.

Macon squeezed off a couple of shots, making Sean duck down.

Sean jumped out from the side of the feed bags, firing off several more rounds.

Macon dived to the side, coming up in a crouch by the counter, firing again.

A cruiser skidded across the gravel out front as it sharply turned into the parking lot. Macon jerked back toward the exit just in time to see Sean running for the trees.

Macon ran out the front door as Margaret Avery hopped out of her car. Just Macon's luck that one of the few officers without a K-9 was the first one to arrive. He could have really used a K-9 right now.

He motioned for Margaret to run to him as he headed back into the store.

She sprinted inside, skidding across the tile floor. Her eyes widened when she saw Jason.

"He's alive," Macon told her. "I think he has a punctured lung. Tell the EMTs that when they get here. Guard him, and Emma. She's in the truck outside with Bogie."

He drew his pistol, checked the magazine.

"What are you going to do?" she demanded.

"I'm going to finish this."

"No, Macon. Not by yourself. And I can't back you up if I'm guarding Jason and Emma."

"Then let's hope I don't need backup." He took off running through the back door.

He didn't bother checking the maze of feed bags stacked in the loading area. He'd seen a flash of white just inside the tree line as he'd spoken to Margaret. Sean was in those woods, trying to get away. That wasn't going to happen. Emma had suffered enough. And Macon didn't want to risk letting Sean get comfortable out there in the trees where he could start shooting at the officers as they arrived. Macon had to stop him before someone else got hurt, or killed.

More sirens sounded down the road, reassuring him that help would be here in a matter of seconds. Knowing it was a huge risk, he took off running again, zigzagging toward the trees in an evasive maneuver.

A shot rang out, barely missing him as he zagged to the right.

Macon fired toward where he'd seen the gun flash in the dark woods.

More shots rang out. Macon swore and fired repeatedly toward the trees.

Engines roared out front. Tires spun on gravel. Sirens shattered the serenity of the forest.

Macon zigged left again. But his boot slipped on some loose rocks, knocking him off-balance. He fell to the ground just as Sean Hopper dived out from behind a huge oak tree, leveling his pistol at Macon.

A dark blur ran past Macon as he twisted around, trying to get his gun aimed at Sean before Sean shot him.

Sean screamed and fell back beneath a hundred pounds of snarling teeth and black fur. Bogie.

Macon frowned. Bogie was supposed to be protecting Emma. He turned around. Emma stood at the corner of the building, watching him. She'd left the safety of the truck and had ordered Bogie to protect him. Fury swept through Macon.

"Get him off me! Get him off me. He's killing me!" Sean screamed and thrashed on the ground as Bogie sank his teeth into his arm.

Cal and Dillon both sprinted to Macon, pistols drawn and pointing at Sean.

Macon slowly holstered his pistol, his chest heaving from exertion.

"Help me!" Sean cried.

Cal arched a brow at Macon. "You gonna call him off or let him keep playing with his new chew toy."

Macon yelled an order in German. Bogie immediately let Sean go and backed away. But he didn't go far. He stood guard, hackles raised, teeth bared, as Cal moved in to handcuff Sean.

Macon didn't wait around. Instead, he motioned for Dillon to come with him back to the building. They stopped in front of Emma.

Her eyes were wide as she stared up at him. "Macon, thank God you're okay."

He leaned toward her, so angry he was shaking. "You were supposed to wait in the truck, with Bogie. You could have been killed."

She blinked in surprise. "But Sean was shooting at you. There wasn't any backup. You needed help."

"I needed you to be safe," he gritted out. He motioned to Dillon. "Get her out of here."

Macon headed into the store to check on Jason. But not before he caught the hurt look Emma aimed at him as Dillon led her away.

Chapter Twenty-Three

Emma curled her legs under her on the couch as Chief Walters sat beside her, droning on about everything that had happened in the past few days since the shoot-out at Sampson's Feed and Grain.

"Sean knows the DNA will come back proving he was here," Walters continued. "And of course, there's no way of getting out of what happened at the store. Too many witnesses, not to mention the security cameras. He's trying to make a deal with the prosecutor. But he doesn't have anything to bargain with. He'll do hard time, might even get life when you take into account attempted murder of two different police officers."

She tried to smile. "Sounds good. He won't be out to hurt Celia anymore. Or Anna. And you said Jason's doing well?"

Walters laughed. "He was, until Tashya walked in on him flirting with one of the nurses. It was all in fun. I know he didn't mean anything by it. And the doctor said he was half out of it because of the pain meds and probably didn't realize what he was doing. But he'll have to grovel for a long time before Tashya forgives him."

"I'm sure she will, though. It's obvious how much

they care about each other. Jason was always anxious to go home to her after his shifts were over here at DCA."

"I'm sure she will. What about you? Are you going to forgive Macon?"

She blinked. "Excuse me?"

He sighed and took one of her hands in his. "Emma, you know I love you like you're my very own daughter. And I understand all the pain and trauma you've been through in your life, probably better than anyone else. But you continue trying to ignore and avoid love to keep from getting hurt. You and Macon are meant for each other. And you need to forgive him and move past how he treated you at the store after the shoot-out."

She tugged her hand from his. "What is with everyone trying to dissect my feelings and act like they know what's best for me? Besides, you have it all wrong. There's nothing for me to forgive. Macon was right. Logically. And I understand how he feels and why he was so angry with me. But at the same time, even if I could go back and change what I did, I wouldn't. Because Macon could have been killed. There's no way past that."

His brow furrowed. "Have you even spoken to him since that day?"

She crossed her arms. "Was there anything else you wanted to tell me about the investigation?"

He sighed again, his eyes sad. "Just that your pickup is still in evidence. The wheels of justice move slowly, even when a suspect is going to plead guilty. It might be a few weeks before I can get it released."

"It's okay. Barbara has offered to take me anywhere I need to go. And Piper picked up the dog food we needed in order to get us by until another feed store makes a delivery."

"Good, good. Where is Barbara? I thought she'd be here with Anna."

"Now that we're no longer under lock and key, she's taken Anna to a park in town. And after that, she's keeping her at her place overnight. She said I've been hogging Anna and it's her turn to play mommy for a few days." Emma smiled. "She also said it was high time she let Anna gum a French fry and get a taste of Idaho heaven."

"Fry sauce?"

"Of course."

They both laughed.

The chief leaned over and pressed a kiss against Emma's forehead. "I love you, sweet daughter. You take care of yourself, all right?"

She reached out and hugged him tightly against her. "I love you too. Dad."

When they pulled back, his eyes were suspiciously bright.

Once he'd left, Emma stood at the back door, looking up at the mountains. They were already wearing little caps of snow in the higher elevations. Winter would be here before long. It was so peaceful looking at the beauty of nature, and she was so lucky to have a little piece of Idaho all to herself. But she was beginning to realize something else. After the aggravation of having someone in the house with her 24/7 for so long, the quiet and solitude she'd longed for wasn't what she'd hoped it would be. Instead of feeling restful and relieved, she felt…lonely.

She missed Macon.

She missed him so much she couldn't sleep at night. She couldn't eat. She was a bundle of nervous energy most of the time, feeling anxious, as if she was going to jump out of her own skin. Loving him and losing him was even worse than she'd dreaded it could be. And they'd never even really dated, or kissed aside from that one time. How much worse would she feel right now if she had allowed herself to get closer to him? If she'd given herself completely, body and soul? All this time she'd tried to guard her heart so she wouldn't feel this way. But she hadn't been able to guard it and had fallen in love. Now that she'd lost her chance with Macon, she'd learned something she'd never expected to learn.

He was worth the pain.

That cliché really was true, about loving and losing or never loving at all. She was in love with Macon. No question. And even though he was out of her life now, and she'd probably never see him again, she was glad that she'd shared those touches of his hand, basked in his sweet, gentle smile, felt the heat of that amazing kiss. Her one small glimpse into what it might have been like to have a life with him was more than some people had their entire lifetime. She was so blessed to have experienced even a small taste of how it could have been.

She stood at the back door a long time, feeling the pain, thinking about the conclusions she'd drawn. The sun was sinking behind the mountains now, casting long shadows across the deck. Good grief, she'd been here for at least an hour, thinking, mulling things over. And she'd come to a new conclusion.

"What a load of crock."

She didn't want to cherish the time she'd had with Macon and wallow in memories for the rest of her life. She'd been wallowing in memories ever since her little sister and brother were killed. It was time to actually *live*. She wanted more.

She wanted Macon.

And if that meant groveling and begging him to forgive her, that's what she'd do. But she wasn't giving up without a fight. She loved him. Truly, deeply, irrevocably. And for the first time ever, she was going to fight for love instead of being afraid of it.

She headed into the family room and grabbed her phone off the end table. Drawing a deep breath, she punched his number.

He answered on the first ring.

"Emma, hi. I was just about to—"

"Don't hang up on me, Macon."

"I wasn't going to—"

"We need to talk."

"Okay."

"Face-to-face."

"I agree. That's why I—"

"I mean it. No more avoiding the elephant in the room. I wouldn't change what I did at the feed store even if I could. And I understand why that makes you angry. Because you care about me."

"Yes. I do."

"O-okay." She swallowed. "And you were worried about me."

"Yes. I was."

"But I was worried about you, too. I couldn't have lived with myself if I didn't send Bogie in there to help you and you got hurt, or worse. Can you understand that?"

"I understand. Emma, I—"

"No. Don't stop me. I have to say this before I lose my nerve. I love you, Macon. Do you hear me? I. Love. You. I love you so much it hurts. I'm sorry that I hurt you, at the station. I was scared and—"

"I know. The chief explained a lot to me, about the trauma you've gone through. How scared it made you to let someone past that wall you built around your heart."

"He...he did? You understand?"

"I do."

She swallowed. "Can you forgive me? For every-thing?"

"I thought we weren't supposed to apologize?"

"I'm invoking the jerk clause. I was a jerk. I need you to forgive me."

"You've never been a jerk. If you need me to say I forgive you, then okay. I forgive you. But only if you forgive me, too."

She clutched the phone so hard her hand hurt. "There's nothing to forgive."

"Emma—"

"Okay. Okay. Yes. I forgive you. And I love you."

"Emma. I think we should be having this conversa-tion face-to-face. Don't you?"

"Yes. Of course. I just wasn't sure you'd even talk to me so I—"

"Emma."

"Yes, Macon."

"Open the front door."

She blinked, then slowly crossed to the door. She pulled it open, still holding the phone to her ear.

Macon stood there, his phone to his ear, too. And the look of love in his eyes as he stared down at her stole her breath.

"I love you, Emma," he spoke into the phone.

"I love you, too." She threw her phone down, crying tears of joy as she jumped into his arms.

Epilogue

"We pulled it off." Emma leaned against Macon's side, reveling in the feel of his arm around her waist as they watched the chaos taking place inside the training ring.

"We sure did. I think almost everyone in the police department is here, with their families. Even your orange cat, Gus, made an appearance. I saw him stealing a corn dog off someone's plate earlier."

She laughed. "It won't be his last today."

"Probably not. Best Daniels Canine Academy anniversary celebration ever. Or so I've been told."

She smiled. "It will be hard to top it next year. I pulled outstanding dog trainers and K-9s from all over Idaho to put on this performance. And I hired the best caterers I could find to make all that delicious finger food in the tents."

"Not to mention your homemade fry sauce. It's amazing."

"It is, isn't it?"

"I would never lie about something as sacred as fry sauce."

She laughed, looking around, enjoying the sheer joy on everyone's faces as they played games, watched the exhibitions and ate an obscene amount of food. "I understand Rutledge not being here since he doesn't support the K-9 program. But it's still kind of sad since he's the second-in-command. Seems like he should be here with everyone else."

He gently turned her around to face him. "You haven't heard the news?"

"News?"

"Rutledge resigned."

She stared at him in shock. "What? Why? I thought he was looking forward to being the new chief."

"He was. Until Chief Walters told him he's moving up his retirement to this Friday. And that the new chief will be Cal Hoover. Rutledge resigned on the spot and walked out."

She pressed a hand to her throat. "Oh, my. That's… unexpected."

"It was a long time coming. Just in the short time that I've been here, I've seen that the rumors are true. In spite of how smart and gifted Rutledge is with police work, his people skills are lacking. He doesn't treat others with the respect they deserve even with the extensive coaching Walters gave him. It would have been a disaster for morale if he'd become chief. But if you're worried about his future, don't be. He's too talented not to land on his feet with some other police force. Hopefully he'll have learned a lesson from what happened here and will treat people better wherever he goes."

"Maybe. I hope so. Wow, this Friday, huh? I didn't realize the chief was going to retire so soon. I thought he was going to wait another year or so."

"Apparently he wanted to make it coincide closely with your anniversary party. I imagine he'll give a speech to officially announce it soon." He leaned down close to her ear. "And then he'll let everyone know that Theresa is retiring, too, and they're both going to move in together."

She jerked back to look him in the eyes. "Serious?"

"Serious. He told me this morning."

She lightly punched his chest. "How did you get so plugged into the grapevine? He never shared any of that with me."

"Maybe he wanted to surprise you. Or maybe he didn't go into all of that yet because you've been so busy helping Celia and little Anna." He pointed and she turned around.

Celia was sitting with Anna at the face-painting booth. Little Anna was squealing with delight, watching the other children. She was too young to hold still long enough to have her own face done. But she kept bouncing on Celia's knee and clapping her hands together in her excitement.

Emma wiped her eyes and sniffed.

"Are you crying?" Macon leaned down to look at her. "You are. Why?"

"They're happy tears. I love both of them so much. And I'm so happy that Celia has earned back custody of Anna. She's worked so hard to get to that point. I'm also relieved she won't have to worry about Sean any more. He'll be an old man by the time he gets out of prison, no threat to either of them."

He gently feathered her hair back from her face. "I know you miss having Anna around all the time."

She smiled up at him. "I miss her, yes. But my husband makes me happy every day." She moved her hand to her stomach, which was still flat, but soon wouldn't be. "And his love and patience convinced me that I could be a good mom, in spite of my fears."

"You'll be the best. I've zero doubts." He gently kissed her before straightening.

She stared up at him, her heart full. "If it's a boy, I was thinking a nice name might be Ken."

His eyes widened and his arms tightened around her. "Are you sure?"

"Of course. I know how much your partner meant to you, how much he still means to you. You've worked so hard to get past the grief and survivor's guilt. I don't want to do anything to make it worse again. If you think it would be too difficult—"

"No." He cleared his throat, then smiled. "No, it's getting easier every day, partly because of the therapy you insisted on, but mainly because of you. Ken, and his family, would be honored if we name our baby after him. And if it's a girl, maybe we could name her Susan, after your mom."

Her eyes turned misty. "I'd like that, very much. Thank you, Macon."

He pressed a whisper-soft kiss against her lips. "Thank you, sweet Emma."

In reply, she pulled him down for a longer, deeper kiss that had him groaning with regret when it ended.

"When is this dang party going to be over?" he complained. "We need some serious alone time."

She laughed, so happy her heart felt as if it would burst from joy. Macon was the love of her life, and they were building a family together. But it had taken the tragedy of nearly losing him for her to realize that love was worth fighting for. And that families came in all different forms. She'd thought she'd lost her family when she was a little girl. But the moment that Rick and Susan Daniels had opened their home and hearts to her, she'd gained a new family. Then she'd lost them too and thought that was it for her. Macon had shown her that wasn't true, and that all she had to do was look around right now to see just how huge her family had become.

Macon, Anna, Celia, everyone in Jasper PD—they were her family. It didn't matter that they weren't blood related. Their bond was stronger than genetics. Because they chose each other, chose to be there every day, no matter what. Just as she and Macon had chosen each other.

"Ready?" He held his hand out toward her.

She laced her fingers through his. "Ready. Take me to our family, Macon."

He smiled and led her across the field.

* * * * *

COMING SOON!

We really hope you enjoyed reading this book.
If you're looking for more romance, be sure to
head to the shops when new books are
available on

Thursday 10th November

JOIN US ON SOCIAL MEDIA!

Stay up to date with our latest releases, author news and gossip, special offers and discounts, and all the behind-the-scenes action from Mills & Boon...

 @millsandboon

 @millsandboonuk

 facebook.com/millsandboon

 @millsandboonuk

It might just be true love...

GET YOUR ROMANCE FIX!

Get the latest romance news, exclusive author interviews, story extracts and much more!

MILLS & BOON
MEDICAL
Pulse-Racing Passion

Set your pulse racing with dedicated, delectable doctors in the high-pressure world of medicine, where emotions run high and passion, comfort and love are the best medicine.

MILLS & BOON
True Love

Romance from the Heart

Celebrate true love with tender stories of heartfelt romance, from the rush of falling in love to the joy a new baby can bring, and a focus on the emotional heart of a relationship.